Subpoena Colada

Mark Dawson was a DJ at Manchester's Hacienda in the early 1990s. He now works as a lawyer in London. *Subpoena Colada* is his second novel.

also by Mark Dawson

THE ART OF FALLING APART

MARK DAWSON

Subpoena Colada

PAN BOOKS

First published 2002 by Macmillan

This edition published 2003 by Pan Books
an imprint of Pan Macmillan Ltd
Pan Macmillan, 20 New Wharf Road, London N1 9RR
Basingstoke and Oxford
Associated companies throughout the world
www.panmacmillan.com

ISBN 0 330 48944 5

A CIP catalogue record for this book is available from
the British Library.

Typeset by SetSystems Ltd, Saffron Walden, Essex
Printed and bound in Great Britain by
Mackays of Chatham plc, Chatham, Kent

To my family

Acknowledgements

Thanks to

My family – here's one (almost) everyone can read.

Mic Cheetham – for support and savvy.

Peter Lavery – once again, for supplying the drink, the advice, the pleasant weekend retreats, and the editing. And everyone else at Macmillan.

Mette Olsen, Alex Ricks, Emma Sweeney and Sharon Sullivan – for reading early drafts.

Simon Kavanagh – for suggestions and impeccable taste.

Amber Melville-Brown for correcting my law.

Neal Doran – for more ideas than I can remember and help when I needed it most: Gertcha.

Tom Nicholson, Arnie Siva and the guys at Global, Glen Scarlett, Matthew Johns, Ian Hancock.

Outlaw Records, Stoke-on-Trent – for supplying the music.

'In the future, everyone will be famous for fifteen minutes.'
ANDY WARHOL

'Brad Pitt was great. But once you're a fellow celebrity you just treat each other like two friends in a pub.'
'NASTY' NICK BATEMAN, 2000

Wednesday (Earlier)

OFFICER OF THE COURT

Court 39 was full of lawyers, court ushers, pressmen and public gallery addicts. The prospect of legal fireworks or, better yet, celebrity gossip, had sharpened the atmosphere's edge, and the congregation was watching avidly. It was the dog-end of an Indian summer, a sluggish, stifling afternoon, and heat sweltered through the crowded courtroom in sultry, shimmering waves. One of the ushers sponged sweat off his forehead with a damp handkerchief and those unwise enough to wear coloured shirts had their discomfort expressed by dark half-moons of sweat at their armpits.

In spite of the soporific effect of the temperature, everyone was held rapt by the legal drama unfolding before us. The staid atmosphere of the Royal Courts of Justice had been electrified by the glitz and the glamour of the Black Dahlia trial. Nothing excites the public better than a messy celebrity feud, and this was as messy as it got. For the two weeks since the case began, this had been the hottest ticket in town.

The clock showed 4.10 p.m.; a long twenty minutes before we retired for the day. I was drowsy and sweaty and another all-night session of debriefing and preparation lay ahead. Court hearings place heavy burdens on the lawyers preparing them; an hour on the office couch was the only rest I had to look forward to.

This was the biggest court in the building. The circus decamped and moved here after the first day had to be adjourned because of the scrum in the corridors kicking and shoving its way inside. I'd never been involved in a case that had aroused interest like this one did; the media couldn't get enough of it. A thicket of reporters waited outside our office on the off-chance that one of the participants in the legal pantomime would pay us a visit. I lost count of the number of calls I fielded from reporters anxious for a quote on the case, even from a low-life lawyer like me.

THE CONTESTANTS

In the blue corner, the Defendant: Brian Fey, represented by my firm, White Hunter.

Brian had taken everything in his stride. A couple of hundred people packed into a courtroom was nothing compared to the concerts the Black Dahlias had played during their glory days. Concerts *I* saw, events that lit up my youth, lit up the youths of so many others like me: Glasto '91, Reading '92, Wembley '95. Concerts they played before they split up.

In the red corner, the Plaintiffs: the rest of the Dahlias, backed up by a rich record label and a team of crack lawyers from the super-expensive firm, Pattersons.

EVIDENCE-IN-CHIEF

Our QC, Gordon Rittenhouse, called Brian to give his evidence.

'As you know, Brian,' Rittenhouse began, 'we're here because your ex-colleagues and their record label've alleged that the payment to you earlier this year of £500,000 was a mistake. They say you ought to be forced to pay the money back. You don't agree, do you?'

'No, I don't,' Brian said, evenly. 'The money's mine.'

To our collective relief Brian – with Rittenhouse's gentle prompting – put on a good show. The past week had been spent priming him with the questions Rittenhouse was going to ask. It seemed like the time had been well spent – Brian answered the questions, didn't elaborate, didn't get excited, just like we taught him. And he provoked slightly self-conscious laughter, even from the bench, when he explained the band's early raison d'être: 'I s'pose our main objective was to get famous, get loads of girls and be The Beatles.' He smiled bashfully at this, and you could sense the courtroom warming to him.

It was working.

CROSS-EXAMINATION

Rittenhouse finished his questions and the QC acting for the band got to his feet. They'd instructed William Dicey, a Rottweiler with a well-deserved reputation for savaging witnesses. This was always going to be the acid test.

No intro, no pleasantries, no friendly banter – Dicey launched straight in with, 'Mr Fey, isn't it true to say you decided to keep the money because you want to *punish* the other members of the band for forcing you to leave? Wouldn't that be a more accurate thing to say?'

The hacks in the public gallery all pricked up their ears. Like sharks, they could smell blood in the water from miles away.

'No, that's not true,' Brian replied. He looked over at me for support and I nodded grimly. By the time I remembered to smile it was too late; he'd looked away again.

'It's not true?'

'No, not at all.'

'I see.' Dicey faked a puzzled expression, then affected taking notes, then looked up again. 'But isn't it true to say that you feel you've been badly treated by your former colleagues? That you've been let down?'

'They haven't been fair to me, if that's what you mean.'

'I think it's rather more than that, Mr Fey,' he said. 'Isn't it?'

Where was this line of questioning going? I thought we'd already spotted the potential ambushes, and prepared stock answers.

'I noticed,' Dicey said when Brian clammed up, 'that you gave an interview to a Sunday newspaper. It was published last weekend, and a very interesting piece it was. If you don't mind I'd like to read out an extract to the court. Then I'd like to hear what you've got to say about it.'

An usher scurried down from the bench to deliver photocopies of the article to Brian, Rittenhouse and the Judge, Mr Justice Robinson. Dicey fished out a pair of spectacles and pushed them onto the end of his long nose. He slowly flicked through a folder on his desk – by craning my neck I could see the page he settled on was of copied newsprint, large chunks picked out in yellow highlighter. He unclipped the ring binder and took out the page.

HOOK . . .

Holding it in front of him, with one hand folded behind his back, he said, 'This's a direct quote from the interview. In answer to a question about your feelings towards the rest of the band – the Black Dahlias – you said, and I quote: "I can't believe they'd do something like this to me. Is that the kind of thing you do to a friend?" Mr Fey, do you remember saying that?'

'I said *something* like that,' Brian admitted. 'I don't remember it exactly.'

'Look at the article. You can see where I'm reading from, can't you?'

Brian nodded. He was following it with his finger.

'You were asked what your feelings were towards this case. You said, quote: "I don't care whether I win or lose. I'm not paying back the money because it's mine. If they're so desperate to get rid of me, they can. I can't stop them doing that, but there's no way I'm paying back the cash. They can" – ahem – "F-off." I'm paraphrasing here very slightly, Mr Fey, as you chose to use colourful language not suited to this court. But, in general terms, you said that too, didn't you?'

Brian floundered: 'I don't remember . . . Journalists sometimes monkey around with what you say to them, twist everything around, I can't—'

'I think you *do* remember, don't you, Mr Fey?'

LINE . . .

Brian started to stutter something, but Dicey cut him off.

'This interview caught you at your most candid and honest, didn't it, Mr Fey? More candid and honest than you've so far chosen to be today, or at any other time during these proceedings. Isn't it true to say that you *hate* the fact you've been forced to leave a highly successful and profitable business? That you *hate* the fact that your glamorous lifestyle has been threatened. Isn't that really the case?'

Brian gripped the brass guard rail that ran around the witness box so tightly that his knuckles went white.

'Isn't it true to say that you greedily seized upon an honest mistake when you saw a chance for one last big pay-day? At its most basic level, this's a case of *theft*, isn't it, Mr Fey? This's daylight robbery.'

Brian looked lost. He began, 'No, it's not—'

'But it's not just about the money, is it, Mr Fey? This's about settling a score. About *revenge*. You want to make your old friends *pay* for what they did to you. You've been wronged and, by thunder, you're going to make them regret it.'

That did it. Brian stabbed a finger at Dicey and said, 'How'd *you* feel if you were suddenly forced to stop doing something you've loved doing for fifteen years?'

'What *I* would feel is beside the point.'

'Let me tell you,' Brian said. 'It feels fucking *awful*.'

A flutter of commotion from the public gallery. Mr Justice Robinson appealed for silence.

'Mr Fey,' the Judge said, 'please be more careful with your choice of language.' I watched as reporters accelerated their shorthand notes, taking verbatim transcripts for tomorrow's papers. 'You are now in a court of *law*. Language you choose to use in your day-to-day life might not always be appropriate here. Please bear that in mind.'

Brian just looked down at his shoes but it was easy to see his blood was pumping hotly. 'I'm sorry,' he said quietly.

. . . AND SINKER

Dicey went for the throat. 'You kept the money because you want to punish your ex-friends for firing you from the band. Isn't it true that you're determined to take advantage of an honest mistake made by a member of staff at the record company? And isn't it true that you won't pay back the advance, even if this court *orders* you to do so? Isn't that true, *Mr* Fey?' Dicey laid on the contempt with a trowel. 'And isn't it true that you *hate* the rest of the band and that you've *enjoyed* putting them to the time, trouble and inconvenience of bringing these proceedings against you?'

'Yes,' shouted Brian, all the careful hours of coaching back in the office disintegrating in that single moment.

He was bloodless with fury. 'Yes, it's true. I *want* to punish them. What they've done to me's not *right*. It's not about the money or revenge. It's the fucking principle. They shouldn't be *allowed* to do what they've done.'

I couldn't stop myself lowering my head into my hands as the court exploded into pandemonium. We all knew Brian had a quick temper, but this . . . this was turning into a disaster.

There were shouts and exclamations as Dicey turned to junior counsel, a tight smile on his face. They knew the case was theirs now. Reporters dashed outside to make hold-the-front-page-type calls back to their news desks:

BRIAN FEY ADMITS HE STOLE MONEY FROM EX-FRIENDS

EX-DAHLIA FEY IN FOUL-MOUTHED COURT OUTRAGE

BAD BOY BRIAN THROWS IT ALL AWAY

The Judge roared for silence but no one was listening. I looked up at the rest of the band, sitting in the pews behind their expensive lawyers. They were doing a bad job of hiding their jubilation.

THE BEGINNING OF THE END

There was only ever going to be one outcome after that. Brian's case was founded on the already shaky proposition that he was entitled to the money because he had contributed to the creation of the band's latest record. Brian's angry confession, plus later admissions about his minimal involvement in the record, meant the final outcome was severe, onerous and inevitable.

'Mr Fey,' said Mr Justice Robinson at the conclusion of his judgment, six days later, 'I have no hesitation in finding that you have, in effect, *stolen* money from your ex-colleagues. You have behaved dishonestly, disloyally, and with scant regard to the friendship one assumes you once shared. It is my judgment, therefore, that you should immediately pay back the £500,000, and also that you should pay the legal costs that they have incurred.'

The grand total, when White Hunter's fees were added to Brian's other liabilities, would eventually top £900,000.

Money he didn't have.

I got the blame, of course. Everyone needs a scapegoat and I was it. The partners told me I should have kept my client under closer control and should have prevented that damaging interview. They said I hadn't prepared Brian properly for the witness box. He should never have been allowed to lose his cool like that. It was all *my* fault.

Only Brian, who had the most to lose, absolved me from any contribution to his downfall.

'If it was anyone's fault,' he said to me afterwards, 'it was mine. *I* lost the case, not you. I did the interview.

I lost it in the box. So don't beat yourself up about it, OK? After all – it's only money.'

Kind words then, given that Brian lost everything in the weeks that followed. And, after everything that happened to him subsequently, he was still the only person who didn't blame me.

Sunday

A CELEBRITY DEATH

I hear at the party that John French has been found dead. *The* John French, bassist and new vocalist of the Black Dahlias, Brian Fey's replacement in the band. His body was discovered by a friend two hours ago and now the police are swarming all over his flat.

I try not to pay too much attention and concentrate on my drink, but it's difficult to avoid being interested in something as juicy as this. I shuffle along the bar to eavesdrop the gossip.

LOCATION, LOCATION, LOCATION

Hip and trendy Soho. Such a cliché. Ex-sweatshop transformed into modish minimalist lounge bar by society It-girl with too much money and too much time. Art deco steel and brushed chrome. Cold and sterile. The usual crowd is here: media figureheads, record company A&R, the young and the beautiful, the old and the rich.

I look around: Richard Branson and Chris Evans; Liam and Noel Gallagher; Sharleen Spiteri and Sophie Ellis Bextor; Jodie Kidd and Sophie Dahl; Gail Porter and Jade Jagger; Rachel Hunter and Patsy Kensit; David Baddiel and Steve Coogan; hip young things from the soaps.

Lots of lovely celebrities.

We've all been comped for the launch party of the big new album. For a young punk band – Monster Munch, the next Next Big Thing – are about to release their debut. Work obliges me to show up to these hideous occasions, on the sniff for new clients. I've been to parties like this a million times before and they definitely are *not* my scene. Insincerity clogs the air, a veritable miasma of phoniness and mendacity.

A few minor stars stopped by earlier, just long enough to be noticed by the tabloid hacks before leaving for more fashionable pursuits. Now the party has undergone the inevitable metamorphosis from hip to unhip. There was a fifteen-minute envelope earlier when this might possibly have been the most happening event in London – three Big Brother evictees plus both Posh *and* Becks were in attendance – but that was hours ago, or at least it feels that way now.

WHY I'M HERE

Three reasons:

Reason No. 1
I'm avoiding home.

Reason No. 2
I don't want to be sober. I don't want to be awake for hours over-analysing the causes of my new status: *dumped*.

(Rewind: six weeks ago. My long-term girlfriend dumps me for no reason whatsoever. Hannah Wilde. Yes, *that* Hannah Wilde. Hannah Wilde the actress. Hannah Wilde the all-round semi-famous person. One day she was there, mooching around with the kind of edgy neuroticism I'd come to interpret as normal behaviour, the next day she wasn't. More about Hannah later, but for present purposes take it from me that it has *seriously* messed me up.

Let's be honest about it: I'm still in a bit of a state. And when I'm forced to return to the flat tonight I'll have had the opportunity to protect myself properly against the ghosts flapping around the empty rooms because, ladies and gentlemen, I intend to be completely off my head.)

Reason No. 3
I thought Brian might like the chance to mix it up with his old crowd again. Davey, his new manager, had called on Friday to tell me he'd been depressed, and he knew Brian and I got on well. 'Take him out,' he suggested to me. 'Loosen him up. He needs to relax.'

Nerves before the release of his new album and the solo tour? It figured. So a couple of drinks might take the edge off things.

If I'm *completely* honest there's a fourth reason too.

Reason No. 4
Miles Mackay finally popped his clogs last month. 86 when he finally called it quits, found dead at his desk by the cleaner with his head resting on the pages of a letter to Jimmy Tarbuck he was working on, possibly the world's oldest practising lawyer. With his passing, a vacancy opened up in the partnership at work. Only at a junior level and certainly not the full equity package, but partnership is partnership and not something you sniff at.

And if I'm going to get nominated for it I need to get myself noticed.

I'm six years qualified. That makes me a candidate for promotion. If you haven't been made up by the time you've got seven or eight years' experience behind you, you figure you never will be. You're on the shelf.

That's when you resign and set up your one-man high-street practice. An office above a Chinese with my name on a stencilled window (Tate & Co), and a low-rent secretary who comes in whenever she feels like it. The work would be shitty, depressing stuff: wills, boundary disputes, immigration, grimy divorces, custody battles. Beepers going off in the middle of the night because some drunk has put a brick through a pub window and needs the duty solicitor to smooth his passage down at the station.

Hell. I'm not doing it.

McKay's death has come at precisely the right time. It offers me a way out. Partners do zero work for fat salaries. *That's* something to aspire to. So I've been putting myself about more than I usually would (not difficult) and, as I say, it's good to get your face seen at this kind of thing. And it won't hurt my cause to land a new client or two.

MORE INFORMATION

The rumours become more precise. People are saying John French has hanged himself. His body was found swinging in the hallway of his Mayfair pad. The police haven't ruled out foul play; there was no suicide note, and it's difficult to imagine why French – successful, rich, basking in the lavish praise for his new role with the Dahlias – would want to do himself in. The gossipers recall Michael Hutchence and wonder whether this was another kinky sex trip gone 'tragically wrong'. Soon fact and fiction will merge until people like me are called in to start sifting truth from lies.

I wonder how Brian will take the news. He and French were hardly on cordial terms after the nonsense that followed the band split. And then, when French replaced him as singer . . . Brian took it very badly. But they'd known each other since childhood, so Brian is bound to be upset. I'll have to be diplomatic. I tell myself that I can still do diplomatic, despite all this booze.

Monster Munch take the stage and play a couple of songs from their album. Their names are Scooter, Bam Bam and Mooch. I'm not joking; these are the only monikers they'll answer to. I'm supposed to be drafting their record contract but I haven't done it yet. I've already got more work than I can handle and I'm finding it difficult to find the enthusiasm to work for the spoiled, rich, successful brats.

101 REASONS WHY I HATE OLIVER DAWKINS

Oliver Dawkins heads my way as I enviously watch the kids on the stage. I notice the light sparking off the sweaty sheen of his bald dome before my attention is drawn down to his porcine features.

Some facts about Oliver Dawkins:

- Dawkins is a corporate lowlife from the office.
- Dawkins hangs a spare jacket over the back of his chair and leaves his desk lamp on overnight to fool the partners into thinking he's working late.
- Dawkins bills fifteen hours a day (and can justify all of them).
- Dawkins is going places.
- Dawkins is the favourite for that spare place in the partnership.
- Dawkins is the sort of guy I really, really dislike.

His nickname in the office is obvious.

'Tate,' nods The Dork.

'Dawkins.'

'You heard the news?'

'Awful,' I say.

He yawns. 'Strictly entre nous,' he says, already sizing up opportunities over my shoulder, 'this is all *so* passé – I was hoping we'd done away with these *awful* little events. I can't stand half the people here, although of course you can't *say* that. Still – already set up business lunches for the next two weeks.'

'Me too,' I lie. I haven't been on a business lunch for years.

'Good for you,' the Dork says. 'A good spread of clients's the first thing the partnership'll be looking for in the new boy, know what I mean? Keeps the old cash rolling in.'

Dawkins is the odds-on favourite for McKay's place

in the partnership, and he knows it. He's already got a list of blue-chip clients to die for. His Psion is bursting with the details of all the best managers and agents in London, plus a few stand-alone celebs and showbiz personalities. This gives him the ability to dangle lucrative work in front of the partnership's nose. That's a big advantage since the partners know he could just resign and take his clients and their money somewhere else if they overlook him.

'New boy or new *girl*,' I correct.

'Come on, Tate,' Dawkins sports. 'They're never going to pick her.'

'Caroline's a first-class lawyer.'

'Yes, maybe, but let's just say I've got it on good authority that we don't need to worry about *her*. We know who the *real* candidates are, don't we.' He ticks the names off on his fingers: 'Me. You. Cohen.' David Cohen is my room-mate. We know we're both trailing the Wunderkind.

'Maybe,' I concede.

'So that's why you're here tonight?' he says. 'Trying to make a good impression?'

'I'd like to think they're taking other things into account, other'n how often you turn out to schmooze. Legal ability, for example?'

'Where's Brian Fey? I thought he was coming.'

He's feigning nonchalance – badly. The Dork's been hankering after Brian for weeks, ever since the case fell into my lap because he didn't even realize there was kudos in it. His current eagerness to usurp me might be tempered if he knew how impossible the job has become. Not even George Carman could have extricated himself from it smelling of anything other than the sticky brown stuff.

'He's coming later,' I say.

'Listen, come over and get me when he turns up, OK?' he says. 'I'd like to pass on my best wishes. I'm a really big fan.'

I start to respond (like the Dork has even *heard* of the Black Dahlias) but he's already moved on to the next stop on his self-promotional tour of the room. As I watch him shimmy away I'm anxiously wondering who's been feeding him the skinny on the partnership race.

THE THIN WHITE DUPE

At last: Brian Fey, my most important client, makes his appearance with two women in tow. I can see from his agitated carriage that he's already made a start on tonight's party fuel. More power to him, I say, so long as he's got some left for me. I'm in severe need of refuelling myself.

Brian's new album is out tomorrow, his first solo effort since being thrown out of the band. He hasn't had half the publicity that Monster Munch are getting. The official line is that Brian's new stuff is so good it sells itself. There's no need for expensive advertising campaigns and media parties costing thousands of pounds. Word of mouth will be more than enough.

Brian believes all this shit. He buys it. His ingenuousness would be charming if it wasn't so sad.

The truth? Brian's going to get eaten alive when his album hits the shelves tomorrow. No review copies were sent out in advance – what does that tell you? The word from the studio says the album's been cut ten times already and it *still* sounds like something Babylon Zoo would be ashamed to own up to. The label have spent so much on it they have to release it, if only on the off-chance that something remarkable might happen.

Brian says something to Emma Bunton and heads over.

'Am I late?' he asks.

'Only a little.'

'Got held up. Sorry.'

'You heard the news?'

'Yeah. Hence the delay. Terrible. Trying not to think about it.'

He looks pale and drawn. His eyes are red-ringed, like he's been crying for hours, with a dark bruise, partially obscured by make-up, visible on the right side of his temple. There's a little dried blood clinging to the edge of his scalp.

I tell him I'm sorry and he manages a thin half-smile. I decide not to press the point any further.

STARFUCKERS

Brian introduces me to his companions. There is Carmen: a giantess who looks like Grace Jones in negative; she tells me that she's an 'artist'. And Lisa: an assistant at Brian's new record company; blonde, well-proportioned, very cute. Both smile sweetly at me, probably labouring under the misapprehension that I have influence to wield. Leaving them in the dark might give the evening some swing, but before I can make any fraudulent claims pertaining to status and/or occupation Brian flattens my ego.

'This is Daniel,' he says. 'My lawyer.'

MY LAWYER.

Passion-killer.

My plans for an evening of amorous deceit fart away like a punctured balloon. Because, let's be honest, being a lawyer ain't got that much in the way of sexual magnetism.

I'm not jealous of Brian. Really, I'm not. He's got things going on in his life you wouldn't believe. Legal things, personal things – we'll get to them later. Still, it *would* be easy to be envious and I could understand it. He's still in fabulous shape, if a little (fashionably) gaunt. Scrawny? Think consumptive, circa 1750. Thin enough to fit the 'Thin White Dupe' tag the music press pinned on him from the infamous days when he shunned food for other, less legal forms of sustenance. White tracks on his arms from before he kicked the junk. He's still famous for the dismissive 'lightweight' he offered when hearing of River Phoenix's OD on the LA sidewalk outside the Viper Room.

'I brought the blow,' he says, forcing a smile.

I'm immediately optimistic the night will pick up.

'Shall we make a start?' I suggest.

THE REMARKABLE RESTORATIVE POWERS OF BOLIVIAN MARCHING POWDER

The four of us cram into a vacant cubicle in the gents. Brian tips the contents of a silver vial from a chain around his neck onto the back of the toilet seat. The attendant by the sinks didn't appear unduly ruffled as the four of us trooped inside. While we waited for a spare cubicle I listened impatiently to the telltale snorts from behind locked doors.

Blow's everywhere these days. It's not even taboo. Say this quietly: Charlie's even a little *dated*, darling. The missing septum look is *so* last year.

But I'm not complaining.

Brian chops the pile into four lines with his credit card, practised hands slicing and scraping until the lines are roughly equal in length and width. We each hoover up a line through a rolled twenty; the first hit is always the best and I shiver in expectation, waiting for the rush to be released.

After ten minutes, it hits.

'There *is* a God,' Brian says, scrubbing a finger over his gums. He doles out extra lines and hoovers one up.

'Amen to that,' I say, carried away on a euphoric high.

After twenty minutes I start to come down. The high recedes and paranoia seeps into the empty space left behind. I need more powder to force it back again.

CARMEN MAKES A PASS

We're sitting in a booth together when Carmen slides closer to Brian and places a hand on his thigh. I know I shouldn't be watching but the blow is playing havoc with my sense of decorum. And, OK, I admit it: I'm jealous. Any idiot can get laid when they're famous – that's easy. It's getting laid when you're not famous that takes talent.

Carmen nuzzles Brian's ear. He smiles softly at her, reaches down and gently lifts her hand away from his leg. He and Lisa share a knowing look, and Lisa, who has been observing the scene, crouches down to whisper something into Carmen's ear. She blushes, apologizes to Lisa, takes a wrap of coke from the table and heads for the ladies.

A PROFESSIONAL CONFERENCE
WITH MY CLIENT

Later, and I find myself alone at the bar with Brian. The girls have disappeared, finally working out that he's preoccupied, and that I'm a no one. They're right on both counts.

Guests are looking askance at us. Some at the bar are talking in conspiratorial tones, glancing in our direction, nodding. Denise Van Outen pretends not to look while glancing over her cocktail glass. She's probably wondering how Brian's taken the news of his ex-colleague's death. Perhaps some of the less charitable souls might even be wondering if he could be somehow involved. Brian seems oblivious to this attention; he's hunched over the bar, a drink resting between his elbows.

'What happened to your head?' I say, pointing to the bruise.

'Fell over,' he says.

We've been drinking shorts with lager chasers. We've worked our way through most of the spirits upended over in their optics, finally settling on vodka. I'm suffering from a feeling of dislocation, of being in two places simultaneously. I suspect another toot of nose candy would correct this existential imbalance but as I'm about to ask for a portion, Brian tells me he's coming to court with me on Tuesday.

'Don't worry about it,' I slur in reply. 'It's just procedural.' This last word, full of mutinous syllables, is almost beyond my present linguistic capacity.

'No way,' he slurs back, throwing an arm over my shoulders. His eyeballs are pinned from the coke and his breath reeks of booze. 'I've been a terrible client. *Terrible*. I wanna be there to give some moral support. And maybe I'll be useful. Maybe the judge would like to speak to me, or, like, something?'

If it gets to that you're finished, I think, but there's no point arguing. Brian is unshiftable when he's made up his mind; he can be as stubborn as a mule.

'Hey, Brian, gimme a shot,' says a roving photographer, hoisting his camera into our faces. Brian – an old pro – puts an arm around my shoulders and raises his glass in salutation. 'Cheers,' he slurs as the flash bulb explodes.

THE LAW OF DIMINISHING RETURNS

We return to the toilets several times but each subsequent hit seems weaker than the last. And then Brian's supply is exhausted and what was left of the evening withers and falls to dust.

DANIEL THROUGH THE DRINKING GLASS

Even later – and I've no idea when this is – I'm staggering out of a cubicle after snorting some badly cut coke. I bought it from a dealer selling wraps in the toilets. There was so much sucrose in the mixture I could have used it to sweeten my coffee. But at least it's not brick dust or baby laxative, and I'm getting a mild rush like a prickling in the membrane between my brain and my skull, so it's not a total waste of time.

The dealer is waiting outside. He seems to have established a dispensary in the toilets. 'How 'bout a cocktail?' he proposes. 'Viagra and disco biscuits, man – mental combo.'

I politely decline the handful of blue and white pills. They look like children's sweets, and Viagra would be as much use to me tonight as a chocolate teapot.

The muffled thump of the music from the dancefloor resonates with the foggy mush in my head. Repeated freezes have burned up my overheated nostrils. Too much sherbet, buster. In the toilets a dribble of blood crawled out onto my upper lip. I tore off a paper towel and scooped wet red out of my nose.

I can't find Brian. In fact, I can't even remember the last time I saw him. Several hours ago, for sure. I search through the club, bothered by the feeling that things are in the wrong place. The music is different. Europop has replaced Monster Munch's punk-lite. Red velvet drapes have been fixed to the walls. Surely the DJ booth was somewhere else? And there's a distressing dearth of celebrity. No sign of even a children's TV presenter.

The atmosphere is feverish. The crowd are attacking the beat with a furious passion that was absent before. There is sweat everywhere, whooping and hollering, and the smell of amyl nitrate and hormones. I watch kids in love with the world dropping Es, speeding, pouring bottles of Evian over their heads, and dancing like they've been plugged into the national grid. A tattooed boy next to me cracks open a popper under his nose and sniffs greedily.

'In vino veritas,' I slur at him.

He looks at me like I've crawled out of a sewer.

I'm feeling listless. My elbows are propped on the bar in a puddle of spilt beer. I order a double, handing over my last note and receiving a smattering of change. I have to find Brian or else I'll never get home.

'Have you seen Brian Fey?' I ask a cute girl next to me, ducking her head to the beat. Her hair is shaved short and looks like velvet. I wonder if she'd mind me stroking it.

'Excuse me?' she asks.

I repeat myself more distinctly. 'You know: Brian Fey? Rockstar? *Famous*.'

'He's great,' she says. 'We like him.'

'Is he here?'

'Not tonight.'

I notice her T-shirt: the words GIRL BAIT written

across the contour of pushed-up breasts. The floor suddenly tips away. I grab for the bar.

'Where am I?' I ask dizzily.

Bored, she gives me the name of a club on the Charing Cross Road, famous for its gay and lesbian nights, and half a mile away from Soho and the bar I'm supposed to be in. I look around: a lot of guys in tight white T-shirts and a lot of short-haired girls in boots more suited to heavy construction or oil rigs. Jigsaw pieces are mashed into place. I'd feel spectacularly stupid if I wasn't already so spectacularly drunk. I look at my watch. I'm missing two hours, and I don't remember anything at all.

'Don't suppose you've got any drugs?' I ask.

'I'm a nice girl,' she says, faking a sweet smile. 'I don't do nasty things like that.'

FINALLY, HOME

Somehow, I make it back home.

My flat is on the top floor of a converted pub. Given the booze I've been drinking lately, this irony has not been lost on me.

It's a gorgeous place, architect designed and finished with top-of-the-range fixtures and fittings. Hannah and I bought the flat together: it was going to be our own place. We'd both shuttled our things around rented places for years and we were tired of it. The flat was outside our budget and we could only barely afford the mortgage by pooling our joint incomes.

Now I'm on my own, I can't keep up the payments. The bank and the utilities have sent me several letters in increasingly menacing shades of red. I should probably sell up and move out, but that's a Rubicon I can't cross yet; the unconscious sentiment remains that, if I stay put, Hannah will eventually return.

As I stagger around outside fumbling for my key, there comes the familiar boom of a night train as it thunders over the bridge. There are two bridges here, one on either side of the flat: one for the high-speed locomotives rushing people and freight in from the east, and another carrying the more sedate light railway running down to the Isle of Dogs. Opposite is the depot for the buses serving this part of town. Between the three of them, the night is divided into small parcels of calm amid the rumbling and clattering of engines and wheels. And when the buses reverse down the ramp into their parking slots, the angle of their descent sweeps headlights across my bedroom ceiling, criss-crossing like searchlights seeking out escaped convicts – or absent girlfriends.

NELSON

Hannah's cat, Nelson, is waiting for me inside the door. Hannah rescued him from the Cat Protection League after he was found half-dead in a box. His previous owners had mistreated him; cigarettes ground out on his fur, besides kicks and more prosaic abuse. He had broken ribs and needed to have an infected eye removed. The empty socket has been stitched shut, hence his new name.

Nelson is a serial victim: Hannah left him behind with me when she bailed.

Nelson rubs up against my legs. Does he know how much we have in common? Deserted, both of us. I pick him up and take him into the kitchen. His bowl has been licked clean. I open a tin of tuna and scoop it out. He kneads my calf with his forepaws until I put his bowl down. I change his water and his litter tray and leave him to it.

GIRLFRIEND BAIT

Nothing on the answerphone. You live in hope. The telephone always seemed to be ringing before.

Into the lounge. For a short moment I think I've been robbed. But then I realize this is all my own doing: no self-respecting burglar would be as untidy as this. The room is in a real state: pizza boxes with bits of pepperoni stuck to the cardboard like fungi; Indian and Chinese takeout boxes coated with dried curry and noodles, soy sauce and ginger; bottles and cans; newspapers. A mug on the coffee table has a white web of mould coagulating in the bottom.

Stacked next to the wall are three cardboard boxes fastened with tape. These are full of Hannah's things. She took most of her stuff with her when she left – one afternoon while I was at work. The stuff she couldn't carry – her books, a few ornaments, some videos – I tearfully packed when I realized she wasn't coming back. She still hasn't collected them but I've left them just in case, like a small child leaves a glass of milk and a mince pie for Santa. A reason for her to return.

Perhaps I could bargain with her for them. A proper explanation in exchange for her cuddly toys? A reconciliation if she ever wants to see her signed copy of *Captain Corelli's Mandolin* again?

SUITABLE VIEWING MATERIALS

On the table, a stack of videos extracted from my far-too-large collection. I've been collecting movies for years and it was my love of cinema that fed my media law itch. Now I've got hundreds: one whole wall of the flat is devoted to floor-to-ceiling shelving I had fitted especially. I've been sorting through the tapes, distilling a selection to match my mood:

Brief Encounter.
An Affair to Remember.
Fatal Attraction.
God, I'm sad.

WE HATE IT WHEN OUR FRIENDS BECOME FAMOUS

I clear a space on the sofa and rewind the tape in the video I set to record earlier. Nelson struts into the lounge and watches me with disdainful pity while he licks his lips.

The soap Hannah appears in – *Skin Trade* – airs on Mondays, Wednesdays, Fridays and Sundays. I know this because I'm an avid viewer.

The show is set in the world of high fashion. Hannah plays Ella, a catwalk model with a closet full of shocking skeletons. Her storyline at the moment involves the return of the fiancé – played, inexplicably, by Dempsey from *Dempsey and Makepeace* – she jilted at the altar at the end of the last series. Now Dempsey's stalking her and her new man, Jake Cocozzo (played by C-list American model/actor Vincent Haines). Dempsey wants payback and *this* irony isn't lost on me, either. I'm always rooting for the bad guy. I cheer his every psychotic turn for the worse. Wednesday's episode saw him running his finger along the edge of a bread knife; he was at the end of his rope. Tonight, I'm hoping for blood.

VICARIOUS THRILLS

Settling back into the sofa I let the video roll. The familiar title music plays and Hannah appears, in the first scene. As she's undressing backstage, getting ready for the catwalk, I reach for the Kleenex.

Nelson puts his nose in the air and goes into my bedroom.

I squeeze my eyes shut and Hannah's face permeates the red darkness. Her smile. The flecks of green floating within her blue irises. Only the small details present themselves; I try to bring the image into sharper focus but nothing happens. I can see the tiny hairs on her top lip, the way a milky moonbeam curves back across her head – the scalp at the centre of her parting – and the rinds of sleep I brushed out of the corners of her eyes when we woke up.

Just like always, I remember the things I'll never do or see again:

I'll never mould myself into the warmth of her body when I'm cold, late at night.

I'll never watch her sleeping.

I'll never kiss her awake, her mouth tasting subtly with the saltiness of sleep.

I still don't know why these things have been taken away from me.

LAUGHTER IS NOT THE BEST MEDICINE

I'm reminded of a bad joke Cohen told me just after Hannah and I broke up. He didn't know about us then; he doesn't know about us now.

'A man walking along this beach stumbled across an old lamp. He picked it up, rubbed it and out pops this genie. The genie said, "This's the fourth time I've been let out of the lamp this month, so forget about the three wishes deal, you're only getting one." The man thought about it for a while, then he said, "I've always wanted to go to France but I'm scared of planes and tunnels and I get seasick. Could you build me a bridge to France, so's I can drive over to visit?"

'The genie laughed and said, "That's impossible. Think of the logistics! How would the supports reach the bottom of English Channel? Think of how much concrete you'd need, think how much steel! Can't do it, pal – think of another wish." The man agreed and tried to think of another great wish.

'Finally he came up with something and he said, "OK, I've got it. I've been married and divorced three times. My wives always said that I didn't care, and that I'm insensitive. So I wish I could understand women. I wanna know how they feel inside and what they're thinking when they give you the cold shoulder, I wanna know why they're crying when they're crying, I wanna know what they really want when they say 'nothing', and I wanna understand how to make them truly happy."

'And the genie said, "Do you want that bridge to have two lanes or four?" '

Pop star found dead

Police refuse to comment

John French, singer with 80s band the Black Dahlias, was last night found dead at his London home. Police are investigating.

John, 34, had recently re-placed Brian Fey as the lead singer of the popular Romford band who were international icons in the mid-1980s.

HANGED

Early reports suggested the singer hanged himself. One of John's neighbours, Max Pope, said: 'I overheard a policeman say he was found with a rope round his neck.'

See pages 4, 5, 6 & 7 for full story

on and Alex are claimed to be worth
he article goes on:

he exception to
ell be Brian Fey,
the early 90s for
life of unabashed
cently, following a
of mishaps (in-

volving a marriage, a divorce,
an overdose, a suspected
suicide attempt and then a
spell in rehab) it's been
rumoured that Fey is almost
broke.

UMBER ONE WITH A BULLET

my stop. If anything the mercury has continued
The other commuters seem to have retracted in
ll, hunching their shoulders and sloping forwards,
ing any remaining embers of warmth. I get a
to go from the Costa Coffee kiosk at the top of
scalators, and trudge through the slushy mess on
avement. The salt leaves a tide-mark of scurf on the
rs of my shoes.
rian's new album is out today. I'm already late for
office but I can't resist stopping off at the record
re for a look. Vicarious excitement is replaced by
appointment as I survey the aisles. The shelves are
minated by the new releases from the Black Dahlias
d Monster Munch. Brian's offering – *Songs from a
wisted Youth* – seems less popular. The store's buyer
as seen fit to order only five copies, and these are
rammed into an out-of-the-way nook on the bottom

SCOTT DOLAN'S GUEST LIST
World's Greatest Showbiz Column

JOHN FRENCH RIP
Showbiz world stunned by death

I was devastated to hear of the death of **John French** last night (see pages 4, 5, 6 & 7 for full details). In two years of writing for this paper I've rarely come across someone with the talent and modesty of the **Black Dahlias'** new singer. John was a class act.

A message for John from all of us here at the Guest List – you'll be missed.

THORA BIRCH buying CDs and DVDs in the Virgin Megastore as boss **RICHARD BRANSON** looked on.

DAVID and **VICTORIA BECKHAM** were looking at jewellery at Tiffany. Could they be planning to add to their collection?

Mondays

I DON'T LIKE MONDAYS

Couldn't sleep.

The leftover coke is still buzzing around my head when I come around. I've got a monster-sized hangover. Nelson presents himself for his morning stroke. He rolls over on the bed so I can rub his belly. He circles his paws in the air and purrs loudly.

There was a heavy snowfall last night and I have to shove hard at the outside door to open it enough to squeeze through. The skies were the colour of spilt mercury for a week before the first fall. The atmosphere was pregnant with it, waiting for the temperature to drop. It fell gently at first, a dusting as fine as icing sugar, then heavier. A haze in the air, fat flakes I watched gathering in the crooks of buildings and then over-flowing, spilling out onto pavements and roofs until everywhere was white. The odds are shortening for a white Christmas, but I'm feeling very unfestive.

Hannah used to love the snow. I remember a snowman we made last year with pebbles for eyes and

a raw carrot for the nos⋯
lings pecked away. Blue⋯
hands and merry laught⋯
crumpets afterwards.

I shuffle through my p⋯
bills, bills, bills. No idea ⋯
all. I stuff them into a rubb⋯

Three trains stroll throug⋯
them all. I just need a mome⋯
down on the metal bench at ⋯
and watch the fat pigeons sw⋯
streaked girders. Another train⋯
festooned with graffiti and, on th⋯
almost empty. The only evidence⋯
a carpet of discarded papers on the⋯
inside behind a six-foot Rasta sm⋯
with a manic facial tic, and a man s⋯
tapering where his wrists should e⋯
begin.

Inside the carriage, our clothes sta⋯
the change in temperature. I settle into⋯
up a discarded copy of the NME.

There is a retrospective piece on the⋯
tied in with publicity for their new album⋯
entitled 'Spandex Ballet', the nickname the ⋯
given after their first, rubber-encased, app⋯
Top of the Pops. The article alludes to the⋯
band members amassed during their glory day⋯

John, Dan⋯
millions. T⋯

Ironically,⋯
this may w⋯
infamous i⋯
leading a⋯
excess. Re⋯
catalogue⋯

I reach⋯
to fall⋯
the ch⋯
nurtu⋯
coffe⋯
the e⋯
the ⋯
upp⋯

shelf. They hardly leap out at the impulse buyer. I feel almost sheepish as I do my bit for the cause and buy one. The assistant regards me with a pitying look as I hand over my VISA card.

I notice another assistant working in the shop window. He's installing a display for the new Dahlias' album: *The Human Condition*. It's a life-size cardboard cut-out: John French – replacing Brian as singer – is flanked by the others, French having done the minor-instrument-to-frontman-shuffle better than anyone since Phil Collins left his drum kit behind him.

The reviews for it have been ecstatic. As far as the critics are concerned, it's been the most anticipated new album for years. And if the fans now treat it as a post-humous tribute to John French, there would appear to be no limit on how many copies it might sell.

Chastened on Brian's behalf, I head on for the office.

HOW IT ALL BEGAN

So. Daniel Tate, that's me – Dan or Danny if you want to annoy me. Average height, average build, average all the way around. Twenty-seven going on twenty-eight, and just treading water, life passing me by. Stop the world I want to get off. No girlfriend, no money, work my only solace and now even that's losing its lustre.

I wanted to be a lawyer for as long as I can remember. Watching Leo McKern as Rumpole, *Crown Court* on slow school-holiday afternoons, taping the American lawmen on the family's Betamax when their shows came on after bedtime on school days. Thinking *I* could do that, too, practising my lines in front of the mirror in my parents' room: 'Ladies and gentlemen of the jury, I put it to you . . .'

I was a straight-A student, read law at university and was offered a place at a big city firm before I went to law school. Two years as a trainee in the City were followed by a few months as an assistant. But then I determined it was time for a change. Prosaic documents and jejune disputes weren't for me, I decided. I wanted glamour, glitz, grandeur, the cheap and tawdry thrills of Mammon. I wanted to move into the entertainment business, so I swapped the Square Mile for Soho Square.

I've always been a sucker for the bright lights, and media law's where I thought I'd find them. Drafting movie contracts for Tom Cruise, entertaining Brad at the Ivy, or Keanu at Nobu. Robbie at the Bleeding Heart, or Kylie at the Criterion. Libel readings for Salman and Martin. Invited to the Michael Jackson gig, VIP backstage passes, 'Thanks for *all* the great work you're doing.' I wanted to defenestrate TVs. I wanted to be banned from expensive foreign hotels for outrageous behaviour. I wanted glamorous, illicit habits, just like I knew my clients would have.

It didn't quite turn out that way.

WHITE HUNTER

Because I had no experience of media law, I couldn't move straight to one of the big players. But, after a couple of interviews at White Hunter, I was offered a place. I thought about it a bit, then accepted. The way I saw it, I'd do a couple of years here to fill in the blanks on my CV, and then move on again. Maybe switch to Abrahams & Co, or Pattersons, firms where the kudos was.

The firm of White Hunter was established some fifty years ago by the incumbent senior partner, Charles Hunter, and the now deceased Peter White. With a few notable exceptions, its clientele tends towards the grotty end of the media spectrum. We do contracts, broker deals, resolve disputes. We even act as agents for a few desperate clients. A- and B-list celebs generally get snaffled quick by the big boys; for example, the Dahlias went to Pattersons, an altogether classier outfit, when they decided to sue Brian. We tend to swim in murkier waters: wrinkled popstars, out-of-fashion TV hosts, fossilized celebrities from a bygone age, some of which might be described as Z-listers.

BLAMESTORMING

Monday means the weekly early-morning meeting in the office. By the time I arrive, late as usual, Fulton is already speaking. Fulton is the head of my department, litigation. There's an awkward silence as I apologize and shuffle in and sit down next to David Cohen, my room-mate. We're in a conference room on the sixth floor. Everything is beige. It's 10.30.

We call this blamestorming. The main topic is usually why project X or assignment Y wasn't finished in time, and which member of staff was responsible for that shortcoming. Most of us spend the whole hour keeping our heads down; that doesn't mean we don't take sick pleasure in watching some unlucky bastard get skewered. Today's victim is Lucy Stiles. Lucy lost a case last week because her expert witness developed a crisis of ethics and actually told the truth in the box. The *truth*! I know that problem. Brian suffers from the same affliction.

Fulton goes on for fifteen minutes about the importance of witness coaching. Lucy slowly collapses in on herself as he points out to the rest of the group all the mistakes that she made. This is pretty stolid behaviour; I've seen assistants flee the room in tears. It's particularly impressive since Lucy knows she'll be forced to atone with really grotty stuff for a month. She's probably imagining a dozen trips to hospitals and retirement homes to discuss testamentary requirements with decrepit and deathly television executives and washed-up game-show hosts. That'd be the standard punishment. But I've seen worse: after he missed a court deadline last week, Aaron Platt was forced to atone by working on the pet project of a certain golf-loving Liverpudlian comic. Some kind of variety-show idea that needed our advice. A fate worse than death.

Fulton's moved on now. I'm not really listening as he drones on about the current reforms to the civil justice system, just as I ignored him when he was grumbling about the lack of fees generated by our department during the last fiscal quarter. I'm gazing out of the tinted window of the conference room, which is suffused with gold in the morning winter sun, out onto the rooftops of the offices outside. Everything's still cloaked with last night's snow, the sharp edges rubbed away and everything rendered in smooth, rounded slopes.

'. . . and we've got to get our billing averages *up*, people.'

Fulton is trying to motivate. I snag a sticky Danish from the platter on the table.

'That's why, as of today, I'm pushing up the minimum charging target. The firm expects each of you to charge ten hours a day to a file, unless you've got a good reason why that's not possible. From *today*.'

There is a low murmur of dissent, quickly choked back. Ten hours, and that won't include lunch and fag breaks.

'Shouldn't be a problem,' Dawkins chirps up. People shoot him hateful glances.

'I'm sure it won't,' Fulton says. 'You already average more than that, Oliver. That's impressive. But it's an example I want to see followed by the rest of you.'

The Dork can hardly keep the smirk off his face.

'How far can one man get his tongue up another man's arse?' Cohen hisses, much too loudly. I jab him in the ribs.

I switch my attention back to the window.

'Daniel.'

By combining a studied expression with aimless doodling, I can pass off the impression that I'm paying close attention *and* taking careful notes.

'*Daniel.*'

Cohen elbows me.

My attention snaps back into sharp focus. Everyone is looking at me. I noisily swallow the last of the Danish. The icing sticks to my teeth.

'Glad you could join us, Mr Tate. And, now you're here, let's have that update on the Fey case you promised us.'

Bugger. Fulton asked me to fill in the rest of the group on Brian's defence – I was hammered somewhere in Soho during the time when I'd been planning to prepare it.

'Um, well,' I falter. Dawkins leans forward avidly, hungrily; I can't help thinking of a vulture circling above carrion. 'The case's going as well as could be expected, in the circumstances.'

Fulton raises his eyebrows, expecting more. 'A little background for the others?'

Regurgitate: 'Brian Fey lost the case against the rest of the band six weeks ago, like you all know. They were suing him for the return of an advance they said he wasn't entitled to. This after they'd sacked him. Anyway, as it turns out the court went along with them. We fought as best we could but it was hopeless. The result was pretty inevitable.'

THE NEW CORPORATE LEXICON

'But you're managing the client's expectations?' asks Blaine Fisher, the stuck-up public-school cow who handles our crime stuff.

('Managing the client's expectations.' Jesus, what *is* the world coming to? The entire group has started to use phrases like that, ever since Fulton came back from a week at a business school somewhere in Massachusetts with a whole new corporate vocabulary. Now people 'do' lunch, but only if they can find a suitable 'window' to do it in. They talk about 'downloading' ideas, putting 'ballpark figures' into the 'factual matrix'. Fulton once said, when discussing potential marketing strategies for the group, that he'd 'run that idea up the flagpole to see how it fluttered'. Mixing his public school/military experience with these absurd new buzzwords; you see what I have to put up with? It's a point of honour with me to avoid these nonsenses.)

'The client was pretty OK in the circumstances,' I answer carefully. 'I think we kept his feet on the ground.'

There. A good, old-fashioned English cliché. Much better.

MY INSTRUCTIONS

'So what happens now?' asks the Dork.

'They want to execute their judgment. They want their money back. But our instructions from the record label're to hold on to it for as long as we can. They want us to try and settle.'

'I didn't think we were acting for the label.'

'We act for Brian. But the label's said they'll stand behind him, and since they've been paying our bills they've been telling us what to do.'

Blaine: 'Chances of settling?'

'Zero,' I reply honestly. 'The Dahlias' position's too strong.'

'More *positive*, Daniel,' Fulton urges. 'We need to get Fey out of this without any more damage. The label won't be happy if we lose any of his other assets. We're treading a fine line here.'

'There's a hearing tomorrow,' I say. 'I'm going to try and lift the Freezing Order. That might help things.'

The very evil Victoria Wilson chips in. 'Make sure you're properly prepared for it.'

'I'm working on it today.'

IMMEDIATE SUPERIORS

I'm too slow leaving the conference room. Wilson collars me in the lift. She's responsible for most of my work at the moment. Unfortunately, she doesn't like me very much.

The doors close, sealing us in.

Wilson is a slight and dainty lady of late middle-age, as well preserved as you'd expect a woman earning the thick end of half a million a year to be. Cosmetic science hasn't cured everything: her mouth sags like a cantaloupe rind (her permanent expression is sour), and crow's feet reach back almost to her ears from the corners of her eyes. On the surface she's demure, the sort of woman you might imagine cooking world-class fruit cakes while taking sips of sherry in her silver-haired dotage. A favourite aunt, perhaps? This appearance is deceiving: it hides a toxic heart.

But at least you can say this for Wilson: if Fulton disguises his offensiveness behind a mask of urbanity, then Wilson is completely open about it. She makes no bones about the fact that she is an intemperate, irascible old witch.

'Trish Parkes and her new band've had a change of schedule. I've arranged for them to come by the office on Wednesday afternoon. Three o'clock sharp, and don't be late.'

'New band?' I stammer as we leave the lift.

'Yes, those three young boys. I can't remember what the record company's calling them now . . .'

'Monster Munch?'

'Yes, that's it,' she says.

We arrive at the office I share with Cohen. He's already here. I catch a glimpse of Solitaire on his monitor just before he alt-tabs to a legal database and tries to make himself look busy.

'They're flying to Tokyo on Thursday morning,' Wilson continues, 'for some tour. She wants us to address a new matter while they're over there. I left you a memo.'

'I don't remember seeing anything . . .'

Cohen gets up to leave. Wilson's back is facing him and so she doesn't notice the sarcastic thumbs-up he gives me.

'Your desk's an absolute disgrace,' Wilson comments as her eyes search for my in-tray. She finds it, shuffles through the internal post folders stuffed inside, produces one and tosses it at me. 'I sent you this, last week. It asks you to research the areas we'll need to cover.'

'I'm sorry,' I begin, 'I didn't notice it . . .'

'Look, Tate,' she interrupts, 'don't apologize. Just do what I asked you to do. I want a briefing note on my desk tomorrow morning, eight sharp.'

'I've got the hearing in court on the Fey case tomorrow morning,' I quail.

She scowls darkly. '*Wednesday* morning then. No later. I suppose I'll have to review your note during the morning before the meeting.' Her tone suggests I've put her to considerable personal inconvenience, a crime that will not be lightly forgiven or forgotten.

'Thank you,' I say.

'What about the recording contract?'

'Recording contract?'

'Yes, the foreign jurisdiction contract. Where was it for?'

I half-remember. It's the *other* work I'm doing for Monster Munch.

'Japan?' I suggest.

'Yes, Japan. Is it finished?'

'Not exactly,' I say. 'It's, uh, proving to be rather complicated.'

'You've had over a week,' she gripes. 'And I don't care *how* complicated it is. That's plenty of time for you. A *trainee* could do it in less than a week.'

'I'll get onto it right away,' I tender, even though I'm tempted to suggest she find a willing trainee instead.

'I want that finished on Wednesday morning too. No more excuses.'

'No problem.'

'I'm not happy about your work on this, Tate,' she adds sourly.

This sums up the general state of her recent disposition towards me at the moment. I can't say I'm surprised.

'I'll get to work right away.'

I won't be getting *her* vote in the partnership elections.

But everyone already knows that she holds a candle for Dawkins.

WHY VICTORIA WILSON AND ME DON'T SEE EYE TO EYE

I did a lot of work for Wilson just after I joined White Hunter. In those halcyon days, she regarded me with the affection she reserves for Dawkins now. She was doing a case for Chris Evans, before he really made it big, and she asked me for my opinion on an esoteric point of law. I prepared a report that politely disagreed with the way she'd handled the case. She didn't take it at all well, disagreed, and then disregarded my advice. When the Judge ruled against us, endorsing my proposed approach, she passed the buck and the blame. The partner's prerogative: reprove the assistant.

And that, as they say, was that.

BATTERY LAWYERS

Cohen returns as soon as Wilson is out of the way.

The firm has been growing steadily in recent years but instead of moving to more suitable accommodation – as any sensible business would do – the decision was taken to stay put. Having a prime spot in the right location seems more important than the comfort of the workforce. And Soho and Covent Garden is where the pot of gold at the end of the rainbow is for media firms like us. Agents, film and TV companies, publishers, all the best watering holes; everything is here.

As each new lawyer is added to the practice the available space shrinks accordingly. The walls of the offices are temporary plywood sheets that can be disassembled and reassembled in different configurations.

We've seen our office gradually contract, and now it has the dimensions of a roomy rabbit hutch. We're battery lawyers. We could shake hands across our desks if we wanted to.

Cohen has tried to humanize his side of the room. There are potted plants, a couple of framed prints, and ornaments and holiday souvenirs on his desk. And there's a blow-up screen dump from *Star Wars* stuck to the wall: the scene with Han, Leia, Luke and Chewie trapped in the Death Star garbage compactor, the walls slowly closing in. The partners evidently don't get the hidden plea.

I haven't really reciprocated. All he has to face is me and the dun beige wall behind me, unadorned apart from a stapled-on magazine pull-out poster of the Dahlias from before Brian was sacked. Mid-eighties. They look awful.

'*She* was in a good mood,' Cohen says.

'How come I land her as supervising partner? Have

I upset someone? Am I being punished for something I did in a previous life?'

'She's not *all* bad.'

'Wanna swap with me? I'm sure I can manage the Dystopia case.'

Cohen smiles sweetly at me. 'But that'd deprive me of the fun of watching you jump every time the phone rings.'

'Cheers.'

Cohen's my best friend here. We joined the firm at the same time and have shared an office together for the last year. We both specialize in litigation. His cases tend towards the cerebral. They usually involve the legal construction of contracts and the application of fine points of law. He likens his work to the slow unravelling of a ball of string: the untangling of knots and snags until he finds the end piece. I liken my cases to a drunken dust-up: he who punches hardest, lowest, first, wins. The clients I represent would rather gut the other side with a blunt instrument than endure the rigmarole of the legal system.

His big case at the moment is trying to get Alex Culpepper, the ex-manager of Dystopia, out of a nasty contractual bind he's found himself in. Cohen says Culpepper looks like he's going to be ruined.

Cohen has a good reputation among the partners. He puts up a good front but I know things about him that only a room-mate could know. For example:

1. I know he spends a large portion of the day playing solitaire and minesweeper on the computer.
2. I know he spends another large portion of the day baby-talking to his wife on the phone.
3. I know he has the enviable ability of looking busy when he's doing nothing at all. (When I'm doing nothing I just look shifty.)

You get to know these things when you share an office with someone for ten hours a day. Cohen knows things about me that even Hannah couldn't guess.

But I haven't told him we've broken up yet.

MISSION: IMPOSSIBLE

I switch on my PC and check my diary for today.

I have a meeting with Michael Barrymore at midday. Wonderful.

I open the folder and review Wilson's memo. It sets out what she wants before the meeting with Monster Munch on Wednesday. A briefing note on Japanese contract law. And a marketing agreement for use in Asia. It really is that vague.

'Look at this,' I say to Cohen, tossing the memo over to his desk. 'She wants this by 8 on Wednesday.'

'And that would be 8 in the a.m. or 8 in the p.m.?'

'The former.'

'Ouch.'

'You don't know anything about Japanese law, do you?'

'Nope. But I know a man who does.'

'Go on.'

'You won't like it.'

'I'm desperate. I'll try anyone.'

'Anyone?'

'Anyone.'

'OK,' he says. 'The Dork. He did something similar to this a couple of months ago. He mentioned it in one of the team meetings you missed.'

'I can't ask *him*,' I protest futilely. 'I mean . . . I just *can't*.'

'That's understandable,' he says. 'He is, after all, an arrogant, supercilious shit who'll remind you for months that you needed his help.'

'It'd be humiliating.'

'Definitely.'

'I'll never be able to live it down.'

'Probably not.'

'I can't ask him.'

'The alternative's to sweat it out in the library all night or throw yourself on Wilson's mercy . . .'

'Ohmigod.'

Which would I prefer: measles or mumps?

CONTACT WITH THE GUTTER PRESS

I notice the display on my phone blinking: voicemail. Then the phone rings. I pick up.

'Daniel Tate?' says the caller.

'Yes,' I say. 'Who's this?'

'My name's Scott Dolan. I do the celebrity gossip column for *Extravaganza*. You know, the "Guest List", page 17?'

'Yeah. I've seen it.'

Extravaganza: it's almost compulsory reading for us. The UK's first daily newspaper devoted entirely to news of the glitterati. The secrets of the rich and famous served up for you fresh, each and every day. WORLD EXCLUSIVES and plenty of exclamation marks. Pictures of flabby stars caught out in bikinis by paparazzi with long-range lenses. Snaps of people leaving flats they shouldn't have been in. Kiss-and-tells a speciality. Salacious scandal just the right side of legal. Take one part *Hello!*, add the worst excesses of the red-tops, blend with the *National Enquirer* and you'd still be nowhere close.

And the Guest List, this esteemed organ's gossip page, is the lowest of the low.

'I'm working on a story and I'd like to ask you a few questions – is now a good time to speak?'

'About what?' I'm automatically wary. We get calls from the press occasionally, and have strict instructions not to divulge client information. Transgression is a firing offence.

'Nothing heavy,' he says. 'Just background stuff.'

'About what?'

'You're the solicitor working for Brian Fey, right? In the case against the rest of the Black Dahlias, yeah?'

'Mmm,' I say hesitantly.

'I'm doing something on John French's death. I was wondering if I could get a quote from Brian about it?'

'I'm not really the person to be asking. You should be speaking to his manager.'

'What about you, though,' he says, without pausing. 'Maybe you could give me something? How about it?'

'I don't think that'd be appropriate.'

'What do you think about Brian? Could he've had anything to do with it?'

'Don't be ridiculous.'

'Why d'you say that? That's not what I've been hearing.'

'I'm sorry. I don't think it's appropriate for me to be having this conversation.'

'How's he feeling?'

'I'm not going to be drawn on that.'

'You sure?'

'Quite sure.'

'Well, in case you change your mind, here's my number.' He recites a number which I only pretend to take. 'You'll give me a ring if you change your mind?'

'Goodbye.'

A FRIEND IN HIGH PLACES

As I'm returning from the library with a textbook on Japanese law – hoping against hope there's enough in here to render an appeal to the Dork unnecessary – I pass Richard Tanner's office.

'Daniel,' Tanner calls out, 'pop in for a moment, will you.'

Richard Tanner is one of the senior partners at White Hunter. Mid-forties, always beautifully well-dressed, a brilliant lawyer blessed with a superb rapport with his clients. He and Fulton interviewed me originally when I was thinking about changing firms, and we hit it off straight away. He was one of the main reasons I decided to come here.

I've never been in any doubt he persuaded Fulton I was worthy of an offer. Fulton prefers his lawyers to share his public-school and Oxbridge heritage. He prefers people like Dawkins, the silver-spoon brigade. Tanner, on the other hand, was educated much like me: comprehensive schools and red brick Uni, pulling himself up by his boot straps. He's been my backer ever since that interview, feeding me great files to make my reputation on. The case I did for Bob Monkhouse last year, when even Wilson had to acknowledge the quality of the work, was all down to him.

'How's it going?' he says.

'Really busy,' I say, sitting down. 'Wilson's got me sweating on some tight deadlines.'

'Victoria on the warpath, is she?' he chuckles. 'Rather you than me.'

Mild indiscretion when it comes to his colleagues in the partnership is one of Tanner's charms. 'I'll be fine,' I say, 'touch wood.'

'Look, I wanted to tell you something. I probably shouldn't say, but I will anyway. You know, with Miles dying, there's going to be a place in the partnership up for grabs. I just wanted you to know that I've put your name forward for it.'

I feel like punching the air. Tanner comes through for me, yet again.

'Richard, thanks, I don't know what—'

'You deserve it. You've done some great work for me since you left the City. I think you'd make a first-class partner, so I'm prepared to be your sponsor. So, you know, good luck. You know who else's going to be up for it?'

'If I had to guess? David Cohen. Caroline Lewis. Oliver Dawkins.'

'Dawkins – Jesus,' Tanner says with a gently derisive laugh. Tanner has told me on more than one occasion how little he thinks of Dawkins. He – alone amongst all of the partnership as it sometimes seems – has seen through him: 'A toadying, mealy-mouthed, spineless brown-noser,' as he once told me over a pint.

'He's popular with Fulton and Wilson,' I say.

Tanner nods. 'I know he is,' he says, 'but they're not the only ones who get to vote. It's a majority decision.

Look, there're no guarantees on this but I just thought you ought to know.'

'Thanks,' I say. 'I really appreciate it.'

'You owe me a beer.'

A NEW FACE AT THE PHOTOCOPIER

Despite my elation at Tanner's news, the morning is still dragging by. I'm still tired from last night; I'd love to be able to find a quiet corner and curl up to sleep. I've been drafting a fifty-page witness statement spelling out the reasons why the court should release the Freezing Order over Brian's assets. Freezing Orders freeze bank accounts, stop you doing anything with your property, your cash, your assets. But it's difficult to summon up enthusiasm for arguments I know have absolutely no chance of success. The court was eager to make this Freezing Order; in the Judge's opinion, Brian Fey was up to no good.

I'm lazily running the statement through the photo-copier when I realize someone is waiting behind me.

'Won't be a moment,' I say, immediately trying to look industrious. I've been caught daydreaming in here too many times before.

'There's no hurry,' replies a voice I don't recognize. I turn around as the copier punches staples through the documents for me. 'Hi,' I beam.

'Hi,' says the slim, good-looking girl standing in the doorway.

'We haven't met, have we?'

'I'm Rachel.'

She can't be more than twenty-four, fresh out of Chester or Store Street law school. She looks keen and determined. There's a spread of light freckles across the bridge of her nose, ducking down onto her cheeks. Red hair tied back in a bunch with a scrunchy. Lightly tanned, probably the product of six months' travelling between the end of college and the beginning of training. She's laden down with a double-armful of law reports.

'Here, let me help you.' I unload the books onto the counter next to the copier. I take her hand and squeeze it gently. 'Daniel Tate.'

'Hello, Daniel.'

'Those look interesting,' I grin, pointing at the spread-eagled books. Some of the dusty spines date back to the late nineteenth century.

Nervous laugh: 'I just hope I've got the right references. I'm supposed to be researching contractual capacity. At least I *think* that's what he wants. It's been six months since I did that. There was this course at law school but now I can't remember a thing about it.'

'I shouldn't worry. Listen, a word of advice: one of the first things you'll find out working here is that no one ever actually does any law. It's all letter writing and presentation these days. The barristers do all the interesting stuff.'

'Great,' she says. 'Letter writing and presentation – two of my strengths.'

'You're new here, aren't you?'

'I'm Mr Fulton's new trainee. Started yesterday.'

'Fulton . . .' I pause melodramatically.

'He's not *that* bad, is he?'

The look of mild terror my allusion to Fulton provokes is familiar, and even a little appealing. She's probably finding the whole experience terrifying. Just like I did.

'No, not *that* bad,' I say. 'I mean, comparatively speaking, he's an angel.'

She brightens, then starts to blush. 'You must think I'm pathetic, don't you? I never thought doing this would be so – I don't know – so *daunting*. It's like another world. So much to learn.'

'Law school seems irrelevant now?' I grin.

'Exactly,' she says. 'So you do know what I mean?'

'I can just about remember,' I say, 'although it was a while ago.' My copying finished, I collect it from the tray. 'All yours.'

'Well, it was nice meeting you,' she says.

I shine what I hope is a friendly, reassuring smile. 'You too. If you need any help, my office's just around the corner.'

She looks up from angling an opened book on the copier plate and follows the direction of my pointed finger. 'Thanks,' she says cheerfully. 'I might take you up on that.'

'And if you want the low-down on the office, let me know. We could maybe do it over a coffee or something?'

Whoah, back up. I can't believe that I just said that.

'That'd be nice,' she says.

And I can't believe that she said yes.

'I'll give you a call,' I say.

APPRAISAL

'Have you *seen* the new trainee?' I blurt to Cohen as soon as I'm safely back in the office.

'Fulton's new trainee?' I'm *that* obvious.

I nod vigorously. 'I'll say one thing for the recruitment policy here. Apart from the odd boiler to keep the average seeming respectable, the partnership signs up some bloody great women.'

'Easy, tiger,' he says, 'you're off the market.'

I remind myself, Cohen doesn't know about Hannah. 'Yeah,' I agree.

'So keep your sweaty paws to yourself.'

'It's not like I fancy her or anything,' I protest weakly.

'Course you don't,' he says with a lascivious wink.

UNDER A TUSCAN SUN

The mention of Hannah trips a switch.

Memories spool:

Last September in Tuscany: the sun-bleached bricks of an ancient farmhouse on the crest of a sun-dried valley; Hannah and I dozing in hammocks strung up between the brick pillars of a derelict barn. Two weeks away from London, swapping the noise and smoke of the metropolis for brilliant blue sky and birdsong. Swapping sandwiches and soft drinks from Pret for fresh pasta with herbs from the garden and red wine from the vineyard at the bottom of the track. Books folded face down on our chests, a pitcher of iced-water slowly warming in the shade, ice-cubes knocking against the glass.

I looked over at my girlfriend and remembered why it was I loved her.

Perhaps feeling my eyes on her, Hannah looked over at me and smiled.

For that brief moment, everything was perfect.

The sun shone down into our eyes. The brown earth baked. We closed our eyes and dozed off again.

GETTING READY FOR BARRYMORE

I'm not sure what Barrymore wants, but he often pops in for off-the-cuff advice. Fifteen minutes before the appointment I follow my usual pre-meeting routine. I hide in the toilets, take a few long swigs from a half-pint of Jack Daniels, straighten my hair and tie, and gargle a mouthful of Listerine.

This routine started a month after I moved to White Hunter from the City. Terry Wogan had asked me for some impromptu advice on the law of inheritance and I had no idea what to tell him. I had no experience; the City firms don't touch things like that, there's no money in it for them. I realized then that my expensive corporate education would be completely useless in my new job. These new clients, used to getting what they wanted, had no compunction in seeking snap advice, and no problem assigning blame when that advice was wrong. When my fumbled explanation of the law of intestacy proved wide of the mark, Wogan complained to Wilson and I was hauled over the coals.

And it was the insincerity of sucking up to celebrities I found, to my surprise, I really couldn't stand. For example: in a conversation with a famous television magician (who shall remain nameless) and a few others, the subject of the London Underground was somehow raised. In response to a general question put to the group, the magician responded haughtily, "Of course I don't know how much the bloody tube fare costs, I don't have to, do I?" It's tough to feel professional loyalty for these kinds of people.

So I started to take little drinks before going into meetings. Just small ones, enough to take the edge off.

They relaxed me, loosened me up, made me much more convincing when I, inevitably, found myself winging it.

After a while, a nip of whisky become a regular occurrence. Presentations to the partners were made easier by a small libation. Applications to court went more smoothly after a couple G and Ts. Quite soon after that a drink first thing, the hair of the dog, began to seem like a good idea. The more the pressure, the more I drank.

That took care of the daytime.

In the evenings, we were expected to hit the media scene in order to schmooze. There were clients out there just waiting to be stolen away from their incumbent advisers. The expense account and my liver both took a hammering two or three times a week. It got so that I was a regular face at the Ivy and Teatro, on nodding terms with surly French waiters who silently recharged my empty glasses.

I drank for lubrication and to drown out the disgust at my own insincerity.

And the celebs we were entertaining brought their own entertainment, too, illicit contraband of which a dusting or a handful would occasionally come my way. And it's rude to refuse a gift when offered, don't you think?

I started to develop an assortment of insidious little habits. But it's nothing to worry about, nothing I can't handle. Just as soon as work allows, I'm going to cut back.

Barrymore is waiting downstairs. I pass through reception, where Richard Madeley and Judy Finnegan are comparing tans with Mark Perryman from the property department, and stop by the door to the conference room. I can see Barrymore's silhouette in the smoked glass. He looks down at his watch.

I smooth out my suit, tug down my French cuffs and walk confidently inside.

SEAGULL PARTNER

The meeting goes well. Barrymore has an idea for a new game show and he wants some legal input before he takes it to the ITV execs. I listened, pretended to take notes, made encouraging noises when they were required. He leaves more than happy to pay the £500 he'll be charged for my time.

I walk him to the door and then pop outside for a chilly fag break. I nod at Gloria Hunniford as she exits the building. As I make my way back inside I'm intercepted by Tim Renwick, one of the younger partners in the litigation department.

We call Renwick the Seagull Partner. This on account of the fact that his attitude to problem-solving is to fly in, make lots of noise, crap over everything and then fly off again. His main negotiation tactic: shout louder than the other guy. He's known for loud braces and an insistence on good-looking female trainees to whom he suggests it'd benefit their careers if they'd let him shag them. They often agree. He's only five years older than me and we've never really hit it off. Jealousy and the fact he earns at least three times as much as I do have *nothing* to do with it, OK?

'Tate,' he says, stepping into my way, 'how was Barrymore?'

'He just needed some reassuring on this idea he's had.'

'Don't know why we bother with him, but Hunter insists.'

'Maybe he thinks he'll make it back again.'

Renwick flashes a superficial smile that tells me what he thinks of that proposition. But he changes the subject: 'What's your capacity like at the moment? I have to do a beauty parade for the new Clooney movie. He's looking for UK lawyers.'

Like our grotty little firm has *any* chance of landing George Clooney. He'll be snapped up by Abrahams & Co or Pattersons double quick.

'I'm pretty busy,' I say.

'You can find time for something for me,' he insists. 'Don't forget what Fulton said about targets. We need to get the billings up. Here's your chance.'

'Look, I don't know . . .'

'I'm not really asking.'

Listen to him, the macho bastard. 'What is it?' I sigh wearily.

'One of my clients needs a witness statement

drafting,' he says. 'Nothing fancy. It ought to be straightforward.'

This really takes the biscuit but what can I say? Turning work away is a cardinal sin at White Hunter. And, despite his lack of seniority, Renwick has a vote in the partnership election. He's not someone I can afford to upset.

'I've had my secretary copy the pleadings, the previous statements and a summary of the case that Counsel prepared. The facts're a bit complicated and you'll need to study them before the meeting.'

'When's that?'

'I've set it up for 3. He's in London for a shoot – some show he's appearing in – and he can only do today. He's got a busy schedule. Wants to meet you at his hotel. The details're all with my secretary.'

'It's already 2.30.'

'Then you'd better get going.'

'But—'

'It's nothing too demanding – the other statements're all in the eighty-page ballpark and we're probably looking at something around that kind of length.' His tone says: this better not be a problem.

I say: 'I'm sure I'll manage.' I think: Bye-bye social life.

'We're exchanging evidence with the other side on Thursday so I'll need it to review with Counsel by Wednesday morning at the latest.'

Wilson's deadline for the stuff on Monster Munch is Wednesday morning.

'Go and see my secretary for the details. And you'd better get going now. You're going to be late.'

IT'S A SMALL, SMALL WORLD

As I leave in a taxi headed to the hotel I flick through the thumbnail summary of the case Counsel has prepared.

I can hardly believe it.

White Hunter is representing Vincent Haines, the American actor who plays one of the male leads in *Skin Trade*. Haines has been sued by an LA production company for breach of contract after he ditched a project there, a police movie – *Defence of the Badge* – so he could appear in the series here. We're defending the claim on his behalf. Haines is staying at the Sanderson while the series shoots, and I've been slotted in to see him this afternoon.

This is a scary coincidence. I already know plenty about Vincent Haines.

Most pertinently: I know he's Hannah's current screen boyfriend and that he's kissed her far more recently than I have. I'm now wondering whether I should pump him for the details, refresh my memory a little?

The thing is, the showbiz gossip columns have been suggesting for a couple of weeks that there might be an explanation for why their screen kisses look more passionate than you might expect.

AN EXTRACT FROM *HELLO!*

There was a picture of Haines and Hannah in *Hello!* last week. The caption beneath the picture read:

> *SKIN TRADE heartthrob VINCENT HAINES, stepping out (again) with luscious co-star HANNAH WILDE. Rumour has it that these two lovebirds are doing* far *more together than simply rehearsing their lines. From the looks of things they're taking method acting to a whole new level!*

Vincent Haines, the star of such sub-Hollywood pot-boilers as *Body Double IV, (Still) Crazy for You* and *Police Academy IX: One More Mission*, films that generally by-pass theatrical release on their way to late-night satellite broadcast and the video store bargain bucket.

Vincent Haines, twenty-five, devilishly handsome in a vapid sub-Keanu way.

Vincent Haines, currently sporting a greasy mop, an immaculately trimmed goatee, and my girlfriend on his arm.

LIFESTYLES OF THE RICH AND FAMOUS

Even wearing my best suit I'd feel totally out of place in the lobby of the Sanderson. The place reeks of money and class. I'm waiting for the receptionist – an impassive beauty who sneered disdainfully at me when I rang the desk bell for attention – to relay news of my arrival to Haines's suite. She nods at whatever the person on the other end of the house phone is saying, and then cups her hand over the receiver.

'I'm afraid Mr Haines isn't expecting any visitors this afternoon.'

'I'm his lawyer,' I explain.

'One moment.'

While she relays this information to the person on the other end of the line, I'm worrying about the work beginning to pile up on my desk. In order of urgency, the briefing note and the marketing agreement Wilson wants me to draft for Monster Munch come first. Plus Wilson shouts a lot louder than Renwick does. I'll have to do those tonight and tomorrow, and then work late to type up whatever inane drivel Vincent Haines comes up with now. Brian's case will have to take a back seat as soon as I've finished with the hearing tomorrow.

My credentials check out. 'Mr Haines's suite is on the top floor. It's that lift over there.'

I follow her instructions and find my way to the door to the suite.

73

YOUNG AMERICANS

'Hold on,' calls a muffled voice after I knock on it. The door is opened on its chain and a blandly handsome male face peers out at me.

'Yeah?' the owner of the face says. He's blond, tanned and considerably younger than me.

'I'm Daniel Tate. From White Hunter? I'm here to see Vincent Haines. I've got an appointment.'

The kid turns and bellows into the suite, 'Hey Vinny – your lawyer's here. Do we like let him in, or what?' The muffled response is in the affirmative; the chain is unhooked and I am admitted.

'Sorry about that,' says the kid. 'We've been having problems with fans wanting to see Vincent. London chicks are like *so* crazy. Can't keep 'em away. I'm Rip, by the way.' He extends a broad hand. I take it.

All the curtains in the suite are closed and the atmosphere is wreathed with smoke and the smell of hash. Copies of this week's *Extravaganza* are scattered on the floor. A TV set is on, with the sound muted, and changing scenes flicker chill blue light through the room. As my eyes adjust I make out Haines lounging on a sofa, flicking through a copy of *Time Out* and chugging from a bottle of Absolut. Haines is wearing an unbuttoned Hawaiian-print shirt and has rings through his nose, ears, one of his exposed nipples and an eyebrow. A spliff is smoking on a saucer balanced on the back of the sofa. As I pick a careful path through the debris on the floor, he rises unsteadily and offers me his hand.

'Vincent Haines,' he says.

I shake his hand. 'Daniel Tate.'

'Good to meet you, Danny. Call me Vinny.'

I ignore the annoying contraction of my name and say, 'Shall we make a start?'

Haines sweeps a newspaper off a chair and sits down. The air is thick, sweetly intoxicating.

'You wanna drink? Spliff? Rip's been on the phone to this dealer he knows. Maybe we could do a few bumps later when the order comes.'

'I told you,' interjects Rip, 'it's not blow, man – blow's *so* last century. It's Special *K*.'

'Coke, ketamine, who gives a fuck?' Haines says and then, explaining, 'All the same to me.'

'Your nose is so shot you wouldn't know if you were sniffing brick dust,' says Rip.

'Hey, shut up and go fetch the cookie jar from the kitchen. I've got the munchies.'

'Yeah, *right*,' says Rip. He lobs a training shoe limply at Haines, who bats it aside.

I'm about to decline his offer of a drink when I have a change of heart. The drink I had before I met Barrymore has long since worn off. Another fortifying blast is just what the doctor ordered; I can see this is going to be a long afternoon. 'A vodka'd be great.'

'Rip, get the man a vodka.' Rip diffidently rinses a glass and pours me out a generous measure.

'I love this town,' Haines says, lounging back into the sofa, 'don't you? You want something to eat? We got take-outs.' He points over to a table with a dozen McDonalds's brown paper takeaway bags on it. I can smell the sweet burger meat and the saltiness of the fries. I decline politely.

'About your case—' I begin, braced by a sip of the vodka.

'What a fucking *drag*,' he interrupts, 'don't you think? Can you believe those stress puppies would actually wanna *sue* me? Me? Jesus. But it's not like this's a first. One of the crosses we've gotta bear in the trade, fucking litigation. *Way* bogus. So, anyways, that's why I'm paying you guys the big bucks, right? So you can nuke their case. Nip it right in the bud. Nix it for me.'

This is heavy going. 'I know all the details of the case' – a lie – 'but I need your angle on things. Then I can write up a statement taking your point of view into account. I'm going to tape this, if you don't mind.' He shrugs disinterestedly and so I take out my Dictaphone, click it on, and set it down on the coffee table between us.

Haines leans forward and starts to lecture, making explanatory gestures with his hands. 'It's pretty simple, man,' he says. 'Jerks had a shit, straight-to-video movie planned. My agent goofed and signed me up for it. *She* got her ass fired, let me tell you.' He high-fives a passing Rip.

'So don't fuck up, OK?' Rip adds. 'Vinny's, like, totally ruthless.'

I smile nervously and finish the vodka.

Haines continues, 'Then *Skin Trade* came along and I decided it was a better vehicle for someone like me. So I jumped town and came over here. And here I am.'

'Whoah,' I say. 'You can't actually *say* that.'

'Say what?'

'That you left to come and do *Skin Trade*, knowing about the film.'

'Why not?'

'Because that proves their case. You'll *lose* if you say that.'

'Listen.' He pours a handful of roasted peanuts into his mouth and munches on them noisily. 'I *know* that, man,' he says slowly, as if he considers me stupid. 'We *both* know I probably *am* in breach of their precious fucking contract. But I'm just giving you the big picture. I leave it to my lawyers to decide what to leave in and what to leave out. That's what I pay you for. If I say anything that's not good for me, you can just strip it out. I never said it, right? And if this case goes to trial, and I hope to God it doesn't, you can tell me exactly what I have to say to make the bad man go away. Got me?'

This is impossible. Quite apart from his blasé attitude, Haines is so completely stoned I'm never going to get any sense out of him. I click off the Dictaphone, put it away, drain my second vodka.

'Another?' he asks. I nod. Rip, orbiting the two of us, refills me.

I decide to change subject. 'So – Hannah Wilde.'

'You know Hannah?' he says.

'Who doesn't? She's a big star.'

'She's a hot chick.'

'What's it like to kiss her? You know, on the show?'

'Pretty great.'

'Yeah? Tell me about it.'

'Get outta here,' Haines laughs.

'No, seriously – I'm interested. How'd you two get together?'

'Come on, spill the beans, man,' says Rip, flicking through the muted channels on the TV. 'It's safe – he's your lawyer. There's that whole client confidentiality thing going on, right?'

'He's right,' I say, 'tell me the story. I'd love to hear it. And I swear I won't tell anyone. Scout's honour.'

CONFESSIONS OF A MOVIE STAR

Vincent Haines doesn't need any more encouragement to talk about his favourite subject: Vincent Haines.

He leans forward conspiratorially.

'OK, Hannah: not bad-looking, great tits, legs that just keep on going, you know; just like this extremely fuckable piece of pussy. Well, as you can imagine I'm pretty happy when I find out she's gonna be the love interest in the new show. Never seen her on TV before, but those raw showbiz virgins're always the keenest to impress, if you know what I mean . . .'

Rip whoops, leans over and slaps him a high-five. I look at the overflowing ashtray on the table and wonder how heavy it is, how much damage a quick swipe would do to the back of his head . . .

Haines continues: 'Anyways, I turn up for a day's shoot and we're getting on pretty well, we've got this neat on-screen chemistry thing going, everything's just *sizzling* and the director's real happy with the both of us. So I think to myself, Vinny, why not see if she's as wild as it looks like she is. I get her number from my PA and start calling. At first she was reluctant – I think maybe there might've been someone else – but I was persistent. Sent her flowers, presents, the works, eventually managed to persuade her to go out for dinner with me. Went to the Ivy. Nothing happened but I ain't giving up just like that. After like a month of this I get my first kiss. She says she feels bad about it afterwards, won't take things along to the next level, starts to get this major guilt trip about the other dude she's still seeing.'

'And this guy's a lawyer,' Rip adds. 'Just like you.'

'What an amazing coincidence,' I manage to say.

I'm thinking about the flowers I didn't buy and the presents I didn't send when I notice Haines is continuing the story. 'After a couple of months I took her out again and this time I got the invite back to her place. She said this other guy had gone off her. We hooked up and, like they say, the rest is history.'

'Hey, man, show's on,' hollers Rip, unmuting the TV. I look over. The opening titles to *Skin Trade* are playing. I realize: time for the Monday afternoon repeat.

'This episode rocks,' Haines says, putting his feet up on the coffee table. 'This's where Hannah and me get it on out back of the fashion shoot.'

One of Hannah's female co-stars is slinking down a catwalk to a chorus of camera flashes.

'Man, that broad is *hot*,' Rip says.

'That's Jessica,' Haines says. 'Got a date with her next week.'

Haines and Rip become engrossed in the show and quickly forget about me. I filch the half-empty bottle of Absolut for the taxi ride back to the office, and shuffle out of the suite.

I stand outside the door for a moment, sweating in the sterile cool of the corridor, trying to stop myself from throwing up my lunch.

DISPATCHES FROM THE FRONT

'You'll never guess what the Dork has gone and done,' Cohen says.

I feel like telling him he'll never guess what Hannah has gone and done.

'Surprise me,' I say. Cohen's calling me on my mobile while I'm in a taxi heading back to the office.

'His seccie told me he's asked her to book out a restaurant for a party to celebrate him being made up to partner. Can you believe that?'

'Jesus, they haven't even started to interview yet.'

'You might call it somewhat presumptuous.'

'He can't've been told already, surely? No one's said anything to me.'

'He hasn't been told, not according to her. She said he told her that he was, quote, "quietly confident of getting the nod," unquote. I'd love to see him fall on his face.'

'Don't hold your breath,' I say, despite agreeing with the aspiration wholeheartedly.

'You hear there's been a press conference on the John French death?' he says.

'What do they reckon? Suicide?'

'They're still investigating. The word is they've found something not right, you know, something making them think he didn't do it himself after all.'

'Shit.'

'I still reckon it's some kind of kinky sex game gone wrong,' Cohen adds. 'Just wish I could persuade some of my less agreeable clients to get themselves into that kind of scene . . .'

THE HABITS OF HIGHLY
EFFECTIVE PEOPLE

It's now the early evening and I'm in the partners' luncheon room for the group's monthly social meeting, sipping at a cold beer and trying to look as inconspicuous as possible. I can think of a dozen things I'd rather be doing, but these meetings get a three-line whip from Fulton. He thinks it important that the assistants take these regular opportunities to 'bond' with each other. It helps perpetuate the delusion that he's presiding over a happy ship – rather than over a bunch of infighting, eye-gouging, socially maladjusted misfits.

Once, Fulton invited a motivational speaker to attend the meeting. Fulton called him a 'facilitator'. I believe he may have been responsible for one of the psychological self-help books that seem so popular at the moment. We had an uncomfortable meal and then suffered two hours of New Age mysticism which would, we were assured, bring us closer together. Words like 'family', 'team' and 'togetherness' were bandied around. There was a lot of awkward hugging. All that was missing was the clasping of hands, and an hour of tantric chanting, before each participant floated unaided up the lift shafts.

You might not be surprised to hear I find these evenings a strain. The only way of getting through the ordeal is to drink. I've corralled a clutch of cold beer bottles from the fridge to lubricate the hour or so until I can make a discreet exit.

I'm next to Cohen. We're standing up against a wall on the periphery of the group. A series of framed portraits of some of Charles Hunter's more famous clients are hung around the room. Stars he served loyally for twenty years, stars from the golden age of entertainment, long since in their graves: Diana Dors, Kenneth Williams, Dusty Springfield, Tony Hancock, Morecambe and Wise. Hunter's problem, if anything, was too *much* loyalty; he stuck with them even as their stars began to wane, when he should have ditched them and sought out a slate of ambitious young turks. While we have held onto a few stars, the firm has since acquired a somewhat geriatric reputation. It's been struggling to catch up with the competition ever since.

Dawkins is talking intently to Fulton and Wilson. He's in his usual office uniform: chalk pinstripe suit, two-tone blue shirt with white collar, red bow tie, braces. He makes a comment and gets polite laughter from both partners.

'I'd love to shove that bow tie up his arse,' I say.

'A word to the wise,' Cohen says into my ear. 'You ought to keep an eye on him. He's been sniffing around your cases. Something about a closed-door meeting with Fulton.'

'He's been after Brian Fey for ages. He'd be right up his alley.'

'Especially with the John French thing happening,

everything in the papers like it is. I've never seen anyone so self-obsessed. Anything with even a *hint* of glory and he wants it. You know he's got a three-paragraph eulogy in this month's *Media Lawyer*? Best young lawyer or something like that?'

In truth, the Dork *is* a good lawyer. Good, but not brilliant. He's superbly organized; what he lacks in creativity he more than makes up for with solid methodology. And he's the best self-publicist I've ever met.

'He gets on my tits,' Cohen continues. 'He's desperate for partnership and he's going to clamber all over us to get it.'

I nod. The Dork qualified a year after Cohen and me. He ought to be behind us on the ladder to partnership, but everyone knows he's miles ahead.

'Who do you reckon'll sponsor him for the partnership election?' I ask.

'Fulton or Wilson. They both love him.'

'You know Tanner's put me forward?'

Cohen clinks bottles with me. 'Nice one,' he says with a big, genuine smile. 'I'd love to see you get it.'

'What about you?'

He pauses and cautiously scans the room. Satisfied he won't be overheard he leans forward and says quietly, 'Between you and me, that might not be something I have to worry about. I'm thinking about moving on.' I raise an eyebrow. 'I put my CV out with a few agencies on the off-chance, out of curiosity mostly, got a few interviews and now I've been offered a job at one of the New York firms. General litigation with little bits of arbitration thrown in. Hardly rocket science, I know, but they've offered to double my salary. Six figures, plus massive annual bonuses and free trips to the States. I'm thinking I might take it.'

'That's great,' I say. 'Wow.'

'I mean, you have to at least *think* about that kind of deal,' he says. 'It's tempting.'

'You don't have to justify it to me,' I say. 'God, it sounds amazing.'

'Like I say, I'm tempted.'

'Be sad to see you go,' I say. I'm pleased for him, and more than a little jealous.

'I haven't made up my mind yet. It's a big decision. I need to get it right.'

We both drink to that.

'Listen,' I say, changing the subject. 'Keep an eye on my desk for me tomorrow, will you? I'm in court early on and I don't want the Dork sniffing around.'

'No problem,' Cohen says. 'You got an application?'

'Yeah,' I say glumly. 'A big one.'

'The Fey case?'

'Yep. I'm going to have to go back to the office in a minute to get ready for it. We're supposed to be trying to discharge the Freezing Order – not that we've got any chance of doing that, of course. I need to finish off a witness statement and get my notes sorted. The client won't stump up for a barrister, so yours truly's on his hind legs.'

'Daniel Tate QC?'

'Best there is.'

'Good luck.'

'I'll need it – his record company seems to've got the idea that the Order's just going to be automatically lifted. If it isn't . . .' I leave the sentence hanging.

Cohen draws the edge of his hand horizontally across his throat.

'Exactly. They'll know who to blame.'

A DATE

I'm scratching my head as Rachel wafts past my open door two hours later. The floor is quiet, the only sounds the hum of the air conditioning and the whirring of my computer's fan. I've been trying to get my head around the case law for tomorrow, but I've just been reading the same sentence over and over again. I did think about making a start on Victoria Wilson's work for Monster Munch but the prospect of being under-prepared for the hearing was too worrying for me to concentrate on anything else.

I'm getting nowhere. For the last five minutes I've been zoned out, staring vacantly through the window at the black wedge of the building across Soho Square, office lights still shining and snow falling like static between. Dozens of people are heading to and from Oxford Street, in transit between various bars and restaurants, Christmas and the holidays more than reason enough to celebrate.

'Rachel,' I call out. There's a pause as she reverses direction and puts her head around the door. I'm either impressed or mortified by her dedication, I can't quite decide which; she hasn't been here a month and already she's settled into the midnight oil routine.

'Hi,' she says. 'Working late?'

'Tell me about it,' I say. A thought establishes itself and I let it out without thinking: 'Fancy that drink when you've knocked off? I could give you the low-down on the office, like I promised.'

I'm surprised I'm able to finish that sentence without my voice climbing octaves and fluttering away in self-conscious scraps.

She pauses and looks at her watch. 'I've just got to finish this copying for James, but that won't take long. A drink'd be nice.'

James? She's already calling him *James?*

'Ten minutes then?' I suggest.

'Why not,' she says. 'Ten minutes.'

GETTING TO KNOW RACHEL

I take her to a quiet bar I know. The kind of place I'm confident we won't be observed by anyone from the office. My intentions might be perfectly innocent (they're not) but I know from experience how quickly rumours spread.

Rachel is drinking a Diet Coke. I've got a double whisky, rocks. I expected the atmosphere to be awkward, the way it usually is when two people with no shared history struggle for common ground. But it's nothing like that at all. She has an easygoing nature and we get along well.

She's already confirmed my suspicion of a recent foreign trip. She worked her way around the southern hemisphere for five months: stops in India, New Zealand and Australia. There's a wistfulness in her recollections: vivid memories probably iridescent compared to the numb dampness of a December London. I let her talk for twenty minutes, but now the exchange has moved on and I'm presenting colourful thumbnail sketches of the rest of the department.

She points at my fast-emptying glass. 'Another?'

'Love one,' I say.

She returns from the bar and settles back onto her chair. 'Now, *Wilson*,' I say, continuing the earlier theme, 'has a bit of a reputation. You want to tread carefully if you ever have to work for her. And if you can't avoid her, get ready to duck when you make a mistake. And you *will* make a mistake – she'll make sure of that.'

'But she looks so . . .' She leaves a pause hanging.

'Nice?' I suggest. 'She eats trainees for breakfast.'

She lifts her eyebrows in surprise. 'And what about Mr Dawkins?' she asks. 'What's he like?'

'*Mr* Dawkins?' I splutter, since formality equals seniority at White Hunter. 'Dawkins isn't a partner. He hasn't told you he's a partner, has he?'

'No,' she says. 'I was just guessing. He gave me some work to do for him this afternoon. He just has this air about him, know what I mean? Kind of dignified – don't you think?' She looks concerned. 'Um, Daniel – have I said something out of turn?'

I smile tightly at her, shake my head in the negative, check how much longer there is to go until last orders, and then accelerate my drinking accordingly.

SCOTT DOLAN'S GUEST LIST

World's Greatest Showbiz Column

JOHN FRENCH
Tributes pour in

The showbiz world united yesterday in paying tribute to **JOHN FRENCH**, the singer of the **BLACK DAHLIAS** found dead at his London home yesterday.

ROBBIE WILLIAMS told me: 'The Dahlias were a massive influence on me and I knew John well. He was a top bloke.'

GEORGE MICHAEL said: 'When I was in WHAM! we got to know the Dahlias pretty well. John was quiet – but a really nice guy.'

MARTIN VALENTINE, one of John's ex-bandmates, said he felt numb. 'I don't know what to feel. It's such a terrible shock.'

I tried to speak with **BRIAN FEY**, the Dahlias' ex-singer. But heartless Fey wouldn't take my calls. His lawyer, City whizzkid **DANIEL TATE**, said he 'wasn't prepared to be drawn upon' how his client was feeling. Not the kind of thing you'd expect from someone you'd imagine to be more upset than most.

More on this story tomorrow.

80s wildchilds **AMANDA DE CADENET** and **NICK KAMEN** looked like they were enjoying each other's company at the Groucho Club.

A once-famous movie star is being investigated by police for tax evasion. This ex-icon certainly hasn't been filling out his returns properly...

Tuesday

RUNNING LATE

The next morning and I'm in the back of a taxi, crawling through the traffic on the Embankment. Everyone is gridlocked except the bike couriers in layers of brash Lycra, zipping in and out of the narrow gaps like multi-coloured pilot fish. Snow is all around. The radio tells us the temperature is minus five today. *Minus five!*

For the tenth time, I recalculate the time it will take to reach court. In my best-case scenario, I'm going to be horribly late. I'm having a difficult morning.

FORTY-FIVE MINUTES EARLIER

Rewind:

The gritter woke me, grinding along the road beneath my bedroom window, spraying salt over the icy surface. Granules pecked against the downstairs windows and the bodywork of parked cars. I just lay there, on my back, filtering the sudden barrage of noise: the rumble of engines from the bus garage, a train, a radio playing, the distant sounds of playground voices, muffled traffic on the main road.

Nelson was stretched out on the end of the bed. He yawned expansively.

My first thought: why didn't the alarm go off?

I rolled over and raised myself onto an elbow to check the time. The hands showed 5.15. I knew that couldn't be right; the curtains were glowing with morning sunlight through the fabric. The clock must have stopped in the night. Not for the first time. The electricity has been cutting out recently and I still haven't gotten around to fixing it. I'd have an electrician around if I thought I could afford it.

I swung my legs onto the floor. The walls tilted towards me and the floor plunged away; the full glory of my hangover became apparent. What did I do to deserve this?

Did I really want to know? How bad had I been last night? How embarrassed should I be this morning?

I scraped the sleep out of my eyes and looked for my watch. I noticed a long cut curling from my knuckles down the back of my hand. Dry blood crusted around the gash, mounting tiny shards of powdered glass. I had no idea of how I'd come by it.

I found my watch: it said 9.15.

Forty-five minutes to get up, get dressed and get to court. I polished the dust from the mirror of the wall cabinet in the bathroom and confronted my reflection.

My eyes were slits ringed with red loops. Chunks of white debris had collected around the corners of my mouth, I was heavily stubbled and my hair looked like I'd been sleeping in a wind tunnel. I slapped on a handful of gel and patted it back into shape, scrubbed a toothbrush around my gums, cleaned the cut on my hand, rinsed my face in cold water and took the electric shaver back into the bedroom with me, in search of my clothes.

Another piece of last night's events recalled: I'd lost my jacket, must have left it at the bar. And my spare suit is still at the dry cleaners. All I had in the flat was an unironed shirt and a pair of trousers which were, I noticed, covered in vomit. When was I sick? Puking up isn't something I'd forget in a hurry.

I try to remember the conclusion of the evening. I can't even remember saying goodbye to Rachel.

I hope I haven't disgraced myself.

By this time it was now 9.30.

I filled Nelson's bowl with biscuits and ran him some clean water. No time for any breakfast for me. I tried to wipe off the sick on my trousers with a damp cloth. Partial success. It smeared and the water revitalized the smell. I felt sick again. I *was* sick again. Dry heaves mostly, my head down the toilet bowl spitting out phlegm.

SOME NEIGHBOURLY CONCERN

Fast forward:

Hodgson, who owns the flat beneath mine, was scrubbing at a red palm print with a sudsy sponge when I passed him in the communal hallway on my way outside. The shirt sleeves under his tank top were rolled to the elbows, exposing podgy forearms. He'd covered a broken panel with a neat square of gaffer tape and had swept broken fragments of glass into a dustpan.

'Morning,' I said.

'Yes,' said Hodgson, shaking soap from his fingers.

'What happened?'

'You must've forgotten your keys again,' he said. 'I heard a smash in the middle of the night. You broke the window to get inside.'

'Oh,' I said. 'Sorry.' I made the connection between the cut on my hand and the blood on the walls. I must have used the spare key hidden under the mat outside my flat to get in there. The spare key under the plant pot for the outside door must have been overlooked in my stupor.

There was a long, drawn-out pause. A sluggish blue-bottle, way out of season, settled on the rim of Hodgson's bucket. Awkward silence ensued as we both watched it totter. I felt like a character in a Harold Pinter play.

'Not at work today?' I asked.

'I didn't think it'd be sensible to go out leaving the glass broken like this. I took a half-day's holiday.'

Another uncomfortable pause. Hodgson then shook his head and started to scrub away another palm print.

'Well, then, bye.' I backed away through the door, kowtowing as I went.

It got worse at the tube station. The PA announced that the westbound service was suspended. A passenger had been 'taken ill' at Liverpool Street. I wasn't fooled. Everyone knows this is London Underground double-talk for some fruitcake launching himself under a train. Of all the days to end it, why today? My career is now hanging in the balance because some loon forgot to drop his Prozac.

AT HER MAJESTY'S ROYAL COURTS
OF JUSTICE

I arrive outside the Royal Courts at 10.15. I'm late. If I'm suitably contrite I might be able to exchange the dismissal of my application for a judicial ear-bending. I've been before a few of the Judges before and if I'm lucky I'll get one who likes me.

A group of windswept protesters in brightly coloured cagoules is protesting on behalf of the appellant in a criminal appeal. A crocodile of French exchange students is being lectured by their tutor on the history of English jurisprudence. The usual gauntlet of photographers is gathered around the entrance, their Starbucks' espressos steaming in polystyrene cups, cameras holstered, ready for action.

I wonder if Brian is still big enough news for the paparazzi to even bother taking his picture. Probably, yes. I should stay close to him when we leave, just in case. Maybe I could even get myself in the papers. Or on the news. Hannah might see me on the early-evening bulletin and realize the error of her ways. She would come back to me tearfully, loving and penitent, asking me to take her back.

Passing through the metal detectors. Keep moving. Murmurs, telephone chirps and dozens of heels clicking against the flagstones of the hugely vaulted entrance hall. An excited buzz with the air cool and dark. A scrum of human traffic: bewigged and cloaked barristers scurrying down myriad corridors like black rats into a maze, junior clerks tugging trolleys laden with files and textbooks behind them; solicitors with mobile phones reporting back to the office; tourists gathered around the cause lists – the order of play – scanning them for any whiff of a celebrity appearance.

I jog on.

The case is being heard in Court 64, across the quiet cloister-like courtyard separating the old building from the redbrick bulk of the sixties annexe. There are usually a few matters to be heard before the more substantial cases and, despite the trifling nature of these applications, they quite often eat away an hour or two. This is my only hope. I'm already fifteen minutes late. I check the list outside the door and groan. My case is being heard by Mr Justice Atkins.

Atkins is a stickler for tradition with a ferocious temper, and we've never really seen eye to eye.

My exertion has covered me with sweat. My shirt is stuck against the small of my back and there's a sticky sheen on my forehead. I mop it away with a shirt cuff. It stains wetly.

COURT 64

I'm too late. That's obvious even as I tug open the second set of double doors to enter, and bow to the bench. The atmosphere is instantly frosty. The band's counsel, William Dicey, pauses mid-sentence and turns to address me with a look of withering disdain.

'I believe *this* is Mister Tate,' he says archly.

'Please accept my apologies, Your Honour,' I pant, sliding onto a bench on the side of the court reserved for respondents.

'Very well,' Atkins says, 'but we're not going to retrace our steps. Mr Dicey was just finishing his submission as to why the Freezing Order over Mr Fey's assets should remain in place. I'll hear you when he's done.'

'I'm obliged,' I say. I peel the shirt from off my skin

and think cool thoughts: ice-cubes, arctic vistas, cold showers. Nothing works.

Dicey finishes off, but I only hear him as a background buzz. I'm trying to ready myself, honing the dull edge of my legal blade.

Before I get to my feet, a quick scan of the courtroom. I spot Brian: he waves, sporting black fedora and shades from the back of the public gallery. His T-shirt has a picture of the luminous yellow mother ship that zoomed across the top of the screen in *Space Invaders*. His manager – Davey MacHale – is alongside him. Davey is glaring down sourly at me. Slouching fashionably to one side are Martin and Damon, the lead guitarist and drummer of the Black Dahlias. They're also wearing black, perhaps in mourning for John French, although Martin, ever flamboyant, is wearing a white lace choker around his throat. It doesn't appear that French's death has softened their attitude towards their ex-frontman.

Dicey finishes with a flourish. He petitions the court to maintain the Freezing Order, then sits. There's an expectant pause as all eyes turn to me. Brian gives me the thumbs-up sign, which doesn't help; it just tickles my conscience, telling me I'm letting him down. Like I needed the reminder.

ADVOCACY

'Um, th-th-thank you,' I say, bracing myself against the bench in front. I suddenly feel light-headed. Usually, I love advocacy. My old firm sent me on courses, taught me the tricks of the trade. I'm *good* at it.

But I'm only good at it with the benefit of preparation. Ad libbing is something I can't do. Today, I have no proper notes and my mind is a blank. Needing a decoy, I shuffle my almost-empty papers newsreader-style while trying to put my thoughts in order. Nothing much happens, so I dive in regardless and hope for the best.

'I don't intend to take up too much of the court's time,' I say. 'My client, Mr Fey, who has come to court this morning, has no intention of putting his assets beyond the reach of his creditors. He's never intentionally followed such a course of action, despite what m'learned friend might like us to believe. It's true that my client has incurred certain *expenses* which may not have been authorized, strictly speaking, by his creditors, but any such expenses were incurred as a result of ignorance as to the terms of the court's order and not through any more sinister motive . . .'

I look up: Dicey is glaring down at me. I remember what he did to Brian in the witness box and temporarily lose my train of thought.

'Have you finished, Mr Tate?' Atkins asks.

'No, sir,' I reply.

'Mr Tate, I need not remind you that you are in open court. You will refer to me as Your Honour.'

I can't hold his steely gaze. 'I'm sorry, Your Honour. I lost my way for a moment.'

'Do let me know when you've found it again.'

I manage to pull myself back together. 'My client has now been fully informed of the restrictions that've been imposed on him by this court. He will obey them to the letter. Furthermore, his creditors've already adequately secured themselves with charging orders over various properties belonging to him: residential properties in this country and also abroad. I understand that they intend to seek orders for the sale of these properties. My client is also presently investigating several possibilities of refinance that've been made available to him, in order that he might settle this matter. If the judgment debt is paid, the matter of the Freezing Order becomes moot. Indeed, I submit that it is moot even today. In the circumstances, it is an unnecessary impediment to my client and I submit that it should be discharged.'

What am I talking about? That stuff about seeking refinance for a settlement? – pure fiction, but I had to say *something*. I breathe out sharply. What's left of my strength exits with it and I slump back into the seat. I turn to the gallery to see what reaction my performance has elicited. Brian lowers his shades and winks at me.

'Is *that* it?' asks Atkins. 'Are you finished *now*?'

'Your Honour, I am,' I reply.

'*Stand up* when you address me.'

I stand. 'I'm sorry. Yes, Your Honour, that's my submission.'

Davey's expression says he's also trying to work out whether I have anything else to say. I feel a dozen sets of eyes boring into me. I'd love to have been able to flourish a killer authority, some obscure eighteenth-century decision that would demolish their case, but I couldn't find one.

They have the law on their side.

JUDGMENT

A judge will often retire to his chamber for an hour or two to consider the competing arguments put before him, weighing up the opposing authorities and deciding with which party the balance of justice lies. Not today. Atkins is ready to pronounce my fate without any further delay.

'In twenty years on the bench, rarely have I been presented with such a shoddily prepared, poorly presented piece of legal argument as has been put before me this morning. Not satisfied with being fifteen minutes late for this hearing, Mr Tate chose to come before me in a state of personal unkemptness – unshaven, wearing an unironed shirt, without a jacket and with stains on his trousers. He then proceeded to present an argument with absolutely no legal basis whatsoever. The thrust of his submission appears to be that I should release the Freezing Order over his client's assets because his client is a good person who now knows the extent of his legal obligations to his judgment creditors. This may well be so, but it is not a compelling reason for me to prefer it to Mr Dicey's comprehensive and well-argued submission that the order should be continued. Smoke and mirrors will only get one so far, and their influence does not extend inside my courtroom doors. Accordingly it is my judgment that the Freezing Order over Mr Fey's assets should remain in force for as long as needs be in order to protect the judgment secured by the judgment creditors.'

Atkins' tone is full of the repugnance with which he might address the man who has just molested his family.

But he isn't finished. He turns to face me.

'Mr Tate, I can recall other applications that you have made before me. My recollection is that you are an excellent young advocate with some not inconsiderable talent. I can only guess at the personal circumstances that have led to you appearing before me today in such a fashion. I do not intend to enquire as to what they might be. However, should you *ever* come before me in such a condition again I will refuse to hear you. I also consider such slovenliness to be tantamount to a contempt of court. Please bear that in mind before your next application.'

CONSOLATION PRIZE

'Bad luck,' Brian says. He's waiting for me outside, puffing on a cigarette. Davey, his manager, has disappeared.

'Sorry,' I say.

'Don't worry about it,' he says. 'I'm not about to sack you.'

'Where's Davey?'

'Not in the best of moods,' Brian says diplomatically. 'He had to go.'

'Great. Now he hates me too.'

'Look, don't worry. I've got something to cheer you up.'

Five minutes later, I back away from a cistern in the gents and let the rush chase my hangover away. I seem to be spending all of my time in toilet cubicles lately. Brian, having himself already sampled the vintage, is barring the outside door to prevent unwanted interruption. Doing coke in here has made me think of fags and bike sheds all over again. Master Nott, one of the court officials who hears interlocutory matters, was taking a leak in the cubicle next door as I hoovered up two fat lines. It felt like sacrilege. We even smiled at each other in the mirror as we washed our hands.

'I needed that,' I admit to Brian.

'Thought you might,' Brian says. 'Back to my place for some lunch?'

It's a little early for lunch but I figure they won't be expecting me back at the office for a while. The hearing should have taken longer than five minutes. I'm also of the strong suspicion that Brian's lunch will be of the liquid variety, spiced with exotic and illegal powders. This is an attractive proposition.

'Why not?' I say.

MEMORIES OF THE BLACK DAHLIAS

1990. Jessica Williams and me, riding the ghost train at the fairground that pitched up every year on the promenade. Sixteen years old and never been kissed. The tang of sea salt in the air, lazy evening heat, her hand in mine. 'Love Me and Leave me to Bleed', the Dahlias' massive summer hit, came over the stereo, just audible in the hot darkness over the bored screams of the others on the ride. I leaned across and pressed my lips to hers.

1992. My first week at University. The Freshers' Ball, too much drink, my first ever E, dancing all night and now covered in sweat. Back at my Hall of Residence room, lying on the hard mattress, Eleanor Morton lying next to me. The graphic equaliser on my cheap Aiwa stereo the only light in the room, glowing green and red in time with the music. The Dahlias, again, but this time a classic cut: 'Heart of Darkness'. Eleanor dragged painted nails downwards as Brian's wretched vocals played out.

1995. Summer, hot and dry, a late evening sitting on the wooden decking of a pub near London Bridge, where I'd met Hannah for drinks after work. A cool breeze blowing in off the water. We both sat with our feet dangling in the cold water, watching matchbox traffic crawl along the opposite bank, and ice-cream scoops of cloud blowing overhead. I remember the smell of warm wood, her menthol cigarettes, sharp diesel fumes from pleasure boats bobbing by, her perfume. The Dahlias were playing, I forget the track. We drank until we were both pleasantly oiled and then she took me back to her flat. There was no discussion: it was understood.

She had a poster of Brian on the wall.

That settled it. She was perfect.

MOODSWING

I call my secretary, Elizabeth, as Brian's chauffeur drives us towards his apartment.

'How'd it go?' she asks. Elizabeth is studying law at night school and is always interested in my cases. With a couple of weeks' training she could do my job for me. I would then happily take her place in the cube farm and answer the phone for her all day.

'So-so,' I say. 'Any messages?'

'Miss Wilson called. She wants to know how you're getting on with the work for tomorrow.'

'How'd she sound?'

'Agitated,' she says delicately.

'What'd you say to her?'

'That you'd call her back.'

'Could you call her for me? Tell her I'm busy or something. Tell her I'm in court. Tell her I'll call her when I get back.' I ring off.

The driver aims the car through the Rotherhithe tunnel. Brian is agitated as we swoop under the river towards the Isle of Dogs, chain-smoking his way through a packet of menthol cigarettes. His mood has changed.

'They didn't even want to speak to me – again,' he says forlornly, tossing a dog-end out of the open window. It splashes red sparks against the retreating wall behind us. 'I tried, but they wouldn't have it.'

'They're probably just upset about John.'

'Oh, *yeah*. Come on, man, you saw them. They won't talk to me – not even now. I mean, *especially* after John, you'd think they'd want to sort this fucking mess out.' He rubs at a bloodshot eye.

'I'm sure it's not personal – their solicitor will've told them not to have any contact with you. I'd say the same thing if I was advising them.'

'It's like they think they've got a monopoly on grief or something,' Brian says. 'Jesus, I've got more reason to be upset'n any of them.'

'Give it time,' I say, just throwing out those platitudes.

As the car bounds up and out of the darkness, he turns to me and says, 'We were friends for twenty years. Twenty years and then it comes to this.'

'Litigation is war,' I say, feeling super-transatlantic. 'That's the way the game is played.'

(Listen to me! Jeez. Look how easily this noxious flimflam slips out. You try and insulate yourself against the business-speak that gets zapped around the office, but you can't keep it all out; some of it X-rays through the defences and seeps into your bones.)

LIFESTYLES OF THE RICH AND FAMOUS, PART II

We pull up outside Brian's apartment. He has the entire top floor in a converted red-brick warehouse. I wouldn't even like to guess how much a place like this must cost. Too much, anyway.

I've been there once before: a party just after I started to work on the case, to celebrate the end of the recording sessions for his new solo album. I was nervous and already drunk by the time I got there, so I can't remember much of it now. The party was on a wide terrace above the penthouse; trance music pumping out from enormous bass bins, chairs and tables loutishly thrown into the leaden waters of the Thames below, me with my legs dangling over the roof watching them bob away on the sluggish current. There were drugs. Lots of drugs. I remember: semi-famous musos and showbiz folk and a feeling of insubstantiality, frothiness, everyone else two-dimensional, almost transparent.

'You've got visitors,' the concierge says. Brian asks who. 'I didn't recognize them, sir. They said they'd wait for you upstairs, outside your flat.'

'Probably fans,' Brian says to me with a faux-embarrassed smile; he's secretly pleased by such attention. 'They track me down now and again. Sometimes they manage to slip past security. I'll sign whatever they want me to sign, then we can get something to drink, OK?'

THINGS START TO UNRAVEL

The four men waiting outside Brian's flat don't look like fans. Three are dressed in matching blue overalls and the other is in a tatty grey suit. There are two goods trolleys propped up against the wall. They look like delivery men.

'Hello,' Brian says. 'I don't think I've ordered anything, have I?'

'We're not here for a delivery,' says the man in the bad suit. 'It's the opposite, actually. I'm the sheriff's assistant, south London district. We're here to confiscate the items in your flat, further to this Order.'

He waves a clutch of documents in front of us.

Brian looks baffled. 'What're you talking about?' Then, to me: 'What's going on?'

With a brusque, 'I'm a solicitor,' I take the documents from the sheriff. It's a writ of fieri facias, enabling the band to confiscate and sell all of Brian's stuff. Everything in it seems to be in order.

It was just a matter of time before they decided to get personal; this is about as personal as it gets. An order for the confiscation and sale of goods that pale in value compared to the debt only achieves one thing: you let the debtor know you're going to ruin him. It's a slap in the face. Pushing for bankruptcy is usually the natural complement. It's standard tactics: I've done it more times than I care to remember.

'The band're enforcing their judgment against you,' I explain. 'The sheriff's people can take your things and sell them.'

'We've clamped your cars in the basement,' the sheriff adds. 'But we'd like you to confirm we've got the right ones before we put them on the back of the low-loader. Black Porsche and red Ferrari, isn't it? Maybe you'd go down with my colleague and check them? Once you've let us in?'

Brian looks at me helplessly.

We could just refuse to open the door. The sheriff doesn't have the power to break it down, so he'd have to camp out in the corridor until Brian tried to go inside. But I'm figuring a Mexican stand-off with a bailiff and his goons is probably the last thing Brian needs right now, especially since the other side could just go to court for an order to break into the flat. Why prolong things? It's not going to help. They've already got the cars. Just get it over with.

'Let them in,' I say. 'Then go down and check the cars. I'll keep an eye on things while they're up here.'

CLEANED OUT

After much sweaty work, the sheriff's crew has cleared out Brian's flat. Gone: his furniture, his televisions, his stereos, the pictures on the walls, even his light fittings, crockery and cutlery. An enormous original canvas by Derek Jarman was carefully removed from the wall and manoeuvred through the door. Small items were packed into wooden cargo boxes and stacked into bigger crates. They reversed two large white Luton vans up outside the front entrance and ferried everything down the fire escape and into them. They were practised and efficient, and for the most part we watched impotently as they went about their work. A small crowd gathered to watch.

Brian wore a dazed expression on his face. I knew what he was feeling because I've seen this before. Losing in court means little in real terms; the judgment is just another piece of paper in a sea of legal papers. It's only when your personal things get confiscated that the severity of the mess you're in comes home to roost.

Seeing your sofa manhandled out the door hits you like a punch in the gut. It's reality-check time.

The flat has been reduced to dusty wooden floorboards and whitewashed walls. All signs of habitation have been removed. Brian's cars have been backed onto a truck and driven off to a pound somewhere. They'll be advertised in the trade papers and sold to a dealer for half their list prices. Brian has been left with the absolute bare minimum: his bed, some clothes, a few plates, the fridge and its contents.

And still they haven't finished. We're standing in what's left of the lounge. The sheriff is sizing up a wall of framed silver and gold discs the Dahlias received in the eighties.

'Come on, guys,' I say, seeing Brian's face fall even further. 'You don't need those.'

'Might be worth something,' the sheriff muses. His crew nod docile agreement.

'Only to him,' I suggest, pointing at Brian. 'Sentimental value. No one else's going to want them.'

'They're not *real* gold and silver,' Brian adds disconsolately.

'Might be right,' the sheriff says, 'but I've got instructions to take *everything* that's not screwed down. Very particular, they were.'

They unhook the framed discs roughly and slot them into a case, leaving clean white squares on the dusty wall where they used to be.

MINIMALISM

'That's not something you see every day,' Brian says, putting on a brave face. His flat is an empty, lifeless shell. 'Still, I hear the minimalist look is in vogue this season.'

I press a smile I'm not feeling onto my face.

'I didn't know they could do that,' Brian says. 'What happens to it all now? My stuff?'

'It'll get auctioned.'

'Cheap?'

'Won't make half of what it's really worth.'

'Oh, well,' Brian sighs. He moves over to the bar and forces a smile himself. He fetches a bottle of whisky and two glasses from beneath the counter. 'At least they didn't take my booze. I could use something to steady my nerves. I mean, just *look* at this.' He holds up his hands: they're shaking.

'Good idea,' I agree.

'Want one too?'

'Love one.'

He pours out two generous measures.

'Brian, look, we really need to talk about the case. I was meaning to bring it up yesterday. There're some things I need to explain to you. Important things: like what happened today, for example.'

'Here,' he says, handing me one of the glasses. We both sit on the floor, leaning up against a wall.

'It's partly my fault. I mean, I should've told you before . . .'

'Are you hungry?' he says. 'I had some cheese in the fridge. It's probably still there. I could fix some sandwiches or something? Might even have frozen pizza. I *know* I've got a tub of Ben & Jerry's.'

'Brian . . .'

He's not listening. He's distracted – it's hardly surprising. I tell him I'm not all that hungry. He wanders over to the window. It's as big as a cinema screen and offers a view of the listless river and, over the turn of brown water, the blister of the Millennium Dome.

'Can I ask you a question?' he says.

'Sure,' I say. I put my best game face on: the one I use to try and persuade clients that I'm competent to answer their complex legal queries.

'What d'you think of the Dahlias now, without me? Their new album?'

'It's, um, interesting,' I say hesitantly. 'I've heard it. In a shop, or the radio. I mean I didn't actually *buy* a copy.'

'But you prefer our old stuff?'

'Yeah,' I say. 'The old stuff is, well, *classic*, special.'

'And John?'

'What about him?'

'What was his singing like?'

The truth is I think John French's vocals are great. Technically, as a singer, his voice was better than Brian's – better range, more power, more versatility – but I've

113

got so many memories invested in the songs that Brian sang. Looking at him now – nervous, expectant – I can see it's time for a diplomatic lie.

'OK-ish. But you can tell he hadn't sung much before.'

'I'm glad you think that. I was beginning to doubt myself.'

'Come on . . .'

'No, listen to this.' He takes out a piece of scrunched-up paper from his pocket. ' "Brian Fey's new material is the nostalgic whining of an 80s brat who refuses to grow up." Or this: "While the Black Dahlias have pushed the envelope once again with new singer John French, Brian Fey has produced the sort of album only a mother could like." '

'They're just reviews. Ignore them.'

'I know they are, but they all add up. And then compare them with what they've been saying about John. It gets me down.'

'Its just opinion . . .'

'I've been thinking about it all,' he says, tapping a finger against the review. 'Fame, celebrity – all of it. And the more I think about it, the more I'm sure that people want their stars to *fail*, to be miserable, just like them. They don't want heroes; what they want is to see you fall.'

I try to lighten the mood but it's no use. We morosely finish our drinks before Brian walks me to the front door. He tells me it wasn't that long ago that it was usual to have five or six fans camped outside in the hope they'd catch a glimpse of him leaving the building or, in their wildest dreams, at the window unawares. They don't come any more, he says. He misses them.

'I miss being famous,' he says. 'I mean, *really* famous. It's the little things: the money, getting a good table at Quaglino's, getting laid when I want to, you know? The usual stuff.'

He smiles a rueful smile. I wonder whether this is tongue-in-cheek.

I watch Brian through the back window of the taxi as we pull away. He's standing, hands in pockets, leaning up against the front door of the expensive warehouse conversion where he now has an empty, dead flat. And he won't even have that soon.

He turns, notices me, and smiles.

APOLOGIES

I get back during the lunch hour. The office is almost deserted.

Cohen is out. I close the door of the office, remove the phone from its cradle and pour myself a plastic cupful of superplonk from the two-litre carton I got at Tesco's last week. It's warm, and tastes as cheap as it should, but I need to take the edge off the afternoon. I munch on a cream-cheese and bacon bagel from Pret. By recent standards this is a nutritious and filling meal.

My office suffers from the same lack of order as my home. The desk is covered with stacks of papers: contracts I'm supposed to have analysed, pleadings I'm supposed to have drafted. These stacks are weighed down by several half-finished cans of full-sugar, full-caffeine Coke and numerous folders and binders. Junk.

I toss the bagel into the bin. Last night with Rachel is worrying me. Too many occasions lately when I've been unable to remember the ends of evenings. I hope I haven't disgraced myself. I've already checked the computer for flame mails: none. I tap out a message:

From:	Tate, Daniel
To:	Delgardo, Rachel
Subject:	I hope . . .

. . . last night wasn't *too* excruciating. When did we leave? Trying to patch together events – may have had *slightly* too much to drink.
A million apologies,
  Dan

HUNTING HANNAH

Since Cohen is out I decide to try and make indirect contact with Hannah. I need to speak with her.

I thumb through the old-fashioned Rolodex she gave me as a wry birthday present last year. She said it was something to do with me selling out. She used to call me a corporate lackey, and never really understood that this was what I actually *wanted* to do. She couldn't reconcile my ambitions with her more artistic temperament. I find the details for her agent, tap the numbers into the phone and wait for the call to connect.

'Suzy Pugh,' says her agent. 'Hello?'

'I'm calling about one of your clients,' I say. 'Hannah Wilde. I was wondering if you had an address for her.'

'We don't give out our clients' addresses to strangers over the telephone,' she answers haughtily. 'Who is this?'

'It's just that, um . . .' Flash: 'I'd like to set up an interview with her.'

'Which magazine do you work for?'

'I'm f-f-freelance?'

'If you can prove you've been commissioned to write a piece, *then* we might be able to have a conversation about this. Until then, don't bother – I'm rather busy. Goodbye.'

COHEN'S INVITATION

Since I'm feeling sorry for myself I step outside to get a coffee. The office is a little busier and Elizabeth has returned. She smiles as I greet her and then fixes me with a look of maternal concern. I must look as bad as I feel – and I *feel* awful. I hurry away.

When I get back Cohen is rooting around for something at my end of the room.

'Hole punch?' he asks. He looks uncomfortable. I find the right drawer, take it out and hand it to him.

'Listen, I don't mean to be nosy, but d'you really think you ought to have that in here?' He points at the empty wine carton on the desk. 'I don't think the partners'd be all that impressed.'

'It's nothing,' I say, dropping it into the bin and then jamming it further down with my foot. 'I just like a drink now and then.' I suddenly feel defensive.

'Listen,' he says, perching on the edge of my desk. 'Beth and I were wondering if you and Hannah'd like to come over for dinner this week. We haven't done that for a while, have we, and we thought it might be nice. Fancy it, then?' His tone is cautious. I can't think why.

'Hannah's pretty busy at the moment,' I reply, still unable to come clean. 'I'm not sure she can get away from work this week.' Then I add by way of explanation, 'They're shooting at nights.'

Cohen gives me a strange, almost pitying, look.

'Then why don't you come over on your own?'

I'm not feeling much like socializing at the moment. I'd much rather avoid two hours of enforced jolliness. 'Thanks, but I don't know—'

'Come on,' he says. 'We could even order in if you can't stomach Beth's cooking – which I'd understand. And there's this *great* little Indian opened up down the road. We could have a Madras delivered, wash it down with a few beers.'

This continues until I relent and accept his invitation. I agree to dinner at his place on Thursday.

AN AUDIENCE WITH PHILLIP SCHOFIELD

Elizabeth reminds me I have another appointment. Phillip Schofield is negotiating with British Airways to take over the pop channel on their in-flight radio. Small beer for him, small beer for us, but Hunter likes to keep Schofield sweet in case one day he makes it back to the big time. I get to babysit until that happens, then one of the big hitters steps in and swipes him away from me. I know the drill.

But now I have to put up with him reminiscing about glove puppets and broom cupboards for thirty minutes.

Another trip to the toilets, another slug of Jack, and I'm feeling ready for action again.

VOICEMAIL

It goes well. We ended by talking about how the quality of British broadcasting has gone down the pan. I tell Phillip I think he could be the man to herald its renaissance if he could just bring back the gopher. He's happy with this and we part with big grins and firm hand-shakes – another happy punter. I go back to the office and my stuffed in-tray.

I settle down at my desk, trying to find the energy to do some work. I check the phone. Someone tried to call, and left voicemail. I play it back over the speaker.

'Daniel? Scott Dolan again. From the Guest List at *Extravaganza*. We spoke yesterday morning? Listen, Daniel, I was wondering if you'd had a chance to consider what we were talking about? I'm not looking for any major scoop or anything like that. Just a few quotes for background colour, that's all. I was wondering if you could, maybe, gimme a steer on how Brian's bearing up under the strain of John French's death, the police investigation, that kinda thing. What d'you say? By the way, I've got information about Fey's past that I'd like to put to you. Something I think you *really* ought to know about. Maybe you could give me a call and we could have a chat? Or if you'd prefer to speak face to face I can easily just come to you. Anyway, in case you've forgotten it here's my number again.'

He recites his number and signs off with a jolly farewell. I press erase.

A SHOULDER TO CRY ON

The coffee from the machine is worse than usual and I leave it half-finished. I wander outside to get fresh supplies from the Italian stall in the square. The air is taut with cold.

I bump into Jonathan Williams.

We end up sitting at a wooden table, watching the tourists drifting into Soho Square, both of us clutching hot lattes in polystyrene cups. Two of the Barron Knights walk past and head into the lobby.

Like me, Williams transferred here from one of the magic-circle firms in the City. He probably expected more civilized hours in exchange for a trimmed pay packet. The way he tells it, the partners waited until his probation period ended and his notice went up to six months, and then hit him with a massive disclosure exercise that'll last until the summer. Now most of his time is spent in a muggy room in the basement going through six hundred boxes of royalty statements from a record company we're defending in a fraud case. His job: to check every statement in case it's relevant to the case and then list each one. Everyone knows disclosure is hell, but we've got limited sympathy for him. There but for the grace of God and all that.

Williams slumps abjectly against the table. He has the unhealthy pallor of someone kept out of natural light for too long. His eyes are ringed with a red the colour of pomegranate juice. I know what he wants to talk about even before he opens his mouth.

'Work getting you down?'

'It's just such a *slog*,' he sighs. 'It'd be better if someone else could help me out. Or even if I had someone to *talk* to. I'm going to go mad if I stay in that basement much longer.'

'Keep your chin up,' I say. 'I've heard a rumour the case might be about to settle.'

'Really?' he says, brightening. 'I haven't heard that.'

I've heard no such thing either. I'm just being nice.

In for a penny, in for a pound. I say, 'Another couple of weeks and that ought to be the end of your problems. Or so I heard.'

BETWEEN THE DEVIL AND THE DEEP BLUE SEA

Back at my desk again. I look at my list of things to do.

I ignore the small pieces of research and correspondence that are still outstanding since no one has chased me for them. My policy: wait until the second chasing email before moving something up the list. If the partner can't be bothered to chase, it can't really be all that important.

My eyes fall on the two bits of work Wilson wants from me for Monster Munch. The deadline is tomorrow morning. I haven't started either of them yet. The contract is a serious piece of work, requiring original thought and a lot of hard graft. I'm not in the mood for it now. It'll keep until tonight. I work best when the office is quiet. The marketing agreement should be easier, especially if I can manage to get a precedent from the Dork. Detesting the necessity of throwing myself upon his mercy, I walk around the perimeter of the building to his office.

It couldn't be more different to mine. He has a window, for a start, and he doesn't share the room with anyone else. He also gives the impression this is somewhere he doesn't mind spending the majority of his waking hours. His files are neatly stacked in alphabetical order on the shelves, with separate folders for precedents, legal authorities and internal correspondence. He's managed to persuade the librarian to buy him a full set of statute books. The desk is otherwise empty except for a stylish banker's lamp, a dictation machine and the pages of the document he is amending.

The Dork has hung a framed photograph on the wall behind his chair. He's mugging for the camera next to Tom Jones, one arm draped across the crooner's shoulders. From the look on Tom's face – wide-eyed with panic – Dawkins probably has an unseen pistol pressed against the kidneys of the greatest living Welshman.

I nervously tap on the door.

'Tate,' he says.

'Dawkins,' I respond, as standard. 'Not disturbing anything, am I?'

'Not at all.' He puts his pen down and takes off his glasses. 'We don't see you on this side of the office much.'

'You know how it is. Busy, busy, busy.'

'That's the truth,' he says. 'I've just negotiated an end to the builders' dispute at the opera house. Working on the settlement agreement now. Just one more thing that needs to be done, and the client wants it done yesterday.'

'I'd offer to help . . .' I leave the sentence hanging.

'No, no, wouldn't dream of it. Fulton's new trainee's helping me out.' He lowers his voice to a lascivious whisper. 'Have you *seen* her yet? She's quite something, isn't she?'

My hackles rise. The Dork has always seemed a vaguely asexual creature. I've always found him damply effeminate. I let his comment about Rachel wash over me.

He sweeps his hand across his desk. 'I ought to be getting back to all this. What can I do for you?'

I take a deep breath. God, this is *embarrassing*.

Force the words out: 'I need a favour. Japanese contract law? I heard you've had some experience?'

'Japanese law,' he ponders, pulling down a precedent file from the shelf. 'I've done a couple of contracts over there. Let's see – ah, here we are – "agreements incorporating Asian law". One of these ought to do the trick. There's a selection of possible clauses depending on your circumstances. And at the back of the folder you'll find some general information about their legal system – background stuff. Copy what you need and bring it back.'

I take the folder and flick through it. A dozen precisely worded clauses listed with brief descriptions of their effect and judicial commentary on their application. I'm taken aback by his thoroughness. I can't imagine ever being as diligent. Or is it anal? Whatever, it's just what I need.

'Which case is this?' he asks. 'Not Brian Fey?'

'No, something else,' I say. 'Something for Victoria Wilson.'

I regret this at once. He'll craftily slip the information that he helped on this case into his next conversation with her. And no, I'm not being paranoid: he's done it before. So now there's no way I can claim the credit for it, *plus* she'll think I'm more of a slacker than I really am.

'Well,' he says, 'let me know if you need any of it explained.'

I leave with my jaw, and my fists, clenched.

EMAIL

From:	Delgardo, Rachel
To:	Tate, Daniel
Subject:	Re: I hope . . .

I can't believe you don't remember (although maybe actually I *can* believe it . . .) You walked/staggered off at about eleven saying you were going to find a

late bar. I tried to persuade you to get a taxi but you
ran off. I was going to pop down to see if you were
OK today, but James and Oliver have kept me busy.
Rachel

From:	Tate, Daniel
To:	Delgardo, Rachel
Subject:	Re: I hope . . .

Ohmigod. I'm sooo embarrassed. Please tell me
I didn't do anything toooooooo humiliating.
PS: Oliver = Dawkins?

THE CRITICAL ESTABLISHMENT

4.15 p.m. Brian calls. He sounds flustered.

'I mean, why do I fucking bother? I put six months
of my life into this and in six fucking sentences these,
these – no, I'm not gonna say it – these, these *critics*
dismiss it.'

There's no introduction to this rant. He launches
right into it.

'I just don't understand how they can be so cruel. I
mean, OK, they might not like it themselves – fair
enough, I can take that. It's not like we ever appealed
to *everybody* anyway, not even in the old days. But
when they fucking condemn my stuff like this, I just
feel like packing it all in and pissing off somewhere in

the middle of a desert or something and never coming
back.'

'*Slow down.* What's the problem?'

I can hear him taking deep breaths. 'Listen to this,
from today's *NME*. I just got it. "Without the judgment
of more accomplished musicians – let's say the Black
Dahlias – to keep him in check, Fey's clumsy lyrics scale
the heights of pure absurdity. He is trying to reinvent
himself as some kind of tortured modern genius, misun-
derstood and under-appreciated, but the brutal fact is
that John French had more creative ability in one
painted fingernail than Brian Fey has in his entire skinny
body." I mean, what is *that*? That's not criticism – that's
assassination.'

Brian reads out another less than enthusiastic review,
and then another. There's no reassuring him. I get the
impression he's using me as a sponge to soak up his
bile. After five minutes he says, 'There's something I
have to do,' and rings off abruptly.

AN APPEAL TO HANNAH'S BETTER NATURE

I check my inbox for email. I have a few newcomers,
all of them work-related. Worrying: nothing back from
Rachel yet. I imagine her working on a tactful reply
that won't upset me too much. Then I imagine her
soaking up Dawkins' bonhomie, working with him on

the opera house settlement agreement, the two of them in his perfect office, the Dork leaning over her shoulder and looking down her dress as they read through a draft agreement. I picture them talking about me, sharing a joke. Maybe she's told him about last night and the fool I made of myself.

Bad thoughts! I force myself to skip through the messages.

Nothing from Hannah either. Maybe she hasn't received the legion of messages I've sent. I've been mailing regularly for the past month or so, ever since I took the decision not to passively accept her dumping me, and try and do something about it.

I try again:

From: daniel.tate@whitehunter.com
To: wildeh@hotmail.com
Subject: Hello stranger

Just a quick message to see how you are. You haven't been answering my mails . . . is everything OK? I was wondering whether you'd like to meet up for a drink one evening? Or a meal? Nothing heavy, just some issues we need to sort. Miss you! Mail me?

I mull over the 'Miss you!' Is this a sign of weakness? I don't want to give the impression of desperation. I think about it for five minutes, add an extra exclamation mark, delete it, add it, delete it, send it anyway. Three times over. And with multiple delivery and read receipts.

WORK: THE CURSE OF THE DRINKING CLASSES

After looking through Dawkins' precedent, I decide to revise my plan of attack. The facts on which his example is based are almost analogous to the vague facts Wilson's note described. This is lucky; the job should only take me half an hour. I can do it later. I decide to take advantage of this modest upswell of enthusiasm and harness it to the larger and more difficult task of drafting Monster Munch's recording contract. I should've finished it ages ago.

I'm out of wine and I don't have time to go and buy a replacement bottle. Another refill of weak coffee and I fumble around until I find a sample contract from the firm's store of precedents. I scribble out the title of the recording deal on the precedent and insert the title of Monster Munch's eponymous debut. I place my pencil on the desk in satisfaction. A good start.

RELIEF

From: Delgardo, Rachel
To: Tate, Daniel
Subject: Re: I hope . . .

You were fine, just a little drunk maybe. Don't worry
– I'm not offended. I've seen much worse.

PS: Yes, Oliver = Dawkins!

BRIAN IN A BRIGHTER MOOD

Before I can get back into the drafting the telephone
rings again.

'It's me,' Brian says.

'Is everything all right?' I ask.

'Everything's fine,' he says. 'Sorry about earlier. I was
upset. I've put the reviews behind me. I'm gonna ignore
them from now on. You either like my stuff or you
don't. *He* didn't. Live and let live.'

'His loss,' I agree.

'That's what I said to him.'

'You *spoke* to him?'

'Yeah. I went down to his office to have it out with
him.'

'You what?'

'We had – how would you put it? – "a vigorous
exchange of views".'

'Nothing too vigorous, I hope?' Why am I suddenly
uneasy? Reason: stories I've heard from Brian's past.

'I think he came around to my point of view in the
end.'

Ignore it and hope. 'Um – OK.'

Brian changes the subject. 'Look, I wasn't calling

about that. I've got a proposition. What're you doing tonight?' I'm about to tell him I'm busy but he interrupts. 'And don't say you're busy. You need a break. You looked pretty wiped out in court this morning.'

'I'm sorry, Brian, I—'

'Relax, man. It's no sweat.'

I've completely lost control of this conversation.

'Guess what? We're going out. You need some R and R and I've still got blow and stuff and I thought maybe we could take it into town and get a table somewhere? Oh, and don't tell your woman, OK? What she doesn't know, et cetera, et cetera.'

A REMINDER FROM WILSON

From: WILSON, V
To: TATE, D
Subject: Tomorrow

By way of reminder:
1. Briefing note by 8 a.m.
2. Marketing agreement by 8 a.m.
3. Draft recording contract by 8 a.m.
Without fail.

The fact Wilson has gone to the effort of dragging her mouse across the final two words and then clicking underline is evidence that she is taking this very, very seriously.

NOSE TO GRINDSTONE

I spread out the precedent recording contract and begin afresh, striking out previous details and inserting new ones.

I make good progress but it's heavy going. I struggle on until I eventually conclude nothing else is going to happen tonight. The spark has gone out. My eyes are heavy. I check the clock: 5.20. Perhaps a change of scenery will give me second wind. A short nap, perhaps. I scrabble the papers into a pile and jam them into my briefcase. I give Elizabeth the cheeriest smile I can muster and head for the tube.

VINTAGE DAHLIAS

Home.

I take off my coat and switch on the radiators. I turn the knob: nothing happens. Perplexed – and fearing the worst – I check the boiler. Freezing cold. I scrabble through the post on the floor of the hallway until I find a letter I vaguely remember from the gas company. I rip it open. The letter is a final, final, final warning: unless I pay my outstanding account within two days my supply will be disconnected.

The letter is two weeks old.

Great. London's in the middle of the coldest December for years and I haven't got any heating.

Nelson is curled up on the sofa. I scratch his head and he wiggles his ears. I wander over to the shelf next to the stereo and run my finger along the spines of the records in my vinyl collection. I take out the Dahlias' first record, and reverently remove the vinyl from its dust jacket. A mint pressing like this is probably worth £100 to the right collector – not that I've got any interest in selling. I lay the disc on the platter and lower the stylus. There's a moment of scratchy static as the needle slides into the grooves, and then the sound of the Dahlias from their disposable electro-pop period – still darker than any of their New Romantic contemporaries – fills the room. I turn over the sleeve and look at the shot of the group on the back: four flamboyant dandies, Brian even sporting a feather boa around his neck, together with black nail varnish and lipstick. But there's no getting away from it – even their early stuff is good.

NEWS OF AN ENGAGEMENT

I potter around, but in no time I'm restless. I try to find a comfortable spot next to Nelson with no luck. I squirm this way and that, then wander around the lounge, trying to keep warm. My mind is buzzing. Plus I can smell Hannah's perfume. It must have sunk down into the fabric of the room.

It's freezing cold. I'm wearing two jumpers and three pairs of socks. My breath steams the air in front of me.

Maybe I should harness this energy. Clean the flat. Clear away this rubbish, treat it as a personal metaphor for a fresh start. The half-life for this idea occupies a nano-nano-second. I start pacing again, imagining a cool breeze flowing through chemically seared nostrils; the tang of alcohol on the back of my throat.

No, I won't give in so easily. I switch on the TV and mute the sound. At least the electricity is back on again. The usual early-evening fare: a soap, regional news programmes, a cartoon. I flick over to a channel running a showbiz gossip programme.

This is more like it.

I watch a segment on the failed love life of some B-list Hollywood actress and then another with the royal family riding horses across a bleak moor. I'm already feeling more like myself, observing all this wonderful celebrity misery.

The show segues into the next segment: twenty-second snippets of hearsay and scandal packed together in an MTV-style montage. One snippet is shot outside a cinema on Leicester Square. The event seems to be a premiere.

I don't recognize Hannah's face immediately – not until she turns to smile into the camera.

Without taking an eye off the screen, I fumble for the remote, unmute the sound and set the video to instant record.

She's wearing a full length cocktail dress made from a reflective silver material that glitters in the flashbulb explosions. It looks expensive. I don't remember her owning anything like it and I've memorized every outfit she ever wore with me, even the sloppy jumper and comfort socks from lazy Sundays staying in. She gives the photographers a spin to demonstrate that the dress is backless. This exposes a long stretch of nut-coloured skin. She was never this tanned, this healthy, when she was with me. And it is obviously not of the bottled variety, either. I wonder where she could have been to get a colour like that.

'Hannah,' says the interviewer, off-screen. 'What's it feel like to finally be engaged?'

Engaged?

'Wonderful,' Hannah says. 'Just *wonderful*.'

My jaw is on the carpet.

'Could we get a word with the lucky guy?'

Engaged? As in engaged to be married?

Hannah tugs at the arm of a figure standing just out of shot. As he allows himself to be pulled closer to her, I see the arm belongs to Vincent Haines. He's wearing an expensive dinner jacket.

'Vincent, tell them how you proposed to me,' Hannah says.

He fakes bashfulness. She playfully chides him. He gives in.

'I got down on the knee and took out the ring. I don't usually make a mess of my lines, but I've never corpsed like that before . . .'

His wooden delivery reveals that this is entirely scripted.

The segment ends with a close-up of Hannah's left hand: a new ring with an enormous diamond is on her finger.

I rewind the tape and play it back.

The ring with the enormous diamond is still there.

I rewind it again.

I play it again.

A SMILE ON DEMAND

I don't want to think about what I've just heard. I mute the sound and hit PLAY.

By using the video's shuttle pause function I manage to halt the frame so Hannah is caught looking straight into the lens, out into the living room. Despite the dress, the neon background and the handsome actor onto whose arm she is clinging, the footage reminds me of the photo I keep on top of the television. An autumnal scene. Reds and golds and yellows. Hannah's smile all for myself behind the camera.

There's a moment during the segment, before she is accosted by the interviewer, when Hannah is wearing an aloof, cool expression. As soon as the paparazzi make their demands, flashes popping, her face lights up magically, a real pro. By jogging backwards and forwards between these two points I can make her smile on demand at the push of a button.

This doesn't make me feel any better.

LONDON, '96

We met because of work. White Hunter was acting for the writer of a television soap opera. I'd been at the office for a few months but I was still wet behind the ears when it came to media law, and I was given clients of little or no consequence. The firm considered this purveyor of low-brow entertainment a suitable stone upon which I could whet my legal blade. He'd been offered a modest deal with a production company intending to film the script he'd been working on for years; an offbeat comedy, he said, although I couldn't find the laughs in it. I remember him vividly, a little red-faced man who looked like Stephen Fry if Stephen Fry was five foot three, fat and bald. He clutched the contract close to his breast as he left the office, as if worried that a gust of wind might snatch it away and rob him of his colourful future. With the benefit of hindsight, he really needn't have been so concerned. His labour of love was savaged by the critics and he went back to the soaps, tail between his legs, lit-cred in tatters. His descent was obviously complete when I noticed his name in the credits for *Skin Trade*. He'd sunk as low as you can go.

Hannah had just graduated from the Old Vic in Bristol and was temping in the reprographics department of a firm of London accountants. She was earning barely enough to support herself between auditions, appearing in an amateur production of *The Iliad* during the evenings but holding out for proper television work. TV was the way to the prizes – intellectual satisfaction and material reward – that acting had to offer.

I noticed her at an audition for a part in my client's film. I'd headed down to the theatre at the NFT which he'd rented for the auditions, to have him sign his copy of the contract. It was a sunny day and I was happy as a sandboy; not only would I take the bus back to the office and claim the expenses for a taxi, but I'd take my time doing it and enjoy the weather. A stroll along the river, a pint at one of the riverside pubs, watching the cruisers and barges working the water.

Hannah was up for a minor part in the film but quickly decided the material was below her. She gave a perfunctory reading and left. Even to this day I'm not sure where I got the bottle to approach her. She seemed so far out of my league, the only possible response to my advance was rejection. She was artistic, quietly intelligent and with a brooding beauty, a dark gloss. Twenty years old and beautiful. In short: a heartbreaker.

I caught her up outside the theatre, scrunching her red hair up beneath a kelly green New York Jets cap. She'd dumped the balled-up script into an overflowing rubbish bin.

'I didn't like it either,' was the first thing I ever said to her.

I was surprised when we started talking, not cramped by the usual awkwardness of strangers, then shocked when she gave me her number after we had shared a coffee and a Danish at the NFT's café under Waterloo Bridge, and stupefied when she agreed to meet me for a date.

That first date: I cowered in the darkness of a theatre, gaping at her on the stage as I waited for her to finish a performance. She looked so beautiful and aloof that I felt hopelessly out of my depth and almost walked out. I screwed up my courage and took her to a branch of a ubiquitous pizza and pasta chain. That first date led to another, and then another. Within a month, we were together, and before I knew it she had moved in.

The relationship was low-maintenance; it suited us both. We'd spend the evenings at home doing little except enjoying each other's company. I was saving up for a bigger place and so we lived frugally, enjoying a simple bucolic existence. She read voraciously, devouring print, and stirred in me an appetite for art that had long lain dormant. She provided the books that had changed her life, and I read them all: *Nostromo*, *Brighton Rock*, *Howards End*, *Ulysses*. We went to exhibitions together and joined the Tate, things I'd never have done without her, but now things I can't imagine being without.

We huddled together in the smoky darkness of the

NFT and watched black and white movies by Chabrol and Zeffirelli. My shelves were soon stocked with her long rows of books: slim tan volumes for her favourite plays by Shakespeare, Wilde and Stoppard, doorstop anthologies for Wordsworth and Tennyson. And all the pulpy ephemera: remaindered paperbacks she picked up from the bookshops on the Charing Cross Road but never read. She just liked to have books, she said. She liked to fill the house with the smell of slowly yellowing pages.

BIRMINGHAM, '80

She was two years my junior, although you'd never have guessed it. Her maturity was forced onto her by a difficult childhood. Her father flew the nest when she was five. He moved to another city and set up another family. To him, families were like franchises, a new one in every town. She never saw him again, which seemed to suit her well. He sent scribbled cards for birthdays and Christmas for a few years after his departure, but he eventually tired of even that small chore.

Her mother was an alcoholic who spent her days marooned in an armchair in front of the television, hypnotized and docile, drinking Bacardi and Pernod straight from the bottle. Their relationship was inverted; more often than not it was the infant Hannah who put her slaughtered mother to bed. There were no siblings to share the burden. Other men came and went, surro-gates who were amorous or abusive to both mother and child. She had to grow up fast, and did. One such boyfriend threw her down the stairs when she con-fronted him for beating her mother. Another thought it amusing to hold her by her ankles from the communal balcony, her dress around her ears, looking down at the cracked flagstones of the car park seven storeys below. My modest middle-class upbringing seemed cosseted by comparison. I was impressed with her gritty determi-nation to escape her roots, but I could never properly empathize with it.

There was a period when her mother called her every day, drunk and sobbing. Whenever I thought of Hannah's clipped responses to unheard maternal suppli-cations as cruel and icy, I pictured her aged seven or eight or nine – dutifully flicking off the lights in their scabby council flat and sliding the bolt on the thin front door – and reprimanded myself for passing a judgment I was not qualified to make.

LONDON, '97

These glacial moments were rare, fortunately. I was deliriously happy during those first months, while I waited for the gleam of passion to fade, as it always does, to be replaced by comfortable familiarity, security by routine, relationship by rote. It never did. During the flush of that early enthusiasm, I had found myself working long hours, and often stayed at Hannah's Holborn bedsit, closer to the office than my place in the suburbs. There would always be a plate of food in the fridge waiting to be heated, and sometimes a warm bath unwinding coils of steam onto the moist ceiling. I'd stare at the shape her supine body made under the duvet, and stroke the fan of hair that spread around her head like a russet crown.

I observed her career unfold with a mixture of pride and dread. Pride: as her résumé filled out with increasingly impressive parts, chiefly on stage, with occasional forays into television drama. She quickly moved from amateur dramatics to fringe theatre, and then found a role as Rosalind in *As You Like It*, in a well-reviewed production. Dread: as her career took off, it took her further from me. She landed roles with repertory companies across the capital. Then minor parts in the West End. She played a whimsical Gertrude in Wilde's *An Ideal Husband* – one of her favourites – then Abigail Williams in *The Crucible*. Her star was in the ascendant. She soon played a shoplifter in an episode of *The Bill*, and then had a semi-frequent part as a barmaid in a long-running soap opera.

She started to return from the theatre later than I got home and rose just as I was leaving for the morning tube. The margins of our free time overlapped less and less. She'd bring me a sandwich for lunch and we'd eat together in Soho Square, outside the office, tossing crumbs to the pigeons. She was happier than I could remember; she could see a destination emerging from the mist of her uncertainty, and she was determined to strive harder and harder to bring it nearer. I accepted that sacrifices would be necessary. I knew that trying to constrain her ambition would be folly: do that and I'd lose her. So I basked in the reflected glow of her excitement and encouraged her as best I could.

LONDON, HERE AND NOW

A while ago, at home, as I was filtering a stack of papers sent by Davey for Brian's defence, she started crying. I asked if everything was all right and she said that it was. Just nervous about her upcoming performance as Cordelia in *King Lear*. *Skin Trade* was doing well and there was talk of a role in *EastEnders*. Of course she was nervous.

When I got home the next day the flat was empty. And not empty as in simply empty of her. It was as if a magician had chosen to erase all proof that I'd ever shared the place with her. Apart from the miscellany I tearfully packed into boxes, everything was gone: her clothes, her plants, her books – all gone. She'd even cleaned the place before leaving; penance, maybe, and the last time either duster or hoover were exercised properly within the place.

Just Nelson and a note: *The cat always liked you more than me.*

I called her mother and endured a drunken rambling for ten minutes before I could extricate myself. She didn't know where her daughter was. I looked for Hannah's address book, but of course it was gone. I thought about wandering the restaurants and pubs she liked. Crazy of me. I had insane thoughts: a murderer with an obsessive-compulsive disorder had broken in, done away with her, then neatly tidied up after himself. Or that this was all an elaborate joke and she would appear, mischievously grinning, after a suitable pause.

I couldn't sleep. Feverish thoughts sprouted into my mind like weeds pushing through the gaps in paving stones.

Two days later she called me. She sounded distant, flat-voiced.

'Where are you?' I demanded.

'That doesn't matter.'

'I've been worried sick.'

'I'm so sorry, Daniel, I'm leaving you. I'm sorry.'

'What?'

'I'm so sorry.'

I paused for a moment to let this information seep in.

'Who is he?'

'That's not important.'

'What d'you mean it's not important?'

'This's about us. I just wanted to tell you I'm not

coming back. And that I'm sorry if I've upset you. I just want this to be as painless as possible.'

'Painless? That's easy for *you* to say. Off fucking your new boyfriend with me left alone in *our* flat. The one *we* bought *together*.'

'Don't be melodramatic.'

'That's rich coming from you.'

'The flat'll have to be sold. I think you should put it on the market as soon as you can. I don't see any reason to wait.'

'Hannah . . .'

'I'll be around to pick up my things in a couple of days.'

'They'll be in the yard. Can't promise they'll be in one piece, though.'

'Don't be like that.'

She left a sad pause and I could hear her breathing, across the crackling line. The same breathing that I used to listen to hushing in and out as I fell asleep.

'Why? What did I do?'

She sounded tired. 'Nothing. You didn't do anything.'

'So why aren't you here?'

'It's a long story, Daniel. I'll explain later. I'll call you. Goodbye.'

Then she hung up. And that was that.

And she never did call again.

TIME FOR A DISTRACTION

My mind is made up. I know exactly what I want to do. I switch off the television, take my coat and head for the tube.

ON THE TOWN

Attica is busy when I arrive. Bored paparazzi quaff cups of black coffee outside the door, juicing themselves up in case the celebs inside stagger out drunk and foolish. Bono and The Edge leave as I'm being frisked by security; they pause on the stoop for an impromptu, impassive photocall. Bono is wearing shades, as usual. As I watch the flashes catch in the lenses, I realize, with a flash of insight, that a celebrity is someone who works hard his whole life to get noticed, then wears dark glasses to avoid being recognized.

Brian is sitting with Dave Gahan from Depeche Mode, and a couple of girls I don't recognize. They must be transient attractions – Brian doesn't even introduce them to me. Dave smiles at me and leaves. The girls follow him. Several bottles of champagne have been emptied and stand discarded on the table. Brian motions for more from a waitress. She brings a bottle over and Brian slaps a twenty down on the table.

'Have yourself a go on this,' Brian says, slipping a vial into my hand. 'A trip to Disneyland.'

He doesn't need to ask twice.

Returning from the toilets I hand the vial back to Brian, wiping stinging nostrils. My head is buzzing with activity and I have that familiar unquenchable desire to speak.

'I've been thinking,' Brian says. 'About this morning in court. Maybe I ought to pay more attention. What'd it all mean?'

Somehow, I manage to click into law mode. 'It means you're not allowed to spend more than you need for reasonable living and legal expenses. This kind of thing –' I tap the empty vial still lying on the table – 'wouldn't qualify, for example.'

'You're my lawyer,' he says. 'We could call this a conference. How's that?'

'I don't think a judge would be impressed.'

'I don't see *you* complaining.'

'Selective blindness.'

'Hypocrite.'

I hold up my hands helplessly. 'Guilty as charged.'

We watch a couple of girls on a table opposite, in silence, until Brian looks over to me again and says, 'Thanks for this afternoon.'

'For what?'

'Cheering me up.'

'I didn't do anything.'

'You put up with me moaning. And it's good to have someone else to talk to. I could talk to Davey, I guess, but I don't like to worry him.'

'Fair enough.'

'He's got a lot on his mind. The album, the solo tour – you know.'

'It's no problem,' I say. 'I don't mind.'

There's a pause and I study Brian over the top of my glass. For a brief moment I see the same vulnerability that was evident in the police mugshots from his drug arrest, years ago. I have to remind myself that this is Brian Fey, rockstar, famous person, icon from my youth.

Vulnerability isn't something you associate with him.

This is what you associate with him: 100,000 screaming fans calling out to him. Him shouting 'Good evening Pasadena' from a stage in California during another mega-concert on another world tour. His face on magazines around the world. His songs on everyone's lips.

I'm almost feeling sorry for him, and I'm not entirely sure why.

He says, 'How'd you explain tonight to your girl-friend?'

'I'm not seeing anyone right now,' I admit, suddenly confident I can tell Brian about Hannah. I don't know why I feel this way. Perhaps his own vulnerability has struck a chord.

'But you said—'

'I know what I said, but I'm not. She left me. I just didn't want to talk about it then.'

'You don't mind now?'

'No, I don't think I do.'

'When'd it happen?'

'A while ago.'

'Why?'

'We just grew apart. You know how it is: you think you know someone, and then you realize you don't know them at all.'

'I know what you mean,' he says emphatically.

'Things change. You look at people in different ways. But then it was her who left me, so I'm just guessing that's what happened. I don't really know.'

'Was there anyone else?'

'No,' I begin, then, recanting, 'Yes. He's an actor.'

'Anyone famous?'

'Not really.'

'You upset about it?'

'For a while.'

'I'm sorry,' he says.

'It's no problem,' I feign. 'Not now. I hardly even miss her.'

I don't know whether he buys my bravado. He lets it sink in as he picks at a packet of crisps on the table.

'We've got more in common than you think,' he says.

There's a companionable pause which doesn't detract from the feeling of surrealism that Brian Fey should be the first person to get the low-down on my new, single status.

He changes the subject: 'You're coming tomorrow, aren't you?'

'Tomorrow?'

'The gig. *My* first gig. The first one on my own, I mean.'

I'd forgotten. Brian's new album gets its live debut tomorrow at a medium-sized venue in town. Brian mentioned it before, I think. He may even have provided me with a ticket. In the confusion of recent events it slipped my mind.

'Course I'll be there,' I say. 'Goes without saying.'

'Good,' he says. 'It'd mean a lot. I'm actually pretty nervous. Can you believe that? After everything I've done, that a little concert like this'd have me scared?'

THE NOBLE ART

Later on a couple of guys approach the table. Both are swaying badly, sloppy drunk. They have the unmistakable look of music executives; ten years ago, they would have been wearing pony tails and shiny suits.

'Are you Brian Fey?' one of them slurs, bracing himself with both hands on our table.

Brian half-smiles. 'No,' he says, 'you've got the wrong guy.'

'Are you sure?' says the other guy. 'You look just like him.'

'I wish I was,' Brian says.

'You wish you were him?' says the first guy, eyes swimming. 'Why'd you wanna be a loser like him?'

'Why'd you want that?' echoes the other.

'What?'

'Why'd you wanna be a loser like Brian Fey? I've heard his new album's a pile of shite.'

'And I always thought,' opines his companion, 'the rest of the Dahlias were carrying him.'

Brian gets to his feet, and I'm suddenly very nervous. 'Yeah?' he says.

'Yeah. He had an OK voice but even that's gone now. Everyone says he's completely lost it. Too much toot, I reckon.' He puts a finger to his nose and gives an expressive sniff.

I look up at Brian; a dark scowl has settled across his face.

The two of them close ranks. 'He oughtta realize he's over the hill and just get it over with. There's nothing worse than seeing someone lose their dignity in public.'

'And slagging him off makes you feel good?' Brian asks. He prods the first guy in the sternum. 'Make you feel better, does it?'

'Don't do that,' warns the guy, scowling. His friend takes a step towards us.

'Let's not argue,' I intervene tremulously. 'Let me buy you both a beer.'

'I'm not thirsty. And your mate's upsetting me with his attitude.'

'I'm sure he's very sorry,' I say reasonably. 'You're very sorry, aren't you?' I almost call him Brian but manage to bite my tongue.

Brian leaps at the bigger man, catching him under

the chin with a looping right-handed uppercut that started from somewhere around his knees. The suddenness of the swipe must have taken him by surprise because he staggers backwards into a table. Brian follows in with another punch, this one left-handed; it lands in the man's gut with a fleshy thwap. He doubles up, wheezing. Brian raises his knee sharply; it thuds into chin, jarring teeth. Something drops out of the guy's mouth as he drops to his knees – a streamer of bloody spit. Brian lands a kick in the man's ribs.

He goes down. Brian keeps kicking, firing out words with each fresh kick.

'Mind . . . your . . . fucking . . . manners.'

He stomps on him; his arms, his torso, his legs. The guy pulls himself into a tight foetal ball, his arms protecting his head but exposing his ribs. Brian's face is stretched into a brutal rictus, flooded with anger and hate. I try to pull him away but he shrugs my hands away from his shoulders.

The other guy shoves Brian back against the table. Brian hits the table but bounces right back at him.

I try to pull him away again. He shoves the guy hard with both hands. I loop *my* hands around his waist and yank him backwards, mid-kick. He teeters back into me and we both collapse. His body is tight, throbbing with energy. He tries to get up, but I don't let go.

As we are lying on the ground, wrapped around each other with him struggling to unlock my arms, the first guy gets up. Blood is pouring from his nose. The two of them step over the furniture until they loom over us.

SUBSTITUTE

The second man pulls me to my feet with one hand locked around my throat. Rather than struggle, or tell him that Brian is the man they should be taking care of, I do something immeasurably dumb.

I aim a hopeless head butt at his nose.

Even from this range, close enough to smell prawn cocktail on his breath and see the fragments of crisps in his oh-so-trendy goatee, I miss. My forehead glances off a solid cheekbone and catches the side of his ear.

'Oh dear,' he says. 'That wasn't too bright now, was it?'

PUNCHBAG

It's Rocky Balboa on the ropes, sucking it up and taking it from Apollo Creed. All I can remember: curling up to absorb the punishment and telling myself that you have to swallow a pint of blood before you're sick, and risk choking on your own vomit.

CONVALESCENCE

Later.

We're sitting in a kebab house nursing our drinks and our wounds. Well, *I'm* nursing wounds; Brian's swizzling a straw around in his glass of 7-Up, watching the bubbles crawl up the glass and break on the surface.

The second guy soon put paid to me, dealing me a head butt and following that up with a kicking as I lay mewling on the sticky floor of the bar. All Brian got was a clip around the ear. This was despite him leaping to my defence; he was thrown back to the floor by a flat-palmed shove to the sternum, and by the time he had got back to his feet for some more the bouncers were there and we were thrown out into the snow, blood from my head staining the white.

Why did I do something so stupid? This wasn't heroism, not even panic, not even the over-enthusiastic application of the professional duty owed to my clients.

This was pity and fear. The look of hatred on Brian's face as he went for the first guy – maybe it was that that pushed me to defend him. I didn't want him to get hurt, and I could see that he was in the mood to go for the second guy as easily as he had gone for his mate. It was almost as if he was inviting the beating he was inevitably going to take once they were both on their feet.

I've never seen him like that before. It's hard to attribute that kind of anger to him. Look at him now, casually slurping up his drink and rubbing idly at the back of his head where it hit the edge of a chair. It's almost as if he was a different person.

'What happened?' I croak painfully.

'You heard them. They were winding me up. I just lost it.'

He looks sheepish now, sucking noisily at the straw like a child; different in the artificial light of the café – washed-out, his colour fading – like the way clubbers look when the house lights are brought up at the end of the night.

He stares down at the table. A heavy silence has fallen.

I apply my amateur cold compress – a cold can of Coke – to my bloody nose. The tin is stained again with a bloom of blood, red on silver-and-red.

'I'm really sorry,' Brian says, looking up. 'It's my temper. I can't always keep it under control. It makes me do stupid things.'

'You only had to ignore them,' I say painfully. There doesn't appear to be very much in the way of space between my cracked and swollen lips – just enough for a taut grimace.

'I know, but I can't, not always. Red mist, you know, I snap. I've tried everything to stop it – even had anger-management classes once. They didn't fucking work.'

Another awkward silence, filled by more sucking noises from the straw.

A sip of whisky from the bottle on the table will ease the pain. I pour myself a generous measure, down it, then pour again. We bought it in a twenty-four-hour supermarket after being thrown out of the bar.

'I'll try to make sure it doesn't happen again,' Brian promises.

SCOTT DOLAN'S GUEST LIST

World's Greatest Showbiz Column

BRIAN FEY: OFF THE RAILS?
Shocked muso considers charges

Ex-BLACK DAHLIAS singer **Brian Fey**, 35, seems to be falling to bits.

Fey, his new album not doing as well as might have been hoped, now stands accused of starting a fight in a trendy London bar.

Media worker **Guy Roberts** was enjoying a night out with a friend at swish bar Attica when Fey and his lawyer, **Daniel Tate**, got into an argument with them. The argument ended with Fey punching Guy, 32.

'He's off his rocker,' said Guy. 'I thought he was going to kill me.'

PULP frontman JARVIS COCKER spotted watching French art house movies in London's Curzon cinema.

CATHERINE ZETA JONES and MICHAEL DOUGLAS at a signing to promote a book by Michael's father, KURT.

Wednesday

SWEET DREAMS (ARE MADE OF THIS)

Hannah sits at the bottom of the bed, cross-legged, in my pair of brown tracksuit bottoms. She likes the soft fabric, made fluffy by dozens of washes in the days when I used to work out. She smiles down at me as I rouse myself. She brushes an errant strand of red hair away from her nose. The Sunday heavies are spread around her. It's the smell rising from the tray on her lap that's woken me: freshly-baked rolls, strips of bacon, eggs, a pork sausage and two pieces of fried bread. A tall glass of orange juice stands next to the salt and pepper pots and the two sauce bottles, brown and red.

She teases her fingers against my toes, cool outside the duvet. She says good morning, tells me it's cold outside, a frost still on the grass in the park. She's already been to the corner shop, so this must be a Sunday, when she always rises before me to get breakfast and buy the papers. She offers me the tray.

REALITY BITES

Nelson wakes me, nuzzling my chin with his head.

I decide against looking over at the clock on the bedside table. I haven't removed the picture of Hannah I took outside St Paul's, which stands beside it, and I know that if I see it the remorse will be unbearable.

I decide to sink deeper into the sweaty clutch of my sheets for a few extra moments. Just a little longer. I watch dust slowly turning in a slanting diagonal of fresh light. The disc of the sun, muffled by glowing curtains the colour of marmalade, is already at its mid-morning position.

As I fumble around the kitchen, hoping to find something fresh for breakfast, I reach back and collect the fragments of the previous evening. When did I ever drink enough to feel this bad? Where?

I don't even know how I got home.

I fork tinned salmon into Nelson's dish. He stands on his hind paws and miaows hungrily.

The frequency of these memory lapses has been increasing. It's become the rule, rather than the exception, for me to wake up with no idea what I've been doing the night before. This should concern me, I know, but it interests me only as empirical evidence of my accelerating decline.

LE PETIT DÉJEUNER

I steady myself against the frame of the door as bubbling nausea sends its tendrils clambering up my throat like magma. I open the fridge. An overdue bottle of milk, turned to sludge. A half-used tin of sweet corn and some fruit salad, also off. A half-eaten ham sandwich. Not too mouldy, so remove that infected crust *et voilà*: breakfast is served.

My cat eats better than I do these days.

I look at a box of Nurofen in the kitchen cabinet. Maybe take a couple? Consider the relief it might offer? A sign that I'm ready to make a conscious effort to get out of this funk; to shower (lack of hot water notwithstanding), iron a shirt, get dressed, go to work. A new start, of sorts.

I decide to leave the pills where they are. I'm not ready to stop drinking yet.

I take out a half-empty bottle of gin and the ice-tray from the freezer compartment. Tip the gin into a glass until it laps halfway up. Top up with tonic water, add chunks of ice and a thick slice of lemon, a bonus discovery from the vegetable compartment in the fridge. Take the sandwich and glass into the lounge to polish off at leisure. Take the bottle also, in case refills prove necessary.

WINTER WONDERLAND

Outside, the naked skeletons of trees outlined against the bus depot opposite the flat. A big jumbo cruising overhead, heading for the sun, patterning the sky with frozen crystals. The queue waiting at the bus stop wrapped snugly in scarves and heavy coats, closed against the chill as, slowly at first and then in a thick white curtain, fat flakes of snow begin to fall. The ending of another year.

MIDWEEK PROGRESS REPORT

On my arrival at Liverpool Street, I divert into the record store to check the progress of Brian's album. The new Dahlias' album has sold out. Monster Munch's is doing well.

I crouch down to flick through the copies of Brian's record. There are still four left. I'm the only person to have bought a copy from this store.

Not good.

TOP TEN

LONDON: Come-back kings the BLACK DAHLIAS look set to trounce all-comers in this week's album charts. The Essex rockers

– their first (and last) album with JOHN FRENCH as singer – have launched to the top of the midweek charts, selling three-times more than their nearest rival, DESTINY'S CHILD. The hip-again DAHLIAS look like scoring one of their biggest ever hits when the charts are officially confirmed at the weekend.

1. THE BLACK DAHLIAS
2. DESTINY'S CHILD
3. TRAVIS
4. MONSTER MUNCH
5. HEARSAY
6. SEAN DARBO
. . . .
92. BRIAN FEY

SAMARITAN SECRETARY

It's almost 12.30 when I finally slink inside the building.

'What happened to your face?' asks Elizabeth, dabbing ginger fingers in the direction of my temple. I tell her I tripped and fell on a loose paving stone.

Clucking like a mother hen she ushers me into my office, presses me down into my chair, collects various salves and lotions from the medicine cabinet, and dabs at a hardened scab on my forehead that's started to leak a thick white pus. The sting of the disinfectant is numbed by the booze. I wonder whether she can smell it on my breath? She tells me I should've stayed home. I tell her I'm absolutely dedicated to the Law. She laughs and gives me a disapproving smile.

'You really ought to take better care of yourself. I'm going to have strong words with that girlfriend of yours.'

A lump in my throat; I swallow it. I don't want her to feel sorry for me. Maybe she knows already, from the TV or the article in *Hello!*, maybe she's just probing me. But I want to bear this cross alone. I *want* to be martyred. Pain is all I have left of my relationship and I don't want to share it with anyone else.

'I saw her on the telly last night,' she says. 'Doesn't she look *great*?' No mention of the engagement to Haines. Maybe she was just watching *Skin Trade*?

I force a thin smile and try not to think about how gorgeous Hannah's looking these days.

Cohen – engaged on a long telephone call – cups his hand over the mouthpiece and says, 'The other guy's eating his meals through a straw, right, champ?'

I give him the finger but he's already back into his call.

Elizabeth takes out her make-up compact and shows me my reflection. A puffy chocolate doughnut around my right eye, the lid half-closed by the swelling, and the whole right side of my face discoloured by a bluey-brown bruise like an ink stain.

'Doing anything tonight, handsome?' she says playfully. I manage a painful smile and shoo her away.

ANY LAST REQUESTS?

Wilson pays me a visit. She seems ready to deliver a broadside but she shudders as she catches sight of my wounds.

'What happened to your head? Have you been in a *fight* or something?'

'Oh no,' I say, thinking quickly. 'It was a crash. A, um, a car crash. I was waiting for the lights when he hit me. Didn't even see him coming. Right up my backside. My head bounced off the steering wheel.' I prod the scab. 'The car's a write-off,' I add for effect.

'You had a car crash,' she repeats slowly. She's wondering whether this is true and whether it's worth calling my bluff. 'When'd this happen?'

'Last night.' When she frowns at me, I elaborate, 'It happened on the way home from the office yesterday.'

'I see.'

'You'll be after the briefing note?'

'And the recording contract,' she adds. 'Where are they? Are they finished?'

Tentative: 'The contract's coming on but I haven't had time to do the note. I was planning on doing them last night at home but I ended up in casualty for three hours.'

This appeal for clemency is brushed aside.

'Trish Parkes has called several times this morning. She wants to move things forwards as quickly as possible. And she wants urgent advice at the meeting. We won't be able to do either if you haven't finished the work I asked you to finish. The work I asked you to finish *last week*.'

'I'm sorry.' It dawns on me that if my story really was true, a flash of indignation might be appropriate here. So I insert one: 'It's not exactly my bloody fault – I didn't *ask* the other guy to crash into me.'

She flinches. 'I realize that. But we've still got a very important meeting this afternoon and at the moment we're not prepared for it.'

'I'm working on it.'

'Are the documents finished enough for me to look at them?'

I suddenly notice the amended pages on my desk. They're covered with red ink. I cover them with a folder.

'Not really. It maybe needs a few hours of extra work.'

She reddens. 'All right, I'll call Trish and tell her the agreement won't be ready until tomorrow morning. I want you to change priorities now and look into that briefing note. You can worry about the agreement after the meeting. And don't let me down, Tate. I *hate* going into meetings when I don't understand the legal problem I'm going to be asked to answer. I need that note.'

'I understand,' I say. 'I'll get right onto it.'

She turns to leave and then stops, a thought occurring. 'Do you need any help?' she asks. 'Oliver Dawkins's done this kind of thing before. I think he even speaks the language.'

I don't believe it – he can't have told her already that I borrowed his precedents?

'I'll be fine,' I say. 'Let's not bother him.'

'It's up to you. Just get that briefing note finished and have your secretary bring it over to me as soon as it's done. I want to review it before the meeting.'

'Leave it to me,' I say.

'And don't be late for the meeting.'

'I won't.'

She turns to leave, pauses, then swings back for a second time. 'And the Fey case? How're we getting on with that?'

'It's going, um, as well as might be expected.'

'And yesterday's hearing?'

'Went really well.'

Each word is a fresh shovelful excavated from my soon-to-be grave. I can't hold her gaze. If she asks for elaboration, I'm doomed. Why is it proving so hard to own up? Making a clean breast of the mess Brian is in may be the best chance I've got of saving my job. A slim chance, for sure, but when Wilson finds out the truth my feet won't touch the ground on my way out.

She nods sternly, temporarily appeased.

'Briefing note. My desk. As soon as possible.'

WITH A LITTLE HELP FROM
MY FRIENDS

'What've you done to upset *her*?' Cohen asks.

'My inability to perform miracles is being unfairly held against me.'

'You sure I can't help out?'

'It's not as bad as it looks. Provided I get a clear couple of hours I ought to be able to break the back of it.'

'I'm here if you need a hand.'

Cohen's a good friend to have in a sticky situation.

'And what really happened to your face?' he asks. 'I took a policy decision not to mention the fact that you don't own a car.'

'You wouldn't believe me if I told you.'

'Try me.'

I tell him.

He gawps. '*You* got beaten up because *he* got lippy with another punter?'

I nod. 'I said you wouldn't believe me.'

'You were right. I don't.'

IF AT FIRST YOU DON'T SUCCEED

From: Tate, Daniel
To: Delgardo, Rachel
Subject: Penance

Following my intolerably bad-mannered behaviour on Monday evening, I was wondering if you could be persuaded to risk another date with me? Maybe dinner? My treat.
Daniel

CAPTAIN OF INDUSTRY

I settle down to work on the briefing note. I open a new file and begin to crib from the notes in the Dork's precedent folder, my eyes flicking from the pages to the screen. I can't believe how thorough his work is. Everything I need is here.

I could kiss him on the top of his shiny bald head.

I finish typing the note at 1.15. I skim read it, marking up the obvious changes in red ink and then hand the pages to Elizabeth to amend. I figure I'll have one last chance to proof-read it and make any final, minimal changes.

'Busy busy busy,' Cohen says.

'No rest for the wicked.'

EMAIL

From:	Delgardo, Rachel
To:	Tate, Daniel
Subject:	Re: Penance

There's nothing to apologize for, really!! If I said sorry
for every time I was a little drunk I'd be apologizing
forever. And dinner sounds good but I can only do
tonight this week. Is that going to be OK? If not,
then maybe next week?

I don't email a reply at once. Best not to appear too
keen or, horrors, desperate. Fifteen minutes seems to be
the appropriate interval. I email back and tell her that
tonight will be fine and that I'll mail later with some
suggested venues.

THE LATEST FASHION

I feel guilty. Thinking about another girl feels like
cheating. My mind rolls another memory to punish me
with:

Hannah and I were invited to half a dozen weddings
last year. We were both at that age when school and
university friends begin to get picked off by the spectre
of matrimony, sucked down into wedded bliss. Our
summer weekends became a series of ceremonies and
gatherings, raising a glass to the next couple to throw
in their lot together. Morning suits, new hats, confetti
in the air, bouquets to be caught: it was difficult to
remember where one weekend ended and the others
began.

We were standing by the lychgate of a small village church in Somerset, apple trees in the graveyard and swallows darting in a picture-postcard sky. Hannah's friend Laura had just been hitched to Joseph, and the two of them were pausing for photos next to an antique Daimler. The car was waiting to take them to the reception in a marquee in the grounds of Dunster Castle.

Hannah, pink and blue confetti in her hair, leant in close.

'I can imagine us doing that,' she breathed.

'One day,' I said.

'Daniel, I'm serious.'

Twenty-six years old and not ready for this, I pushed out a smile.

'One day.'

SOME ADDITIONAL RESEARCH

Cohen leaves and with Elizabeth still amending my work I decide to risk calling Suzy Pugh, Hannah's agent, again.

'I'm calling about Hannah Wilde.'

'Go on.'

'I'm producing a movie – lottery money, romantic comedy, very zeitgeist, big hit written all over it – and we're auditioning the cast. I've seen Ms Wilde's work and I think she's just perfect for the female lead. I was, um, wondering if you had an address I could contact her on?'

'Did you call me yesterday?'

'No.'

'Yes, you did. I recognize your voice. Listen, I don't know who you are but please stop calling. If you bother us again I'm going to call the police.'

'Come on, *please*.'

'Goodbye.'

I listen to the dialling tone buzzing in my ear for twenty seconds and then put the receiver back.

I'll have to try another avenue.

THE HEART OF THE MATTER

Why am I even *trying* to get hold of Hannah? I don't know what I'd say to her if I managed to get through. I might ask her about this marriage business, I guess, and then there's the whole business of why she left me in the first place. That's never been properly explained, although I can guess: my failure to commit. My refusal to give her what she wanted: a ring on her finger.

Of course I've thought about this. Why couldn't I give her that? Why, when everything was so perfect, was I unable to offer to make an honest woman out of her? I know now: I wasn't able to satisfy myself that Hannah was with me because she wanted to be. I was always half expecting some loathsome TV host to appear and announce that I was the victim of an elaborate joke. That the last five years of my life had been for someone else's entertainment. Did I *really* expect a gorgeous, talented, successful actress like Hannah Wilde to be interested in an ordinary, mediocre, everyday lawyer like me?

The longer our relationship lasted, and the more she wanted from me, the less I was ready to commit. Previous relationships had ended messily. I wasn't ready to invest so heavily again, only to tremulously wait for the inevitable crash.

Every time I rebuffed her gentle suggestions, the worse she felt. Her history was littered with untrustworthy male figures: her father, who left her and her mother when she was tiny; a boyfriend at university who fucked with her head; the wannabe actor she shacked up with when she moved to London – the one who beat her every time he was rejected for parts. My behaviour fed her insecurity. My every refusal made me out as just another example of my duplicitous sex.

I told her I was happy with her, happier than I had ever been before, so why wouldn't I prove it? That was all she needed.

I see it all now. Now I understand. But the knowledge has come months too late.

MORE DECEPTION

I skim through the Rolodex until I find the card I've dedicated to Hannah's personal numbers. I realize I haven't contacted any of her friends yet. Perhaps one of them will be able to tell me where she is. Or provide me with the hint of a clue. I run my finger down the card until it alights on a name I recognize: Karla, an actress she met shooting a commercial for a supermarket chain a year or so ago. An image: the two of them in skimpy dresses pushing trolleys around empty aisles. The memory stirs carnal thoughts.

The number belongs to a mobile. Karla answers after a short pause.

I try to sound nonchalant as I ask her whether she has heard from Hannah.

'Not for a while,' she replies. 'I only got back from Cannes yesterday. You guys aren't having problems or anything, are you?' Her tone is suspicious, concerned that I'm after information not to be divulged. Her trip abroad might explain her apparent ignorance about Hannah and Haines.

I tell her it's nothing like that – I've lost her mobile number and some urgent family business has come up. Does she have it? I'm cringing as I say this, wondering whether it sounds as lame out loud as it does in my head.

'The only number I ever had was the one for your

place,' she says doubtfully, 'and, anyway, I haven't spoken to her in months.'

Another dead end.

SCOTT DOLAN TRIES AGAIN

Phone call:

'Hi, Daniel, Scott Dolan from—'

'The Guest List,' I complete it for him. '*Extravaganza*. Yeah yeah, I know. You don't give up, do you?'

'Danny, I was wondering – have you had a chance to think about our conversation on Monday? I left a message yesterday?'

'I know you did,' I say, teeth gritted. 'I listened to it.'

'And . . .?'

'I erased it.'

'But have you thought about what I said?'

'My position hasn't changed. I haven't got anything interesting to say to you.'

'Why don't you let me be the judge of that? Tell me – what *have* you got?'

'You don't understand,' I say firmly, striving to keep my patience. 'Professionally, I *can't* say anything to you. I'm not about to break the duty of confidence I owe to my client by blabbing to a reporter.'

'Listen, all my sources are confidential,' he says. 'You've got my word on that.'

'That's nice to know.'

'Come on, Danny.'

'No. I'm sorry. I can't help you. Please stop bothering me.'

'OK, but before I go let me offer you some free information that might surprise you. You know what Brian Fey did yesterday afternoon?'

'I really couldn't care less what—'

'He beat up a journalist at the *NME*.'

I remember the change of tone during Brian's rant to me yesterday afternoon; the note of resolve, a decision made.

'He did what?'

'I thought that might interest you. He went to the *NME*'s offices, forced his way inside and found the journalist who'd just given his new album a slating. They argued; he decked the guy. It took two security guards to pull him off. I've just got off the phone with the victim myself. He was pretty battered: suspected broken nose. Probably gonna bring charges. It'll be in the paper tomorrow and I'm just working on the headline now: BRUTAL BRIAN BASHES HACK. What'd you think?'

'No, no—'

'How about SPITEFUL SINGER STRIKES SCRIBE?'

'No – I don't care about the headline. This hasn't got anything to do with me.'

'Come on, Danny, don't play stupid—'

'It's *Daniel*.'

'You know that this's got everything to do with

you. You know Brian's got a temper. And you also know that someone who wasn't exactly on his Christmas card list was found dead on Sunday.'

'That was suicide.'

'Was it?'

'This's ridiculous.'

'Let's say it *wasn't* suicide, just for the sake of argument. Brian's got motive. And now *we* know he's got a violent streak, too. You don't think he's capable? You *know* he is. All I'm doing's giving you a chance to put his side of the story before the rest of the press get hold of this. It could get ugly. Why not let him get a shot in first?'

'I'm sorry, I've still got nothing to say.'

'I might have something else to tell you tomorrow. Something much worse. I've got researchers digging up stuff at the moment, and I don't wanna mention it over the phone. Why don't you at least *think* about talking to me? Discuss it with your boss or do whatever it is you've gotta do?'

'No, please, don't call me tomorrow, don't call me again. How many times do I have to say it – I'm not interested.'

Before I can put the phone down, he squeezes in, 'You've got my number, Danny.'

AN INVITATION TO LUNCH

This whole briefing note thing is getting bogged down. It's 90 per cent finished now; just the final small amendments to sort out.

Elizabeth tells me that Davey MacHale – Brian's manager – is waiting for me in reception. This comes as a shock. I check my diary, suspicious that I've forgotten an appointment with him. I haven't: this is an unannounced call. I ask Elizabeth to finish off the amendments to the briefing note, and to leave it on my desk when it's done. I want to check it before I take it along to Wilson.

THE SENIOR PARTNER

I share the lift down to reception with Charles Hunter.

Hunter's face is as wrinkled as a fossilized flannel. He always wears the same suit – navy-blue and chalk pinstripe – and carries a pocket watch in his waistcoat. He's the epitome of tradition, and no one can imagine the office without him.

Despite his impeccable bearing, Hunter is driven by one thing: profit. Consider this as anecdotal evidence: a slap-up meal thrown by an infamous society girl after the successful conclusion of a rather notorious case in the sixties. 'Whatever can I do to repay you?' the society girl asked. 'My dear woman,' answered Hunter, 'ever since the Phoenicians invented money there's only been one answer to that question.'

'Afternoon,' he says as the doors seal us in.

'Mr Hunter.' I return his pleasantry with a shaky smile. I count the floors sliding gradually down to reception. It takes for ever.

'What's happened to your face?'

I repeat the car-crash sob story. He raises an eyebrow and nods sympathetically.

'That sounds unpleasant,' he offers. 'I hope it isn't too painful.'

'It was,' I say. 'But it's not too bad now.'

'Miss Wilson tells me Mr Fey's case is going rather more smoothly now. We might even've turned the corner?'

'Oh, yes,' I say, glad to change the subject, although I'd prefer it to be something else, something that my hot cheeks wouldn't betray me with. 'I'm going to meet Brian's manager now, actually.'

'Excellent. Keep me informed.'

The bell chimes as the lift reaches the ground floor, and I follow him out.

'Keep up the good work.' He smiles sagely, and heads towards the conference suite.

BEEF ENCOUNTER

Vanessa Feltz and Dale Winton are waiting in reception with their own agents. Some new TV show we're giving advice on. Davey is there too. He looks dapper in his black pencil tie, white shirt, camel-hair overcoat and winkle-pickers. His fat cheeks are flushed from the cold outside.

He asks how my evening with Brian went. I tell him it was very enjoyable. It doesn't sound as if Brian has divulged the conclusion of our proceedings, and maybe Davey hasn't seen the papers, so I follow Brian's lead and omit the details. Davey doesn't appear to have noticed the protrusion on the side of my head, or else he's keeping his own counsel to spare my blushes.

He asks if I'd like a bite to eat. I accept.

We get a taxi and Davey takes me to one of the trendy new media hang-outs in Covent Garden, an upmarket steakhouse called, ridiculously, Beef Encounter. Decor: whitewashed walls and sterile lighting. Floor: untreated concrete. Long metal-framed mirrors hang on the walls, with tiny bull's-eye spotlights aimed into them. Tables and chairs made from chunky aluminium. Plates of plain white china. Single red roses in aluminium holders shaped like test-tubes. Knives and forks like surgical instruments. The waiters are dressed in black suits and shirts, no ties.

The maître d' glides ahead of us to a table that, if not quite front of house, is close enough to offer a good view of the stars. Courtney Cox is talking with Maria Kelsey, ultra-thin, über-trendy, super-agent to the stars. Matthew Perry is sitting with a glam blonde.

The maître d' raises a haughty eyebrow as I sit down. I feel like a charlatan: he can see right through me. Beyond all reasonable doubt, I don't belong in a place like this.

I wonder if Davey is making a point.

The menu is examined. The prices are stratospheric.

'The fettuccini's great,' Davey says, 'but don't let me influence you. And don't worry about the price. I'm paying.'

The soundtrack here is deliberately kitsch. Lift muzak versions of camp seventies tracks. Abba's 'Gimme Gimme Gimme' is playing over the sound system right now. I assume every reference in the place is some sort of deeply ironic gesture. If so, most of them are whistling right over my head.

A waiter – six foot plus, swarthy, thick hair, male-model-stroke-resting-actor – impassively takes my order.

SOME PROFESSIONAL FEEDBACK

Fifteen minutes of excruciating small talk follows during which we both tiptoe around the fact that we're obviously here to talk about something else.

The waiter returns with our starters. The portions

are minuscule, artistic. The satisfaction of appetite is secondary in this sort of restaurant. This is self-advertising. Image. You're paying for exposure.

Davey says we need a frank discussion as I pick lamely at my starter: a stringy spinach ravioli. It looks vaguely intestinal splayed out on my plate. He didn't want to have this discussion over the telephone, he says, and when he says 'discuss' I know he means chastise. This isn't promising.

'It's like this. I'm – no, *we* – we're worried about how the case's going. I was told Brian's defence was good. I know you can't guarantee success in these things, I mean we *knew* there was a risk of not settling with them before, but we never thought it'd pan out this way. It's looking like a disaster from where I'm sitting right now.'

'Like you say, you can't predict how litigation's gonna turn out.'

'It's the damages. Look at them! I mean, fuck me Daniel, there's no way on *earth* Brian'll be able to pay the money the court wants him to pay. No *way*. The label can take a small hit, we're standing behind him to an extent like you know, but we thought this was gonna be a minor problem and then Brian's free to get on with the rest of his life. Make some *music*. Sell some *records*. Do what he's good at. This's taking so long. *Too* long—'

'Maybe we should set up a proper meeting to dis—'

'—and all we seem to be doing's bailing water. We

never set the agenda. I want to be positive, go out there and make proposals, settle things, get all this shit over and done with. I want *pro*active, not *re*active. And I'm not getting it—'

DAVEY HITS HIS STRIDE

'—and it's really upsetting Brian. I know he plays it pretty cool and you'd never really know it, but it *is* bothering him. He's a delicate character. He likes stability. Typical bloody artist, yeah, I know, but what can you do?' Davey leans over and lowers his voice conspiratorially, worried perhaps that what he's about to say might be overheard by Matthew or Courtney. 'The rehearsals for the tour have been just *terrible,* between you and me. Fucking *awful.* He doesn't seem able to concentrate on the music. His voice isn't the same – too tense. And now he needs a gram to even get out of bed, which's even more expense apart from anything else. And, yes, I suppose we ought to be thinking about his health and well-being too, especially given his history, but when that's the only way to get him going and into the studio what else're we supposed to do? And it's all the distraction of the court stuff that's doing this to him, I know it is. So I need you to get it out of the way.'

He slices open a parcel of pasta with the point of his knife. Pesto sauce seeps out. I'm expected to offer something in response here, but my mind is an empty white space.

So he keeps going: 'The label's concerned. There's no blank cheque here, Daniel, there's no money tree at the bottom of the garden. The directors want an urgent review of this. We heard the band had his cars and furniture seized yesterday, by the way. That doesn't help things. When will this all end – that's the question?'

I've finished my ravioli. It's had no effect on my hangover. If anything, it's made me feel even worse. This makes my answer maybe too abrupt.

'When Brian pays over £900,000, like the court ordered.'

Davey laughs edgily. 'We both know that won't happen. He doesn't have that kind of cash. And the label won't pay it.'

'Then the band'll just execute the judgment on whatever else they can get their hands on.'

'Meaning?'

'Meaning the band could sell Brian's flat in London and his villa in the South of France. They could divide his rights in the Dahlias' back catalogue between them, choke off his entitlement to any future royalties. They could tell his banks to pay the contents of his accounts over to them. They could bankrupt him and investigate his private life with a fine-tooth comb. And if he refuses to cooperate with them they could commit him for contempt of court, arrest him and have him locked up. That's just for starters.'

He looks shell-shocked. 'Then let's appeal.'

'Too late,' I say. 'We're way out of time.'

'Why didn't we do it before?'

'Because we would've lost,' I say. 'It wouldn't have been worth the time or the effort. And it would've been very expensive.'

(Let's not mention it was because my girlfriend binned me around then and I forgot the deadline for filing the application at court and I've been a negligence suit waiting to happen ever since and my once-glittering reputation is in danger of being irreparably tarnished and . . .)

'I can't believe this, Daniel,' he says in a low, tight voice. A nervous tic just above the left corner of his upper lip has started to vibrate. I watch it tremble. 'I'm not happy about this at all. The communication between us can't've been up to scratch because I've had too many nasty surprises.'

I expect a stronger rebuke, but none comes. He just hunkers down around his plate, scowling.

DAVEY COMES CLEAN

He finishes a mouthful. 'You know how much I've got riding on Brian?' he asks bluntly.

'I'm not sure what you mean.'

'I gave up a lot for the chance to manage him. You

know that new punk band everyone's talking about? The young lads? Monster Munch?'

'I'm . . . familiar with their work.'

'That was my project. I put them together.'

'I don't get it.'

'You don't think they're a proper *band*, do you? They think they're the new Sex Pistols but they're more like the Spice Girls. Think S Club 7 with guitars and nose rings. Or Steps with nasty attitudes and profanity. Except it's all fake, of course. Manufactured, they're manufactured and fake and they're making a shitload of wedge for someone else.' He takes a bitter sip from his glass. 'You want to know something about those boys? They're all good as gold. Mooch – his real name's Stephen – he's at this Catholic boys' school when he comes to the audition. Scooter – that's Colin – was working at Sainsbury's. And Bam Bam – Richard – was recommended to me by a mate setting up a boy band who turned him down 'cause he couldn't dance for toffee. None of them can play their instruments and all their songs've been written for them. All they're good at is sneering and swearing, and that's only 'cause we taught them how. They're puppets, Danny; talentless, half-witted mannequins.'

'Jesus,' I say, although I suppose I shouldn't really be surprised by this news.

'I dropped them as soon as Brian got chucked out of the Dahlias. I thought he was the better bet. So much for going with your gut.'

'What, then Trish Parkes picked them up?'

'Yeah. And now look at them. Selling albums by the bucketload. Lucky bitch – and I don't get a penny out of them.' He dead-eyes me, switches back to Brian again. 'Thing is, Danny, I had to put a lot of my own money down just to get Brian's bloody album finished. The label got nervous the fifth time he had to lay it down and they wanted out. It was costing them a bomb. They were ready to write the whole thing off, and that would've been the end of his career. Finished. So I paid for the last month in the studio and the mix. I thought it'd just be a short-term loan thing, six months tops until his new album started to shift copies then we'd all start raking it in. So now you can see why I'm upset this isn't going like I want it to. The show's gotta go on because I personally haven't got any money left. If Brian goes down the toilet that's my career in the music business done and all my money pissed up the wall. So you've *got* to sort this thing out, see?'

I'm not sure what to say. We finish our meal in awkward silence. To drown out my discomfiture and guilt, I accelerate my consumption of the excellent red the sommelier recommended for my very bloody steak. Matthew Perry and his date are replaced by Jude Law and Ewan McGregor.

This really is an *excellent* restaurant. I should leave business cards behind, maybe snare some passing trade. When the sweets arrive, I push the boat out and order a bottle of dessert wine. After all, Davey's paying. And if my hangover won't quit, then I'm just going to drown it in more alcohol. Hair of the dog.

Davey's grim expression gradually gets grimmer.

PANIC

'Where's that briefing note?' I ask Elizabeth when I return to the office. I'm running late for the meeting. My head is heavy from the wine.

'I put it on your desk like you asked me.'

I scour the desk a second time.

'Are you sure?'

Elizabeth comes in and looks for herself.

'I put it right there,' she says, pointing. Save the jumbled pile of papers that usually litter my desk, there's nothing.

'Doesn't matter. Could you print me off another copy?'

She goes back outside to her station. It's 3.10: already ten minutes late for the meeting downstairs. I pace impatiently, waiting for the sound of the printer firing up. It doesn't happen.

'It's disappeared.'

I join her outside. 'What d'you mean?'

She scrolls through the files on the server directory. 'It was right here,' she says, indicating the location with a stab of the cursor. 'Right between these two files. It's just vanished.'

'Files don't just *vanish*, Elizabeth.'

'I know, but . . .' She falters. 'Maybe I could call IT?'

'No time for that,' I say. 'I'll just have to do without it.'

I head downstairs and sheepishly open the conference room door, edging in. Renwick is talking to Rolf Harris. I apologize and back out.

I ring Elizabeth to check where the meeting is supposed to be, and she rings Wilson's secretary. Elizabeth calls back: the location changed just after lunch. The band is shooting a video before they fly out, and they wanted us to come over to them.

No one told *me* anything about this.

I sprint outside and flag down a cab.

Wilson will gut me for this.

VIDEO SHOOT

By the time we get to the derelict warehouse where the shoot is taking place I'm forty minutes late and jumpy with nerves.

I have to negotiate my way past the security guards keeping out the twenty or so anxious girls gathered around the entrance. I can hear muffled music coming from the inside of the building and then it stops. I walk inside and follow open stairs down into a basement with a half-collapsed ceiling, patches of damp on the walls and pools of brown scummy water all over the floor. I pause at the bottom of the stairs, as Scooter – the singer – is talking to a guy I guess is the director, and Mooch is having make-up applied. Bam Bam is alternating between a can of Red Stripe in one hand and a spliff in the other. His drum kit is set up in the room and two guitars are propped against Marshall amps. I move inside, stepping over the wires and cables and monitors and spotlights.

Wilson is standing to one side, self-consciously, completely out of place here in her power suit and knowing it. I'm about to go over and face the music when the director calls for quiet and tells the band to take their places. They do, sullenly, and then the director checks the camera crew is rolling and, after counting in the band, shouts, 'Action.'

The video is basically Monster Munch playing straight to camera, with no storyline or fancy special effects. The director's pitch was probably 'gritty urban angst', or something similarly post-modern and trite.

The song plays out through the monitors and the band mimes to it, only Bam Bam actually playing – and he's a couple of beats off the pace but not really giving a shit because he knows the soundtrack will be wiped when the film is edited.

YOU CAN'T SING, YOU CAN'T DANCE, YOU LOOK AWFUL. YOU'LL GO A LONG WAY

I don't like their music. They're loud and noisy: the aural equivalent of a mugging. I feel brutalized by their blitzing guitars and wrenching vocals. I wonder whether my inability to recognize talent within this cacophony is proof that I'm ageing, losing touch, that my tastes are becoming obsolete, just like the 28-inch-waist Levi's in my wardrobe, and my Young Person's Railcard. Still, after what Davey told me I feel my views have almost been vindicated.

The band smash up their instruments, looking totally bored, driving them into the concrete floor and then flailing the ruined pieces around their heads. When the director calls for the cut, the broken bits of fret board and drum kit are thrown on top of a pile of other broken instruments and new ones are set up for the next take.

These guys are so bogus even their 'spontaneous' instrument-trashing is faked.

DOWN TO BUSINESS

Trish Parkes – their gorgeous, super-important manager – spots that I've arrived and heads over to Wilson. I join them and we're both shepherded outside to a luxury tour bus. The band follow slowly behind us. Inside, there are beds and a luxury bathroom, and the back has a small arcade stocked with vintage games cabinets and pinball machines. In fact, their bus looks like a much nicer place to live than my flat does. It's certainly warmer.

They slouch around a table in an office space halfway down the bus, ignoring the polite small talk passing between Wilson and Trish, and all of them eyeballing me sourly. They are dressed in an unkempt slacker style: T-shirts with skateboard logos, bandannas or reversed caps, chunky trainers, cargo pants with wallet chains, lots of tattoos and piercings. You can't help but feel aggrieved at their good fortune; their three-album deal pays each of them more than I'll earn in five years. Still, it's difficult to take them and their inane act seriously, knowing what Davey told me in the restaurant.

Wilson gives me an evil glare.

'Thanks for coming over,' says Trish. 'You know the boys, don't you?' Her current charges study Wilson and me with languid contempt.

'Joke,' Scooter says. 'What's the difference between a lawyer and a vampire?'

Wilson smiles uncertainly. Trish glowers.

'Vampires only suck blood at night.'

'Lame-o,' groans Bam Bam.

Wilson manufactures a laugh. She's adopted her client face. It is, I have to admit, very charming. But

191

then the citizens of Pompeii probably thought Vesuvius was a picturesque sight before it went nuclear on them.

'I wanted to talk through the details of the Japanese contracts we need,' Trish continues. 'I think there're two outstanding?'

'Yes,' Wilson says. 'The recording contract and the marketing agreement. We haven't finished them yet. It shouldn't take much longer.' Wilson gives me another eloquently evil glare.

I find myself nodding even though I still have no real idea why we're here save for talking about some kind of new contract they've landed. We could have done this over the telephone. Scooter leans all the way back in the chair and laces his fingers together behind his head. Slowly, deliberately, he puts both feet on the chair opposite him, reaches into his trousers and scrubs at his balls. Trish looks over at him in exasperation. He sneers back at her and slurpily starts to chew on a wad of gum.

'I was hoping they'd be ready by now,' she says. 'But maybe it doesn't matter – the circumstances've changed a little. You can amend your drafts.'

'Why not just run through what you need?' Wilson says. And then, to me, she adds brusquely, 'Take a full note.'

Trish goes through the list of things she now wants included in the contracts. It's all vanilla stuff: the kind of things I would've put in as a matter of course. This whole session is pointless.

'Bor-ing,' Mooch yawns.

'Yeah,' agrees Scooter. 'Do we have to be here?'

I feel like concurring with them.

'Yes, you do,' snaps Trish. 'This's important.'

'We'd rather just leave this to the *lawyers*,' Bam Bam says, stacking his scorn on the final word.

'I know what *you'd* rather do,' says Trish, 'but *you're* not managing the band. I am.'

'But we're supposed to be a *punk* band,' whines Mooch. 'We're *supposed* to be doing crazy stuff, not sitting in the trailer listening to this kind of bullshit. We're supposed to be swearing on teatime TV shows, and shit.'

Scooter apes the infamous Bill Grundy interview with the Sex Pistols: ' "Well keep going, chief, keep going. Go on, you've got another five seconds. Say something outrageous." '

Mooch, playing the Steve Jones part: ' "You dirty fucker." '

'The filth and the fury,' Bam Bam concludes. 'That's where it's at.'

Trish angles a fearsome glare in his direction. 'That's *enough*,' she barks. They pipe down like chided schoolboys. I'm left feeling mildly depressed at the state of the British music industry; they really don't make them like they used to.

'Now,' Trish moves on, addressing Wilson again. 'You promised you'd be able to give me a little preliminary advice, and that'd be helpful. I told the board I'd report to them before we leave.'

Wilson shifts uncomfortably. 'Would you mind if I delayed that until tomorrow? I don't want to advise you until I'm absolutely sure of the facts.'

'The facts are pretty simple, Victoria,' Trish says disdainfully. 'And, anyway, we won't be in the country tomorrow.'

'I'm sorry,' Wilson apologizes awkwardly. 'I forgot about that. And I know the facts're simple, but, if it's all the same, I think I'd still rather wait. I want to make sure whatever I tell you's absolutely correct. I could give you a call?'

Trish fidgets with annoyance. 'I have to say,' she says, 'that this isn't at all what I've come to expect of White Hunter.'

A DRESSING DOWN

Wilson and I are in the back of a taxi, heading back to the office.

'You were late,' snaps Wilson. Her voice is quivering with fury. '*Fifty* minutes late!'

'Forty actually,' I correct, then wish I hadn't when she aims an ultra-high-beam death stare at me. 'I was lunching with a client. Brian Fey's manager—'

'You *knew* we had an appointment. You should've rearranged. You made me look *amateurish*.'

'Plus I didn't know the meeting was supposed to be here. I thought it was at the office. I had to get a cab. It was late. The traffic was heavy, it took us ages, and—'

'What do you mean you didn't know?' she seethes. 'I asked Olly Dawkins to tell you the venue had changed.'

A cold knot forms in my gut.

'You told *him*?'

'Your secretary was at lunch and I bumped into Oliver when I tried to find you myself. He was in your office, so I asked him to pass on the message.'

Would the Dork deliberately withhold information to make sure I was late, to make me look bad? Of course he would. But what's the point of telling Wilson that? She loves Dawkins – bad-mouthing him will only upset her more.

And what was he doing in my office?

'I'm sorry. You're right. It won't happen again.'

'But that's the least of it,' she continues. 'Where was the briefing note? I told you it was essential.'

'It disappeared.'

'What?'

'It disappeared. It was on my desk – then it wasn't.'

She shakes her head disdainfully. 'You're in enough trouble already. Don't make it worse by insulting my intelligence. We're not talking about late homework here. This could be a disciplinary matter.'

'My secretary put it on my desk. It wasn't there when I arrived back from my lunch. And someone deleted it from the file server.'

'Quite apart from being unlikely, that's also completely irrelevant. If you'd done the work when I asked you to, none of this would've happened.'

I sigh; time to cut my losses. 'You're absolutely right. I'm sorry.'

'No. Sorry's not good enough – not this time. Call my secretary and arrange a meeting so we can discuss what's happened here. I'm thinking very seriously about giving you a formal warning.'

A formal warning. That would be getting off lightly.

'And in the meantime I want that marketing agreement and the recording contract drawn up and on my desk *tomorrow morning*. I won't hear any more excuses this time, Tate. This's your last chance. Don't – *do not* – mess it up.'

'I won't.'

She stares ahead for thirty seconds, boring a hole into the cabby's neck.

'And there's another thing,' she says. 'It's a little delicate.'

'Delicate?'

'I understand you've been drinking in the office.'

Silence.

'Is that true?'

I don't know what to say. So I say nothing.

'Put a stop to it. If you've got a problem with stress or something, go and see a doctor. The firm won't tolerate drinking in the office. Is that understood?'

I nod dumbly.

EXTRACT FROM THE MUSIC PRESS

Following the MASSIVE success of **THE BLACK DAHLIAS'** new album – **The Human Condition** – the band have announced plans for a 100-date, greatest hits world tour. They plan to take in cities on four continents in a five-month trip they say will be their most ambitious to date. And in a HUGE surprise, band-members **MARTIN** and **DAMON** unveiled their replacement for the late, great **JOHN FRENCH**: American heart-throb **SEAN DARBO**.

'I've always been a huge fan of the **DAHLIAS**,' **Darbo** said. 'When **Marty** asked me if I'd like to stand in on the tour, it took like half a second to say yes.'

Martin said, 'When we were thinking about a singer **Sean's** name just leapt out at us. He's not here to replace **John** – no one could ever do that – but we think he'll give our old stuff a fresh new sound.'

'We're really looking forward to getting into rehearsals with him,' concurred **Damon**.

TAKING STOCK

I fix myself a strong black coffee to try and clear my head.

Trouble on every side. Davey hates me. Wilson hates me. Wilson thinks I've got a drinking problem. I've got a mountain of work to do, and only so much time to do it in. Deadlines are piling up. I haven't begun to draft Haines's witness statement for Renwick. I'm not even sure I can find the stomach to get around to that.

EMAIL

There's an email waiting for me. It's been sent to Cohen too; he's scrolling down it and chuckling to himself. I zoom the cursor over to it and double-click:

From:	Hunter, Charles
To:	Dawkins, Oliver; Cohen, David; Tate, Daniel; Lewis, Caroline
Cc:	Partners (London Office)
Subject:	Partnership

As you know, the death of Miles Mackay has led to an opening in the partnership. All four of you have been nominated for the partnership. Unfortunately there is only room for one person to be made up this year and so, in the interests of fairness and to ensure that the right candidate is selected, we would

like to invite you each to give a short presentation to the partnership council setting out your respective cases. My secretary will email you individually with an appointment in due course.
Charles Hunter

'This's it,' Cohen says, reaching for his paper knife. 'Now I have to kill you.'

'Save yourself for the Dork.'

'I'd probably enjoy that more,' he admits.

'Is that knife blunt?' I ask.

'Very.'

'Excellent.'

LAST CHANCE SALOON

I scoop an armful of papers off my desk to clear a space. Elizabeth makes a photocopy of Dawkins' precedent marketing agreement. I hunker down to my task.

To my surprise, perhaps buffeted by a following wind of panic, I make decent progress. This is good; the success even makes me enthused. I scribble my amendments on the photocopied sheets and Elizabeth collects them, one page at a time, and types them up. By the time 5.30 comes around, I'm halfway through my first draft and, fortified by multiple caffeine fixes, I'm even relishing the task at hand.

'Shall I stay late?' Elizabeth asks.

'I'll be fine,' I say. 'I should be able to finish the amendments this evening and then you can type them up tomorrow morning.'

'Don't work too hard.'

'I'll see you tomorrow.'

A VISIT FROM THE COMPETITION

Dawkins comes over.

'How's it going?'

There's no point in bothering with pleasantries.

'Why didn't you pass on the message from Wilson this afternoon?'

'What message?' says the Dork innocently.

'About the change to my meeting?'

'Oh God,' he says, slapping his forehead with the palm of his hand. 'It must've slipped my mind. I'm *so* sorry.'

'You devious little fuckwit.'

'Don't be like that, Tate,' he says. 'These things happen. I've been busy. I forgot.'

'Look, what do you want? I'm busy.'

'Is my precedent helping?'

'Not really,' I lie. I'm not about to tell him I'd be lost without it.

'When d'you have to have it finished?'

'Tomorrow,' I reply tersely.

'Well, glad to've been of service,' he says. 'But I've

got to dash. I've got dinner with Anthea Turner tonight. Don't want to be late.'

RACHEL

Rachel calls at six.

'Any ideas for tonight?' she asks.

'I thought I'd surprise you,' I fib. I'd forgotten about dinner.

'What time do you want to go?' she asks.

'I've got some things to finish off. How's eight sound?'

'I suppose I could find something to keep me busy until then.'

'Are you sure?'

'Yeah. It's no problem. Call me when you're ready to go.'

ANOTHER FORGOTTEN APPOINTMENT

The office slowly empties and by 7.30 mine is the only room still lit. I've managed to carve out a solid two hours of quality work. The agreement is almost ready. It's even looking good.

I'm beginning to remember why it was that I used to love law so much.

I'm doodling on a scrap of paper, mustering up the energy for a final blitz, when the telephone rings.

'Where are you?' It's Brian. Laughter and the sound of partying in the background. I hear a guitar being strummed.

I'd forgotten: tonight is Brian's concert and I promised him I'd go.

'I'm in the office,' I say. 'I was just finishing up and then I was gonna come over.'

'Fine,' Brian says. 'I'm on stage in an hour. I've left a ticket on the door for you.'

I've nearly finished the first draft and, now I come to think of it, I'm feeling tired. My best work today is behind me; staying longer won't accomplish anything. I should call it a night, go to the concert and arrange to meet Rachel as soon as Brian's finished his set. Then get in early tomorrow morning to finish off.

I call Rachel and explain.

'Could we do a late dinner instead?'

'Sure.'

We arrange to meet at a little Italian I know down in Spitalfields – the kind of intimate place she won't be able to help falling in love with – at 10.

PRE-GIG NERVES

A modest crowd is loitering outside the doors to the venue. I feel a minor flush of importance when security confirms my name is on the guest list and ushers me inside.

Brian is picking at the strings of an acoustic guitar in his dressing room. I recognize the melody from one of the Dahlias' early hits.

'What's the crowd like?' he asks.

'Not too bad,' I reply. 'Quite a few.'

'Tonight's *so* important,' he says. The veins on his neck are standing out like cords. I recognize the symptoms: he's all coked up. 'Oh, man, I'm actually feeling nervous.'

'You'll be fine,' I say.

'Look, my hands are shaking – can you believe that? For a little concert like this?'

'You'll be fine.'

'I'll be fine,' he says, as if repeating this will make it true.

There's a small pile of coke on a silver platter and Brian takes a long sniff through a straw from an empty milkshake carton. He offers the platter to me. I feel I ought to decline. But I *am* tired and perhaps a little pick-me-up might be just what the doctor ordered. It couldn't hurt, could it? Just a quick toot. I accept the straw and join him over the platter.

Soon I'm feeling immeasurably better.

Brian plucks out something I don't recognize – one of his new tunes. Gradually the session musicians arrive. No one talks – none of them knows each other – and everyone is fixated with their own image, their own neurosis. They look like eighties throwbacks, identikit rockers: Iggy or Ozzy or Alice or Slash. Brian does some scales and reminds me of the Dahlias. I wonder if *they'll* be in the audience tonight? Probably not.

Davey walks in.

'Ready to go?' Davey asks. He doesn't acknowledge me.

'Born ready.'

'Good-sized crowd outside,' Davey reports.

Brian is winding himself up.

'I'll prove them wrong. I'll show them who was the driving force in that fucking band.'

'*You* were, Brian. It was all you. We know that, right? Yeah?'

'Yeah,' I say awkwardly, realizing that I'm being tapped up for moral support. 'You're going to be, um, completely amazing.'

'I'm ... going ... to ... be ... amazing,' shouts Brian, slapping the heel of his hand against his head with each syllable.

Just as Brian shrieks out that he can't find his leather jacket, Oliver Dawkins creeps uncertainly into the room. He looks nervous and out of place. I've no idea who could have invited him here but then, as Davey disengages from our group and goes to greet him, the picture becomes clearer. I find myself digging nails into the fleshy heel of my hand and clenching my teeth. The Dork sees me and the uncertainty washes from his face. It's replaced by a sly, knowing smile.

MUSIC FOR THE MASSES?

I watch the concert from the wings. The grey mass of the crowd bulges upwards in a darkness underscored by the blinding glare of the spotlights aimed down from the roof. I'm troubled by a vague feeling of unease as Brian performs his new songs, none of them really any good, the feeling gradually taking on shape and form until I realize the source: *he looks out of place without the rest of the Dahlias behind him.* I wonder if this solo career was really such a good idea after all. Maybe he might have been better advised to just retreat and lick his wounds. I can't help the feeling that he's taken things further than they were naturally meant to go. Like a prize-fighter fighting on after his punch has gone.

'There're a lot of people outside,' Brian squawks out. (There aren't any – I checked.) 'I think you should tell them what we're doing in here.'

The crowd lets out a slightly self-conscious holler, quickly choked back. They're too old for this, and they know it. I wince.

He cuts into a collection of covers: a hard-rocking 'Sweet Dreams' by the Eurythmics, 'Master and Servant' by the Mode, a strictly-by-the-numbers version of Hendrix's 'Purple Haze'. The crowd tightens in recognition. The dancing spreads a few rows further back. Half of the crowd are dancing, the other half standing arms-crossed, foot-tapping, head-nodding. There's an under-current of agitated expectation.

Brian prowls across the front of the stage, goes offstage to do more coke, kicks the microphone stand, thrusts his hips, launches himself in a mad stage dive as his final encore fades out. An upsprouting of hands emerges to support him. He sinks down into the sweaty quicksand of the crowd.

As the house lights are brought up, a puzzled murmur passes through the hall. A few shout for more. Surely there's a final, final encore? There are so many songs he hasn't played. When they realize that this really is the end, the atmosphere takes on a harder, restive edge.

I figure it out: they were expecting Brian to reprise some of the Dahlias' material. This is confirmed when the title of the band's most famous hit rises up in a ragged chant. There is a volley of boos as the PA announces the show is over. Brighter lights snap on and the doors open.

Brian is retrieved from the crowd by a wedge of yellow-shirted security. The crowd parts politely for them, almost apologetically. It's hard not to contrast this with the scenes of bedlam from the Dahlias' infamous tours of earlier years, when Brian pulled fans to safety as the surge threatened to crush them against the railings, and security drenched the moshpit with fire hoses. A notorious film recorded a stage dive he took in Rio; the crowd ripped his clothes away and left him near-naked by the time he was dragged out.

The fervour from those who were once dedicated enough to risk injury in the moshpit has been eroded, replaced with a more mature, sensible appreciation. Three words spring to mind: impending middle age. Brian's audience is growing older but I doubt he's mature enough to have noticed, let alone adapt to it.

Would he even want to? He still wants to be the subversive kid, but the benchmarks have shifted without him noticing. What was subversive in the eighties is conventional today. No one bats an eyelid now at a boy dressed in leather and rubber. Addictions are common-place, even required. Mainlining is mainstream. Perhaps he remained insulated within the band. Maybe together they could have ridden their reputation through this transition. Other bands have managed it. But on his own Brian looks vulnerable and confused.

He looks almost sheepish as he is led backstage.

HONESTY IS NOT THE BEST POLICY

'How'd it go?' he asks me. 'Honestly?'

He seems so earnest, so delicate, the truth seems unnecessarily cruel. 'Fabulous,' I say. 'Like nothing's changed at all.'

'Feels so good to be on stage again. Best fix there is.'

He tokes on an enormous jumbo spliff, slumps against the wall and exhales a long jet. He's taken off his sopping shirt. You can count his ribs against the drum-skin flesh of his chest.

'Like I said, I thought it was great, *you* were great.'

He hands the spliff to me. I suck in a lungful and let it out through my nose.

'I would've liked to sing some of the old songs,' he says. 'I wasn't being precious or anything, but you know how I couldn't.'

I *do* know. The Dahlias had got an injunction preventing him from playing the old songs – tonight that seems gratuitously spiteful. I reassure him again that the concert was a success but I can almost hear the reviewers sharpening their pencils.

Brian heads off for the toilets, and the Dork sidles over. He's been talking to the record company staff, shuttling between them with his little jokes and anecdotes . . . Badmouthing me, promoting himself – don't think I don't know.

'Quite a concert,' he says.

'What're you doing here?' I ask.

'Davey invited me. I met him at the party on Sunday. We had lunch on Monday.'

'We had lunch *today*.'

'I know,' he says.

'How?'

'I suggested it to him. He said he wasn't altogether happy with the way things're going, so I said he ought to take you out and talk to you about it. It's better than doing it over the phone, isn't it?'

I can't believe this. 'Why don't you just piss off.'

'As it happens I *do* have to go back to the office.

There're some things I need to do. Anthea's got me running about all over the place.'

It's late. I can't even begin to imagine what could be so pressing that he has to go back to the office to do it now. He gives me a mocking little wave as he leaves, his coat slung over one arm.

IS THERE A LAWYER IN THE HOUSE?

It's only as I'm leaning against the damp black-painted walls, busying myself with a bottle of beer from the rider, that I remember Rachel. I curse and check my watch: 10.30.

I remember the last call I made on my mobile was to the restaurant to book the table. I just need to press redial and ask to speak to Rachel, apologize and explain what's happening. She seems professional enough, she'll understand: sometimes the client has to come first.

I take out my mobile. The batteries are dead.

If I got a cab now I could still be in Spitalfields, in time if the traffic isn't too bad. I'm searching for my overcoat, ready to leave, when Davey bustles over.

'Where's Oliver?'

'Oliver?'

'Dawkins, from your office. Have you seen him?'

'He's probably gone home. This isn't really his scene. He's a bit of a wallflower, between you and me.

In fact, I don't think he enjoyed the concert all that much.'

'Then you'll have to do. Come on.'

His tone is urgent. Something's happened. It must be Brian. I get a picture of him slumped in a cubicle with his back against the cistern, sliced wrists throbbing with blood or a fatal syringe quivering in his arm. He did look depressed when he wandered away, but I thought he was just coming down from the coke and was on his way to reload.

I start to jog, overtaking Davey.

PROCESS SERVING

It's not what I was expecting. The men's room is a squalid affair, unfinished either through artistic design or basic slovenliness. Blocking the path from the urinals to the door is a man dressed in a charcoal-grey three-piece and pricey shoes that don't belong on the urine-soaked concrete. He's facing the nest of cubicles, one of which is closed.

'I can wait out here all night if I have to,' he says. 'Why don't you deal with this *sensibly*. It'd be better if you just came out.'

He's holding a large white envelope in one hand and a mobile in the other.

'I'm not doing anything without my lawyer.'

'Your lawyer's not here.'

'He's coming. My manager's gone to get him.'

'This really is very silly, Mr Fey. Why don't you just come out?'

'You just wanna give me more papers – and I don't want them.'

'It'd be easier—'

'Just leave me alone.'

Davey turns to me and shrugs in a deal-with-it gesture. Given his current dissatisfaction with the performance of my duties, and his obvious preference that the Dork should deal with the problem, this might be a chance to impress him with my legal ability.

I clear my throat and step further into the room.

'What's going on?'

'None of your business,' the man says curtly.

'If that's Mr Fey in there, I'm his solicitor. I'd say that makes it my business, wouldn't you?'

He swings around. Now I have his attention.

'Are you authorized to accept service on his behalf?'

'Am I authorized to accept service?' I call out to Brian.

'Um, would that be a good or bad thing?' Brian asks.

'It'd be convenient.'

I'd also prefer it if the band's lawyers were not given the opportunity to gather evidence of Brian's coke habit. Because I know that's what he's doing in there; he's hardly using the facilities for their intended purpose, is he?

Brian: 'I guess so, then. I mean, if you think it's OK.'

'Well?' says the man.

'Serve away.'

He hands me the envelope. 'I'm serving you with details of a Sale Order brought against your client's properties. As of now, my client is now authorized to enter your client's premises for the purposes of offering them for immediate sale.' He fiddles with his mobile and waits as a call connects. 'I'm going to instruct the locksmiths to change the locks now. Good evening.'

And he leaves.

'What'd all that mean?' Davey hisses in a voice only I can hear. 'The stuff about his properties?'

'It's complicated.'

'But not good?'

'Not good.'

'Go on . . .'

'The band've persuaded the court they should be entitled to sell Brian's flats. So they don't technically belong to him any more.'

'Has he gone?' Brian calls. The top of his head pokes above the top of the cubicle.

'He's gone,' Davey says. 'It's safe.'

Davey looks at me sternly and puts a finger to his lips. 'Not a word,' he says. No doubt he wants to break the news to Brian himself. The toilet flushes – redundantly – and Brian reappears. His nostrils are an irritated red.

'I feel so stupid,' he says helplessly. 'I didn't know what else to do.'

THE KING OF SCHMOOZE

Later, sitting with Brian on a plum-coloured sofa at the after-show party. I'm seething: Dawkins has come back. He's sliming all over Davey. Whatever he needed to do in the office for Anthea Turner didn't take long. Now he's all friendly gestures and big toothy smiles. Every now and again he book-ends Davey's comments with peals of phoney laughter.

'You see that guy?' Brian says. He points at the Dork with the neck of his bottle.

I nod.

'He came over to me earlier – when you were in the gents – and asked if I was happy with the work you were doing for me. Said he works in the same office as you. He says he might be put on the case soon.'

'He said that?'

'Something like that. Is he helping you out or something?'

'What'd *you* say?'

'That I was well happy and that I didn't think we needed anyone else.'

I could kiss him.

'Thanks,' I say.

'I don't think he likes you very much.'

'Be fair to say the feeling's mutual.'

ANSWERPHONE

Much later:

I get home. A message on the answerphone. The blinking red light fills me with a mixture of joy and nervous anticipation. I've been like this ever since Hannah left.

I hit PLAY:

'Daniel, I'm really sorry to bother you at home like this but I'd like to talk to you again about our conversations.' It's the reporter, Dolan. 'Something's come up that I think might interest you. You remember what I was telling you about the other day? Could you give me a call? I'll give you my mobile number and I want you to call me anytime, night or day, OK? It could be *really* big. Sorry to be so vague, but I don't really want to just leave this as an answerphone message. And remember: discretion *absolutely* guaranteed. The number you need is—'

I stab erase before he gets any of the digits out.

ANY PORT IN A STORM

Can't sleep. My head won't switch off: I can't stop thinking about Hannah, about Rachel, about Brian, about work.

I thought there was some Valium in the bathroom cabinet but all I could find was a bottle of Hannah's herbal relaxants. I took six of them two hours ago. They've had no effect, except to make me feel nauseous.

I'm still trying to sleep when the intercom buzzes. The glowing red digits on the clock radio show 3.30. I was hoping to catch at least five hours' sleep so I could report to the office at eight, ready to do battle with the work I need to finish. I'm going to be busy tomorrow.

The intercom buzzes again. I don't get out of bed. It buzzes more insistently. I fumble for the lamp, knock over the pint of water I left unfinished on the bedside table, curse, and shuffle into the hall.

'Who is it?' I ask into the intercom.

'It's me.'

'*Brian?*'

His voice sounds dulled and weary.

I slump forward, forehead pressed against the wall.

'It's 3.30, Brian.'

'Yeah, I know,' he says. 'Sorry about that.'

This must be a bad dream. Ignoring it might make it go away.

'Can I come in?' Brian asks. 'It's kind of snowing out here.'

I look out of the small window in the hallway; a heavy fall is wafting through the orange streetlight. I buzz the lock and let him up.

He looks terrible. He's still wearing the same clothes from the concert. They smell of dry ice, reefer and sweat. He doesn't have a coat and is shivering uncontrollably. I give him a spare blanket to wrap around his shoulders and put the kettle on.

'You want some toast?'

'That'd be nice. Got a bad case of the munchies.'

I clear away enough debris from the sofa and chairs to uncover two places to sit. Brian slouches down on the sofa. I make a pot of black coffee and pour him a mug. He looks like he could use it.

'Sorry about the mess,' I say.

'It's freezing in here.'

'My boiler broke down,' I lie. I'm not going to admit to Brian that I've been disconnected for not paying my bill. I still have *some* pride.

'I really appreciate this. Didn't know where else to go.'

'Where'd you get my address?'

'I called your office and said it was an emergency. The night porter gave it to me.'

The surrealism isn't lost on me. Here I am: dressing-gown over my boxer shorts, and Hannah's fluffy cartoon slippers on my feet. Slumped out on my sofa is the ex-lead singer of one of the most famous bands of the eighties. I used to dance to his songs at the sixth-form disco. The girls were crazy about him.

'Well, it's not a problem,' I say, handing him a plate of toast and dropping into an armchair.

He warms his hands around the coffee mug.

'What's happened?' I ask.

Brian had returned to his flat after the concert to

find the locks were changed. He glimpsed removal men locking up their transit van and driving off with his few bits of remaining furniture. The band is moving fast. They've probably already had the sales particulars and advertising boards prepared, ready to offer the property to the market first thing in the morning. They might even have a buyer lined up.

'I looked in through the letterbox,' he says. 'I could see a couple of people inside but they wouldn't answer the door. I made a bit of a fuss. In the end someone called the police and they told me I had to go away. I tried to check into a hotel but all my cards've been cancelled. I couldn't get cash out of the machines either. So I got the night bus over here.'

'Where's Davey?'

'He left just after you did. I don't know where he lives. I mean, I hardly even *know* the guy.' Brian leans back on the sofa and scrubs at his forehead. 'Oh man, what am I supposed to *do*?'

'Look, it's too late to worry about that now,' I say. 'We'll think about it in the morning.'

'I haven't got anywhere to go,' he says.

'You can crash here.'

'Really?'

'Sure. No problem. I've got a spare room you can use.'

The room was once intended to be my study but I never got around to sorting it out, so I use it for storage

now. There's a folding bed somewhere amidst the junk
– I think.

'Never thought I'd get into such a *mess*,' he says as
I refill his mug. He looks pale and drawn, his eye-
shadow running like tears. I realize how thin he really
is: his wrists, his ankles, even his neck, they're all as
slender as sticks. And, for the first time, he looks *old*.

'It'll sort itself out,' I say. 'And things always look
better in the morning.'

SCOTT DOLAN'S
GUEST LIST

World's Greatest Showbiz Column

THE MADNESS OF BRIAN FEY?
Black Dahlia says he's worried

BLACK DAHLIA **Martin Valentine** has expressed fears that ex-bandmate **Brian Fey** is suffering from mental illness.

'We were worried even before we decided to split,' he told MTV. 'And I've heard his behaviour's been really erratic lately.'

Martin also suggested that Brian's well-reported drug hell might not yet be behind him. 'He was still doing a lot of drugs the last time I saw him,' Martin said. 'I just hope he's got it all under control.'

Fey yesterday assaulted a journo at the offices of music rag the *NME*. Fey's ex-colleague in the Dahlias, **John French**, was found dead on Sunday.

Celebs I've spotted this week: KATE MOSS outside Soho House after a night on the tiles.

1990s baggy-rockers EMF and JESUS JONES rumoured to be planning comebacks and a joint tour.

Thursday

THE STAR IN THE SPARE ROOM

I check my reflection in the bathroom mirror. The welt on one side of my face has settled into a livid bruise, but the signs of healing are evident. I got only about three hours' sleep. My eyes are ringed with fatigue and red- and brown-coloured bags bulge out beneath them. I've occasionally felt better.

I listlessly run the iron over a shirt, find a pair of cuff-links and pull on the spare suit I picked up from dry cleaning a couple of days ago. It's only as I'm eating a bowl of cereal and watching chatty breakfast TV that I remember my visit from Brian last night.

The door to the spare room is still closed. I mute the television and press my ear against it, but I can't hear anything. I didn't hear him leave, but my eventual sleep at last was probably deep enough not to have noticed. Rather than opening the spare-room door to check, I find a pen and paper from the mess on the floor and leave him a note.

Dear Brian, I begin, feeling absurd to be penning something so mundane to someone like him. *Help yourself to anything in the kitchen. Apologies for the mess. I'll call Davey as soon as I get to the office, to tell him what's happening. Daniel.*

But I'm not ready for work yet. I need something to kick-start the day. I find a bottle of cherry schnapps I bought during a holiday to Bavaria, years ago. It'll have to do. I take it into the lounge and pour myself a glass.

Nelson jumps up onto the sofa next to me and settles down on my lap.

A CRITICAL REVIEW

I buy a paper outside the tube station and unfold it as my train rattles through bleak drizzle into the city. The snow outside is slushy and grey. I scan the pages for news. There's a review of Brian's concert last night.

Brian Fey

London, LA2

Let's be honest about this: **Brian** ain't much of a name for a rock god. In the grand scheme of things, it doesn't sound *right*. Axl, yes. Ozzy, hell yes. My God – even *Bruce* is better than Brian . . . But if only that was the only thing that didn't sound right about the first solo concert of ex-**Dahlias'** frontman **Brian Fey**. Whilst we're being honest, try this – **Brian Fey** sucks. His solo album, *Songs from a Twisted Youth* (aka The Album Nobody Owns), is full of maudlin rock balladry and petulant stabs in the direction of his ex-bandmates, and while his God-awful compositions can be tarted up in the studio by a decent producer, when he actually knocks them out live the fact that he can't write/sing/play for toffee is painfully obvious. By the end of the evening even the die-hard **Dahlias**, who were distraught at the jettisoning of their idol, would have to admit the band knew what they were doing. **Brian Fey** – in his pomp one of the best rawk voices of the 80s – has lost it. The moshpit didn't mosh. They were too stupefied with boredom to care. Brian Fey's like a loveable but somewhat mangy family pooch that's just had a stroke – someone, please, put him out of his misery. 0/10

Ouch.

I wonder whether this reviewer has private health insurance?

THE POLICE MAKE A BREAKTHROUGH

At my stop, I struggle out of the tube and continue reading on the escalator as it carries me towards the surface. The lead story on the front page updates the investigation into John French's death. The police are conducting a detailed investigation into his final weeks in the hope of finding clues. They've examined his telephone statements and recent mail. They've interviewed the other members of the band, and his neighbours in the usually peaceful Mayfair street where he lived. They believe French was being stalked immediately before his death. Neighbours have reported a car parked outside his house for hours, its chain-smoking occupant leaving a pile of dog-ends on the snowy pavement before he left. The police have invited this person to come forward, believing he could assist them with their inquiries.

They also announce their suspicion that the cassette from French's answerphone was deliberately removed from the machine. A fingertip search was conducted and the tape has not been found anywhere in the house.

And also they report that a large sum of cash has gone missing. On the afternoon of last Saturday, French withdrew £10,000 in cash from his bank. There is no sign of this money anywhere in his house.

Scott Dolan's name appears in the by-line. So, he's graduating from the gossip columns. Clearly, Brian is his ticket to the big time.

The fresh fall of snow last night has transformed the walk to the office into a stroll through a Christmas-card idyll, but I'm not in the mood to appreciate it. Sounds are muffled as the cars crawling carefully along scrunch on compacted snow and ice.

I buy a bottle of Scotch from Tesco's and hide it in my bag.

And I haven't even started worrying yet about the work I've got to do.

VOICEMAIL

There's a voicemail waiting for me when I reach my office. I let it play. It's Renwick:

'Where were you last night? We were supposed to be having dinner with Chas and Dave – celebrating that Press Complaints Commission thing. I didn't know where you were, so I had to tell them you'd come down with food poisoning. Dave seemed to buy it but I'm not sure about Chas, he's pretty smart. And you don't just snub these people, Daniel. You don't just snub *stars*. You'd better have a good excuse, that's all I'm saying.'

THINGS GO FROM BAD . . .

Elizabeth is already in, sitting at her desk and reading one of those free magazines handed out at the station.

Her screen-saver is busy sending random shapes hurtling around the monitor.

I guess she decided to make an early start on the agreement I had drafted. From her relaxed bearing it looks as if she's already finished it. I'll proof-read my amendments, tweak any loose sections until they're taut and unambiguous, and have it ready for Wilson by nine.

'Morning,' I say.

'Morning,' she says. 'I thought I'd come in a little earlier and get started on the amendments to that document you were working on.'

'That's great,' I say. Must remember to buy her a bunch of flowers or something.

'Thing is, I couldn't find it anywhere. What'd you do with it?'

'It's on my desk. I left it there when I finished last night.'

'Are you sure? I couldn't find anything.'

I'm not panicking – not yet. There's a rational explanation for this. Lightning can't possibly strike twice. Perhaps I put the agreement into my drawer for safekeeping. It was late when I left, and I was flustered by Brian's call. It's not surprising a detail like that slipped my mind. Or maybe Wilson has already been in to see me and took the amended draft away with her. Unlikely but feasible. Dozens of potential explanations. No need to panic. Not yet.

Deep breath.

I check my desk. Nothing. I open out each drawer

and scoop out all the everyday debris that I've allowed to accumulate. Nothing. Perhaps it's fallen onto the floor. I get down onto my knees and root about. I can't see it anywhere.

'Are you sure you haven't moved it?'

'No,' Elizabeth says. 'I haven't even seen it.'

'Well, someone moved it,' I say. 'It's not where I left it.'

'Where did you leave it?' She's starting to look upset.

I point at my desktop.

'Should I call housekeeping? Maybe the cleaners took it by mistake. We still might be able to find it.'

'Worth a try.'

'I could print it off again?'

'It'd take hours to go through it and put the amendments back in again. Unless we can find the original, there's no point. We might as well just give up.'

. . . TO WORSE

I slump into my chair, my forehead pressed down into my palms. I can feel hot blood pumping against the backs of my eyeballs. I'm reaching for the Scotch when Elizabeth comes back inside.

'There was one other thing,' Elizabeth says in a low, hesitant voice. 'Miss Wilson's secretary called just before you came in. She's set up a meeting with you and Miss Wilson for this afternoon. She said you'd know what it was about.'

Great, now I'm going to get sacked. Maybe if I'd been able to present the agreement in decent shape I might've earned a second chance. Can't even do that now. I'm going to look like a lazy, negligent idiot.

Elizabeth calls housekeeping. Bad news. If the agreement was collected by mistake, it's too late to get it back now. Last night's rubbish has just been pulped.

'Is there anything I can do?' Elizabeth asks.

'No, don't worry.'

'Don't forget you've got lunch with Gaby Roslin,' she reminds me.

DOMESTICITY

With nothing better to do while I wait for my meeting with Wilson, I call the flat to check my messages. After two rings, and before the answerphone can pick up, someone answers. I can hear a loud, whining drone in the background.

'Hello?' Brian half-shouts.

'It's me – Daniel.'

'What?'

'*Daniel*.'

'Hold on.'

The droning sound falls away.

'Sorry, had the hoover on. Who is it?'

'It's me.' I don't even start to consider what use Brian could possibly have had for my hoover.

'Daniel?'

'Yes. I thought you'd gone?'

'Sorry, slept late. Hope you don't mind. Or me answering your calls like this.'

Brian taking my messages is either amusing or terrifying, I can't quite figure out which.

'No problem at all. Make yourself at home.'

'Where're you?'

'At the office.'

'I'm glad you called: you've had a few calls. Some guy called Dolan rang, said he was a reporter.'

'Don't talk to him,' I say wearily. 'He's trying to get quotes off me about you. Don't say anything if he calls again. Definitely don't tell him who you are.'

'OK.'

'Anyone else?'

'Yeah, some girl. Didn't want to leave a message.'

My heart falters. 'Did she leave her name?'

'Nope. I asked if she wanted me to pass anything on. She said it didn't matter.'

'Were those her exact words?'

'Um, no, I think she said something like, "It doesn't matter, it's OK, I'll call later," or something. Why, are you expecting a call?'

Hannah! Who else could it be? But I can't think of a sensible reason why she'd call me.

'No,' I say, 'not really expecting anyone.'

There's a pause. 'There's something else,' Brian eventually continues, a little self-conscious. 'I don't mean to be demanding but do you think you'd be able to come with me to John's funeral today? I wouldn't ask, but the others'll be there and I could do with some moral support.'

'Of course I will,' I say. A plan hatches: perhaps Brian could put in a good word for me with Wilson. If he said how impressed he's been with me, maybe that'd count for *something* . . . Maybe it'd get me a reprieve. It's worth a shot.

Brian gives me the details of the crematorium, and I tell him I'll see him there.

I call Wilson's secretary and ask her to rearrange the meeting. She'll be furious with my presumptuousness, but I can't see what difference it would make if she's already resolved to get rid of me.

EMAIL

I check my mail.

From Hunter's secretary:

From:	Templeman, Jean
To:	Tate, Daniel
Subject:	Presentation to partnership council

Further to Mr Hunter's email yesterday, I have

scheduled your presentation to the partnership
council for this afternoon at five p.m. I've checked
your diary and you appear to be free. Please let me
know at once if this is inconvenient. Please also let
me know if you will require any equipment, i.e.
overhead projector, PowerPoint slides, etc.
Jean Templeman

And another:

From:	Tanner, Richard
To:	Tate, Daniel
Subject:	Re: Presentation to partnership council

GOOD LUCK!
R

THE RETURN OF THE RELENTLESS SCOTT DOLAN

Then the phone rings.

'Hi, Daniel, it's Scott Dolan—'

'How did you get my home telephone number?' I
snap.

'I asked around,' he says with the aural equivalent
of a shrug.

'Well, don't call me there, OK? In fact, don't call me
at all.'

'I was just wondering—'

'No!' I slam the phone back down.

After a couple of seconds, it rings again. I pick it up and leave it off the hook.

LUNCH WITH GABY

Early lunch with Gaby Roslin. Joy! She's unhappy with the long-lens photos taken of her on holiday that have been appearing in all the papers. Some adventurous paparazzo snapped it from halfway up a tree. I know what she wants: a Q&A on how we can get the pix withdrawn. There's no time to do any legal research, so I swallow down some Dutch courage, collect my thoughts, and go to work.

FIVE MUSICIANS, A FUNERAL
AND A FIGHT

Just past lunchtime. Lunch with Gaby got boozy, and now I feel wiped out.

Brian and I are standing outside, stamping our feet in the cold and watching the crowd of black-suited mourners file slowly out of the crematorium. So far, from the world of music: Peter Gabriel, Adam Ant, Elton John, Simon Le Bon and Nick Rhodes, Boy George, both Communards, Marc Almond, Billy Bragg,

Kevin Rowland, Stephen 'Tintin' Duffy, Suggs, Limahl, Chrissie Hynde, Feargal Sharkey, Paul Weller. And, from the world of showbiz: Zoe Ball, Dani Behr, Chris Tarrant, Vic Reeves and Bob Mortimer, Ben Elton, Steve Coogan, Patsy Palmer, Al Murray.

Bob Geldof is talking to Midge Ure; the Dahlias' set at Live Aid was one of the London gig's highlights. Norman Cook and Mark King are reminiscing; two bassists-made-good lamenting the loss of another.

Everyone is wearing shades, which qualifies this as one of two possible funerals: a dead mafioso or a dead celebrity.

Thanks to our vantage point during the service, hidden in a rear row at the back of the chamber, we were the first to exit just as soon as the coffin slipped through the red scarlet drapes and into the furnace beyond. Brian didn't want the rest of the Dahlias to spot him, for fear they would try to exclude him from the further proceedings. So we meanwhile just hid at the back and watched, and no one paid us any attention.

Brian choked back sobs; tears rolled down his cheeks.

The band sat in the front pew, looking grim. Traditional hymns were replaced by their music as Paul Oakenfold mixed a ten-minute medley of their hits, his decks set up in the pulpit, and music thumping from bass bins rigged up next to the altar. It was all pretty surreal, my experience of it not helped by me having finished off the Scotch in the taxi on the way over. I've got the taste for it now, and I'd like more.

Outside, I scan the crowd of mourners and double-take when I notice Oliver Dawkins talking to Davey. The two of them are conferring intently just outside the chapel's porch.

Brian is staring down at his feet, his eyes red-raw. The snow is dotted with flattened-out cigarette butts from where the next party have been waiting to go inside. He drops another into this collection and scuffs snow over it with the tip of his boot.

'Ten to one they won't even talk to me,' he says glumly.

I have a crumpled packet of cigarettes and a Bic lighter in my inside pocket. I gently pull one out, kinked and crushed as it is, and offer it to him. He takes it. I take out another for myself and light both, shielding the flame behind my cupped hand. I smoke mine quickly, then light another. They taste good.

'Coming with me?' Brian asks, walking towards a guy shaking the hands of the mourners as they leave the chapel. 'It's Giovanni, John's friend. He found John's body on Sunday.'

'What're we doing?'

'Gio's a nice guy – I ought to say something.'

Giovanni – buffed up, tanned, shaven-headed – scowls at us as we approach.

'I'm really sorry,' Brian says to him, awkwardly squeezing his shoulder. Giovanni shrugs Brian's hand away, and looks at us disdainfully.

'I noticed you skulking at the back,' he says.

'The place was full,' Brian explains.

'I haven't got anything to say to you.'

'I just wanted to say how sorry I am. John was a good friend.'

'Oh, *please*.'

'Sorry?'

'If it wasn't for you, none of this would've happened.'

'That's not fair,' Brian argues.

'Please leave now,' Giovanni says. 'Just go.' He turns away.

Brian is about to follow him but I catch his arm. 'Maybe now's not the right time?' I suggest.

We walk away as another group of mourners approaches.

'You're right – he's probably upset. It's understandable.'

'Call him later, or something,' I say.

I'm not sure, but I'm suddenly getting the feeling that Brian isn't telling me everything.

RECONCILIATION?

We resume our vigil at the edge of the garden of remembrance. Eventually the band and their entourage emerge from the chapel. Theirs is a united and public show of grief as they press celebrity flesh. I feel sorry for Brian, stuck with me on the lonely fringe of the crowd, next to this bleak scrap of grass.

'Why don't you go over?' I suggest to him. 'You don't have to mention the case. Maybe they'd just like to talk? A chance to mend some fences.'

'You think?' He looks unsure. I hope I'm not misjudging this.

'Worth a try. If it doesn't go well, you can always just leave.'

'Would you come with me?' he asks. 'I'd feel outnumbered on my own.'

Davey and Dawkins are shaking hands and beaming happy smiles at each other. The Dork saunters off towards the main road, looking smug. He waves when he spots me looking at him.

'Sure,' I say, ignoring the wave.

The three surviving members of the original line-up of the Black Dahlias are standing under the eaves of the chapel, accepting commiseration from the dispersing mourners. Sean Darbo, the new singer for their Greatest Hits tour, walks over to join us from where he's been talking with record label execs.

POSTER BOY

Sean Darbo.

Heart-throb. Cover star of a thousand teenage magazines. Dreamboat. Multi-million seller. Hip young gunslinger. Money-making machine.

That's if you believe what you read in the papers.

The inside line is a different story.

The truth from the industry grapevine: Sean made a mint out of his first album but things have since taken a turn for the worse. He's been working on a follow-up for months. The label sent him to Miami to record, and the temptations there proved too much for him. No one had remembered the great idea of shipping the Happy Mondays out to Jamaica to record the follow-up to *Pills, Thrills & Bellyaches* ... Some people never learn.

The demos since have been awful; the label keeps sending him back to the studio to re-record them. There's a new producer every time: the Dustbrothers, Mirwais, William Orbit. No joy for any of them. None of them can salvage the dross he's laying down.

Then there are the stories that Sean's taken the rock-and-roll lifestyle a little too far: hookers, gambling, booze, nose candy. Living the cliché and loving it. He'd started to believe his own press. But now the money has dried up. Sean Darbo needs a boost.

His solution? Hook up with the Dahlias, tour the world, coin it in, bask in the publicity, write the new album on the road. It's a can't-miss plan.

But how does this make Brian feel? He's been replaced once by a *bass guitarist*, no less. That was bad enough. But it gets worse. Now he's overlooked for a one-trick pony who's been asked to sing the songs *Brian* made famous.

He must be seething.

THE BLACK DAHLIAS' GREATEST HITS

'What're *you* doing here?' Martin asks as we edge alongside them.

'I'm here for John,' Brian says.

'Come *on*, no one's buying that.'

'He was my friend too.'

'Bullshit,' Martin says. 'You never got on with him.'

'You were always at each other's throats,' Alex says.

'I'm as upset about this as you are.'

'Yeah, *right*,' says Damon. 'You hated him, admit it. And he hated you.'

'You don't know anything about us. You don't know what you're talking about.'

'All the bad feeling we had was because you two couldn't get on,' Alex says. 'It was *you* being such a bastard that led to us breaking up like we did.'

'I was closer to him than any of you were.'

Martin finally turns to face Brian directly, open disgust on his face.

'You wanna know how much he thought of you?' he asks. 'I wasn't going to ever mention this but you are so lost in the clouds, man, so deluded, I'm gonna do you a favour and tell you. It was John who suggested we needed to dump you. *John* – it was his idea. Big mark of friendship, right? You two were really close, really tight.'

'That's not true. The label made the decision,' Brian says, with a catch in his voice.

This accords with the official line in the papers, at least.

'Only after John persuaded us and them that you had to go,' Martin says. 'That's the bottom line, Brian,' Alex adds. 'So just accept it and stop all this nonsense. It's tedious, and it couldn't be further from the truth.'

Brian has tears in his eyes.

'Yeah, man,' Sean Darbo says. 'Plus it's *bor*ing.'

'What do *you* know,' Brian snaps, 'fucking prostitute.'

A heavy silence.

'What did you just say?' Sean takes a step towards us.

'You heard.'

'I want to hear it again.'

'I called you a whore.'

I nervously look for the photographers. Thankfully, they all appear to be distracted by some glamourpuss or other. I take Brian's shoulder and start to tug him gently away. I can feel the muscles in his arm stiffening. 'Take it easy,' I say.

'Something else before you go,' Alex says. 'Just so you know, we've got better ideas out of Sean in two days'n we *ever* got out of you. In fact I'm not sure we ever got any ideas out of you at all. And your new album – we've heard it. You suck, Brian, face it.'

Brian starts to answer but the words choke back in his throat. Nothing comes.

'And now,' Martin says, 'if you don't mind, we're

grieving. If it's not too much to ask we'd like you to just fuck off now.'

Brian wrenches his arm free of my grip. Before I can reach out to hold him back he launches himself at Martin. They collide, Brian's bony shoulder driving into Martin's stomach before they both end up on the ground, wrapped around each other. The other mourners instantly stop their conversations to stare over at us. The members of Spandau Ballet gape in amazement. Vince Clarke and Andy Bell gawp. A heavy silence settles over the grounds of the cemetery; somewhere a crow squawks.

Brian draws back his fist and strikes Martin full in the face. Blood splashes down onto the snow. The rest of the band seem too stunned – or afraid – to move. Brian punches Martin again, harder. He has his hands around his throat. I slip my arms underneath his shoulders and yank him away.

'Get off him,' I gasp.

Sean jumps at us. With me pressing his arms to his sides, Brian can't defend himself. Sean pulls his arm back and punches Brian hard on the bridge of his nose. Brian's neck cracks back and his head slams into my chin. We both hit the deck. There's a lot more blood.

I remember a photo I once saw in *Hello!*. Sean Darbo, dressed in a loose white jacket, attacking a piece of wood, the photo's caption: BLACK BELT SEAN HITS RING TO UNWIND.

Damon and Alex have formed a barrier in front of

Martin. He's spitting out bloodied teeth. Sean stands over us, fists cocked, ready for more.

'Come on, then,' Brian hollers at him, panting hard, struggling against my loosening grip.

'You want some more?'

'This isn't going to help you,' I hiss at Brian. 'Calm down.'

'You fucking moron,' Alex says. 'You never learn. It's always violence with you, isn't it?'

Martin has been helped to his feet. His mouth is a mess, two teeth missing.

'I wish I could say this was the first time,' he says thickly, a trail of intermingled blood and spit running down his chin. 'You're an animal. You ought to be locked up.'

Brian strains against my arms, but I've linked my fingers again and he can't unclasp them. 'Take it easy,' I repeat. I rise to my haunches, then upright, and yank him back a couple of steps.

'Get him out of here,' Alex says to me, 'before we have you both arrested.'

'Let's go,' I say quietly to Brian. 'You don't wanna get into any more trouble.'

'Don't think about showing your face around here again,' Sean warns.

He hawks noisily, and then spits full in Brian's face.

'Loser.'

MORE REMORSE

We slipped around to the back of the church after that. I was worried the police might have been called, or that someone from the press might have got a picture. Once we were out of sight, Brian's tenuous grip on his composure faltered, then failed. I could see he was really upset as soon as I pulled him off Martin. He was clenching his teeth to stop his face quivering and his eyes had misted over. Out of sight of the others, the tears started to fall freely again. The knuckles of his right hand were cut and bleeding from Martin's teeth, and his nose was a mess after Sean's punch. He used the sleeve of his shirt to wipe away the blood and spit and tears from his face.

'I'm sorry,' he said in a dead tone.

'What happened?'

'I don't want to talk about it.'

I didn't know what to say to that.

He added, 'I hate myself.'

Now he's headed off into town. He said he had something he had to do urgently and that he would call me later, that he would want to see me tonight.

SOME FRIENDLY ADVICE

I'm just about to leave when Alex and Damon beckon me over.

'I'm sorry about that,' I apologize nervously. 'He's really upset about John. He's not himself.'

'Yes, he is,' Alex says. 'That's exactly the Brian I remember.'

'We haven't got anything against you,' Damon says. 'You're just doing your job. We know that.'

'He tell you where he was last Sunday?' Alex asks without preamble.

'Who, Brian?' I say, perplexed. They both nod. 'No, and I haven't asked.'

'You might want to,' Damon suggests. 'Just a bit of advice.'

'You don't think he knows anything about John, surely?'

'Let's just say he took John's success badly. He gatecrashed one of our signings and made a bit of a fuss. It was obvious he was jealous, and Brian's got what you might call a volatile personality.'

'We've known him for years,' Alex adds. 'We know what he's like.'

'Jealous?'

'We're not saying anything,' Alex says. 'Just that maybe you ought to ask him where he was last week, OK?'

AN INTERVIEW WITH SCOTT DOLAN

As I'm walking out the crematorium, towards the main road, a black-suited mourner detaches from the crowd and jogs over to join me.

'Danny,' he calls. His voice is familiar. I've heard it half a dozen times on the telephone.

Not *now*.

Scott Dolan is tall and stringy, with red hair tied back in a ponytail that reaches down to between his shoulder-blades. He looks uncomfortable in his suit and his choice of footwear, a pair of scuffed eight-eye DMs, looks like a petty act of mutiny.

'Not again,' I groan.

'Danny,' he says, extending a long thin hand. 'Scott Dolan from *Extravaganza*. Great to meet you at last.'

I don't take his hand. He tries to disguise the snub by smoothing out his rumpled jacket.

'I only just got here,' he says. 'Did I miss anything?'

Brian's been lucky. I can just imagine tomorrow's front pages if his assault on Martin had been caught on camera. The police would have pulled him in double-quick.

'I told you already. I've got nothing to say to you. Don't call me in the office. Don't call me at home. Please stop bothering me.'

I start walking, more quickly.

'Just a moment of your time,' he says, trotting to catch up with me. '*Please.*'

'Look – what is it?'

I swivel to face him. This gives him the opening he was looking for. He edges in front of me, subtly blocking my way out to the road.

'You know what I want. I want to talk to you about Brian Fey.'

'For the last bloody time, I've got nothing to say to you. I *can't* say anything to you.'

I side-step him and continue walking even more briskly towards the road. He matches my pace and falls in alongside.

'How about this, Danny? You know I told you that we were close to digging up some interesting information on Brian?'

'You mentioned it.'

'Well – look, slow down – I've got it with me. Here.'

Dolan pulls a brown manila envelope from inside his jacket. He hands it to me.

'What is it?'

'Dynamite. There was an incident in California ten years ago. The band was in the US on their world tour. The one that stopped halfway through for no reason, remember? It got covered up by the label, but we've managed to get hold of the police report. That's a copy of it there.'

'And?'

'Just read it – and then call me. You've got my number.'

I try to hand the envelope back to him. He refuses to take it.

'Look, I'm doing you a favour. And if you don't take this away and look at it I'm going to use it in the story tomorrow. If you humour me I'll hold the story back a couple of days so you have a chance to think about it. I might even make sure that this never comes to the public's attention.'

'I still won't have anything to say.' I keep walking.

I flag down a passing cab and get inside.

'Danny, please.'

He pulls the half-open window further down.

'Look, Danny – just remember my offer's on the table, OK? Read that report and call me. I'll buy you lunch. We'll talk.'

SOME THINGS I DIDN'T KNOW ABOUT BRIAN FEY

Later, as the cab comes to a halt in heavy traffic, waiting for the lights ahead to change, I can't resist sliding a finger inside the envelope and tearing it open. I take out a collection of photocopied documents. It looks like a criminal report. The front sheet bears a stamp: Davis County Police Department, California.

A police mugshot of Brian. The shot was taken ten years ago before the drugs had really left their mark and wasted him. One eye is half-closed and a bruise has formed around the socket. I turn the papers over and flick through them again, from the start.

The lights change and we edge slowly forward as I start to read.

Brian was arrested for a serious assault after officers were called to a waterfront hotel in San Francisco. The police had been alerted by other guests at the hotel, who had become concerned at an increasingly heated altercation taking place on the balcony of the room above them, two floors up. Brian was arguing with another man, and the guests witnessed their argument turn violent. There were raised voices and a punch was thrown. I assume from the mugshot that it had landed on Brian's face. Tests conducted at the scene indicated that both participants in the argument were intoxicated. Both of them were later charged with possession of cocaine, marijuana, and various drug paraphernalia. All charges were subsequently dropped although the reason for that was unclear.

The other man then lost his balance and fell backwards against the rail of the balcony. The rail itself was in need of repair and unable to hold his weight. The man fell, landing on a grass verge next to the swimming pool. He suffered a broken leg, a broken pelvis, and four cracked ribs. He was lucky to survive, but the ground had been softened by several days of rain. Usually, it would have been as dry and unforgiving as concrete. In usual circumstances, he would have been dead.

This other guy was John French.

I check the date on the front page of the report: 1986 – the start of the Black Dahlias' year off. I remember: the band claimed they were tired from all the touring and needed some time to recuperate. There was also talk of burn-out and frayed nerves. The rest of their world tour was cancelled, and no one heard anything from them for months. Then they came back with a multi-platinum album, like they'd never even been away.

Now the reason for the absence is obvious. Not a matter of choice but of necessity: it was forced upon them. French needed time to recover from what Brian had done to him.

I stop the taxi. We're nowhere near the office but I need a walk.

Dolan claimed that the report had been suppressed – no wonder. The record company must have moved heaven and earth to make sure the newspapers never got wind of it. I'm guessing French was persuaded not to press charges, for the good of the band. They were all coining it in back then, and it would have been stupidity to upset things.

Now I know Brian has a history of violence.

I know he hasn't conquered it. I've twice seen him lose control in the last two days.

And John French is dead. And the police still haven't ruled out foul play.

I try to put it all out of my mind. This isn't something I want to think about right now.

I make my way along the quiet residential streets I've wandered into towards the noise and bustle of a main road. A taxi approaches with its amber light lit. I half-raise my arm and then drop it, just as the cabby slows down. As he slows he gives me an exaggerated shrug of enquiry: what do I want?

An idea: I ask him to take me to Hackney and the studio where they film *Skin Trade*. If Hannah did call this morning, then she won't mind me stopping by to pay her a visit. And I need to talk to someone.

SKIN TRADE

The studio has been built inside an old converted warehouse. I've been here once before, when Hannah originally got the part. Its cavernous space has been sub-divided by thin wooden screens to fashion a dozen locations that recur throughout the series: rooms, offices, a bar, a catwalk. The roof leaks in places and the concrete floor is half an inch deep with water. Vandals have broken the windows and one wall is blackened with soot. The sets, sheltered within the bright arc of the klieg lights, shiver inside the vastness of this space.

I make my way into the loading bay that runs alongside the main body of the building. There are three big trailers parked up on one side of the bay.

I walk forward assertively. A security guard looks up from a newspaper and blocks my path.

'I'm here to see Hannah Wilde,' I announce confidently.

'That so?'

'My name's Daniel. She knows me. Could you tell her I'm here, please.'

The guard shakes his head. 'Can't do that.'

'Why not?'

'No shooting today. The cast're doing press interviews in town.'

'You know where?'

'At the Sanderson, I think.'

'Cheers,' I say.

VINCENT HAINES MEETS HIS PRESS

I taxi into town and blag my way into the Sanderson by telling the receptionist that I'm Vincent Haines's lawyer and that I have urgent legal business. I'm shown through into a suite of conference rooms filled with the ladies and gentlemen of the press, the crowd expertly handled by a crack corps of publicists. A table has been placed at the far end of the room and on it has been arranged a nest of microphones and wires. Bright TV lights shine onto the table and promotional posters of the show have been fastened to the wall behind. Vincent Haines is sitting next to an attractive redhead whom I recognize as one of the other 'models' from the show, and an anonymous man in a black polo neck whom I assume to be a publicist. Vincent and the girl are fielding questions from the hacks. There's no sign of Hannah.

'Tell us about the perks and price of fame, Vincent,' asks an attractive reporter with a notepad.

'The price? You can't sleep with all of them,' Vincent replies with a libidinous wink.

'That's a joke,' adds the publicist, with a half-panicked laugh.

'What's happening with *Defence of the Badge*?' asks another reporter. 'I heard you might be getting sued in the States for dropping out.'

Haines spits out, 'I can't believe what those two-bit—'

'No questions on anything other than *Skin Trade*, please,' the publicist interrupts hastily, a pacifying hand on Haines's arm. 'Vincent'd *love* to talk about *Badge*, but I believe the correct phrase is sub judice. We'll leave it to the lawyers.'

'Vinny,' says someone else, 'what's all this stuff about you and Hannah Wilde?'

Haines calms down. 'I'm gonna plead the fifth on that one too, guys,' he says with a shit-eating grin.

'Let's just say Vinny and Hannah've been getting on really well, lately, and leave it at that,' the publicity guy smirks suggestively, perhaps sensing a useful angle to land some column inches in tomorrow's papers.

'Yeah,' Haines adds, catching the drift, 'we've been enjoying *working* together.'

A prurient sniggering goes up – I clench my teeth to prevent an unfortunate outburst.

The questions continue for thirty minutes, Haines's answers monitored hawkishly by the publicist throughout. We unearth a treasure trove of important information about everyone's favourite American soap star: Vincent's preferred ice cream is chocolate chip, although he has a soft spot for mint; he won a regional surfing competition when he was eleven, back in LA; he's suffering sleepless nights over the fate of the Giant Panda in south-west China.

Vincent Haines: a multi-faceted, complex enigma.

Oh, please.

During the conference, Haines excuses himself on three occasions to visit the men's room; the good news about his 'successful' stint in rehab – the question clearly planted by his PR team – is given the lie by the manifest purpose of these absences. I'm reminded of a visit to another of these events: a down-at-heel Brit-pack movie star we were acting for handed a reporter his bowl of pot and asked him to pick out the stems and seeds, while proclaiming it felt great to be clean. Haines might not be quite so blatant, but the red crescents around his nostrils leave no one in any doubt what he's been getting up to.

As we file out, an attractive girl wearing a *Skin Trade* T-shirt offers me a bag full of novelty items bearing the show's logo. I take it.

'I'm Vincent Haines's lawyer,' I say. 'Do you think you could tell him I'm here? I need to speak to him.'

'Wait here,' she smiles, and heads towards the door through which Haines exited.

LOSING IT

I'm shown through into the room where Haines is finishing off a one-on-one interview with a reporter from a national daily. She's pretty, and Haines is unashamedly hitting on her. The interview is as rigidly policed as the press conference was; gentle questions are lobbed at the charming, handsome star, who obliges by fielding them with pre-scripted answers of wit and esprit.

Haines leans over to plant a kiss on the reporter's cheek when her final question has been answered. The reporter is followed out of the room by the publicity guy. For the moment, Haines and I are alone.

'Dude,' he says.

'Thanks for seeing me.'

We shake hands. 'No problem. What's up? You got more questions?'

'Yeah,' I say, 'something like that.'

'No problem. I could get the caterers to fix us up

with a couple of cheeseburgers or something. How's that sound?'

'Sounds perfect,' I say, feigning a friendly smile.

'Take a seat,' he offers.

'I'm fine standing,' I say.

'Suit yourself, man. Can I get you a beer? Something stronger?'

'No, I'm fine.'

He takes a can out of a fridge and spikes it. 'No drinking on the job, right? I totally admire your dedication.'

He sinks down into the room's sofa and rests his feet on the table.

'No Hannah today?' I ask.

'Left twenty minutes ago. She's done for the day. I'll catch up with her later. Some shit at the theatre she wants me to go to.'

I suddenly know exactly what it is I want to say to him. It's so obvious.

'So – what can I do for you?' he asks me.

'I was just wondering—'

'Yeah?'

'I was just wondering what it feels like to fuck my girlfriend.'

A flicker of confusion passes over his beautiful face. 'Come again?'

'I was just wondering,' I repeat, 'what it feels like to have sexual intercourse with my girlfriend.'

He laughs nervously. 'You've completely lost me, man.'

'Simple question. I just want you to tell me what it feels like. I can't remember, see – since she stopped fucking me when she started fucking you.'

He laughs again, more nervously this time. 'This's a joke, right? Someone's put you up to this? Is it Rip? It is, isn't it – this is Rip's lame-ass idea of a joke.'

'No, no joke,' I deadpan, taking a step towards him.

'Hey, man, I've got like totally no idea what you're talking about.'

Now he looks concerned. He's upright in the sofa, eyes darting left and right, working out angles of escape.

I step forward again. He shuffles away from me. I catch a glimpse of myself in a mirror: with the bloody scab and the bruising on the side of my face I actually *do* look threatening.

'You told me all about her when we met on Monday,' I say. 'You said you took her off another guy, remember? And then I heard on TV how you've got engaged to her. So I'm assuming you've slept with her by now?'

'You're talking about Hannah? Hey, man, help me out a little – I'm lost here. Are you saying you're her *ex* or something? I mean, if you are, man, what can I say? I'm completely sorry. I had, like, *no* clue.'

The door to the room opens and the publicity guy returns.

'Get security!' Haines shrieks.

The guy takes one look at me, snarling at Haines,

and takes a step backwards. Laying down his life for his charge obviously isn't in his contract.

'Get this kook out of here!'

The publicist spins and sprints towards the hotel lobby.

I turn to Haines.

'Get out,' he orders, his spunk reinvigorated by the promise of imminent reinforcements.

'We're not finished,' I say, doing my best *Dirty Harry* impression.

I make my way back outside before the cavalry can arrive.

A FAMILIAR SOLACE

I need a drink. I feel wiped out – all the emotion has been sucked out of me. I also feel slightly pathetic; putting the frighteners on Haines was childish, and, now that the adrenaline has drained away, I'm disappointed to find that all I'm left with is embarrassment. After stopping at an off-licence to buy a bottle of whisky, I aim my taxi back towards the office.

'Liverpool Street,' I say as we pull out into traffic.

'You all right back there, mate?' the cabby asks me. I must look as bad as I feel. 'I don't want no mess in my cab.'

I repeat myself, 'Liverpool Street, please,' and wrench open the cap of the bottle as we set off.

En route, I tip out the contents of the novelty bag that was given to me after the press conference. There is a T-shirt, a poster, a collection of signed postcards with photographs of the stars, and a mug. I turn the mug in my hand: it's decorated with a group shot of the cast, all of them either handsome or beautiful, all of them smiling for the camera.

It gives me at least a measure of satisfaction to pull down the window, feel the cold air sting my lungs, and toss the mug outside. The china ruptures into a million fragments, scattered in the gutter.

I rummage in the pack and slip the postcard of Hannah into my pocket.

RUMOURS

It's getting late when I finally make it back. I feel nauseous, so I divert into the toilets to freshen up. It also occurs to me as I position myself at the urinal that I've been going more often than usual. It's probably nothing but maybe I ought to mention it to the doctor the next time I see him for a check-up.

Jonathan Williams walks out of a cubicle and washes his hands at one of the basins.

'So what's happening with you and the Fey case?' he asks as I zip up.

'Nothing much,' I say. 'It's running along.'

'I mean, even I finally heard the rumours,' he adds. 'They get to me eventually, even down in the basement.'

'What rumours?'

'I thought you knew?' He sounds embarrassed.

'Knew *what*?'

He fidgets. 'It's probably nothing. Listen, I probably shouldn't have mentioned it. Just forget I said anything.'

'No,' I say, finishing up and joining him at the basins. He's squirming, looking ready to make a quick escape. 'You can't leave it at that. What rumours?'

He speaks slowly and carefully. 'I heard you were coming off the case. I heard you're going to get reassigned.'

'You what?'

He nods.

'Where to?'

'That's what I was kind of pleased about. Everyone seems to think you're gonna be working downstairs with me. I mean, that'd be great news. I could certainly do with the company.'

A LAST-MINUTE REPRIEVE

'Any messages?' I ask Elizabeth when I get back to my room.

'Only one. Miss Wilson's secretary called to cancel your appointment with her. She said something about Miss Wilson being ill. Food poisoning, apparently.'

Double take. 'Sorry?'

'I think she's got food poisoning.'

'Are you sure?'

'That's what her secretary told me. She said she left the office to go to the doctor's this morning. I could check if you like.'

'You beauty,' I exclaim. She looks slightly confused. I plough ahead, 'OK. This's what we're gonna do. Print the marketing agreement off again. Maybe I can still sort this out.'

She nods and turns to her screen. In five minutes I have a warm copy of the agreement in my hands. This is amazingly good luck; Wilson's definition of sickness is being hospitalized. Someone is smiling on me for once. Perhaps this marks an upturn in my fortunes.

MORE APOLOGIZING

From:	Tate, Daniel
To:	Delgardo, Rachel
Subject:	You have no idea . . .

. . . how sorry I am and how utterly *stupid* I feel. I will completely understand if you don't want to talk to me again. Brian Fey had an emergency that I had to go and deal with at once. It was really hectic and I only realized I'd stood you up when I was finished, and by then . . . it was too late. Anyway, what I'm

saying is SORRY!!! and I hope you don't hate me
although I'd understand it if you do.
PS: If you don't hate me, maybe you'd let me make
it up to you?

She mails back after only a couple of minutes. So there's
still hope.

Of course I don't hate you although I was pretty
annoyed last night. But these things happen and it's
no one's fault. So apology accepted. But I'm not sure
I'm going to risk dinner again with you at the
moment! Perhaps we can have a talk at the staff
Xmas party?

The annual Christmas bash on Monday evening. The
yearly orgy of drink, inappropriate staff liaisons and
badly dancing Partners, providing enough licentious
scandal to fuel the gossip until February. Great. I'd
almost forgotten about it. I was going to stay away this
year, but I suppose I could make a flying visit. Plus the
drink is free: a persuasive argument in favour of my
attending.

THE LAST LAST CHANCE SALOON

Wilson's absence has given me a last chance. I'm determined to seize it. Also, I need something to put thoughts
of Brian out of my mind.

Cohen is meeting Keith Chegwin and so, until he gets back, I've got the office to myself. To my surprise, I find that I remember most of my amendments to the agreement that I made yesterday evening. The work is tedious but I'm cutting through the pages at an encouraging clip. When Cohen returns at 4.30, I've finished making amendments and I've even managed to proof-read two-thirds of the changes Elizabeth has typed up.

I haven't had time to prepare for my presentation to the partnership council but at least I've made a fist at recovering my position with Wilson.

THE DORK HAS REASON TO CELEBRATE

Dawkins walks past my office. He backs up as soon as he realizes that I've spotted him. His fat face has a gloating cast to it.

'Just going for a quick drink, men,' he says cheerily.

'A little early for that, isn't it?' Cohen says.

'I'm celebrating,' he says. 'I've had a good day today. The interview went very well.'

'Wonderful,' I say.

'Isn't it,' he says. 'And I've got a charming date to tackle the champers with me.'

'Anyone we know?' I ask despite myself.

'All will be revealed, Tate.'

'How enigmatic,' I say.

He smiles another of his bogus smiles.

'Don't let me keep you,' I say.

'Pip-pip,' says the Dork over his shoulder.

'You think that means he got the job?' Cohen asks.

'Probably.'

'What an arse.'

RED HANDED

Dawkins' early departure presents me with an opportunity to take the Japanese precedents I borrowed from him back to his office without having to endure ten minutes of his crowing. I collect the papers and wander round.

I slip into the Dork's office and quietly close the door behind me. I stand at his window, raise the blind and take in the view. Stone and glass and shimmering darkness. The Christmas lights in Soho Square look gorgeous from up here, framed against another fresh covering of snow that must have fallen this afternoon, not that I'd know it from my own vantage point. London's modest skyline glitters in the darkness. I watch as the blinking lights of a jet slowly move from left to right across the window.

I could get used to a view like this.

I drop the papers on Dawkins' spare chair and then go around behind his desk and open up the drawers, one by one. They are all unlocked. I'd like to find a copy of his appraisal just to see how good the partnership really thinks he is.

Even his drawers are efficiently organized. More ringbinders, a few books, a bicycle helmet and his fetid gym kit. I run my finger along the spines of the folders until I reach the one labelled 'personal'. Crouching down beneath the desk I pull the folder out and flick through its contents.

I find a copy of his contract and note glumly, although without much surprise, that he's paid £10,000 a year more than me. There are summaries of timesheets confirming that he's averaged over 11 hours a day of chargeable time over the past twelve months. He probably deserves the extra he's making. There are reams of inter-office memoranda, the kind of thing I usually read once, bin, forget about. And then, filed loosely towards the back of the folder, a document I recognize at once.

The missing briefing note.

I stare at it dumbly. I'm trying to work out why the Dork would have it in his office. Without even thinking about the significance of the find or what Dawkins is up to, I put the document back in the folder. I close the drawer, check quickly to make sure everything is as it should be, and return to my office.

I've only got ten minutes before my presentation to the partnership council.

HOW TO LOSE FRIENDS AND INFLUENCE NO ONE

Nausea has settled heavily in the pit of my stomach. Nerves? Plus I'm feeling light-headed. I need a good blast of fully sugared-up black coffee.

Caroline Lewis finishes her spiel. Inside, the lights have been dimmed and she is projecting slides from her laptop onto the wall at the end of the room. When I press my face against the glass panel in the door I can make out vague pie charts and graphs. And there's Caroline, silhouetted by the cone of light from the projector, emphasizing the data with explanatory swoops of the cursor. In the brief periods of darkness, as one slide is replaced by another, I can make out the dark shadows of the partnership council. When she finishes, they applaud politely. I recognize Hunter's syrupy-smooth voice as he adds a few concluding words. Although I strain my ears hard, I can't make out what it is he's saying.

'Thank God that's over and done with,' Caroline mutters as she backs out of the room. She's got a large leather portfolio folder under one arm and a sheaf of spare handouts in a spare hand. The handouts have been glossily colour-printed and neatly spiral-bound.

'Cheers,' I say, feeling utterly inadequate.

'Are you feeling all right?' she asks quizzically, peering into my face. 'You're not looking that good.'

'I think I'm coming down with something. It's nothing. I feel fine.'

'Best of luck,' she says.

I flash her a smile and step inside.

The tables in the conference room have been rearranged to form a horseshoe, with a single desk in the centre at one end. On this desk sits an open laptop and a projector. Caroline has left one of her handouts behind. I flick through it as I'm waiting for the partners to finish making their notes on her presentation. Hunter and Fulton are conferring quietly. Surely only for show, though? I can't imagine they haven't already given the Dork the nod.

These presentations are being given to the entire partnership council. The council comprises the five senior partners in the firm: Charles Hunter; James Fulton; Victoria Wilson; Richard Tanner; David Turner. Any hope that Wilson might be too unwell to attend is immediately dashed. She's sitting next to Fulton, fixing me with an icy stare.

Tanner catches my eye and gives me a smile of encouragement. Hunter and Fulton finish their hushed conversation, and Hunter then addresses me with a toothy smile.

'Thanks for coming down, Daniel,' he says. 'Have you got any slides you'd like us to look at?'

'I wasn't planning to use any,' I admit. 'I'd rather just make a quick speech if that's all right.' I scrutinize his face for a reaction but he keeps it diplomatically blank.

'Well, why don't you get started? We're all very keen to hear what you've got to say. We'll interrupt if we have any questions.'

I clear my throat, rub my sweaty palms against my trouser legs and scrabble around for somewhere to begin.

'As you all know, I've been at White Hunter for a few years now. During that time I've worked on some excellent files and, I think it's fair to say, I've had some good results.' Tanner nods conspicuously. 'I'm an ambitious person, and I'm very interested in developing my career here. I'd like to acquire my own list of clients and I think I'm well on the way to doing that.'

'You've certainly got a good reputation outside the firm,' Tanner acknowledges – bless him.

'Although it wouldn't hurt you to get your name mentioned in the legal press a bit more,' Fulton suggests. 'I'd like to see you in the *Media Lawyer*, something like that.'

'Bob Monkhouse speaks very highly of you,' Tanner says.

'I enjoyed working for him,' I say.

'And I received a letter of thanks from Geri Halliwell after the work you did on her new recording contract.'

'It was interesting – and she's very kind.'

'Where do you see yourself in five years' time?' Hunter asks.

'Here, I hope. Established as a partner with a great list of clients and a couple of assistants working for me. Making the firm a lot of money.'

There's a pause. I smile in anticipation of a question.

'Before you go on, Daniel,' Wilson says, 'there're a couple of things I'd like to ask.' She opens a folder and takes out a document. 'I've just got off the phone with Trish Parkes. As everyone here knows, she's one of my clients: a very important manager with a lot of industry clout. Daniel's been working on her file. It seems Trish received this document this morning. I think it's relevant to Daniel's presentation.'

She hands me the document, and I scan it.

'Do you recognize it?' she says.

It's the half-finished marketing agreement Dawkins stole from my desk. It has the scribbles and swirls of my manuscript amendments on it.

'It's a draft marketing agreement I've been working on,' I say. 'But I haven't sent it to Trish. Someone else must've.'

'Someone *else* sent your unfinished work over to Trish?'

'Yes.'

'Who'd do something like that?' she laughs scornfully.

'Oliver Dawkins.'

'That's ridiculous.'

'No, it's not. He stole some papers from my desk. I

just found them in his office. He must've taken this too and then sent it out.'

Wilson throws her hands up. 'That's utter nonsense, Daniel.'

'I have to agree,' Fulton says.

'He's trying to discredit me. He obviously sent it to Trish because he knew she'd get straight on the phone to you.'

'Daniel, that's ludicrous,' Fulton says.

'Come on, then.'

'Come on what?'

'I'll show you.'

BROUGHT TO BOOK

I lead Hunter, Fulton, Wilson, Tanner and Turner up to the second floor and around to Dawkins' room. To my surprise, he's sitting at his desk, working.

'Is everything all right?' he says.

'I'm sorry to interrupt, Oliver,' Hunter says, 'but Daniel says you removed some documents from his desk and sent them out to one of Victoria's clients.'

'That's preposterous,' the Dork splutters.

'He says he found some documents in your office. Would you mind if he showed us where they were?'

'There's nothing here,' he says.

'I'm sure it won't take a moment.'

'Go ahead. I don't mind at all.'

I go around to his side of the desk. He's hidden an open bottle of champagne and two glasses underneath his chair. I look up at him and sneer. I tug at the drawer. He's locked it.

'Unlock it,' I say.

The Dork takes out his keys and opens the drawer. I flick through the contents. Nothing. I pull out the folders and book, his gym kit and cycling helmet, and dump them onto the floor. I empty the drawer completely. There's no sign of the stolen report. The corners of the Dork's mouth rise ever so slightly.

'It was in *there*,' I point.

'Daniel, it's empty,' Dawkins says faux-apologetically.

'Thank you, Oliver,' Wilson says.

'Sorry to bother you,' says Hunter.

DEBRIEFING

We return to the conference room. I have nothing else to say. Wilson and Fulton glare at me malevolently. Hunter seems embarrassed. Even Tanner can't look me in the eye. There's a minute of awkward silence before I thank them for listening to my presentation and leave.

I'm finished. I'm not going to be made up to partner, that's obvious. But, worse than that, I've just made a complete fool of myself in front of the entire partnership council. I've just killed any chance I had of a successful career at White Hunter.

Cohen is outside, waiting to go in. Like me, he hasn't prepared any slides or handouts. Unlike me, he's glacially cool.

'How was it?' he asks.

'I don't want to talk about it,' I say.

'Come on, these things're just like job interviews,' he reassures me. 'You think they've gone terribly but you've never *really* got an idea. I thought I'd fucked up my interview for this place but they still made me an offer. Just wait and see. Don't get down about it. You never know.'

'On this occasion,' I say, 'I've got a pretty good idea.'

I'm still sweating. I really need a drink – a hard one. I've got the whisky upstairs and now Cohen is going to be out of the way for twenty minutes.

'Don't forget about tonight,' he says. 'Beth's cooking aside, we'll have a great time, right?'

'Right,' I say.

IN SEARCH OF CLUES

I'm on my knees in the photocopying room, streamers of shredded paper all around me, some bunched in my fists, when Dawkins comes in.

'What on earth're you doing?' he says.

'You know what I'm doing,' I say, pointing at the shredder. 'Trying to find the document you stole.'

'You've lost it, old son,' the Dork laughs. 'And you should've *seen* old Hunter's face back then.'

'What did you do with it?' I say.

'I have no idea *what* you're talking about,' he laughs.

'We'll sort this out later,' I say.

'Whatever you say,' Dawkins says, leaving me to my spaghetti paper.

SOME MATERNAL CONCERN

The new version of Monster Munch's marketing contract waits on my desk, the amendments typed up by Elizabeth. I can hardly bear to look at it. I sweep it off the desk and into the bin. I replace it with the postcard of Hannah.

I really, really need a drink.

I only intended to drink two fingers of the whisky but by the time Elizabeth comes in to tell me she's leaving I've sneakily worked my way through half of the bottle. And now I've started it, I might as well finish it off, so I keep going.

'Do you need anything else?' she asks. 'I'm happy to stay if you need me.'

I cover the postcard with a piece of paper. 'No,' I say, 'I'm all set up here, thanks. I'll see you in the morning.'

'How's your head?' she asks.

'What?'

'That bruise isn't getting any better.'

'I'm fine.'

'No, you should go and see a doctor about it.'

'Maybe.'

'I'm serious. I'll book an appointment for you before I go.'

It seems easier to say yes than argue. So I accept.

'Tomorrow morning,' Elizabeth comes back to announce.

'Fine.'

EVEN MORE THINGS I DIDN'T KNOW ABOUT BRIAN FEY

One of the evening messengers comes in to leave a package on top of the surfeit of work brimming in my in-tray. It's unusual: a jiffy bag. I examine it, turning it over in my hands. Smaller than the usual size, and it looks brand new. The address is neatly printed on a white label stuck to the packet. There are no stamps on the envelope, so it's been hand-delivered or couriered. I heft it in one hand and then squeeze it: lightweight with something solid in the middle. I tear it open and tip out the contents.

Out falls a small cassette like the ones found in answering machines.

I think back to the newspaper report from this morning and the missing tape from John French's machine? Could this be it? Intuitively, I pick up my Dictaphone and try the tape. It fits.

Sudden nerves. I thumb the machine to play.

Static, then a few messages. I don't recognize the voices or any of the names mentioned.

Yet another message plays, rendered tinny and indistinct both by the quality of the original recording and the cheap speaker on my Dictaphone. It takes me a moment to identify the speaker.

'John? Are you there? Pick up, you selfish bastard, come on.' There's a pause, a long damp snuffle. 'OK, you're not there, or ignoring me. Jesus, I can't believe it's got to this.'

It's Brian.

'John, listen, I want to talk to you . . . I'm confused and I really need to see you. I want to know what happened. Why didn't you stick up for me? I never did anything to you to deserve being treated like this . . . What did I do? I just wanna know, that's all. Losing your bottle was bad enough, for fuck's sake, but now you just stand by while they chuck me out of the band? It's not fair, John, and you fucking know it's not. I mean, I know we don't have as much success these days – not like we used to have before and all that – and I know we've had our problems but it doesn't mean you had to sit and watch while they fucking got *rid* of me, does it? Huh? And who was it? Who decided? The label, right? I mean, it must've been. I hope it was the fucking label, you know, 'cos if I ever find out someone pushed the others into doing this I'm gonna make whoever it was fucking *regret* it, I am: I'm not joking.'

Brian is drunk. The ends of his sentences descend into slurred jumbles, the sibilant sounds drawn out into thick wet hisses. At one point he starts to sob; mawkish snivelling abbreviated by long sniffs. This monologue continues for several minutes, eventually disintegrating into an incoherent stream of seemingly random words.

I let the tape run on. There are a few other messages – several from the Dahlias, and one from the band's label congratulating John on an ecstatic review. As they play back, I reach into the jiffy bag to see whether there is a letter, something that might identify who sent this to me. Nothing.

Then another message from Brian plays out on the tape. It sounds as if he's calling from a mobile. I can hear the sound of an engine in the background, growing and then fading out as a car passes by.

'John – fucking pick up! Come on, man, I *know* you're in there – I saw you just go in. I'm right outside. Look out the window – I'm waving, look. *Look!* There's no point hiding – I'm not going away until I've spoken to you, you understand? Come on, dammit, pick up. I just want to, I don't know . . . we've gotta talk or something. It's just . . . it's just that I don't understand what's going on, why this is all *happening* to me like this. Do you know – have you got any *idea* – how humiliating this is for me? I'll tell you.' A pause, and I can hear a can being spiked. 'It's got to the stage where I can't even pick up my phone 'cos it's some fucking stupid journalist asking me how it *feels*. How it *FEELS*? As if I could explain it so they'd understand – but of course they'd call it sour grapes or wounded pride or something stupid. They won't understand. They don't understand why I'm so upset, because you fucking made me swear not to tell anyone.'

He carries on, ranting futilely for five minutes, the end of his monologue dissolving into ragged sobs just before the tape runs out, choking him off mid-sentence. I feel awful for Brian, but then a sense of foreboding settles in. I can see how bad this all looks.

This almost looks like a confession.

Should I be calling the police?

DINNER WITH THE COHENS

Cohen and his wife, Beth, have a two-bedroom house in Wapping, a twenty-minute walk from the office. Beth works on the trading floor of a City bank and earns more than Cohen and me combined. Her Christmas bonus last year was three times my salary. They're probably the richest couple I know but they are probably also the nicest, so it's impossible to feel anything other than pleased for them both.

As I walk the short distance along Bishopsgate I'm

thinking about those messages Brian left on the tape. I can't get them out of my head. They could be very easily construed as threats. In the present circumstances – Brian already being a person with an axe to grind, if what Martin Valentine said at the funeral was true – that kind of thing will leap him to the top of the police's list of suspects if they decide French didn't die by his own hand.

I'm not sure what I should do with the tape.

Take it to the police? Confront Brian? Or sit on it?

I arrive at their house and we enjoy a pleasant meal, although my thoughts are elsewhere. Eventually, Beth goes upstairs to check on their two-year-old, Michael.

Cohen and I finish our coffee at the half-cleared table, a candle flickering between us.

We somehow bring up Rachel Delgardo.

'I hear you took her out for a drink.'

'Let's not talk about that. I think I made a fool of myself.'

'She seems sweet.'

'She is.'

'And pretty.'

'Can't argue with that.'

'So – you interested?'

I'm nonplussed. I haven't told Cohen about Hannah.

'I'm a one-woman man,' I say.

He smiles.

We talk for another twenty minutes, all the time I get the sense we're both waiting to broach a more important subject. This is conversational sparring: gentle feinting and jabbing, and waiting for the right moment. I get there first.

'I want to tell you something,' I say, 'but you have to swear you'll keep it between us.'

He smiles sympathetically. He looks like he knows what I want to say. 'Go on.'

'You remember how two documents I was working on went missing?'

He looks disappointed. Maybe he was expecting something else. 'Yes,' he says.

'I found one of them in a drawer in the Dork's office. He took it.'

'Really?'

'And then, in the middle of my presentation, Wilson comes out with this half-finished version of the agreement he must've stolen too. It got sent to the client – I told them it must've been sent by the Dork after he nicked it, but when I went to show them where I'd found the other one he'd taken it out and got rid of it.'

'Jesus, Daniel, why'd he want to do something like that?'

'Isn't it obvious? He takes the briefing note I was working on and then deletes it off the system so I can't give Wilson the advice she wanted before her meeting yesterday. So I'm on her shit list straight away. Then he sends the half-finished agreement off, knowing that when the client complains that'll be the end of my chances of making partner, at least as far as Wilson's concerned.'

'You think he'd go that far? I know he's ambitious, but . . . I mean.'

'What?'

'Look, don't jump to any conclusions. Maybe there's another explanation.'

'You're kidding me?'

'Maybe he just found your papers somewhere and was planning to give them back to you?'

'Come on, David. They were in his *drawer*.'

'And then they weren't.'

'Whose side're you on?'

'I'm just saying—'

'What about the draft agreement being sent to the client?'

'You ask your secretary about that?'

'No fucking way. She's too *good* to make a mistake like that. It's *him*. He's sabotaged my chances of making partner.'

'Then why hasn't he done that to me, too? Or Caroline Lewis?'

I can't answer that.

THE REAL REASON FOR DINNER

The evening proceeds. We drink whisky and listen to jazz. It's still obvious Cohen wants to bring up some topic of conversation himself, but is reluctant to do it. Beth has made herself scarce again; I get the impression her frequent absences during this evening are part of a prior arrangement made with her husband. She has provided him with opportunities to talk to me alone that he hasn't yet taken up. And I've had the feeling he's been beating around the same bush for the last twenty minutes.

'What is it?' I ask. 'It's obvious you want to say something.'

'Am I that transparent?'

'You've been itching to get something off your chest.'

'Well, I—'

'Is it the American job? You've decided to take it?'

'It's not that,' he says. 'And, no, I haven't decided what I'm going to do about that yet. Still weighing up the pros and cons.'

'Something with you and Beth?'

'No. Everything's fine.'

'Dawkins? Something else at work?'

'No.'

'So?'

'It's . . . well, ah, shit, this isn't an easy thing for me to bring up.'

'Go on,' I prompt. 'I won't be offended.'

He takes a slow breath. 'OK. Look, I've been wanting to talk to you about this for a while, but it's not something you can bring up in the office.'

'So you asked me over here to do it?'

'Well, yes,' he says, 'partly for that. The thing is—'

'Go on.'

'The thing is, I've noticed you've been drinking a lot recently. Not just social drinking but full-on, all-day heavy drinking. It isn't like you – I just wanted to know if everything was all right with you?'

I have a spurt of indignation. 'Have you been talking to Wilson?'

'About what?'

'Like you don't know.'

'You've lost me.'

'Have you told her I've been drinking in the office?'

'No – course not.'

'So it's coincidental that Wilson tells me yesterday she knows I've been drinking in the office, and you ask me about it today.'

'Daniel, I haven't said anything to anyone, I swear.'

'It's none of your business anyway. And it's out of line you trying to intrude like this,' I explode.

'I'm *not* trying to intrude,' he says. 'I'm just worried about you. I mean, drinking in the office – that's hardly normal, is it? There was that carton of wine and then I found a whisky bottle today.'

'You've been going through my drawers?'

'Come on,' he says, 'you're in no position to criticize me for that. You did the same thing to the Dork. And at least *my* motives were good ones.'

'Frankly,' I say brusquely, getting up off the sofa, 'I can't believe you're trying to butt in like this.'

'It's not just me, Dan,' he says. 'Rachel mentioned that you got hammered when you took her out. Don't look so pissed off – she only made a jokey comment about it – but the fact she said anything at all ought to be a warning to you.'

'I'm not pissed off. I just think you snooping around like this is out of line.'

'Come on, any friend'd do the same thing.'

'Bollocks they would. Nosing around in my private life doesn't seem to be a very friendly thing to do at all. Telling a partner about it's even worse.'

'I didn't tell her.'

He sighs and starts to pace the room. We're both standing now. The conversation, at least on my side of it, is already out of control. Tension crackles in the air between us. I'm close to an outburst.

'I *knew* you'd react like this,' Cohen says. 'That's exactly why this has been so difficult to do.'

'Excuse *me* for making your life awkward,' I snap.

'Beth had to persuade me to bring this up.'

'Oh, great – so you *have* told other people, have you? How many others've you told? You mention it to the partners at your interview? "Be careful with Tate, he's a fucking alcoholic"? Did you?'

'Stop being so melodramatic. I haven't told anyone else. What d'you take me for?'

'I'm not sure any more.'

'Come on,' he says. 'Be reasonable. It's not like I've

got so many friends in the office that I can afford to throw my best ones away.'

'Well, you've got one less to worry about *now*,' I say.

I know this is theatrical, and that I'll regret it, but in the heat of the moment it's the automatic thing to say. I snatch my coat from the banister and shrug myself into it.

'Ignoring it won't make it go away,' he says. 'If you can't talk to me, for God's sake talk to *someone*.'

EMBARRASSMENT

I stand in the street outside Cohen's house for five minutes, smoking a fag and trying to calm down, smoke and warm breath clouding in front of my face. The flash of irritation at being interrogated has been replaced by a crushing weight of embarrassment that I've reacted so petulantly. I'm trying not to think about the apology I'm going to have to make to him in the office tomorrow.

And even an apology won't seal off this subject. There will still stand between us our unfinished conversation. Is Cohen right: am I drinking too much? That will have to be discussed before we can return our friendship to its usual footing. I drop the cigarette into the gutter and grind the cherry tip under the sole of my shoe.

This is all I need. Now I'm starting to doubt myself. At the corner of a junction ahead the warm golden glow from the windows of a pub casts a latticed square of light onto the snow. Music is playing and I can hear laughter. I'd like to order a pint or two and breathe in some second-hand smoke. Zipping up my coat I trudge through the drifts towards it.

SCOTT DOLAN'S GUEST LIST

World's Greatest Showbiz Column

RUSSELL CROWE at an exclusive gym in posh Chelsea.

BRAWL AT GLAMOUR FUNERAL
Brian Fey attacks ex-friends

As our EXCLUSIVE picture shows, EX-BLACK DAHLIA **Brian Fey** went loco yesterday at the funeral of **John French**. Fey PUNCHED ex-bandmate **Martin Valentine** and was RESTRAINED by the Dahlias' new singer, hunky **Sean Darbo**.

Stud Sean, 27, said: 'I guess he's under a lot of pressure what with his career going down the toilet but that's no excuse for what he did.' What Fey DIDN'T know was that heart-throb Sean is a black belt in kung-fu.

A witness told me: 'Sean tried to calm things down, but Fey wasn't having any of it. So Sean hit him. Someone else dragged Fey away.'

Fey's recent behaviour has been worrying. On Tuesday he attacked a journo from music rag, the *NME*. If this is all a plan for publicity, it's not working: yesterday his new album fell to 97 in the charts.

RONAN KEATING forced to cut short his holiday to Caribbean because of Hurricane Violet. CALISTA FLOCK-HART was also on the same island.

Friday

AND SO TO BED

I wake up cold and sore. I look around. It looks like I've managed to make it inside the communal lobby on the ground floor, but that's it. My key protrudes from the lock above my head, still unturned. I've been asleep under the post boxes, leaning against the clammy unfinished bricks with my head half in the pot where the anaemic cactus plant lives. My muscles are locked together from the sheer cold. I try to stretch out.

My attention is drawn down, beneath my chin, by a rancid odour. I find I've been sick down the front of my suit. It's coagulated there in thick, gelatinous chunks; I'm lucky I didn't choke. I only picked this suit up from the cleaners the other day, and I have no alternatives save a mauve mistake I bought for my unsuccessful interview at Cambridge ten years ago. I'm not even sure I'll be able to get into it these days.

'Morning,' says Hodgson, stepping gingerly over my splayed legs.

'Morning,' I reply, feeling utterly ridiculous.

'Lost your key again?'

'Nope,' I say. 'Here it is, in the lock. Just forgot to turn it this time.'

'What's happened to your suit?'

I try to laugh it off. I'm beginning to realize I'm feeling very ill indeed.

AN UNCERTAIN DIAGNOSIS

I haven't been to the doctor for months. My last check-up? – I couldn't tell you. Elizabeth had made the appointment for me and left a reminder on the answer-phone.

'Mr Tate. We haven't seen you here for a while.'

'I've been busy at work.'

The bruise on my head is examined; it is prodded and poked until the doctor satisfies himself that it is healing. He looks down at my notes, and then back up at me.

'And how are you? Generally, I mean. Everything all right?'

'I'm fine, feeling great.'

'You don't look great.'

'Bit of a hangover. Nothing to worry about.'

'Do you drink much?'

'No more'n anybody else.'

'How much?'

'A bottle here and there.'

'Do you know what the recommended alcohol intake is for someone like you?'

'No.'

'No more than, say, three glasses of wine a day. Together with two days a week when you don't drink any alcohol.'

'Well, I don't drink anywhere near as much as that, not normally.'

'In that case I'll just give you a quick check-up and then you can be on your way.'

The usual: height and weight, blood pressure and pulse, light shone into the eyes, a barrage of questions all answered 'No'.

The doctor looks at my notes, then addresses me quizzically. 'Would you mind if I did a quick test?'

'What for?'

'Just routine.'

He takes my hand and holds a small black box against the tip of my finger.

'This won't hurt.'

He presses a button. There is a sharp prick and a bud of blood forms. He wipes the blood onto a glossy strip of thin paper and puts it into a machine. After twenty seconds the machine bleeps; he checks the screen.

He frowns: 'How've you been feeling lately?'

'I told you, great.'

'No excessive thirst?'

Just the booze; best keep that to myself. 'No.'

'Mood changes? Any nausea? Vomiting?'

'No. Everything's fine.'

He rubs his chin. 'I'd like you to come back in a couple of days. I want to take some blood and run a few more tests. Best to be sure.'

'Of what?'

'Your blood sugar's a little outside where it ought to be. I'd like to test you for diabetes.'

'Diabetes?'

'I saw from your notes that your father had it. It's not unusual for it to be passed on. It can set in quickly and you don't want to take chances with it.'

Diabetes?

'You're kidding.'

'Don't worry about it, it's probably nothing. Stop off at the desk on your way out and ask Cheryl to book you in for thirty minutes on Tuesday. We'll have this checked out in no time.'

THE NET CLOSES IN

Cohen isn't in our office when I finally make it in. I check that with Elizabeth; he has a meeting with Richard Whiteley and Carol Vorderman for most of the morning. I have two client meetings scheduled for today, so I can probably arrange my time so that our contact is minimal, if any. The shame of last night's humiliation is still fresh, and I'd rather have the weekend to put my thoughts in order. I'm still angry, mostly with myself, and the last thing I want is another – maybe worse – argument.

'Have you heard the news?' Elizabeth says. 'The police've said they're close to arresting someone with something to do with that John French's death.'

Apprehensive: 'It's not suicide, then?'

'Well, they're arresting someone, so I suppose it can't be.'

'Did they say who it was?'

'Not really. They said something about a new lead – that sort of thing – and that they expected to have someone in custody before the end of the weekend.'

I slide the fresh bottle of whisky I've bought into my desk drawer – after taking a couple of mouthfuls.

A VERBAL WARNING

My phone is blinking red with a call-me-back message. It's from Wilson. I'm feeling too numbed to worry or to think about waiting to call her back, so I dazedly dial her number.

'What in the *hell* did you think you were playing at yesterday?' she bellows as soon as the call connects. 'I had Trish Parkes on the telephone for over half an hour complaining about the work you sent over to her.'

'Dawkins stole the original—' I begin.

'No, no, I'm not listening to that cock-and-bull story

again, Tate. You've made a very serious mistake this time. She's threatening to go elsewhere. Mr Hunter is livid, of course, and he insisted you be removed from the matter at once. But I'd decided to do that already.'

To my surprise I'm actually relieved by this. It's not the way I would have chosen to finish my involvement on the file, but at least I don't have to worry about it any more.

'This isn't the first time I've had to apologize for your mistakes. I've given you the benefit of the doubt before. But now I'm beginning to wonder if you've got the skills for this job.'

'I'm sorry,' I say, devoid of feeling.

She pauses; I can almost picture her steaming.

'I'm too busy to deal with this today. Call my secretary and arrange an appointment with me on Monday.'

When I put the phone down my ears are ringing.

THE FINAL HUMILIATION

Things get even worse.

At 11.15, Fulton pays me a visit.

'Daniel,' he says awkwardly, perching on the edge of Cohen's empty desk. 'There's something we have to discuss.'

This absolutely *has* to be bad. I've never seen him looking so uncomfortable.

'We're all a little worried about what happened yesterday, obviously. We think you might've been putting yourself under too much pressure. I know you've been working very hard.'

'I'm fine,' I protest.

'I've got some rather bad news. Well, I say bad, but maybe it's for the best in the long run. I've just had a long conference call with Davey MacHale and the directors at Mr Fey's record label. I've dictated a detailed attendance note, and of course you're more than welcome to look at it and discuss it with me, if you want. But the short version is this – they want you to step aside from the case.'

Because it's the reaction Fulton expects, and because it won't do what's left of my employment prospects any favours to reveal how far I've fallen into the dull funk of fatalism, I manage to reach down for some jaded umbrage. '*What for?*' I ask.

'It's not so much a matter of what you've done *wrong*,' Fulton explains, 'but more what you *haven't* done. I think they feel there's been a breakdown of communication of some kind. They've lost confidence in us and I think they'd rather someone else took up the reins.'

'Who?'

He coughs, awkwardly. 'Oliver Dawkins is taking things forward from here.'

'Dawkins?' This time my dismay is 100 per cent genuine. '*Dawkins?*'

Apparently he's met Mr MacHale several times. They got on rather well from what I can understand. Mr MacHale requested him especially when we spoke yesterday.'

'Dawkins doesn't know anything about the Dahlias. I mean, he hasn't got a *clue*.'

'I'm not sure that's fair. I've just been in to see him, actually. He's just gone out and bought all of their records.'

'So, when am I off the case?'

'Well, as of now actually. We're reassigning you to help Jonathan Williams with the discovery exercise he's doing. I think his work'll benefit from a little supervision and because of this you'll obviously have the time to give him that. Plus it'll give you some time away from the front lines, as it were. I think it might be just what you need.' He stands and straightens out his shirt. 'I'd like you to go around and talk to Oliver now. I want to make sure that the transfer's as seamless as possible.'

Before he goes, Fulton mentions a small matter that he'd like me to take care of for him. A failing star, only recently the subject of lurid tabloid allegations relating to his sexual preferences, wants us to find out who owns the copyright to *Runaround*. He wants to stage a revival – Channel 5, apparently, are interested.

And so the punishment begins.

WINNER TAKES IT ALL

I sit and seethe for ten minutes after Fulton leaves. I can't believe this is happening. Now I find myself regretting Cohen's absence. I need someone to talk this one out with, someone to remind me how petty and pointless this firm can be, and how there really is no need to get steamed up about it. It's just a job, right? Don't take it personally. But he isn't here and so, as I collect the double-armful of correspondence and document folders I've accumulated since I started Brian's case, and head over to Dawkins' desk, I'm probably not in the diplomatic or constructive mood Fulton was suggesting he'd like me to be in.

The Dork is already preparing for his new case. A pile of CDs is arranged on his desk. He's watching a documentary on the history of the Dahlias when I stomp into his office. He stabs the remote control in the direction of the video, and pauses the tape.

'This,' he says, pointing at the screen – Brian frozen at the edge of an anonymous stage – 'is surprisingly good. They write some catchy tunes, don't they?'

'Happy now?' I ask, dropping the folders on the floor next to his desk. Loose papers spill out around his feet.

' "Happy"?' he says, placing his tortoiseshell glasses on the desk.

'You've been after the case for weeks, haven't you? Don't think I didn't notice.'

'Settle down,' he says.

'You couldn't wait, could you? I bet you were *really* cut up to see me land the firm's best case.'

His tone hardens. 'Listen – I was merely chatting with Mr Fey's manager after the funeral, and we got on very well. That's all there is to say. The fact that you couldn't handle the case properly hasn't got anything to do with me. Your incompetence is hardly *my* fault, is it?'

'So it's unfair to say you've been angling to get me off this case?'

'Unfair, paranoid, obsessive,' he says with a sugar-coated smile. 'I *could* go on.'

'You make me sick,' I say. I head for the door.

'I'm just doing what's been asked of me,' he replies. 'Just doing my job.'

As I reach the door, he adds, to my back, 'I had a date last night.'

I shrug. 'I really couldn't care less.'

'It went very well. Rachel really is a *lovely* girl, isn't she? A really good sport.'

'Rachel?' I say.

'You know. Rachel Delgardo. Fulton's new trainee.'

I can't help myself. 'You saw *Rachel* last night?'

'That's right,' he nods. 'She was telling me about you getting drunk when you took her out on Monday. Bad form, Tate. Bad form. Not the way to impress the ladies.'

I try to put the images of Rachel and the Dork out of my mind but they are insidious and I'm only partially successful. I try to imagine what Rachel could possibly find attractive about the Dork. It can't be his looks or his personality. Perhaps she finds the prospect of his imminent promotion to the partnership appealing. Some women are turned on by money and power, I suppose, even the petty influence that junior partners can wield in an office like this.

This prompts a truly terrifying thought, something I should have realized long ago. If (no, check that: *when*) the Dork does become a partner, and assuming I haven't been sacked, I'll almost certainly have to work for him. The office isn't big enough to avoid a particular partner, especially one that shares his legal specialization with you. The prospect of having to take orders from the obsequious little bastard . . . I try not to think about that, too.

MY NEW HOME

I ride the lift down to the basement and find the case room Williams has been cooped up in for the last six months.

I have a morbid desire to look around my new home.

There are no windows. Sunlight filters down through the glass bricks set into the pavement above, slanting through in insipid lozenges. The hallway is full of junk that no one knows where else to dump: sheaves of yellowed, decades-old paper; out-of-date marketing brochures; obsolete computers. This is where broken furniture comes to die. It's a graveyard for office trash.

The rooms around me are murky and depressing. The firm uses the rooms to store closed files and junk but also as space suitable for the undertaking of the document-intensive tasks for which there is no room in the office above.

A light shines from one of the four doorways leading off the hallway. With a heavy tread, I investigate.

Williams is sitting with his back to me, hunched over a table covered with papers. Stacked up to the ceiling along three sides of the room are dozens and dozens of cardboard boxes, each marked with a number in black magic marker. I spot number 312 and stop looking. Williams has one of these boxes on the desk and has pulled out a sheaf of papers from it. As I watch, he goes through each document individually, skim reading at first and then carefully applying adhesive labels to obscure certain passages of text.

Some documents contain information that doesn't have to be disclosed to the other side. His task is to locate this irrelevant or legally privileged material and obscure it before the documents are copied. Then the copies have to be checked. In a case with a lot of documents the task can take months, sometimes even years.

It is apparent that this case is one with a lot of documents.

I can see my life draining away like the last dirty suds sucked down a grotty plughole.

A WORD WITH MY PATRON

I bump into Richard Tanner on the way back to the office.

'Are you OK?' he asks.

'I've been better.'

'Look, I've spoken with Wilson and Fulton. I've heard what's happened. Do you want to talk about it?'

'I don't know, Richard. I'm having some difficulties.'

'Is everything all right at home?'

'Fine.'

'All right, just keep your head down for a week or two. I'll try and smooth things over with the others. You know what Victoria's like – she loses her rag sometimes. She'll cool down. And I'll have a word with Hunter if it comes to that. Now, I've got a big case coming in next week, something juicy for Bruce Forsyth, and if you want it, I'll make sure it comes to you. You won't have to do anything else for either of them – not until you're back to being yourself again. OK?'

'They're gonna fire me, Richard,' I say.

'No, they won't,' he says, although you couldn't call his tone confident. 'Look, we'll say you've been under a lot of pressure. These things happen, Daniel, they happen to the best of us. Leave it to me. I'll talk to them.'

'What about the partnership thing?'

He shakes his head.

'So?'

'It's between David, Oliver and Caroline. Maybe you'll get a chance another time.'

MEDIA ONSLAUGHT

The memory of Brian's messages on French's answer-phone, suppressed by the weight of the morning's tribulations, slips free and bobs to the surface. I try and put it aside. I don't want to have to deal with it now.

Then, in the space of three minutes, my telephone rings twice (I ignore it). Then my mobile, stowed in my briefcase, starts up. I try to ignore the merry ringing tone, and check my mail instead. As I stare dumbly at the screen, trying to shut out the mobile and the tele-phone, both of which are coalescing in a jarring symphony, a new email lands in my inbox. I crawl the cursor across and double-click:

From:	dolan.scott@extravaganza.co.uk
To:	daniel.tate@whitehunter.com
Subject:	Answer your phone

You might as well answer your phones. I'm not going

to go away. I just want to talk. We can make it worth your while.
Scott Dolan

Before I can make a decision, a piercing sensation lances up from my chest. My vision dims, as if someone were lowering a muslin drape over my head. I slap a hand onto my forehead; my temperature has gone through the roof. My heart is jackhammering. The shock leaves me breathless. I regulate my breathing until things return to something like normal and then glug down rancid mineral water from a bottle of Evian that has stood on my shelf for a month.

I'm sweating.

I go to the toilet and dunk my head in a basin of cold water.

I didn't bother booking that return appointment with the doctor. Maybe I should.

COLD SHOULDERED

Still no mail from Hannah. All I want to do is talk to her. I call home to see if Brian is there, in case the girl who called me earlier has called again. There's no reply. Maybe he's moved into a hotel.

Then I have an idea. If Hannah is trying to contact me, maybe I should get proactive and try to find her.

EMPATHOGEN

This past summer, three months before she left, Hannah persuaded me that we should go to Ibiza 'before we both get too old'. I was never one for dance music but I let her talk me into it. We flew to the island, splashed out on a gorgeous hotel room in San Antonio, and had the time of our lives. We did the clubs, got drunk, splashed through the Mediterranean surf, half out of our heads.

At her prompting I scored some Ecstasy from a dealer outside Manumission. Hannah had never popped an E before and I was out of practice; both of us were keen to try.

We draped towels over the lights to soften them, poured a pitcher of iced mineral water, placed a tube of Vicks inhalant and a tray of ice cubes near to hand, lay back, relaxed, swallowed.

An hour passed. Waiting for the rush, talking, her talking just to keep the nerves at bay. The pills kicked in and the world billowed open, as if I'd never seen it like this before. Guilt and worry were instantly obliterated. The office, always at the fringe of my awareness, was atomized. We locked eyes; I could see the virgin rapture in her face and, for a moment, I was jealous. But then the drug softened my own hard edges, unravelled tight knots of tension I had ignored for months, slackened my muscles, loosened my tongue.

I talked on for hours: talking about us, talking about

where we'd been and where we were going, what we wanted. She listened, nodding and smiling sadly.

And then, for three hours, we made love. She smelt of apple blossom and tasted of peaches. It was the best, the most intense, the most rhapsodic revelatory sex I have ever, ever, ever had.

MEMENTO MORI

We slowly came down together. Hannah lay on the bed, her back to me. I pressed myself tight against her skin, clasped my hands around her waist and fitted my knees into the space behind hers. The neon of Calle San Vicente rose and fell, sparking against the glass and colouring the ceiling. As I stroked her red hair, full of that smell of lemons that still conjures her today, I noticed a single tear roll down her cheek.

'What's the matter?' I asked.

'Nothing,' she said. 'Just emotional, that's all.'

CHASING FAME

Thirty minutes later and I'm standing opposite the main entrance to the Sanderson. I'm guessing Hannah is staying here with Haines. Maybe she was out when I came by on Monday. It won't take long to check.

As I'm summoning the courage to make an entrance,

not quite knowing what I'm going to say, Haines comes out of the hotel lobby. I freeze. He's wearing a leather jacket with combat trousers and shades and has a back-pack slung over one shoulder. He's already too far away from the entrance to retrace his steps by the time he spots me. Terror chills his face and he starts into a sprint. Perplexed, I give pursuit.

'Stop,' I call out. 'I just want a word with you.'

He speeds up, dodging pedestrians as he powers up the road.

Why are we running? I only want to talk to him.

A delivery man pushes a trolley of boxes through the door of a shop. Haines swerves to avoid him, skidding on an icy patch. He almost falls flat, one hand touching the ground, to keep him from sprawling.

'Haines,' I holler. 'I just want to talk.'

He continues running. We pass a tinted window and for a moment I catch my reflection speeding across the glass: hair blown back against my crown, sweat washing down my forehead into fanatical eyes, lips pulled back to bare my clenched teeth.

'Vinny,' I shout.

He cuts across a slow-moving queue of traffic, horns honking, and clambers over a fence into a park. I follow, but fifteen metres behind, my legs sinking up to the ankle in the drifts of snow. We continue like this for several minutes, both struggling through the heaped-up snow. Haines is athletic and much faster than me – his legs pump like pistons in and out of the snowdrift – and now he's reached a path dosed with grit. I'm starting to lose ground.

As we approach a statue he risks a glance over his shoulder. I'm gasping for air, stumbling like a drunk, just about ready to give up now. His attention distracted, he doesn't see the tiny dog scampering onto the path to fetch a stick thrown by its owner. He trips over it and hits the ground hard. When I reach him, wheezing from the exertion of the chase, his bloody knees are showing through his ripped trousers. He raises his hands to ward me off; his palms are bleeding too, some of the skin scraped away, and studded with tiny stones and rock salt from the path.

I wipe sweat out of my eyes. My heart feels ready to explode. The freezing air throbs as I draw it down into my lungs in hungry gulps.

'What're you running for?' I pant at him.

'Please don't hurt me,' he whimpers.

'What're you talking about? I just want to talk to you.'

'I'm really sorry about Hannah,' he garbles. 'I didn't know anything about you – she said it was finished – I'd've never done anything if I'd've known.'

'Where is she?'

'Filming.'

'So why are you here?'

'I'm not in any of the scenes they're shooting today.'

'Where's she living? With you at that hotel?'

'No – her own place.'

'What?'

'I think she's living with a friend.'

'Where?'

'I don't know, man – I swear it – I've never been there and she hasn't told me – she just moved in last week – she's renting with a friend – she was in a hotel for a couple of months before that – that's God's own truth.'

'All right,' I say. 'Thanks.'

'That's it?' he asks. 'That's all you wanted?'

I turn to leave him sprawled out on the path.

He scrabbles to his feet. Now that I'm leaving, he finds some chutzpah.

'You're crazy,' he calls out after me. 'I'm going to call your boss about this. You're a frigging lunatic. I'm gonna get you fired.'

The emptiest of empty threats.

I ignore him and head for the road.

THE REASON BRIAN WAS
LATE LAST SUNDAY

Back at the office, the air outside is cold and my breath is steaming damply in front of my face. I take a stroll around the Square; I need time to think. I'm still agitated after that chase with Haines. As I'm completing my slow circuit, my attention is drawn to a familiar bald dome: Dawkins, walking in close file with Fulton towards the office. Both of them are carrying cardboard cups from Starbucks. I press myself back against the dark-glass windows at the side of the lobby and watch as they stroll in together, the picture of easy comradeship, joshing together like old friends.

I imagine the things – all violent, all illegal, all very cathartic – I would like to do to the Dork right now.

I'm still thinking dark thoughts when Scott Dolan takes my elbow in his right hand. His grip is firm and insistent and he has a determination in his eyes that wasn't there before. He's holding an envelope in his spare hand.

'Hello again,' he says. 'You're a hard man to get hold of.'

'I've got nothing to say to you.'

'I'm going to show you something and then I'm going to go away. And I won't bother you again.'

'Why do I find that impossible to believe?'

He hands me the envelope. 'Just take a look at the pictures in there and tell me what you think. That's all. Go on – open it.'

'What is it?'

'Open it.'

I undo the envelope and pull out several glossy 10 by 8s, long shots taken by someone with a telephoto lens. The photos show Brian Fey standing outside John French's house. I recognize his fire-engine red front door from the newspapers. Brian is standing at the foot of the steps leading up to the door in one shot, and at the top of the steps in another. He looks agitated, his face turned to the camera, cigarette in hand. Another photo shows him with his arm cocked, apparently while knocking on the door. In another shot the door is open and the inside of the hallway is visible. Brian has a look of surprise on his face, maybe because French has finally succumbed to his siege. In the final picture Brian is, mid-step, halfway across the threshold. I turn the prints over. On the back of each, someone has inscribed the date and the time: they're all labelled last Sunday, each falling between 5.28 and 5.30. This is around the time – give or take 20 minutes – that the pathologist suggests John French died.

'What're these?' I ask superfluously. I know exactly what they are.

'That's Brian Fey – ex-rockstar, your client and soon to be chief suspect in what's about to become a rather notorious murder inquiry – stood outside the door of the victim right around the time the police think he was killed. One of our freelance snappers was tailing Fey last week. We got these back from him. Interesting, aren't they? You see the date and the time on the back? Just before French died. Listen, no bullshit, these're going to the police first thing on Monday. I *can't* hold on to these. Withholding evidence, you know – I'd get into all sorts of trouble. Then we're going to run them on our front page on Tuesday. I just wondered whether you wanted to make a comment before we do? It's a chance – a *last* chance – to save your own reputation.

Brian's in the shit, for sure, but it's not going to look good for you to be seen to've been working for a convicted murderer, is it? Professionally, I mean – careerwise. All kinds of stuff could rub off on you. Onto your firm.'

'Is that a threat?'

'Course not. We're just giving you a chance to fire off a pre-emptive strike.'

'Why would I wanna do that? Brian didn't kill him.'

'You don't sound so sure now.'

'I still haven't got anything to say.'

'Sure? No second chances this time.'

I articulate each word slowly and distinctly: 'No – comment.'

'All right. I'm just gonna say this: my editor's killed the piece I was doing on John French. Not the right atmosphere for the story I had in mind, he says. And I've been doing the fucking Guest List for three fucking years, Danny, three years of my life wasted peddling that toxic shit. The John French exposé was my ticket to proper journalism. So if I can't get him, I'm fucking well gonna nail Fey instead. And anyone else who's caught up in it. Just so you know.'

I walk back into the office.

'Last chance, Danny.'

I keep walking. This time Dolan doesn't try to follow me.

REVIEWING THE EVIDENCE

I spend the rest of the afternoon playing the answerphone tape back, again and again, trying to work myself into Brian's mind, trying to figure out whether he'd be capable of killing John French. Through the booze, the drunken sobbing, his voice has a hollow note of despondency about it – of finality, a quality I hadn't noticed before in him. The thought begins to coalesce in my mind that maybe he *could* have done this. I hardly know him, after all, so how can I say what he's capable of?

Who sent that tape to me? I call the guys in the mailroom in case it was delivered by one of the courier firms that bike our stuff around the City. But they've got no record of receiving the package. I call reception to see if someone brought it in by hand; no one recalls accepting it. I'm at a complete loss.

Whoever it was, he or she obviously had access to French's house before the police got there, although these messages could have been recorded weeks ago.

Dolan's pictures, though, were timed just before the pathologist said French was hanged. Maybe Dolan faked the dates and times to reel me in, but something tells me that's not the case.

This I do know: whoever sent those tapes to me is someone who bears a grudge against Brian.

What should I do? Confront him? Set out the evidence against him and demand an explanation? Go to the police and tell them everything, confessing to my own unwitting complicity?

A thought suddenly dawns on me: perhaps Brian has duped me with the story of his insolvency, winning my pity and trust, my co-operation in a scheme for him to hide out from the police. I mean, how realistic is it to believe that he – Brian Fey, for fuck's sake – didn't have enough money to check into a hotel, or that he didn't have *somewhere* else to stay?

Impossible.

Now I'm actually *thinking* about this, subjecting it to some rational analysis rather than letting the current carry me along in its wake, little epiphanies start exploding in my head. Brian might have a bank account hidden somewhere that he hasn't told us about.

Perhaps he's been readying himself to make a break for it. Perhaps I've committed a crime, albeit an inadvertent one, in abetting him in his escape. I was too starstruck to recognize what was going on. I was too stupid. And now I've been involved in a criminal conspiracy.

I wish Cohen was here. Between us, we'd know what to do.

And then I remember: Brian had a bruise and a cut on his head the night French's body was found. Evidence of a struggle? A fight?

I rest my hand on the receiver, framing what I should say now to the police. But I can't pick it up.

WITH FRIENDS LIKE THESE

Then, without warning, I feel sick again. Another wave of nausea. I rush to the toilet and kneel on the wet floor of a cubicle, my mouth aimed over the bowl and my hands braced against the cistern, waiting to see if I'm going to throw up. I'm breathing deeply, trying to calm my head, and half-listening to the sounds of someone zipping up in the cubicle next-door to mine, and someone else pissing against the china of one of the urinals. The air is freighted with the fragrance of lemon disinfectant, with deeper, more primal odours lurking beneath it. The smell of other people's business.

A toilet flushes and a cubicle door opens. I hold my breath.

'Cohen,' says a voice from the direction of the urinals.

'Dawkins,' Cohen replies.

'How're you? Haven't seen you for a while.'

Cohen: 'Not bad.'

Dawkins: 'Busy?'

Cohen: 'Always. You know how it is. Everything has to be done yesterday.'

The Dork, much too friendly for my liking: '*Tell* me about it. Listen, I've been meaning to ask you something. Is Tate all right? I mean, is he well? He isn't looking that healthy at the moment, know what I mean?'

'Not really.'

'I'm not butting in, I was just wondering. He looks so – I don't know – so *pasty*, washed-out. I thought you might know, seeing as you share an office with him.'

'Well, I haven't noticed anything.'

'You heard about that nonsense yesterday? Bringing the partners up to search my office. I mean, *please* – what does he take me for?'

'I heard about that.'

'He'll never make partner here. Not after yesterday.'

'Come on, that was just a one-off. He made a mistake, that's all.'

'He accused me of *theft*, David.'

Cohen says nothing.

'And his work's been going down the pan – so I hear.'

I'm straining my ears and not even breathing.

'Listen, Oliver – I don't think we should be sticking our noses into his problems. It's best if we just leave things alone, don't you think?'

'So he *has* got problems – you admit it.'

'He's under pressure. The Fey case really took it out of him in the run-up to the trial. He was working all hours for a couple of months putting it all together. I thought he did brilliantly with the shitty material he had to work with. You *know* he's a genius. But it was always going to be a no-win case. But that's it: it's just pressure of work. And we all have *that*.'

'Well, his workload got lighter yesterday. The Fey

case isn't something he's gonna have to worry about any more. He's been taken off it.'

'*Really?*'

I don't like Cohen's tone – too scandalized – and I don't like the fact he's still talking to Dawkins. A real friend would have finished the conversation as soon as the Dork tried to start it. He wouldn't have anything further to do with him. And Cohen is supposed to hate Dawkins as much as I do.

But still they carry on.

Dawkins: 'It's my case now.'

'What d'you mean? I haven't heard anything. Daniel hasn't mentioned anything like that to me, although I suppose I haven't seen him yet today.'

'It's true. He got the hook this morning. Apparently the client complained to Hunter and he was completely *furious*. Hunter called Fulton in a rage, according to him – I was just talking to him about that on the way into the office. If you believe what Hunter says, the client was threatening to sue us for negligence. Can you believe that? The partners took evasive action – they're not going to charge the client anything for the work Tate's done. They're taking a *massive* hit on it. Tens of thousands of pounds. I've been asked to see if I can salvage anything from the mess he's made, although I have to say, on first impressions, it doesn't look good.'

'I had no idea,' Cohen says.

I can't *believe* he's still talking.

Now Cohen's saying something else, completely

unable to shut the fuck up, doubtless blabbing about my so-called drinking problem, but the sudden blowing of the hand-dryer obliterates the rest of the conversation. I strain my ears but I can't catch a word. When the dryer finally stops, the silence suggests that they've both gone.

Finally, at last, I'm sick.

TIME FOR A CHANGE OF SCENE?

Back in my room, I start to wonder: would it be such a bad thing to lose my job? Maybe this is the opportunity I've been waiting for. The motivation I've been lacking for too long, the impetus to do something worthwhile with my life. Something different. The clean break.

As I sit at my desk, looking sadly around at the beige walls that have surrounded me for nine hours a day, five days a week, an intention to do something drastic coalesces in my mind.

What have I got left here? Nothing. My ex-girlfriend hates me. My ex-client might be a murderer. My best friend has betrayed me. I'm going to lose my job and, anyway, do I really still enjoy it? I've got no money and it's just a matter of time before the bank repossesses a flat I can no longer afford. I have no ties, nothing to dampen the sudden enthusiasm for change that is settling over me.

There's no reason for me to stay here.

My mood brightens as ideas start to form.

I'll need funds. I place a call to my financial adviser and ask him to cash in my life assurance policy.

HOLIDAY MONEY

I find one of the letters we received from Pattersons, the firm acting for the Dahlias, and take it to the photo-copier. By placing a sheet of paper over the body of the letter, then carefully positioning both sheets on the plate and copying it onto prime quality engrossment paper, I produce decent fakes of their blank letterhead. I slot them into the printer tray.

I start typing.

The first three letters, one addressed to each of the three banks administering accounts on Brian's behalf, purport to be from the solicitors acting for the Dahlias. I tell them the Freezing Orders securing Brian's accounts have been discharged. Dealings with the accounts may now take place without restriction.

These letters are complemented by the second series of three, these also sent to Brian's banks. These are transfer requests, instructing the contents of the accounts to be transferred immediately. I sign the letters in Brian's name, tracing over a signature he gave us when we opened his file. After a couple of practices, it looks authentic. I stick a second-class stamp to each envelope, ensuring that the first series of fakes will have had time to arrive and be processed first.

I reckon I've got until next Wednesday to make the arrangements for receiving the money.

NOTHING TO SAY

Cohen comes into the office.

'Hi,' he says.

I don't reply. My brows are clenched hard and I can feel the line of my jaw hardening as my teeth grind against each other.

I pick up my briefcase and leave the room.

BECAUSE NOW IT ALL MAKES SENSE

Outside, stomping footprints into the snow as I wait for a taxi, I begin to put it all together. I can see what's been going on. Suddenly it's obvious. I've been a fool. Everyone's been taking advantage of me. Cohen and Dawkins have been conspiring.

Maybe Rachel's involved too. Maybe she got me drunk on Monday so I messed up in court. What's to say the Dork didn't give her instructions before I met her? She admitted herself she'd been doing some work for him earlier in the day. She's certainly ambitious; maybe she sees Dawkins as a better bet than me.

It all stacks up. All the pieces fit.

Cohen keeps an eye on me in the office and passes information to the Dork. I can imagine more secret assignations in the toilets, whispering gossip and noxious rumours. Dawkins passes everything on to Fulton and Wilson and Renwick, anyone who needs to have his or her opinion of me revised.

Meanwhile Rachel gets me so smashed I mess up an important court hearing. And the Dork has been poisoning Davey's mind against me – at the concert, at the funeral – criticizing me, telling him that losing the case was all my fault, that I'm negligent, that I'm a liability. He complains to Fulton and it's the final straw.

I can't *believe* I didn't see this earlier.

And why is Cohen doing this – my so-called best friend? Cohen knows Dawkins is a shoo-in for the partnership. Cohen knows he doesn't stand a chance against him. Maybe the Dork has promised to put a good word in for him to make sure that he gets made up next year.

TRAVEL ARRANGEMENTS

There's no point in waiting around. I need to do this now before I give myself the chance to bottle it and change my mind. I have the taxi stop outside a travel agent's. Inside, I buy a ticket to Rio de Janeiro with the proceeds of my life assurance, a seat on the red-eye leaving early on Wednesday morning.

BRIAN'S PLAN

An eastbound cab headed home. I'm watching the rush hour disperse into the gloaming of the early evening streets, and my mobile rings. The caller ID displays my home number.

'Hello, Brian,' I say slowly.

'Where are you?' he asks.

'Why?' I try to hide the wariness in my reply.

'Because I've got a plan – for tonight.'

'I'm on my way home. I need sleep.'

'Sleep can wait.'

I have no idea how to broach the subject of the tapes and pictures. If Brian figures out that I'm having suspicions about him being involved in French's death, what would he do? If he's already killed once, it would be the easiest thing for him to suffocate me in my sleep, or poison me, or shoot me . . . and no one knows he's staying with me. No one would suspect him if I suddenly disappeared.

'I'm not up for much tonight, Brian,' I say. 'All I want to do is chill out.'

'Come *on* – I was out last night until fuck knows when, but I'm still up for going out again.'

'Where did you go?' I ask suspiciously.

'Just into town. I was upset about what happened at the funeral. Got hammered, not that *that's* anything out of the ordinary. But anyway, the idea for tonight—'

'Listen, I'm not so sure.'

'Let me finish,' he says. 'There's a new club opening tonight, and I've got us both VIP tickets. I thought maybe we could check it out?'

'Don't you ever take it easy?' I ask. 'Is the concept of a quiet night at home *completely* alien to you?'

'There's fun to be had, Dan,' he says. 'We're *not* staying home. I forbid it.'

'I'd rather not. Why don't you—?'

'Enough,' he says theatrically. 'You're coming and that's that.'

I grunt in resignation.

'Oh, and you've got a message on the answerphone,' he adds. 'I was in the bath and I heard it while it was recording. I think it's that girl I spoke to the other day.'

'*Don't touch it.*'

'Easy, man, I wouldn't dream of it.'

Before the conversation concludes I gather that Brian is in the kitchen. I can hear a food processor whirring in the background. And I don't even *have* a food processor.

'Can't you go any faster?' I ask the cabby.

ANSWERPHONE

I fly to the answerphone as soon as I'm through the door. Brian sidles up alongside as the tape spools back and replays:

'Hi, Daniel. It's Hannah. I know we haven't spoken for a while but I need to talk to you. It's very important.

317

I was wondering if we could meet up? How about six-thirty tomorrow, somewhere neutral – let's say Soho. At the Groucho. Is that OK? I'll see you then.'

My first thought: I've missed her call, again. I dial 1471 but she must have withheld the number. I still don't know where to reach her.

My second thought: what could Hannah *possibly* want to see me for?

My third thought: Hannah's the only person who can make me change my mind.

'Sounds positive,' Brian says.

'I doubt it. She probably just wants the rest of her stuff back.'

'Well,' Brian says, 'Saturday night comes around and I'm out of here. I'm not going to get in your way.'

'Where'll you go?' I ask. Perhaps he's ready to disappear. Maybe I should call the police to tip them off.

'Around,' he says. 'I'll be around. I'll crash with Davey for a bit or something. I know I've taken advantage, and I feel bad about it. Don't want to cramp your style with your woman, do I?'

I don't say anything.

'Anyway, if this is my last night here, we're definitely having some fun. I've cooked us a meal – you like steak, don't you? – and then we're going out.'

A NIGHTCLUB, SOMEWHERE,
SOME TIME

Later, after an unpoisoned steak and unpoisoned wine, a dozen drinks, numerous lines of coke and a tab of E each, we hit the town.

Eventually it comes to this: a nightclub somewhere, some time later, that might be Dogstar, Babushkar, Fabric or Subterania, and I'm alone in a booth with Brian, watching the dancefloor, scouting the girls and scoping for dealers, downing more whisky to steady my nerves. Brian suggested this – that we should move on after the party at the new club lost its shine. He said something about the benefits of perpetual motion, of never staying in one place for too long. I was too dazed to pay attention, much less disagree.

My short-term memory: too full of snatches of conversation, glimpsed faces, girls, music, dancing, drink, pills.

We're both drunk. I've been standing rounds for people I've never met, spending money I don't have yet, money that belongs to the Black Dahlias' record label. I've been the life and soul of a dozen different parties. I remember bellowing that drinks were on the house in more than one of the stopovers on our never-ending trip. All I can think of is short-term. And it's all just distraction.

I've been trying to find the right moment to talk to Brian. I don't know where to start. How do you accuse someone of murder? Because that's what I'd be doing – accusing him of hanging someone he once considered his best friend. I can't do it. Maybe I'm too afraid of what he might say. Or what he might do?

Now Brian's talking to me: 'Those videos in the flat,' he slurs, 'of that show – *Skin Trade*? Because of your ex-girlfriend, right?'

Blood colours my cheeks. I don't remember telling Brian that Hannah is on television, much less in which show she appears. It's all too embarrassing. Perhaps he's been watching them, and connected her to the framed picture on top of the TV. I feel discovered, almost ashamed. But I nod.

'I recognized her from the photos in the flat. I've been watching a lot of TV lately. You get to remember the faces.' He squints into his glass, then looks up. 'She's really pretty,' he says. 'I'm not sure if that helps any.'

'Thanks,' I say.

'But doesn't it get to you to see her on the TV? Like, you know, a reminder or something?'

'Not any more,' I say. I feel like telling him that it does bother me. I feel like telling him that watching my ex-girlfriend – the keeper of my heart – kissing Vincent Haines is like having my guts ripped out and fed back to me in raw bloody chunks.

'It's better than nothing,' I say. 'At least it helps me to remember what she looks like.'

Brian nods, thinking. 'That's where we're different,' he says eventually. 'Every time I see John on the TV, it makes me sick. I'm telling you – I hate it. It's like a reminder of all the stuff that's been taken away, how my life's changed, everything I've lost. You don't know what I'd give to bring it all back.'

I don't respond. I'm wondering how far Brian *would* go to bring it back, or what he might be driven to do one day when he drunkenly realized that he couldn't, that it was out of reach for ever.

'But we've got more in common than you think,' he says.

UNUSUAL SYMPTOMS

I don't know why, but I'm finding that I have an almost continual urge to piss. I've been to the toilet about six times already, and here I am again aiming a straw-coloured squirt into the smeared chrome-effect bowl. And I'm getting really bad abdominal cramps, sharp stabbing pains in my gut that seem to come and go without reason. Nothing as bad as the pain I had in the office, but enough to make me wince.

First thing on Monday: a trip to see the doctor. I don't want to be ill while I'm travelling.

3 A.M. AND NOTHING MAKES SENSE

Later still, four or five in the morning, the club is emptying fast, only the last few desperate ravers too wired to notice shuffling on the dancefloor like robots with exhausted batteries, metal shutters half-lowered across the bars, milky streetlight emitting through the open exits. Cleaners starting to dump the spent bottles into black bin-liners, tidying up, removing the evidence.

I'm half-asleep, propped against Brian's shoulder, my eyes feeling as if they've been scoured with bleach and my skin as dry and brittle as filou pastry. Brian clenches his shoulder, stiff with tension, and I look up. All I can think about: how far it is to get back to the flat. Miles – in the full glare of morning. I'll wither and fall to dust like a vampire the moment the dawn light falls on me.

'Come on,' Brian says. 'There's something I want to do.'

BREAKING AND ENTERING

Snow is falling again as a cab takes us through London, into the centre of the City. Brian has given the driver an address in fashionable Shoreditch. I imagine a trendy late-night bar or club, more drinking and drugs. This is not unappealing. My nerves are on edge. They need to be soothed.

'Where're we going?' I ask Brian.

'Patience.'

We stop at a street just off the main road heading east. A crowd of late-night revellers is in evidence, heading towards the bus stops and the night buses. A scrum of hooligans in football shirts stagger across the road, chanting.

'Over here,' Brian says, heading towards a nonde-script side street. I follow. The street is dark and empty. It looks like the warehouses on either side have been converted into loft apartments. So close to the City, I shudder to think how much a place here would cost.

The street smells of money.

Brian checks name-plates, and stops outside the entrance to a low-slung converted warehouse. He pulls out a scrap of paper from his pocket and compares a scribbled address.

'It's in here,' he says.

'What is?'

He doesn't answer. 'Come on,' he says. 'This way.'

'What're we doing?' I ask.

'I just wanna look around.'

'We are *not* breaking in,' I say. 'Out of the question.'

'We're not gonna fucking take anything. Stop worrying.'

He leads me into an alleyway at the side of the building and around to the rear. There is no one around and I suddenly feel very vulnerable. I could be stabbed by him, or strangled, or shot, and my body dumped into the industrial rubbish bin pushed up against the wall. No one would know.

'Up here,' Brian says.

By climbing onto the bin, the thick plastic lid yielding beneath our weight, it's possible to shin up to a ledge underneath a window. Pulling me up onto the ledge beside him, Brian checks the street below for witnesses and then, satisfied, puts a foot through the glass, reaches through and unlatches the window from the inside. He pulls it open and slides through. Teetering on the brink of the ledge, watching the snowflakes slipping through the golden light cast by a lonely streetlight, I have a moment of anxiety that has nothing to do with my vertigo. It passes. I follow him inside.

I find myself on a small landing. Stairs lead down into the gloom below, and three doors face us up ahead. Brian has padded over to one of the doors and has his hand on the handle, slowly opening it.

'What're you doing?' I hiss.

He puts a finger to his lips and gently opens the door. Peering through the dark crack of the doorway, holding up a hand for silence, he scopes the room beyond. I stop breathing and listen, straining my ears for signs of detection. The hubbub from the street outside sounds menacingly loud. Somewhere, the cables and gears of a lift rattle in its hollow shaft. A car horn sounds, muffled by the snow. He goes over to each of the other doors and looks inside.

I stare at him, raising my eyebrows in query.

'No one's in,' he says. He throws a switch and the hall is suddenly lit; I squeeze my eyes shut against the brightness. 'Come on.'

SMASH AND GRAB

The apartment comprises one massive vault-like room with other smaller rooms – bathroom, spare bedroom – leading off the landing. It has a wide-planked oak floor, two-metre-high walls of exposed bricks, iron girders supporting the roof, full-length windows. Brian finds a light switch and throws it.

'Not a bad place,' he approves, taking off his coat and hooking it onto the edge of the door. He picks up a vase from a coffee table and hefts it approvingly in his hand. 'Lots of nice stuff in here.'

'Whose flat is this?' I ask fretfully.

'Sean Darbo.'

He flings the vase against a wall. It smashes loudly.

I yelp, 'What're you doing?' but Brian has already found where the crockery lives.

He flings a stack of plates, Frisbee-style, at another wall. They shatter: explosions of white shards. I watch them clatter to the floor in slow-motion, where they smash again. He reaches up to the top of a free-standing bookshelf and tugs it back towards him. As he dances back out of the way, the shelf comes crashing down onto the floor, spilling books and breaking ornaments around his feet and then itself breaking apart when it hits, the wood tearing and splintering.

Brian moves on to the dining area; there's a ten-seater chrome-and-glass table with gothic-style wrought-iron chairs.

'What're you doing?' I repeat, out of my head with panic, and now almost completely sobered-up.

'I was hoping he might've been in—'

He sweeps a crystal fruit bowl onto the floor. The noise seems impossibly loud.

'I wanted to give him a shock—'

Six long-stemmed wineglasses bounce in pieces off the walls.

'But this'll have to do for now—'

He struggles with one of the heavy chairs and, with it balanced half on his shoulder, tips it forward into the middle of the table. It drops straight through, the glass shattering, fault lines cobwebbing across the surface, and then shards falling out of the frame smash noisily on the floor.

'And I've gotta say – this is making me feel *much* fucking better.'

I should do something to stop this. But I'm hypnotized by his face as he moves on, tipping over the other chairs and then a chaise-longue: naked, unrestrained fury. Was this how he was the evening he visited French? Suddenly fearful, I badly want to leave.

I edge back towards the wall. But, as I'm watching Brian put his coat back on again, I feel a sudden and almost overpowering urge to throw up. I force the vomit back down again and brace myself against a table.

'Are you all right?' Brian asks, slotting the plug into the kitchen sink and then turning on both taps. He comes over to me. 'You look awful. You're sweating.'

'I'm fine,' I say, although I do feel a little dizzy. I brace myself on the frame of the broken table.

The sink fills quickly and the water slops over the side. A puddle begins to gather on the floor, spreading out across the room.

'What was that?' I say. 'I heard something.'

'What? You're slurring.'

'I think I heard something. A door opening.'

'Are you sure you're all right?' He puts a hand on my arm. I suddenly feel very weak. 'You're not making sense.'

Water is washing into the lounge now. The legs of the table are licked by its leading edge.

'I'm fine,' I say as I slide off the table, into the water, my head swimming, Brian tries to catch me, my knees buckle, I slump face-first onto the floor, pain, cheek resting against rough wet wood, the door behind us opens, a brief struggle, someone shouting at us, a pair of polished black boots wobbling like heat haze in front of my face, Brian thrown back against a wall, his face dissolving into rage, losing it, not himself, and then I fall away completely.

SCOTT DOLAN'S GUEST LIST

World's Greatest Showbiz Column

KIEFER SUTHERLAND and STING jamming at a night-club in Venice Beach.

POLICE TO INTERVIEW FEY
Ex-singer to help with enquiries

I've heard police want to speak to Brian Fey about the death of John French. This follows trouble at John's funeral when Sean Darbo had to stop Fey from attacking his old colleague Martin Valentine.

An unshaven JAMIE REDKNAPP buying milk and a newspaper at his local newsagents.

Saturday

NOT A BED OF ROSES

The sound of a shout echoing along a corridor brings me around. As I wake up the shouting has stopped. I wonder if I was dreaming it. I must have been.

I'm groggy and uncomfortable. There's an acrid taste in my mouth. I gradually realize I'm not in my own bed. I squeeze my eyes shut and feel the cold hard surface I'm lying on through the twisted muscles of my stiff back. My right leg is numb from where I've been lying against it. The lobby again? I try not to think about my neighbour Hodgson stepping over me on his way out of the front door. What must he think? It's very embarrassing. I ought to be ashamed of myself.

I open my eyes.

I'm not in the lobby.

I'm definitely not in my flat.

I don't know where I am.

It's a small, square room. The walls are painted with a faded yellow that has peeled away in uneven blistered patches. Graffiti has been scrawled on top of the surviving paint. The floor is tatty red vinyl and there is no furniture. The sick orange throbbing into my eyes originates from a strip light fixed to a high ceiling. There are no windows; I've no idea what time it is. The décor is ascetic, spartan. I could do with some of this austerity in my life right now.

I have a tremendous hangover.

The only exit is a heavy metal door with a closed slot set into the middle. This door is firmly shut and there is no handle on the inside. My resting place is a long concrete shelf, barely ameliorated by a thin mattress. There are no sheets or covers. The mattress is stained yellow. It smells of urine. My belt and shoelaces have been removed.

My legal practice has never called upon me to visit a place like this but I recognize it from television drama. In a way, this was inevitable. It's been coming.

Only a matter of time before I would find myself waking up in a police cell.

AT HER MAJESTY'S PLEASURE

Detective Inspector Lawrence is sipping from a plastic cup of water. He didn't offer me one. His colleague, DC Eagen, has spent the last five minutes skipping through pages of typed print. I try to read the upside-down script but it's impossible to decipher anything from my position.

At the bottom of the page I then notice a signature; unsteady and scribbled, which I still recognize as mine. I don't remember signing anything.

Eagen breaks open a sealed audio tape and slips it into the slot of a tape deck on the table. He presses a button and a red indicator lights up. The tape starts to record.

'For the tape,' he says, 'DI Lawrence and DC Eagen present with the suspect, Daniel Alexander Tate. Interview commencing at –' he checks the cheap plastic clock on the wall – 'six-thirty p.m.'

'Six-thirty?' I panic. 'Are you sure?'

'That's right,' Lawrence confirms. He points up at the clock. 'You've been asleep all day. In a bit of a state when we brought you in. We thought we'd leave you in the drunk tank for a bit, let you sober up.'

'But I can't be here,' I tell them. 'I have to meet someone. It's really urgent.'

'You'll have to be late, then. You've got some explaining to do.'

We're sitting in folding chairs, facing each other across a table patterned with ringed coffee stains, cigarette burn marks and scratched graffiti. The backrest of my chair, a cold metal strip, is cutting into the cramped muscles of my back; it's impossible to get comfortable, but then that's probably the point. Detective Inspector Lawrence is a tall, thin man with a sharp pointed nose and wire-frame glasses. Detective Constable Eagen, by contrast, is short and dumpy with a beard silvered by age. His eyebrows join in the middle and his breath wheezes in and out from between clumps of thick nasal hair.

'So – let's go through this again,' says Eagen. He looks at the notes. 'You said last night that you were "just looking around the place". You were "just having a laugh". That's right, isn't it?'

'Last night?' I ask.

'During the interview.'

'I don't know. I don't remember being interviewed.'

'You don't remember being interviewed last night?' he says.

'I don't even know how I got here.'

'No?'

'No.'

'You *were* drunk,' Lawrence tells me. 'In fact, you were almost unconscious when we brought you in.'

'So I must've forgotten,' I say.

'That must be it.'

'And you interviewed me? In that state?'

'We did.'

'Isn't that against the rules?'

'Don't get chippy,' Lawrence warns. 'The doctor examined you. He said we could go ahead.'

'Let's see if we can't refresh your memory,' Eagen offers. 'You and your friend – Mr Fey – have been charged with burglary and criminal damage. You broke into a flat and wrecked some very expensive furniture. The couple who live there were out at the time, lucky for you, because if they'd've been in, you'd be looking at something more serious than what you've got. Aggravated charges, that sort of thing. You were caught by a couple of the boys after they heard all the noise you were making, from the street.'

'What couple?' I ask. As far as I know, Sean Darbo is single.

'The flat belongs to a couple of accountants. They were working late.'

'Not Sean Darbo?'

'Sean who?'

'It doesn't matter.'

'You smashed up the place,' Lawrence says. 'Flooded it, too. Wouldn't like to think about how much damage you caused.'

I lie: 'I don't remember any of it. Where's my friend now?'

'We've already interviewed him,' Lawrence says. 'I've got to say, we had a shock once we identified him. The rest of the station was very impressed when we told them who we had in here. But we're done with him now. He's been charged and we released him this afternoon.'

'What've you charged him with?'

'Same as you.'

'Anything else?'

'No. He was lucky – we could probably have had him for assaulting a policeman, too. He was a bit feisty when he was brought in.'

'And that's it?'

'What d'you mean?'

'No other charges?'

'No. What else would you like us to charge him with?'

I bottle it, say, 'Nothing,' and ask them what they intend to do with me.

'We'd like to know why you did it. Don't get too many solicitors in here on charges. Most of the solicitors we see in the station are just here to make our jobs difficult. So this's a novel experience for us.'

'By the way,' Eagen says. 'Would you like a solicitor? We could call your office, perhaps? Maybe they could send someone over?'

I shake my head vigorously. The last thing I want is for work to find out about this. I'd be sacked on the spot.

'Suspect declines offer of legal representation,' Eagen reports for the tape.

Lawrence steeples his thin fingers and stares straight at me. 'So why don't you tell us exactly what you were trying to achieve.'

It would take too long to explain so I just shrug. 'I don't know. Like you say, I was drunk. What else do you need to know? It's not like I'm proud of it.'

'You confirm you caused the damage?'

'Yes. I confess. We did it.'

'Then there's not much else to say, then, is there? I'm terminating the interview at – six-forty,' says Lawrence, stopping the tape.

'Look – I really need to go now. I'm missing a very important appointment.'

'You'll go when we've finished with you,' Eagen says sternly. 'There's paperwork to fill out.'

'Why would you go and do something stupid like that?' asks Lawrence, as Eagen seals the tape into an evidence bag. 'We get all sorts in here, but someone like you – a solicitor? It's not like you two even looked like you were trying to nick something. It was just senseless damage.'

'I don't know,' I answer, truthfully. 'I haven't been myself lately. Look, I don't really have time to chat. I'll sign whatever you want. I just need to get out of here, *please*.'

He pays no attention. 'But you've got so much to *lose*,' he muses, with a dour shake of his head.

I don't bother to correct him on this.

TOO LATE

They take me back to the cell. I've no idea how long they leave me there since they haven't returned my watch or any of the rest of my possessions. I bang the door and shout and yell, but after the custody sergeant assures himself there's no cause for alarm he goes back to his office and ignores me. I give up, then.

When the police eventually let me out, another hour has passed. I hurriedly sign for my things and take a taxi to the Groucho. The receptionist takes one look at me – haggard, unshaven, clothes askew – and refuses to let me in.

'I'm here to see Hannah Wilde,' I explain, half-hysterical. 'I'm just a little late.'

With a frown of irritation, the receptionist consults a ledger on the desk in front of her. She shakes her head. 'Miss Wilde left thirty minutes ago,' she reports.

'Couldn't I just go in and check?'

'I don't think so.'

'Look, it's really important. She asked me to meet her here. Could you check your book?'

'Miss Wilde left thirty minutes ago,' she repeats impatiently. She nods to a burly bouncer who gently guides me towards the door. I try to peer through the windows into the hazy interior but there's no sign of Hannah. Eventually, I give up and get a taxi home.

FINALLY, A SECOND CHANCE

The telephone starts ringing as I climb the stairs to the flat. The last ring is choked short as the machine picks up and the message Hannah recorded before she left plays out. The message, I recall, is mercilessly brief. By the time she's invited the unknown caller to leave their message I've sprinted up the stairs, two at a time, fumbling for my keys as I do so. Hannah – the real deal now, unrecorded – is already well into a rant. She sounds like the kind of person who has just been left standing alone at a bar for the past couple of hours.

'. . . and if you can't even be bothered to turn up so we could talk about it, then you're not leaving me with any real choice but to . . .'

'Hello,' I gasp. 'Hello?'

'Oh,' she says. 'So you are in.'

'I'm sorry. I'm *so* sorry. In fact, you have no idea just how sorry I am.'

'And your excuse is, like, what exactly?'

'You wouldn't believe me if I told you.'

'No, go on, tell me, I'm interested. I'd love to know what it was that was so important that you had to stand me up at the fucking *Groucho*. Of all the fucking places you could choose to stand me up . . . I could have *died* in there.'

'Listen, I mean it, I'm really sorry. I'm really, *really* sorry.'

'*Everyone* was there,' she continues. 'The whole crowd, including this director I'm auditioning for next week. How he's ever gonna take me seriously now, I have no idea.'

She hasn't slammed the phone down on me yet, which must be a good sign.

'Please, Hannah, I really need to talk to you. It's very important.'

She takes a breath. 'I need to talk to you too.'

Brian walks in through the still open front door, with

a carrier bag of provisions. He starts to say something, notices that I'm on the phone and heads through into the kitchen.

'Can I make a suggestion?' I'm suddenly inspired. 'Why don't you come over here tomorrow evening? I'll cook dinner. At least if you come here you'll know I won't forget.'

'Fine,' she agrees. 'I'll be there at seven.'

'That's great,' I say, but I'm talking to the dialling tone. She's already put the phone down on me.

I slump into the sofa while Brian prepares a meal. Nelson miaows at me. He hasn't been fed. Brian cooks some chicken and rice and fills his dish with it. Nelson wolfs it down.

My head is spinning again and I feel drowsy. Probably just hunger and lack of sleep. I've had a difficult day.

'I'm really sorry about last night,' Brian says from the kitchen. 'I told the police everything. I told them it was my idea. As far as I'm concerned, you had nothing to do with it. It was all my fault. I put everything into my statement.'

'They charged me too.'

He opens the cupboard and slides something inside. 'They'll drop it once they realize it was all down to me. And, if I have to, I'll get us both a really good lawyer. There won't be a problem.'

'You haven't got any money, Brian,' I remind him.

'I'll find some,' he says.

I look around. To my surprise, Brian has completely tidied the flat. He must have done it yesterday while I was at work, or after he was released this afternoon. I can't remember the last time it was this clean. The rubbish strewn on the floor has been collected. The carpet has been hoovered and all the surfaces have been dusted. The kitchen and bathroom have been subjected to the same diligent attention. I don't even want to *think* about how long it must have taken him – or why he's done it.

'Is the heating back on again?' I say.

'The gas company said you hadn't paid your bill. I paid on my credit card. Hope you don't mind.'

I shake my head dumbly. Brian brings me a bowl of the chicken and rice. It's a struggle to bring the fork to my mouth and I can barely finish it all.

I sip my tea and then put it aside. 'I feel awful,' I say.

'Why don't you try and get some sleep?' he suggests. 'You'll feel better in the morning.'

I remember saying something similar to him earlier in the week. But whereas problems seem to slide off Brian, leaving him untouched and relaxed, they stick to me like glue.

Trying not to think about the answerphone tapes, the photographs – the weight of the evidence against him – I take his advice.

'Thanks for the food,' I say edgily. 'And for tidying up.'

'Forget about it,' he says, sliding a clean plate into the draining rack. 'It's the least I could do.'

Sunday

BREAKFAST

The sun is pouring through the bedroom window when I awake. I check my watch: it's already 3 p.m. I struggle out of bed and tidy up. Hannah's coming round tonight and even though I'm not one for counting chickens, a filthy bedroom would be tempting fate.

Into the kitchen to check the fridge and the cupboards. They've been stocked with items I don't remember purchasing: jars of pasta sauce, tins of tomatoes and baked beans, a whole shelf of microwave meals, eggs, fruit and vegetables, cartons of juice, yoghurt.

On the counter I find a note from Brian:

Daniel – Had to go out. Back later. Bagels and croissants in cupboard – dig in. Spare room is messy – suggest steer clear until I've tidied. Brian.

I open the cupboard to verify this information; the luxurious smell of fresh bread reaches my nostrils, reminding me of how hungry I am. Three different types of bread from the bakery up on the main road have been neatly stacked on the shelves.

I take down a round bloomer and unwrap it from its brown paper bag. Tearing off a chunk, I bite in; the white bread inside the golden crust is still light and fluffy. I butter several slices and daub them with set honey from a jar that Brian has added to my provisions.

SHOPPING

I step outside. The snow has started to turn into grey viscous slush, sludging into the gutters and disappearing down the silted drains into the city's sewers. Rain is falling.

I visit Safeway to pick up the ingredients for the recipe I plan to cook tonight. I'm surprised to find that I'm feeling almost optimistic about the evening. Maybe Hannah wants a reconciliation? Perhaps she's missing me?

I'd change my plans if she asked me.

I squeeze a plump red pepper and pop it into my basket.

I decide on something Italian, and drop in a courgette, an onion, a bulb of garlic and some durum wheat pasta. Two bottles of wine, one white and one red, complete my requirements. As I approach the check-out I remember that I'm out of booze and drop in a selection of bottles.

Brian is still not home when I return. The door to the spare room is shut and I put my ear to it to make sure it's empty. I can't hear a thing. How I'm going to explain to Hannah my now practically sharing the flat with Brian Fey is something I'll have to deal with as the need arises.

I take out the postcard from the *Skin Trade* publicity pack and lay it on the dining table. Hannah stares out at the camera, an enigmatic half-smile playing on her lips. I pour out a whisky and drink a toast.

To second chances. New beginnings.

WHERE DID OUR LOVE GO?

By the time 8 p.m. comes around and the doorbell rings I'm feeling very nervous. I open the door, half-expecting it to be Brian.

Blood floods my cheeks as I smile shyly at my beautiful ex-girlfriend.

Hannah is wearing a long dress, very glamorous, like Audrey Hepburn in *Breakfast at Tiffany's*. Dark glasses obscure her eyes. Expensive-looking jewellery I've never seen before is around her wrists and neck. She's gone to a lot of trouble.

Things look promising.

I can't help saying, 'You look gorgeous.'

I open the door wider for her to come inside.

I then say, 'It's great to see you.'

She doesn't come inside. She stands there, glaring at me from behind her shades.

'Come on, come in,' I encourage. 'I don't bite.'

She grimaces. She takes off her shades; her eyes are like flints. A certain warning that she's angry. I'm going to have to try harder.

'I'll make this quick,' she says.

'What do you mean?'

'I don't want to be here any longer than I have to be. It wouldn't be good for me to be seen in a place like this.'

'What do you mean "a place like this". This is *our* place. We bought this *place* together.'

'Yes, yes,' she says tersely.

'Come on, come inside.'

She pauses and looks at me questioningly. 'Have you been drinking?' she asks.

'Just a little,' I admit. 'Just while I was cooking.' I got through half a bottle of JD but I'm not going to admit to that.

She wrinkles her nose, a familiar habit I always used to find cute. A frown creases her brow but she smoothes it away. She looks resolute.

'I want you to stop pestering us.'

'What?'

'Me and Vincent. I know what you've been doing – and it's very immature of you.'

'You . . . and . . . Vincent?'

'Yes, me and Vincent. My *fiancé*.'

I'm suddenly breathless. 'I don't know what you're talking about.'

'Yes you do. You've been ringing my agent and trying to get in touch with me. And you've been ringing my friends, too – Karla told me about it.'

'I wanted to speak to you and it was—'

'And now Vincent's told me you've been bothering him. Chasing him outside the hotel, trying to intimidate him. That's harassment, Daniel.'

'Come in,' I plead. 'Let's talk about this over a glass of wine.'

'I'm not coming in, Daniel. I'm not staying. I'm just here to warn you. If you don't stop bothering us I'm going to report you to the police.'

I desperately try to change the subject. 'But what about dinner? I'm ready to dish up. It's my speciality—'

'Stay away from us, Daniel.'

'—spag bol.'

'I'm only going to tell you that once. If you bother either of us again – either of us, or *any* of my friends – I'm going to report you to the police. I mean it.'

'I only want to talk to you.' I'm half-wailing now.

'Do I make myself clear?' she says sternly. 'I'm serious.'

'Hannah, please—'

'That's it. I've said what I wanted to say.'

I change tactics, taking a deep breath until my composure returns. 'OK. Just give me five minutes, that's all. Come in for five minutes and let me talk to you and then I promise – I *swear* – I'll never bother either of you again.'

Hannah looks over her shoulder and down into the dark of the stairwell. A flicker of uncertainty.

'Come on, you owe me at least that. I'm not asking you to stay. Hear me out and then that's it.'

I open the door wider and stand aside. With another uncertain look over her shoulder, she grimaces and steps inside. 'Five minutes,' she warns.

THE HEART OF THE MATTER

'Can I get you a drink?'

'No, thanks.'

An uncomfortable pause that I avoid by quickly dashing into the kitchen and pouring myself a large whisky. I finish half in one long drag and then refresh my glass. When I return to the living room, Hannah is fingering a frame on the mantelpiece. The picture is one of us in Ibiza, both coming down from whatever drug we'd been taking, a warm pink dawn breaking over the island. Another partygoer took the picture for us; it's off-centre and slightly blurred.

'Remember that?' I ask her.

An almost wistful look melts her stern glare away. 'Just before you jumped into the harbour, wasn't it?' she says. 'You didn't know the water was going to be so cold. I can still see your face.'

'I've got a picture of it somewhere. After they pulled me out.'

'Remember the night with the Ecstasy?' she says.

As she smiles sadly at the memory, I realize that she must have already been seeing Haines by then. I remember her sadness after we had sex that time. She had suggested the holiday; perhaps it was her giving us one last chance.

I close my eyes and try to forget it.

'Look – are you sure I can't get you a drink?'

'No,' she says again, although the hostility has gone. 'I'm not going to stop. But thanks anyway.'

Nelson, who has been asleep on my bed, walks into the room.

'Nelson!' Hannah exclaims happily.

She takes a step towards him. Nelson arches his back and takes a sudden backwards step. He peers out from behind my ankles.

'He's probably nervous,' I say. 'He hasn't seen you for ages.'

The cat walks carefully to his water bowl.

'Where's *he* tonight?' I continue.

'Who?'

'Loverboy.'

'No – this isn't about Vincent. We're not talking about him.'

'It's just every time I see you on TV with him—'

'Daniel, don't.'

'Do you trust him? He seems so, I don't know, so . . . flirtatious.'

She tells me, with firm resolve, that, 'We're not talking about me and Vincent, Daniel.'

'I miss you so much.'

She smiles a melancholy smile. 'You'll get over me. You've still got your work.' This last sentence is delivered with mild, gentle resentment. I recognize, at last, the reason why Hannah walked out: my fucking job. Ever since I took on Brian's case, I've been devoted to it; it was the chance I'd been waiting for to make my reputation. I've worked long hours, at weekends, cancelled holidays, made every sacrifice necessary to ensure the case got my full attention. Did Hannah, sidelined by my feverish activity, see with me a future where I was married to my job and not to her? I realize, too late, how stupid I've been.

There's an uncomfortable pause before I say what I have to say. There seems no other way to do this, so I just start talking. I tell her how empty and cold the flat is without her in it. I tell her that I'm sorry that we've broken up and how I'd do anything to have her back again. I tell her I've missed her, again. I tell her I can't stop thinking about her, that every time she's on the television is another small torture. I tell her I'm jealous of Vincent Haines, and even though I know bugging him is immature I didn't know what else to do. I tell her again that I want her back. I tell her that I'd try harder. That I'd pay her more attention. That I wouldn't be so selfish or obsessed with work. That I'll make the effort.

When I'm finished she can't bring herself to look at me.

'Well,' I say. 'That's that.'

When she turns back, her eyes have a slick, glassy appearance. 'I'm sorry we broke up, too,' she says. 'And I've missed you as well. It's just . . . God, Daniel, it's just that things are much more complicated now. You can't just rewind to how it was before.'

'Why not?' I press. 'Finish with Vincent. Come back to me. Give me another chance? I'll try harder.'

'It's not as easy as that,' she wistfully half-smiles.

'Why not?'

'It's just, you can't just—'

'I want you back.'

'No, you don't.'

I take a deep breath. Time for the last shot in my locker.

'What if I said I'd quit my job? Get something with more reasonable hours?'

'Daniel—'

'And what if I said I wanted you to marry me?'

'Daniel, I—'

Hannah looks down at her feet. There's another,

heavier pause. Offering to change jobs is an easy concession to make, given the circumstances, but I can see the gesture has had the right effect. She frowns. Something drops to the floor in the spare room but I hardly hear it. She reaches up a hand to brush away a gemlike tear. She looks beautiful. I'd forgotten how beautiful she really is. The television doesn't do her justice at all. She bites her bottom lip to stop it quivering.

AN UNEXPECTED INTERRUPTION

As I'm thinking of what I should say next, wondering whether I could get away with sitting next to her on the sofa and taking her hand, the door of the spare room opens. I start to work out how I'm going to introduce Brian to Hannah.

Only it isn't Brian.

The door opens outwards so my view of the person behind it is obscured. But Hannah has a direct view. And I have a direct view of her. And so I'm able to watch her face as it slowly dissolves and transforms. As it breaks up. The softness there the moment before fades, hardens – and fierce anger settles across it like a dark cloud.

'You sick bastard,' she says tonelessly.

I don't have time to ask her what she means. The door opens fully and Lisa, Brian's groupie from the club, wearing the red cashmere dressing gown that Hannah bought me last Christmas, walks out into the lounge. The dressing gown is only loosely tied together around the waist, and a wide slash opens downwards, half-exposing large breasts, brown skin and a tattoo of a kingfisher above her navel. Her hair is mussed up and, as she saunters towards me, she tousles it with a long-fingered hand. Her eyes are only half-open; she looks like she's just woken up.

'You *bastard*,' Hannah repeats, but with more heat this time.

'No, no, no,' I falter, frantic. 'Ohmigod. This isn't what it looks like.'

'Oh, really? Is that right?' She's on her feet, wrapping her coat more tightly around her.

A thought breeds in the panic – maybe if I changed the subject, appealed to her vanity? I know it's irrational, and probably even a little freaky, but I'm desperate, and ready to try anything. I go into the kitchen and fetch the postcard of Hannah from the *Skin Trade* publicity pack. 'Look,' I say soothingly, card proffered, 'I've been collecting. Maybe you could sign it for me or something?'

She curls her lip in disgust. 'OK. So now you're sick *and* creepy.'

'What time is it?' yawns Lisa, before trailing off.

'I don't even know who *she* is,' I say, pointing. When I realize how crazy this sounds – professing not to know the buxom chick naked except for my dressing gown – I clarify, adding, 'No, she's a friend of a friend. I've got someone else living with me at the moment. A friend, OK? She must be with him – not *me*.'

'Just fuck off,' Hannah spits, jutting her chin in my direction. 'Save your breath for someone who cares.'

'It's Brian Fey. He's been staying here with me. She's a friend of his.'

Her jaw drops in stupefaction. 'Brian Fey?' she exclaims incredulously. 'Oh, *please*, what do you take me for? You're out of your mind.'

I take her wrist in my hand. She jerks it away, disgusted. She pauses at the threshold. 'All those things you just said – I almost believed you were being sincere. But you don't even know what sincerity is. After everything you put me through, *everything*, I can't believe I'm still crazy enough to fall for your stupid lies.'

My temper snaps. 'Everything I've put you through? *You*? What about what you've done to *me*?'

'What were you hoping for? A nice little *ménage à* fucking *trois*? Wanted to get your own back on me, did you? Is that it? Going to reel me back in so you could blow me out? An eye for an eye? You're *sick*, Daniel.' Hannah turns to address Lisa. 'Listen, sweetheart – a word of advice. Don't believe a word he says. He's completely full of shit.'

'Just *listen* to me for a *minute*,' I bellow at her, totally losing my cool. 'Just listen.'

'No, not any more. I've had enough of listening to you.'

Lisa is standing between us, gaping at me. 'Hey . . . you,' she says, the dopey pause between the two words confirming that she has absolutely no idea who I am.

'Just listen—'

'So, like, what's going on?' Lisa asks dreamily. She's gazing absently around the room with no idea where she is.

'*Will you just shut up*,' I yell at her.

Hannah steps outside. 'Bye, Daniel.' She puts her shades back on again.

'No. Don't go. Please—'

'Oh – in case it isn't obvious – I never want to see you again.'

As Hannah turns to go I spot a figure lurking in the shadows at the bottom of the stairwell. Another pair of shades glints darkly up at me in the artificial light. As he takes a step forwards, Vincent Haines's face is briefly lit.

'You bastard!' I roar at him, setting off down the stairs. 'Look what you've done!'

The door to the flat starts to close after me. My keys are inside. I pause uncertainly – caught between propping the door open and following Hannah downstairs – and I wait long enough for them both to get outside the front door. While I hover, undecided, the door to the flat shuts anyway. I ignore it; for now I want to stop Hannah or attack Haines, I'm not sure quite which.

'Wait,' I call out as I scamper down the stairs after them.

'Leave us alone!' she barks out; they're onto the pavement now and heading off towards the main road. A car parked twenty yards away starts up, pop-up lights rising out of the bonnet and flashing on.

I'm suddenly overcome with anger. I'm being treated shabbily. This is *unfair*. Diplomacy seems less urgent now.

'Starfucker!' I shout out.

'Fuck you!' she turns and yells back at me. Haines takes her by the elbow and tugs her backwards, faster, towards the car as it rolls forward to meet them. I can hear Hannah's high heels clacking on a patch of pavement treated with salt. The remaining snow and ice numbs my feet through my shoes as I skid out onto the path.

There's a sudden flash from the inside of a car parked up beside me. As I swing around to face it, there comes another. The driver's door opens into the road and a silhouetted figure gets out.

'Daniel,' says Scott Dolan, shooting off another snap of me. 'What's this all about?'

I stumble. A light flicks on in the bedroom of one of the houses opposite. But it's much too late to worry about upsetting the neighbours.

THE FAN HITS THE SHIT

Hannah and Haines get into the waiting car and slam their doors shut. As it rolls forwards towards me I notice the driver. It's Rip. The car slows as it reaches me, and the passenger window slides down.

Haines leans out and says to me, 'You should get a life or something. You're a disgrace.'

As I lunge at him, he bangs his head on the roof of the car trying to get out of my way, then my clawed hands fasten around his neck. I tighten my grip and squeeze. I'm half in the window, half out of it, and being dragged along in the gutter.

'You don't love her,' I shout. Dolan's flash lights up again and again.

'Get out of here!' Haines chokes, dislodging one of my hands.

Rip hits the gas and the car bucks away. I flail at the handle with my spare hand and the door opens as I grab and pull against it. Haines didn't shut it properly. With my free hand tugging at his neck, all of his weight is being pulled against the door, as it opens, he loses his balance and tumbles out on top of me. Rip stands on the brakes; the wheels lock and skid. I lose my grip on the handle and both of us slide along the icy road, legs and arms entangled, the car slowing down beside us. Haines struggles hard and breaks free of me, his momentum causing him to glide away. As I slither to a stop against a lamppost, I watch with sick fascination as his slow spinning drags one of his legs underneath the car, between the front and back wheels. The car, slowed almost to a standstill now, keeps creeping forward. The rear wheel rolls leisurely onto and over Haines's trailing right leg.

I've never heard the sound of a gun being fired in real life, but the sharp crack his leg makes as it snaps must be similar. The car finally stops with the rear wheel half resting on his leg. Haines screams.

Somewhere, behind us, a camera flashes.

Haines screams again.

I scramble to my feet and take half a step towards him.

'His leg,' I call out, slipping on the road. 'The car's crushing his leg.'

Hannah gets out of the car and crouches down next to Haines. Rip quickly gets back inside again and drives the car slowly off Haines's leg. He screams again, but louder.

'You bastard!' Hannah screams. 'Look what you've done to him.'

'It was an accident,' I stammer. 'I didn't mean to hurt him.'

'Look at his leg!'

I look down at Haines. His foot is pointing backwards at an impossible angle. A sliver of white bone has pierced his trousers and points up at the sky. Blood is beginning to seep out onto the road. He is moaning in pain.

I notice Rip speaking urgently into a mobile phone.

'I didn't mean it,' I plead. 'The door was open.'

Someone jogs up behind me. 'What's going on?' Dolan asks. He's alongside the car, tentatively edging forward. His camera is pressed to his face, the shutter whirring as he takes picture after picture. He notices Haines. 'Fuck. Uh – Vinny? Are you OK?'

'Of course he's not OK,' Hannah snaps.

'Just fuck off,' I yell.

'Have you had an argument with Hannah?' Dolan asks. 'Is that why you're so upset? Hannah? Is that it? I know you two had a thing – before Vincent, of course. I know he's the reason she dumped you, Danny. And how's Brian Fey tied up in all of this? Is Hannah sleeping with him too? Daniel?'

I advance around the car towards him. I've had enough of this. He walks backwards to where his own car is parked. Dolan is encumbered with the camera around his neck and is caught between me and the car. He tries to duck inside, but not quickly enough to escape me. I grasp a handful of his jacket and yank him outside again.

'Mind your own business,' I pant. I enjoy the infusion of fear in his eyes and the involuntary bobbing of his Adam's apple, before I nail him with a straight right on the nose and dump him down onto the seat of his pants. Hannah shrieks. I'm not much of a brawler but it was a pretty solid contact. Solid enough to splash blood all over his face and down the front of his shirt, and sting the hell out of my fist.

I reach down for his camera. I remove the film and pocket it.

'Oh, this is going to look *great* in the papers,' he says nasally. Two streams of blood are pouring out from both nostrils and onto the grey slush. "Hotshot Lawyer Assaults Soap Star *and* Reporter." That's just beautiful.'

'Do I look like I care?' I say, turning my back on them all and heading back inside.

CRIME AND PUNISHMENT

I knock on the door to my flat but Lisa doesn't open it. It then takes me ten minutes to batter it open. It's not a substantial door, but still strong enough to resist my persistent charges and kicks long enough for painful bruises to develop on my shoulders and feet. At one point Hodgson comes halfway up the stairs to complain, but when I swing around to confront him, blood on my knuckles and my eyes wild, he changes his mind and retreats down to his own flat again. I finally push the broken door back on its shattered hinges and rest my forehead against the frame, breathing slowly through my mouth – in and out, in and out. I hear a siren wail in the distance, gradually getting louder.

Lisa is on the sofa, snoring. The bottle of whisky I was drinking from is on the floor next to her, tipped over now, a puddle of liquid staining the carpet brown. I rescue it; there's still a few fingers' worth left.

I run a hand through my hair. I fold the tablecloth over the candles and cutlery on the table and throw the bundle into the trash. I drink off the remnants of the JD in one long slug. I scrape the spag bol I took all afternoon to prepare into the bin. The evening I had planned seems ridiculous now. I feel humiliated. I take the blanket from the spare room and throw it over Lisa.

Blue light from the street below pulses through the curtains. I can hear voices, accusatory tones.

Someone knocks on the door.

'Just a minute,' I say, filling Nelson's bowl with tuna and changing his water and his litter tray.

I don't make a fuss and follow the police docilely down to the squad car waiting in the street. An ambulance is there too, and two paramedics are crouching on either side of Haines, gingerly immobilizing his leg in a long splint. Lights are on in most of the houses, silhouetting my neighbours as they look out at the scene in the street.

Hannah is nervously smoking a cigarette, pacing fretfully as she watches the medics at work. Dolan is there too, his nose plugged with two stoppers of cotton wool. He's loaded a new film into his camera and he snaps away as I trudge towards the police car, its lights flashing, and slide into the back. A constable gets in next to me and the door is shut.

As we reach the end of the street, I turn back. The

houses are bathed in blinking blue light from the ambulance, that light also falling upon Haines as he is lifted up on a stretcher and upon Hannah standing next to the stretcher so she can hold his hand.

As the police car accelerates away from the junction, I know this is the last time I'll ever see her. I watch until we turn a corner and put them out of sight.

FAMILIAR FACES

'Not you again,' Detective Constable Eagen says as I'm handed over to him at the station. 'What is it this time?'

'Let's just get it over with, OK?' I suggest.

The interview doesn't take nearly as long this time. I decline the offer of a lawyer and admit to everything. He asks questions and I provide full answers. I calmly dictate a statement, then am put to wait in the same cell as earlier. When the statement is ready I sign it. They charge me with GBH twice: once for Haines's leg and once for Dolan's nose. I don't complain as they lead me back to the cell. I slump down on the foul-smelling mattress. I expect to be here all night and so it comes as a surprise when the custody officer opens the door and tells me that I've been bailed.

'Bailed?'

'That's right. Come on, out. This isn't some hotel – I need this cell.'

'That's not possible,' I tell him. 'I haven't paid anything.'

'I know you haven't.'

'Then it's a mistake.'

'No, it isn't.'

'So what . . .? It's police bail?'

'A couple of friends have put up some cash for you. They're out in reception.'

BAILED

It's just before midnight when I'm let out. A drab reception room awaits me. The walls are covered with community-action posters, crime-prevention pamphlets and photofits of suspects and missing persons. A weary-looking woman in a dusty saree is sitting on a moulded plastic chair, staring first at the front of her hands and then at the back. A uniformed officer absent-mindedly twirls a spoon in a mug of coffee, the metal clinking against the porcelain.

Brian and Cohen are waiting for me there. The desk officer tells me quietly that Brian's been here for nearly the duration of my stay. I check the clock: that would be three hours.

Cohen is standing with his back to me, reading a poster on domestic security.

'Hi,' Brian says. 'How are you?'

'I'm OK,' I tell him. 'Just a little confused.'

'You look awful,' Cohen says. He's wearing a tux, his bow tie unknotted and strung loose around his neck.

I grunt at him.

'What's going on?' he asks.

'I've been arrested.'

'I know, we heard. What've you been doing?'

I shake my head and stare at him.

'It doesn't matter,' Cohen says. 'We can talk about it later. Let's just get out of here.'

'The press's outside,' Brian reports with a grim smile. 'Lots of them.'

I look through the dusty window; a crowd of journalists and photographers is thronging the pavement.

'Oh, great,' I groan. 'That's all I need.'

'OK, listen – I'm used to this. Or at least I *was*. The best way to get through in one piece is always to keep your head down and just keep walking. Don't stop to answer questions or they'll have you. You'll never get away.'

'OK.'

'Ready?'

'OK.'

MIDNIGHT RUN

There are excited cries of 'Daniel,' 'Dan' and 'Danny' as I emerge outside. The barrage of flashes seems even brighter in the darkness of the night. The predominant enquiry as I struggle down the steps towards the street is 'Why'd you do it?' I ignore them, as per Brian's advice, and concentrate on maintaining my forward momentum. One foot in front of the other, then repeat. Shutters whirr and flashbulbs flash, painting blinding white splashes on my retinas. Lights fixed to TV cameras strobe at us. Microphones and recording machines are brandished beneath my nose. A fluffy boom mike wobbles overhead. Late-night pedestrians – some the worse for drink – gawp in curious amazement and car horns honk as the crowd encroaches into the street.

We struggle forward, an anomalous trio: me looking like death warmed up, leading the way; the famous rockstar behind me; Cohen in a monkey suit doggedly bringing up the rear. 'No comment,' I say repeatedly as I grapple my way through the skirmish. No one is paying any attention to Brian, his hand on my elbow, guiding me firmly towards a black cab idling by the kerb. No one even seems to have recognized him.

A determined reporter prises down the window of the cab and leans halfway inside as we move away.

'Is any of this to do with Hannah Wilde?' he asks. The taxi is crawling forward too slowly in the traffic. We're trapped behind a night bus. 'I know all about her dumping you.'

'I wasn't dumped,' I reply heatedly. 'It was, um, a mutual idea – for the best.'

'Bollocks,' he exclaims, trotting to keep up now. He

only has eyes for me; he hasn't even noticed Brian. 'Come on, Danny, I *know* you must be cut up about it. Just tell me it's true and I'll leave you alone. It'll make it a lot easier for you. Just trust me – I'm on your side.'

'He's got no comment, OK, so fuck off,' Brian says angrily, reaching across me and shoving the window closed. 'Bastards.' He shakes his head. 'They get worse and worse.'

I turn to watch as the taxi pulls into an empty side lane and picks up speed. The reporter is left standing in the gutter, a mobile phone pressed to his ear and a fag clamped between his lips.

'How'd you manage it?' Cohen asks Brian incredulously. 'How'd you ever put up with all that?'

'You get used to it after a while,' he replies. 'The strange thing is, I actually *miss* it now. Can you believe that? I'd give a lot to have it back again.'

'What was it like?' Cohen asks. 'You know, being famous?'

'Specifically?' Brian says. 'Can't say I've got any bad memories. But then I can't say I've got any good memories, either, because I can't remember any of it.' He lights up a fag, blows out smoke, introspective. 'But generally? You know, it's strange – the effect it has on people. You get served faster in the shops, for one.'

'It must've been a shock to the system, at the start.'

'You remember that haircut I had back in the early eighties?' I remember it well: dyed red and blue, with three-inch spikes on top and hair going down all the way to the shoulders. As a ten-year-old, I imagined this to be the pinnacle of cool. Cohen nods at his own recollection.

'God, that was embarrassing,' Brian continues. 'I had that cut when I was working in Tesco's, before I joined the band. People used to walk past saying, "What a tit." As soon as we were on *Top of the Pops*, they started saying it in national magazines. That's what fame does.'

'I don't know what's happening to me any more,' I say. 'I think I'm going mad.'

'He's been under a lot of stress,' Cohen says to Brian. I think about responding, but don't.

As we head home, they explain what happened. Brian was on his way back to the flat when he saw the police car pull away with me in it. He managed to extract a partial story from Lisa, who had watched through the window before falling asleep. Brian took a cab to the station to see if he could help. When bail was set he knew he'd need someone else; following the brouhaha last night his own character was in doubt and the police wouldn't want to deal with him. Without anyone else to turn to, he rang the office and got Cohen's number. They'd met weeks ago, at the start of the case, and apparently I've told him since that Cohen's my closest friend in the office. I don't recall saying that. Cohen excused himself from a dinner party. He said he would stand bail for me but Brian insisted his own money be used. They had both waited there for the last couple of hours while my questioning proceeded.

'How much was bail?' I groan.

'£10,000,' Cohen says.

'Where'd you get that kind of money from?' I ask Brian.

'I've got an account I'd forgotten about,' he admits, too hesitantly. I don't believe him. He's lying. 'The bank told me about it yesterday. I suppose I should've told you about it but it slipped my mind.'

I knew it. I knew he had money somewhere he wasn't telling us about. Look at him now, squirming uncomfortably. But he still isn't telling me everything. There's something else.

'And why'd you get involved?' I say to Cohen. 'What's in it for you?' The taxi stops outside his house and he gets out.

He fakes a puzzled frown. 'Because you're a friend,' he says through the open window. 'Because you'd do the same thing for me.'

'Whatever,' I say.

'I'll call you tomorrow, OK?' he says.

'Fine,' I say.

He pauses for a moment, unsure if he should say something else, before smiling at us and walking towards his front door.

Finally, we get back to my flat. There are three photographers waiting for us outside. I ignore their

questions as we struggle inside. The door won't lock –
I've damaged it pretty badly – so we jam it shut.

Brian sees Lisa asleep on the sofa and groans.

'I'm sorry,' he says. 'I forgot about her. I should've
said something.'

I wave his apology away. 'Don't worry.'

'It's just she didn't have anywhere else to go either.
I mean, after I was kicked out of my own flat, I didn't
know what else to do with her.'

'What – she lives with you?'

'Yeah.'

'I didn't realize.'

'Since my mum died.'

'Sorry?'

'She's my little sister.'

'Your *sister*?' I look down at Lisa. It's difficult to
spot a familial resemblance. 'I thought you were seeing
her.'

Brian laughs, long and hard.

'What's so funny?'

'I suppose it could look like that.'

'I didn't know you even had a sister.'

'Yeah. Look, I'm sorry. I know I should've asked. It's
just that she didn't have anywhere else to go and it was
an emergency. I was gonna take her to a hotel tonight.
I found one I could afford this afternoon – that's where
I've been today. Just looking around.'

'It doesn't matter.'

'So what'd they ask you, the police?' Brian asks this nonchalantly, not looking at me, busy in the kitchen.

'Nothing much,' I say carefully. 'I admitted to everything.'

'That's it? They didn't want anything else?'

'No, nothing.'

'Jeez,' he says. 'What a mess.'

'I'm wiped out,' I tell him nervously. 'I'm turning in.' I head towards the bedroom.

'Night,' Brian says. 'Maybe we can talk in the morning?'

'Sure,' I say. I go to bed. There's nothing else for it.

NIGHT THOUGHTS

But what's the point in that? I can't sleep, anyway.

I've been in and out of the toilet five or six times and now I'm lying on my back, staring at the gloomy ceiling and trying to work out why Brian and Cohen put up my bail money. What's in it for them? The whole mess keeps running through my head. There must be an explanation, as I can't believe either of them would do it out of philanthropy.

Maybe Brian thinks I know more about French's death than I'm letting on. With me locked up and facing charges, maybe he thinks I might be tempted to cooperate with the police. I deliver them the killer in a high-profile murder hunt, they release me with a slap on the wrist. Brian would prefer me to be outside, where he can keep an eye on me, influence me, and, if he suspects that I'm becoming a threat, take steps to shut me up. He couldn't do that if I was locked up. He wouldn't be able to get at me.

Is this paranoia? It seems plausible enough.

And Cohen? If Cohen is working with Dawkins to undermine me, it'd be useful to have something on me, especially now I've found out that the Dork has been sabotaging my work. And they know I've found that out now because I told Cohen at dinner on Thursday night. I could wreck Dawkins' chances of partnership if I could prove everything I know about him to Hunter. And if Dawkins doesn't make partner, Cohen loses his new ally on the inside and his guaranteed promotion next year. But now they can discredit and get rid of me. They can add to my disgrace, whisper gossip and slander and innuendo, and have me sacked. No one will believe a word I say.

Lying here, unable to close down my mind, I'm playing these ideas and theories around, and trying to grasp the threads of an idea that I've been unable to stitch together. It's been bothering me since I got out of the police station, just out of reach at the back of my mind, tantalizingly incomplete.

And then, as a train rattles across the railway bridge, I make a connection and everything becomes obvious. I sit bolt upright in bed, horrified.

I remember the newspaper report that said £10,000

was stolen from John French's house after his murder last week. £10,000 was the amount Brian gave to Cohen to pay for my bail. Brian was supposed to have no access to money.

This can't be a coincidence.

Brian must have killed French and then stolen the money.

I'm suddenly anxious. I get out of bed and lock the bedroom door. I don't want to wake up with him standing above me in the gloom of the bedroom, a pillow ready to press down onto my face. I prop a bookcase up against it and wedge a chair underneath the handle.

I come to a decision. Either I confront him tomorrow or I go to the police.

One or the other.

SCOTT DOLAN'S GUEST LIST

World's Greatest Showbiz Column

VINCENT HAINES IN PUNCH-UP WITH BRIAN FEY'S LAWYER
Skin Trade star has broken leg

Vincent Haines, Jake Cocozzo in raunchy soap *Skin Trade*, was in hospital this morning after suffering a broken leg at the hands of **Daniel Tate**, 27, the lawyer representing Brian Fey. Violent Tate then punched ME after I tried to ask him a question about the incident.

I understand that Vincent and Tate were arguing about Hannah Wilde, who plays Ella in the hit show. My sources tell me Tate was seeing Hannah before she got involved with handsome Vincent.

Manchester United pals RYAN GIGGS and GARY NEVILLE spotted in a Ferrari at a red light.

Clothes empire boss FLAVIO BRIATORE shopping in Milan.

Monday

MEDIA CIRCUS

I'm looking down from the bedroom window onto the street below. The road is blocked with cars, some resting half on the pavement and others crammed up together under the bridges and on the bus depot car park. The owners of these vehicles, a scrum of reporters and photographers, are clustered around my front door. They are strung out in loose formation at the moment; talking, drinking take-out coffees and eating rolls and confectionery from the bakery. As I watch them, a TV reporter takes up position in front of the house and starts talking to camera, a fluffy boom mike dangling above his head and temporary klieg lights ameliorating the morning gloom.

The neighbours over the road are also staring down at this commotion, and I don't even want to contemplate what Hodgson must be thinking. A shout goes up as I'm noticed standing at the window, followed by a loud chorus repeating my name and the sound of flashbulbs going off. The cameraman tilts his lens in my direction. I recoil sharply and twitch the curtains closed.

The flat is empty save for me. There is no sign of either Brian or Lisa, so they must have left. I check out the spare room to be sure. It's as spotless as the rest of the flat, and I nose around. The bin is full; I tip it over and rummage through the displaced rubbish: copies of *Hello!* and *OK!*, an empty bottle of Prozac, dead beer cans. The curtains have been pulled closed.

As I turn to leave, I notice two suitcases resting against the wall. I open one of them: newly bought clothes, some still labelled, two pairs of shoes, toiletries, other personal belongings. I have a vivid picture of Brian walking into shops on Regent Street and buying the things he's going to need wherever it is he's going to set up his new life. The other case is packed with feminine things. So, one case for Brian and one for Lisa. There are only two conclusions that can be drawn from the fact that the suitcases are still here: either Brian is still making the final arrangements for his departure, or he has decided he's been compromised and has already left, taking Lisa with him and leaving these behind in his haste. Maybe he bailed me first to make sure I hadn't told the police anything to imperil him. I remember his questions last night, trying to work out whether I'd dropped him in it. Maybe yesterday was too close a shave to stick around. I re-pack the suitcases carefully and leave them where I found them.

I'm still feeling on edge, even in the daylight – and with forty gentlemen of the press outside.

And, cravenly, I can't help thinking about my own neck; the fact that I let him hole up with me for three days; the fact that I haven't told the police about him when I should have done, when I have incontrovertible proof to place him at the scene of the crime and clear evidence of his motive – the evidence to have had him arrested. I think of Dolan; he only had half of the information. I was – I am – in possession of the full picture but I've sat on my hands and done nothing with it. The thought rattles around my head until it echoes relentlessly: *I'm going to go to prison.* If it isn't for GBH it'll be for withholding evidence or perverting the course of justice.

One way or another – one crime or another – that fate seems inevitable.

I'd rather avoid running the gauntlet outside if I can, so I briefly entertain the idea of calling in sick. I dismiss that. I still have an iota of pride in my work and I'm hardly in a position to afford the time off; anyway, I'm already hanging on to my job by my fingernails. Maybe I can appeal to Tanner to intercede on my behalf with the rest of the partners. And I don't want to stay here any longer than I have to. Rather than have the press follow me all the way to the tube station, I make alternative plans to get to work, and call a minicab.

I'm still not ready to face the music as I watch the cab and its bemused driver pull up fifty yards away.

I collect my coat and a briefcase with which to shield my face and leave the flat.

Hodgson is waiting for me in the communal hallway. He's pacing fretfully.

'What's going *on* out there?' he hisses, as if worried that the sound of his voice will attract the horde of pressmen.

He twitches back the net curtain screening the window a fraction. I glance outside; the scrum looks to be denser and more agitated than earlier. Feeding time.

'You really don't want to know,' I say.

'I've got to get to work through this,' he complains bitterly. His inconvenience is the least of my concerns at the moment but my overwhelming sense of torpor, of inevitability, chokes back my instinctive snapped response.

'I really am sorry,' I say instead, 'but it's not like I asked for this.'

All I seem to be doing at the moment is apologizing.

'Are you going out now?' he asks.

'Yes.'

'Then you can go out first. I'll follow behind.'

'Ready?' I say.

He nods.

I open the door.

THE ATTACK OF THE FOURTH ESTATE

The flashes start popping as soon as I step outside. The crowd surges up from the pavement and I have to force my way through the crush. Dictaphones are thrust into my face and photographers hoist their cameras into the air and start shooting in the hope that they might get a picture of me fleeing my flat. I can see Dolan's ginger ponytail bobbing after me.

'Danny, why'd you attack Vincent Haines?'

'Danny, look over here.'

'Is Hannah Wilde cheating on Vincent Haines with you?'

'Is Brian Fey seeing Hannah Wilde?'

'Come on, Danny, give us a picture.'

I answer everything with the same 'No comment.' When this has no effect I put my head down, raise my briefcase and plough a path through to the minicab that is, miraculously, still waiting. Two paparazzi crouch down in the garden of the house at the end of the terrace and shoot away at me, like snipers. The flashbulbs bleach out my vision.

I have the sense of Hodgson's lumpish presence behind me but the surge quickly separates us. I don't risk a glance back to confirm this but I catch questions from reporters left in my wake redirected at him, a subsidiary target.

What kind of neighbour am I?

Does he know anything about the visitors to my flat?

Does he know Hannah?

Does he know Brian?

Should I feel exhilarated with this new-found attention? I'll admit to a shudder of enthusiasm as the pack surges after me, and the faces of my neighbours stare out from curtained windows. I try to put myself into Brian's shoes and imagine what it would be like to suddenly lose this spotlight. And then I think of Hannah, and the transitory limelight she's getting as the consort of the handsome American film star. For me, this feels like fraud. I'm not the person these men of the press would like me to be, but, right now, I doubt they'd believe me if I told them that.

The minicab is a battered old Nissan with a coat-hanger for an aerial and a jagged crack down the windshield. I dive inside, give the wide-eyed driver the address of the office, and raise my case so it obscures my face. The flashbulbs keep popping.

'This is fantastic,' the driver says, elated, 'like in the movies. I've always *dreamed* of doing this. Are you famous?'

'Only for the moment,' I say as I let him drive on.

The press are ready and give pursuit. A black Jeep pulls away from the kerb and tails us along the Mile End Road and into town. As we wait for the lights to change at a major junction, it slides alongside us in the adjacent lane. The snapper in the back seat winds down his window and pokes his camera through. I cover my face as the flash starts popping. Another guy in the front seat of the Jeep leans out and calls out something to my driver, who has identified himself as Samad.

'He's offered me £100 to pull over,' Samad reports with a wide grin.

'£200 to keep going,' I counter with no idea how I'll manage to find the cash.

'Hey, chill, don't *worry* about it,' Samad beams. 'I'm having too much fun to charge you, man. This one's on the house.'

The lights change and, with a whoop, Samad buries the accelerator and lifts off on the clutch. The Nissan's back wheels smoke, and leaving rubber, we jolt forward. At the last moment, and to an accompaniment of irate horns from the onrushing traffic, Samad slaloms across the junction and ducks into a narrow side-street between two warehouses. Behind us, the Jeep's progress is blocked off by a bus stuck at the lights.

'Short cut,' Samad explains.

'Wonderful,' I breathe. The Jeep is now completely out of sight.

'Wait 'til I tell the missus about this one,' he chuckles.

SUCCESS

Elizabeth guiltily folds a newspaper and stows it in her desk drawer as I approach her bay. She smiles at me but I can tell whatever it is that she's been reading has aroused her maternal concern. Before she can say anything I smile back, trying to look airily unconcerned, and duck into my office. I shut the door.

Cohen isn't here. At least this means I won't have to put up with him spying on me all morning.

I need to speak to Hannah. I call her agent again. This time the phone is not answered with the same acerbity. It is a new, younger voice.

I decide to play the writer-seeking-interview card again with a slight modification. I introduce myself as a semi-famous feature writer for a reputed arts and style magazine.

'I was wondering,' I say, 'whether you might have a telephone number or an address for Hannah Wilde. The magazine's arranged an interview, I'd like to confirm it with her but I've misplaced her details.'

'Just a moment, please,' she says, placing the phone on the desk. I'm breathless with anticipation. She returns, saying, 'Sorry – just had to look it up.' She gives me a South London address. Just as she finishes I can hear someone else asking her to whom it is she is speaking. Hannah's agent, Suzy Pugh, comes onto the line.

'Who is this?' she says irately. 'Hello?'

It is with a measure of some satisfaction that I put the phone down on her and check over the address I've written on the notepad in front of me.

AN INAUSPICIOUS SUMMONS

Jean Templeman, Hunter's secretary, calls me. I am to report to the boardroom on the fifth floor immediately. When I ask what this summons is for, she tells me that Mr Hunter wants to see me – at once. Her tone is grim. I finish off a weekend-old bagel – the condemned prisoner's last meal – and head upstairs to face the music.

AN AWKWARD MOMENT

As I'm nervously waiting in the lobby for a lift going up, Rachel walks out from a corridor. She is clutching an armful of folders to her chest.

'Hi,' she says uncomfortably. She seems surprised to see me, and presses the button to summon a lift going down.

'How are you?'

'I'm fine,' she replies. 'James has got me really busy – *big* surprise – but OK, thanks.'

We both look at each other, smiling and raising our eyebrows, neither really sure what to say. I'm scrabbling for inspiration but there's nothing there. And my smile is as false as hers. I can't see past my certainty that she is involved with Dawkins and Cohen. We both watch the displays monitoring the progress of the lifts.

She finds something to say: 'Going tonight?' she asks.

'Tonight?'

'The Christmas party.'

'Oh, maybe. I think so.'

Her lift arrives. She looks relieved.

'I'll see you later, then,' she says, smiling bashfully, walking off before the lift can leave her alone with me again.

CAUGHT IN THE ACT

Compared to the fourth floor, where the assistants live, the fifth is deluxe. The lift opens onto a marble lobby filled with sculpture and real, non-plastic greenery. Leather sofas that probably cost more than the aggregate worth of my own shabby furniture back at the flat are positioned around the room. Jean Templeman guards Hunter's lair warily from behind her marble desk.

'You'll have to wait a moment,' she says briskly. 'They're busy in the boardroom finishing up with someone else.'

'They?' I swallow nervously.

'The partnership council,' she says with affected sympathy.

As I sit on the edge of the sofa I wonder if the decision to cut me loose has already been made. It doesn't worry me at all.

After fifteen minutes Cohen comes out of the boardroom. He looks uncomfortable to see me. It doesn't take a genius to work out why that is.

'Had your fun?' I accuse, blocking his way to the lift. 'I bet they were really interested in what you had to say.'

'What're you talking about?'

'Told them all about my quote "drink problem" unquote, did you? Tell them what a "state" I've been in?'

'You're not making sense, Daniel.'

'Or did you tell them about me being arrested?'

'I didn't have to. It's in all the papers this morning.'

'I've known what you and Dawkins've been up to.'

He does a pretty decent impression of total bewilderment, then takes me by the elbow and guides me around the corner, out of Jean's earshot.

'Don't worry,' I say. 'I'm not going to tell them.'

'What're you talking about?'

'Oh, very convincing,' I sneer.

'They were asking me about *you*,' he hisses.

'Is that so?'

'I don't understand you. You're not making any sense. Look – *listen* to me – it doesn't look good in there. The papers, everything. There've been complaints. They –' he gestures at the boardroom – 'are *not* happy about it.'

'Who's they?'

'The partnership council. They're *all* in there. Wilson wants your blood – she's completely *rabid* – and I've never seen Fulton so red in the face. He's really lost his cool.'

'But you've sorted everything out for me, right?' I really lay on the sarcasm. 'You've explained *every*thing.'

'If it's any consolation I did my best. They were asking if you've been under pressure lately and so I told them about Hannah.'

'*What?*'

'Come on, Daniel,' he says. 'I'm not blind and I'm not stupid. I figured out what happened ages ago. You've been moping around with a face like a monthful of wet Sundays for ages. And she emailed me last week to ask how you were. She said she's worried about you. So I know everything. I was going to bring it up at dinner last week, before you walked out.'

I'm furious – I can't believe Cohen would betray me so completely. I start to move away but he puts a hand on my shoulder. I push him hard in the sternum and he staggers back.

'Daniel . . .'

'Don't talk to me,' I spit.

'What's going on, Daniel? I don't understand.'

'Don't talk to me,' I repeat, disgusted, and turn away. He stops me again with a hand on my shoulder. I turn around; the evil look on my face freezes whatever it was he was going to say. He points his eyes at the ground, guiltily, and I spin about, stride away.

DANIEL THROWN TO THE LIONS

Cohen wasn't exaggerating. The entire partnership council is waiting for me in the boardroom. They are gathered along one side of the long table. A huge picture of Charles Hunter with Frank Sinatra, Dean Martin and Sammy Davis Jr is on a facing wall. No one invites me to sit, so I sit.

I'm put in mind of an interrogation. The partners are seated with their backs to the open window, winter sun streaming through. All I can see now are their shapes, framed in silhouette. I'm breathing deeply and regularly, trying to impose a measure of composure on my riotous thoughts and to stop the sweat leaking into the small of my back. It's not working. I can't help thinking how much easier it would be to sprint at the window and launch myself straight through it.

Richard Tanner looks at me. He smiles sadly.

In front of each partner is a bundle of photocopied newsprint. Fulton is looking at the front page of *Extravaganza*, and although it's upside-down I can still make out my startled face. The photo editor hasn't bothered to correct my red eye. I look like one of the undead.

'I'm sure you can guess why we want to see you,' starts Hunter without preamble. His congenial exterior has been stowed away. He's all business today.

I nod.

'You've put us in a delicate situation.'

I nod again. I try and imagine myself somewhere else. Somewhere hot, sunny and without any cares or responsibilities.

'What the hell've you been playing at?' Fulton interjects. 'You can't even imagine how embarrassing this's been for the firm.'

I draw a deep breath. 'Could I take a look at that?' I point at the bunch of clippings. Fulton slides it across the table at me. I flip to the front page of *The Times* and read:

City Solicitor Charged with Assault on Soap Star

Daniel Tate, a solicitor working for media law firm White Hunter, has been charged by the Metropolitan Police for an attack on soap star Vincent Haines. Mr Tate, 27, pushed Mr Haines beneath a moving car, breaking his leg, and then attacked a reporter who took Tate's picture outside his East End flat last night. The police were not prepared to be drawn on possible motives for this attack. Unsubstantiated rumours last night suggested that Brian Fey, the ex-singer of the Black Dahlias, and Hannah Wilde, who appears in the same series as Mr Haines, may also have been involved in the argument that led to Mr Haines's injury.

'We've been *inundated* with calls from the newspapers,' Fulton says.

Wilson says, 'You know there're reporters waiting for us outside?'

The thought of propelling myself through the window becomes more attractive; perhaps I might take a few of them out with me when I land.

'I don't think it's you they want,' I suggest.

'The marketing department's having to prepare a statement.'

'Can I ask what it says?'

They all look at Hunter. He looks grim.

'It announces the termination of your employment at White Hunter – effective immediately. You'll be paid three months' salary for your notice period, but I'd like you to clear your desk and be out of the office by three this afternoon.'

Finally, the axe falls. I'm almost relieved. A weight is lifted.

'I think it's fair to say some of us had already resolved that your position here was untenable,' Fulton says, 'after last week's events.'

'Fair enough,' I say.

'We'd appreciate an explanation,' Wilson says. She seems upset that I'm taking this so well.

'I'm sure you would,' I say.

Wilson splutters. She's been itching to spill my blood for a long time. Her cheeks are beetroot red and her hands are quivering with mild tremors. If she had her way this would end with a lynching and my head impaled on a spike in the lobby, as a warning to my peers: *don't fuck up*.

'Dawkins going to get my cases?' I ask.

'Well, yes, at least in the short term,' Fulton explains. 'He's already looking after the Fey case. It made sense to give him the others. But you needn't worry about that. It's all in hand.'

'Well, then, perhaps this is for the best,' Hunter concludes. 'We really didn't have a choice, Daniel. You know the Law Society'll strike you off for this, don't you? There's nothing else for it, not really – no choice.'

'No, I quite understand,' I say. 'Nothing else for it.'

'You're a bloody disgrace,' Wilson says.

'That's enough, Victoria,' Tanner says sternly. 'Just leave it.'

Wilson stares hard at him; he holds her eye until she looks away.

'Are we finished?' I say, standing up. My knees don't seem strong enough to support my weight. I feel sure that they're about to buckle.

Hunter nods gravely. 'I think we are,' he says.

Finally, I open the door.

KNOW YOUR ENEMY

I'm sitting on a toilet seat in one of the cubicles, trying to regulate my breathing so as to take long, soothing lungfuls rather than short, asphyxiating gasps. I'm having only partial success, however. I wonder if I could be hyperventilating? I'm feeling drained and thirsty and then, without warning, sick. I raise the seat and bend over the bowl, and retch up my breakfast in lumpy red chunks followed by strings of icky phlegm.

I rinse out my mouth at the basins.

Another toilet flushes behind me and a door opens.

'I heard the news,' Dawkins says, exiting from that cubicle. I'm humiliated – he must have heard me puking up.

'These things happen,' I say evenly, teeth grinding.

'Listen, no hard feelings? I wouldn't want us to part on bad terms.' He extends a chubby hand.

I'd like nothing more than to take that hand and drag him in nice and close, so I can grab him by the hair and drown him in a basin of icy cold water. Or flip him onto the floor and pummel his head against the tiles, spreading some of his blood on the floor. If I were prone to violence, it'd be tempting. Unfortunately, I'm not; thumping Dolan last night was an aberration, albeit an agreeable one.

'Come on, Danny,' he says, knowing perfectly well that I hate that truncated moniker, 'let's not fall out over this.'

'You should've thought of that before you stole my cases, *Olly*,' I say, leaving his hand hanging in mid-air.

His face wrinkles with disgust. 'What's happened to

your breath?' he says. 'It smells odd – I don't know – kind of *fruity*.'

'Get lost,' is all I say, leaving him to rinse his hands.

THE END OF AN ERA

Elizabeth gets to her feet anxiously when I return. 'What happened?'

'Could you get me a few packing crates?' I ask. 'I've got to clear my stuff out by three.'

'I don't understand.'

'As of – ' I check my watch – 'fifteen minutes ago I ceased to be in the employ of White Hunter. I am now officially without a job.'

'I don't understand,' she repeats. 'They *sacked* you?' I nod. 'But what for? What did you *do*? I mean, I know you were a little late with some work for Ms Wilson, but that's hardly a reason to fire you. *Is* it? I mean, it *can't* be.'

'It doesn't matter. My heart hasn't been in this for a while. This's probably a blessing in disguise.'

'But what're you going to do?'

'I've got a couple of ideas,' I say.

I squeeze her shoulder as I force out a smile and then hide in my room, ready to start dismantling this little, redundant corner of my life.

SETTLING A SCORE

There are things to do. Things I want to straighten out. I find my Dictaphone and slot in the tape from the interview with Vincent Haines. I'm going to make him pay. I back the tape up until I find the precise section I need and, thumbing the Dictaphone to play, I double-check it:

'Jerks had a shit, straight-to-video movie planned,' Vincent Haines says again. 'My agent goofed and signed me up for it. *She* got her ass fired, let me tell you. Then *Skin Trade* came along and I decided it was a better vehicle for someone like me.'

Tim Renwick strolls past the office. He looks in at me and I stare him out until he moves on. I watch for him to move off, and then spool the tape forward a little and press play again.

'We *both* know I probably *am* in breach of their precious fucking contract. But I'm just giving you the big picture. I leave it to my lawyers to decide what to leave in and what to leave out. That's what I pay you for. If I say anything that's not good for me, you can just strip it out. I never said it, right? And if this case goes to trial, and I hope to God it doesn't, you can tell me exactly what I have to say to make the bad man go away. Got me?'

I've got him all right. I address an envelope, put the tape inside, and drop it in the post tray.

A CRY FOR HELP

The news of my dismissal travels fast. Several of my contemporaries pop by to commiserate, although they all want the full story so they can work out how easily it could have been them in my shoes. And of course they're curious about my notoriety, although none of them has the nerve to ask me about it.

As I'm packing my law books into a crate, I notice that I've received voicemail. I punch in my password and play the message back on the squawkbox.

'Um, Daniel, it's me – Brian – listen, I've gone and got myself into a bit of a fix and I could really do with your help. Um, they're only going to let me make one call and I've only got another ten pence left so I can't go into all the details and such like, but I was wondering – could you come over and help me out? I wouldn't ask this usually but I think it's pretty important and I don't really have anyone else to go to, you know, no one else I *trust* anyway. Fuck, anyway, shit, my cash is running out, so, um, I'm at the same police station as last night. I guess you just ask for me at the desk or something, and, um, like, thanks and everything in advance, OK? I'll see you in a bit. Bye. Oh, um, before I go, if Davey calls, you don't know where I am. OK? You haven't even heard from me. OK? See you then, bye.'

So: this is it. Brian's finally been arrested. I'm not sure what to feel. If anything, a sense of relief; if he's been arrested I won't have to do anything with the cassette I've hidden at the back of my drawer nor will I have to report my knowledge of the photographs. If the police can manage without my information, I'll be able to placate my itchy conscience and forget about the whole sorry mess.

I wonder if I should go to see him or whether it might be best just to erase the message and consign him to the past. If I follow through with my plan, I won't even be here. I wrestle with the alternatives for a couple of minutes. Then I decide to go; maybe he *didn't* do it, however bad it might look, and maybe the opportunity will present itself to ask him about the tapes. And I'm curious; I need to see him. He deserves the chance to put his side of the story to me. He's earned at least that.

A FINAL PLEA FROM SCOTT DOLAN

More voicemail:

'This is it. Last chance, Daniel. I'm gonna forget you punched me. I know, you were under pressure and you snapped. It's understandable. It's forgotten. I'm dropping the charges today, so you don't need to worry about that. And listen – I want to talk to you *very* badly. More than before, now the story's broken. The whole attack on Haines – I saw what happened and I know it was an accident, but it's made you big news. Look, it's made you a bit of a star. You're gonna get offers from all the papers once they find out your details, so I'm laying my cards on the table now. If you agree to be interviewed exclusively by me I guarantee you, I absolutely *promise*, you'll get sympathetic treatment. Plus I know I'm close to something really big with Brian Fey and John French. I know he's involved in that death. Anyway, I'm not gonna call again. This's your last chance. If you don't call, all bets are off. We'll unleash the hounds. Goodbye.'

I wonder if now would be a good time to establish contact with this friend in the media. Maybe he could be useful to me. I dial his number and then wait for the call to connect.

SQUARING THE CIRCLE

On the way out of the office I run into Cohen.

'I'm so sorry,' Cohen says.

'Of course you're sorry. Now I'm not going to be around getting made up's gonna be a lot easier for you, isn't it? Your friend'll make sure you get in, won't he? Jesus. I just hope you can live with your conscience.'

'What's the matter with you? I don't know what you're talking about, Daniel.'

'I'm not interested.'

'Come on, Daniel – I'm worried about you. I've never seen you like this before.'

'I let you pull the wool over my eyes. But not any more.'

'You're not making sense. Listen – let's meet for a drink. We have to talk properly. I don't want us to part on bad terms.'

I say, exasperated, 'Fine.'

We arrange to meet for a beer later in the week. I do this just so I can get out of here without a scene. I want this to be as easy and smooth as possible. This is an appointment I have no intention of keeping.

BRIAN'S STORY

I leave the office by the back entrance to avoid the mob of reporters waiting out front. By the time I arrive at the police station Brian is signing forms at the front desk and collecting his personal belongings. This is not what I'd been expecting. They *bailed* him? Lines of fatigue are etched around his eyes and he looks gaunter than usual. He actually looks old and tired.

'They're letting you out?'

'Yes.' His eyes flash with anger. 'They finally believed me.' He says this loud enough so that the desk sergeant can hear him.

Five minutes later and we've found a coffee shop, where we sit with steaming lattes and slices of carrot cake set down between us. He had said that he was famished. A flurry of snow is swirling up against the window and people are hurrying down into the underground. The day is short and twilight is already drawing in, the headlights of cars on the road glowing through the translucent flakes, little yellow bowls of brightness.

Brian is now wolfing down his cake, but I can't bear the suspense. I take a sip of coffee and, attempting an innocuous introduction, say, 'So what happened?'

He polishes off the last forkfuls as he explains. 'They arrested me early this morning after I took Lisa to a hotel. They questioned me for hours.'

'What did they ask you about?' I ask artlessly, even though I already know.

'About John.'

'Go on.'

He looks out of the window into the white. 'This isn't easy,' he says. 'Before he died I'd started to stake out his house. I know it was stupid. But I just wanted to talk to him. We had things we needed to talk about.'

'Like what?'

'I can't say.'

I look away.

'He wouldn't answer his phone so I just waited there for him, sometimes for ages at a time. Some of his neighbours spotted me.' I remember the report in the newspaper. 'When the police found out, they must've thought they were onto something. They traced the car back to me. I guess they figured I was worth talking to – plus they knew John and me didn't always see eye to eye. We had an argument in America during a tour, ages ago – John punched me, I shoved him, he fell off a balcony and ended up with some broken ribs. It was just an accident but they went on and on and on about it.'

Brian tells me this quietly.

'I've never forgiven myself for it. My temper again.'

I tighten my grip around the mug.

'So the police started checking me out; said I've been followed for the past few days. They said they had someone watching us at the funeral – so they saw that argument with the others. Me hitting Martin, that was the final straw.'

He looks out into the darkness of the street, thoughtful. 'I *know* I was stupid to bug John like that,' he says, 'but I couldn't help myself. I wanted to talk to him, just to try and understand what happened between me and him. I could never get my head around it.'

Looking away from him, unable to hold his gaze, I ask, 'Did you? I mean, did you talk to him?'

He swallows a final mouthful of cake. I'm holding my breath as I wait for him to speak.

Brian frowns, troubled, and then hesitantly – *too* hesitantly – shakes his head. 'I couldn't do it. I'd sit out there for hours playing things around in my head, not really paying attention to anything much, drinking, smoking, not thinking straight. I'd eventually get the courage up to go and knock on the door, but then I'd imagine what he'd say and I'd just lose my bottle.'

I look down at my plate, trying to hide my certainty that this isn't true; I've seen the pictures that prove the lie. I try to not think about why he's tendering this fiction, because the obvious answer – his guilt – is too compelling. It must be the reason. Why else lie to me now that he's been discounted as a suspect? A cold shiver passes down my spine.

And I haven't forgotten about the money used for my bail and the cash stolen from French's house – those identical amounts.

Brian gazes outside to where a bus is wheezing alongside its stop. The storm has picked up, an abruptly fierce wind tossing light snow up from the ground, dervishes of swirling flakes. The street is almost empty now, the remaining few pedestrians clasping hats to their heads. Brian takes out a packet of cigarettes and taps one out. He offers it to me. I decline.

'The thing is,' he continues, fishing for his lighter, 'I was outside his house the evening he died. I now can't get the feeling out of my head that if I'd done something then I might've been able to stop him. I don't know.'

I study his face. He lights the fag and the tip flares up briefly, casting an orange glow across his chin and mouth. I look for the clichéd signs of deceit – the darting eyes, the rapid blinking – but he just looks back wistfully at me. Sadly.

He can't fool me: I know too much; I've seen too much.

I want to ask him about the photos and the tapes. I want to ask him about the money. I want to tell him that I *know* he's lying, and why won't he admit it?

Instead of bringing this up, I lamely ask, 'So what happened then – with the police?'

'They were convinced I hadn't told them everything. Eventually I persuaded them that I was with someone else at the time they were telling me John died. They made a few phone calls to check out my story, and when it held up they let me go.'

I guess at the alibi that he must've used. The false alibi.

'You said you were with Lisa and Carmen?'

He nods. 'We'd arranged to go out for a few drinks before meeting you at the party. I'd heard that the band were all going to be there, and I just needed some Dutch courage before I faced up to them. I thought the girls might as well come too.'

One final chance for him to come clean. I say, 'So you weren't outside when the police think he died?' My tone is more suspicious than I intended.

His expression blurs, changes. He glares at me sourly, suddenly irritated. He says, 'No, I wasn't outside when the police think he was killed – I already told you that. Haven't you been listening?'

'I know you told me. It's just that—'

Brian interrupts, voice swiftly raised. 'It's just that what? What? That you don't believe me?'

'I never said that.'

'You didn't fucking have to.'

'Come on, Brian—'

'Don't patronize me,' Brian snarls.

He slams his coffee cup down. The saucer cracks and hot coffee splashes back onto his hand. He swears, wipes it off on his trousers, gets up abruptly. He shakes his head, 'I don't believe this. I thought you of all people would believe me.'

I don't say anything. He looms over me. His fists clench and unclench. The veins in his neck and under his chin are as tight as cords, bulging.

'You're just like everyone else,' he sneers. 'No one gives a shit about me any more. You only put up with me because this case looks good on your CV. Don't think I don't know.'

'That's not true.'

'Fuck off. You can all go to hell. I don't need any of you.'

As he starts to leave I reach for his arm. He swipes my hand away and glowers down at me. He says, 'Leave it. I've had enough. I don't need you any more.'

Brian heads for the door and strides into the storm. And there's no way I'm going to follow him out there – on my own with him in the gloom and the empty streets.

I know what to do now; my mind is completely made up. I put a call in on my mobile as I get up to leave, confirming the details of the appointment I set up earlier.

EXPOSÉ

Scott Dolan is already waiting for me where we had arranged, leaning back with one foot braced against the wall of yet another coffee shop on the way back to the office. There are a dozen of them around here. I spot his hair from a hundred yards away, red against a shifting curtain of white. Snow is gathering on his shoulders. He brushes it off. I can't help feeling a little flicker of satisfaction when I notice the scabbed crust of blood around his nostrils. He smiles a neutral smile as I approach, the corners of his mouth downturned, and I take his hand when he offers it. We find a table inside and sit down. He orders cappuccinos, sets up his recording machine on the table, and thumbs to a fresh page in his notebook.

'I'm glad you've had a change of heart,' he says. 'Now – let's get down to business, shall we? What've you got to say?'

The tape starts rolling. I gesture for him to switch it off.

'It's not so much what I've got to *say*,' I suggest. 'It's more what I can *give* you.'

THE WHIMS OF FASHION

After I'm done with Dolan I've still got half an hour to kill until the rush hour kicks in and the office empties out. I visit the record store to check out how Brian's album is doing.

New releases have taken the place of last week's offerings, although Monster Munch's albums have been moved to a huge display immediately inside the doors, filling the space that was previously occupied by the Dahlias. There aren't many copies of their album left.

I root around the racks devoted to the charts and then, having no luck, browse the alphabetical shelving where back catalogue is deposited. Nothing. As I'm about to leave the shop I pause by the bargain bucket. Among failed singles from soap stars and charity records for obscure causes, I find the remaining four copies of Brian's record, reduced to half-price to clear. This after just one week!

'Why's this so cheap?' I ask the guy behind the counter, another copy of the album in hand.

'Have you *heard* it?' he asks me. I shake my head. 'Worst piece of self-referential garbage I've ever had the misfortune to listen to. You can't even give these away. We've only sold one copy.'

'I thought he was still popular.'

'He *was*, once,' he replies. 'Not any more. And that's the *worst* thing about stars like him. They think they can keep trotting out the same old stuff year after year after year, but they can't. Times change. Tastes change. And if you can't keep up, you might as well quit. You know the album's been deleted by the label, don't you?'

'No.' I shake my head. I didn't know.

'It only sold a few hundred. That's disastrous. You can give it a couple of months tops before his label cuts its losses and drops him altogether. And that'll be the last we ever hear of him.'

PREPARATIONS

En route to the office, I divert to a cash machine and try to withdraw enough money to see me through the night. My request for cash is denied. I eject my card, insert it and punch in my number again. Rejection. I request a balance instead. While the machine clicks and hums to itself I work out how much of my final, abbreviated pay cheque will be absorbed by the mortgage and bills, and realize I'm going to be facing a serious shortfall. The thought that I'll be bankrupt does not fill me with the dread it should, since I won't be around to suffer the consequences.

The machine finishes its calculations and reports back that I have the grand total of twenty-three pounds and change. This should be all I need for tonight.

BURNING BRIDGES AND
THE MIDNIGHT OIL

The office is empty as I creep back inside. Everyone must be on their way to the party. This suits me fine.

Ray, one of the downstairs security guards, is on duty. He's engrossed in a magazine involving motorbikes and naked women. He looks up as I approach and grunts at me.

'You missing the fun too, eh?' he says. The news of my dismissal has evidently not yet been circulated to the support staff.

I nod glumly. 'Pain in the arse.'

'Tell me about it,' he accedes.

Our bond of shared grievance established, I don't even need to show him my security pass. He just waves me inside.

My office is dark. I stumble over packing crates until I reach the anglepoise on the desk. I click it on and hunker down behind its golden cone of light. I still feel nauseous and dog-tired but I push my frailties to one side. I have work to do. It won't take long and then I can relax. The plan is almost fully-formed now. I just have to put it into operation.

Someone has finished off my packing for me. The shelves are naked and my desk is clear. My things have been neatly slotted into place in their crates: books at the bottom, then folders and breakable knick-knacks resting on top. I suspect Elizabeth, and resolve to thank her at the party.

I take the answerphone cassette from where I taped it to the bottom of a drawer and drop it into an envelope. I address the envelope to the investigating officer dealing with the John French inquiry and type a brief note explaining the tape's significance. I leave the note anonymous – a coward to the last – and place the envelope in the tray for the outgoing post. I've missed tonight's late collection; the tape will be collected tomorrow morning and delivered to the police on Wednesday or Thursday, depending on the post.

On the way out, I stop by the big wall-high filing cabinets and, after thumbing through the index, locate six juicy folders, each stuffed full of papers – correspondence, contracts, attendance notes – held together with treasury tags. I slip them into my bag and leave the office for the last time.

SOUTH OF THE RIVER

There's one more thing I have to do before the party.

I leave the office, flag down a black cab, and cross the river to head south into Tooting. On arrival I hand the driver one of my two £10 notes, reserving the other for my return trip.

Only one thing will change my mind about leaving the country. Only if Hannah agrees to see me, listens to what I've got to say; that's the only way I'll still be in this country on Wednesday, and not cramped in economy class with a miniature do-it-yourself chicken chasseur kit on my lap, following the sun halfway around the world.

I know this is pathetic of me, weak-willed to still be

in her thrall after everything she said last night. But her claws have sunk in deep. She's as much a part of the maelstrom in my head as anything else: Brian, losing my job, my decision to steal the band's money and leave. I have to at least try to see her before I can go.

The address I've been given by Hannah's agency is for a mid-terraced house in a quiet tree-lined street. As the taxi chugs away down the road, leaving me shivering and alone on a snowy pavement, I stare up at a large bay window and two smaller windows on the first floor. A light is on in one of the bedrooms, painting a barren flower box in a tawny hue. I pace along the pavement for five minutes trying to compose my thoughts and then sit down on a cold bench at the corner of the street where I can watch the house without being observed. I'm feeling unsteady again. I see a shadow move quickly across a window lit by blue light from a flickering TV.

So she's in.

It's no use just sitting here, freezing. Be a man: do something. I gather my courage, march up to the front door and knock loudly. There is long delay and I'm about to leave, when the door starts to open.

'Yes?' says a girl I don't think I've ever seen before. She's tall, good figure, blonde hair and freckles, wearing a white terry-cloth robe with her hair bunched in a vivid red towel. Her skin is wet and puckered.

'Um, hello,' I falter. 'Sorry if I got you out of the bath.'

'I was already out,' says the girl. 'It's OK.'

'Is Hannah in?'

'She's gone out,' she says warily. 'Who are you?'

It dawns on me that I *have* seen her before – she plays one of the other models in *Skin Trade*. Hannah must have moved in with her. Or perhaps they bought the place together? This confirmation of another, separate life is hurtful, underscoring the finality of our split and confirming she has found an alternative, independent existence – one that doesn't feature me in it. I would have preferred her to be shivering in a freezing bedsit somewhere, like she was when I originally found her. Now I feel even more pathetic; she's gotten over this much more easily than I have.

'I'm a friend,' I stammer. 'I was just passing through. Thought I'd stop by and see if she was in. I haven't seen her for ages.'

'Well, she's not, I'm afraid. She went out earlier – to a party, I think. Do you want me to say you called?'

I'm not about to identify myself and blow my cover, so I politely decline and tell her that I'll telephone later instead. Then, taking me by surprise, inspiration. I say, 'She's with Vinny, I suppose?'

The girl relaxes. 'Yes,' she says. 'He came by with Rip to pick her up fifteen minutes ago. Don't know what he's doing going out – his leg's broken, you know.'

'I should've explained,' I say more confidently. 'I'm a friend of Vinny's. I directed his first movie. I know

Hannah through him. I was going to talk movies with her, actually. I've got one just about to start shooting.'

A half-embarrassed smile cracks the stern face. 'Look, I'm sorry if you thought I was being rude – it's just that Hannah's been having problems with one of her ex-boyfriends. He's been nosing around most of last week and he managed to get this address off her agent this morning. We've both been a little on edge.'

'Don't worry about it,' I say. 'You can't be too careful.'

'I didn't catch your name,' she says.

'Uh, Jeremy,' I say.

'Listen – Jeremy – can I offer you a cup of tea? It's freezing cold out here and I feel awful for being so rude.'

'That'd be really great,' I say. 'Thanks.'

HANNAH'S HOME FROM HOME

The inside of the house has been decorated in an exaggeratedly feminine fashion. The walls are painted orange and there are bunches of bright flowers thrust into jaunty vases. The furniture, a mixture of expensive designer pieces and cheap junk from Ikea that Hannah liberated from our flat, marks the recent swelling of her income. She can afford the stuff now that we could only dream about before; I remember afternoons spent drooling over classy tables and chairs through the windows of boutiques that credit-check you before they even let you inside.

'I'm Jessica, by the way,' the girl says, offering me a hand puckered red by hot water.

I take it, warm and a little damp. 'Nice to meet you.'

'Milk and sugar?'

'Mmmm, two sugars, please.'

'Won't be a moment.' She tightens the cord of her robe and swishes into the kitchen, leaving me alone with Hannah's things.

I wander around the room, carefully lifting ornaments from the mantelpiece, turning them over in my hands, inspecting them. Some of them I recognize, things we bought together; others are new and unfamiliar. Some might be Jessica's, I suppose.

On a bookshelf I find a framed, signed picture of Vincent Haines. I'm tempted to throw it against the wall.

'Biscuit?' calls Jessica.

'Uh, no,' I force out. 'No, thanks.'

I replace the photo carefully.

She comes back into the lounge with a cup of tea. 'I'm just going to go upstairs and get changed,' she says. 'Make yourself comfortable.'

I wait until she's out of the way before continuing my search. In an alcove between the chimney breast and the wall I find a cardboard box full of stuff. I crouch down and scrabble inside it. The box contains several of Hannah's old photo albums and a lot of junk.

I take one of the albums out and flip through pages protected with thin sheets of adhesive plastic. There are dozens of pictures of Hannah and me: pictures of us on holiday; pictures of us at Christmas and at birthday parties; pictures of us looking happy and relaxed at home. I carefully replace the album with the others in the box and take out a picture frame I recognize. Hannah used to have it on her bedside table. It is a picture of us, together, taken by a guard on the observation deck of the Empire State Building when we visited New York last spring. We are clutching each other, hair and clothes tousled by the night wind, everything frozen in the white glare of the flash, the Chrysler Building glowing out-of-focus over my right shoulder, both of us grinning with exhilaration.

'Look at all that rubbish,' says Jessica. I didn't notice her returning downstairs. She's changed into a chunky jumper and leggings. I quickly thrust the picture back down into the box.

'Sorry, I was just—'

'Don't worry, it's just Hannah's old bits and pieces – you know, bric à brac that reminds her of her old boyfriend. Did you know him?'

'Uh, no,' I say. 'Before my time.'

'Me too. But he's ancient history, right? She said she's going to bin all that crap tomorrow.'

I fight to keep my voice from catching, and say, 'She's just going to throw it away?'

Jessica is back in the kitchen again, and she misses

the anguished edge to my voice. 'She wants to make a clean break. He's been totally weird lately – stalking Vinny, trying to find out the address of this place. They went to see him last night to tell him to leave her alone. He broke Vincent's leg. It was in all the papers this morning, front-page news. If you ask me, he needs help. He's, like, a total fruitcake.'

'How long's she been seeing Vinny for now? It must be, what, three months?'

'No – longer than that,' she says.

'More than three months?'

She comes back in with a teapot.

'Easily. She must've dumped the old guy about, what, three or four months ago? She'd been seeing Vinny a long time before that. She was sleeping with him, I don't know, at least six months before she split up with her ex.'

I get up sharply and a wave of giddiness washes over me. I have to steady myself on the mantelpiece.

'Are you all right?' she asks.

'Head rush,' I say.

'You sure?' she asks. 'You don't look well.'

'It's nothing,' I bluff. 'I'm probably just coming down with a cold. It's the weather.'

'Can I get you anything?' She raises the teapot. 'An aspirin?'

'No, I'm fine, thanks. But I should maybe get going.'

'What about that movie you mentioned? I was going to ask you about it?'

'What?'

'The movie? I'm an actress too – sorry to be so pushy, but I'd love to take a look at the script.'

'I'll send you a copy,' I say brusquely. 'Look, I have to go.'

'Should I tell Hannah you called?'

I'm already in the hallway, reaching for the door handle.

'No,' I say. 'Don't worry about it. I'll catch her later.'

THE CHRISTMAS PARTY

An hour later, I reach the ballroom of a hotel off the Strand, full of people from the office, dry ice from the disco, and loud music over a background of chattering and general mirth. I sneak in without anyone seeing me.

The men are in black tie and the women in cocktail dresses. A smattering of celebs: Richard Stilgoe, Paul Daniels and Debbie McGee, Anthea Turner, Peter Stringfellow, Bonnie Langford, Cilla Black, Stock, Aitken *and* Waterman, Shane Richie, Fern Britton, Peter Davison, Carole Smillie, Henry Kelly, Lorraine Kelly, Matthew Kelly, Gillian Taylforth, Tony Hadley, Keith Chegwin, Roger Moore, Richard Whiteley, Keith Harris (with Orville), Terry Wogan, Diddie David Hamilton, The Krankies, Chas (without Dave), Kilroy, Noel Edmonds, Dave Lee Travis.

The Grumbleweeds, lured out of retirement to indulge their lawyers, are providing the evening's entertainment from a stage at the front of the room.

I look at everyone and feel a pang of regret.

The party's been in full swing for a couple of hours and everyone is drunk on the free booze. I'm returning from the toilets where I have just been powerfully sick, but it hasn't made me feel any better; now I just feel empty. I've started to feel dizzy and I can't stop sweating. I had to splash cold water over my face for five minutes just to cool down and I looked half-dead in the mirror. I must be coming down with something. I've been under a lot of stress. I'm probably worn out.

I'm standing at the bar, necking bottles of beer, when I see Brian in the entrance. He stops to scan the room but doesn't see me. As he's waiting there, Dawkins appears at his side and says something into his ear. Brian smiles affably at him and nods agreement. They must have come to the party together; the Dork has already taken my place with Brian. I finish the beer, surprised that this has made me angry, when Brian finally spots me and half-jogs across to the bar.

'What do you want?' I ask.

'I need to talk to you,' he says. 'I want to apologize.'

'I'm not interested.'

'Please, Daniel, there's something I have to tell you.'

'What are you doing with him,' I say quickly, pointing at the Dork. He's already found a couple of the partners to brown-nose.

'Just a coincidence – he got out of a taxi the same time as me. I thought you might be here, and since I'd already been invited by Mr Fulton I thought I'd check.'

'You know he's an idiot, don't you?'

'What? The bald guy? Of course I do. He started schmoozing me as soon as he saw me. I already told you he pisses me off.'

'Make it quick,' I say.

He smiles, looks embarrassed. 'How's this for crazy? That couple dropped the charges against us. I didn't tell you earlier.'

'What couple?'

'The flat we broke into? Well, the one *I* broke into. Turns out they're both big Dahlias fans. All I had to do was sign a couple of albums for them. They said it was obviously a misunderstanding, and if I paid for the damage to be fixed they'd forget it ever happened. Pretty weird, huh? I go ages to find someone who remembers me and then find those two like that.'

'Yeah, weird,' I say dubiously. 'Look, Brian, unless there's anything else I've got to be going.'

He subtly moves until he has angled himself in front of me. 'I want to say sorry. I feel awful about earlier.'

I say, 'Yeah, well,' nervous to be around him again.

'Please?' he says. 'There's something I have to tell you.'

Reluctantly, I nod. As I chug away on another bottle, nervously stripping the label, he explains.

BRIAN'S CONFESSION

'I'm sorry about losing my temper. I've been on edge this last week – Jesus, even longer than that, *months* – and everything's been happening at once. You know? And then I found out this afternoon how badly the new album's doing. I mean, *really* bad – I think I'm gonna get dropped. And I'm not using any of this as an excuse. I'm just explaining. So, anyway, I've checked myself into anger-management courses again for the New Year. I'm gonna give them a real try this time.'

'Look – that's great, Brian,' I say. 'Just get whatever it is off your chest so I can go.'

He takes a long breath. 'You were right about John,' he admits.

I falter, 'How do you mean?'

'I did see him – just after he died.'

'You were in his house?'

He nods. 'The door was open and I went inside.'

'Why?'

'I needed to talk to him and he wouldn't speak to me.'

'Why not?'

'He made me promise that I wouldn't get in touch. He said it wasn't possible, not any more.'

'Look, I'm sorry, you've lost me.' I put down my beer and step around him. 'And I have to go.'

He grabs my wrist and looks straight into my eyes.

'John and me were seeing each other.'

'What?'

'I'm gay, Daniel. So was he.'

Every other noise in the room is silenced for me. My mind is an empty white space. I look at him. He smiles sadly. I fumble for words. All I can manage is, 'What?'

'We were a couple.'

'No way.'

He nods.

'No fucking way.'

'Ten years,' he says sadly.

'What . . . what about all the girls? You were always with gorgeous women. All the pictures, the stories in the papers? Both of you.'

'None of that meant a thing. It wasn't real. It was just something we *did*. I mean, we couldn't've come out in the eighties. Can you imagine what it would've been like for us? We're weren't exactly Erasure or Bronski Beat, were we? We'd've been crucified. It would've been the end of us.'

'But you were married—'

'And divorced. Look, I was confused about myself. I thought maybe if I got married I'd be able to straighten out, you know, *cure* myself. Jesus – I know that's complete bollocks, I know, but I had a *really* Catholic upbringing, OK? It's taken me a long time to accept what I am, you know, to get over the guilt. There's been a lot of guilt.'

'No, I don't believe it—'

'No one else knows about us. Well, I think Giovanni

maybe suspects, but I know for a fact none of the band knows. We always kept things very quiet. All the arguments we had, we always said they were because of "creative differences" – rather than the boy one of us had found the other with. And you mustn't say anything, either. I promised John I'd never speak about it.'

'Fuck, I . . . what happened?'

'We split up when John found out one of the tabloids was about to do an exposé and out him. Someone from *Extravaganza*, I think. There was a rumour they had photos of him at Heaven with his tongue down some bimbo's throat. John was terrified.'

'Of what?'

'He thought if he got outted, that'd be the end of his career – the end of the band. He didn't have a very high opinion of the people who bought our stuff. He had this idea they wouldn't buy anything of ours if they knew two of us were queer. I don't know – these days? Maybe we would've gotten away with it. Fuck it, it might even've *helped*. Music was the most important thing in his life, more important than everything, including me as it turned out. So he finished with me, made me swear I'd never tell anyone about us, and started putting across this bullshit hetero image. And now, if you believe what Martin said, it looks like it was John who pushed me out of the band, too. You know, get me out of the way, avoid temptation, guilt, all that shit.'

'But what about what's-his-name – the guy with the Spanish name?'

'Giovanni? He's Italian, actually. John never could resist good-looking foreign boys. And we had an open relationship. Well, *he* did. I calmed down after I had a close shave with a guy I didn't know was a junkie, but I didn't mind him messing around every now and again so long as he was careful. It was the only way I could keep him. Gio's been on the scene for a couple of years.'

'I had no idea.'

'Of course you didn't. No one does.'

Brian orders a couple of whiskies and hands one to me.

'I couldn't get over him as easy as he got over me. Couldn't stop thinking about him. Every time he was on TV it was fucking murder. Just like with you and your girlfriend – I told you we had more in common than you thought, didn't I? And then, when I got dumped out of the band, I couldn't understand how John could just stand by and let it happen like he did. But Martin was right . . . fuck, I don't know what to think, it's possible. John was ruthless when it came to his career.'

I'm struggling to take this all in. I neck the whisky and ask the barman for another two.

'So that's why you kept the money?'

'Partly,' he shrugged. 'It wasn't the money itself. I just didn't want them to be able to get rid of me quietly, without a fuss.'

I have to tell him about taking the money.

'Look, I know I should've said something sooner about me being outside his house that night. I wish I had, but I was scared – I didn't know what people would think. I was worried everyone'd jump to the wrong conclusion, especially if it came out that we used to be together.'

'*I* did,' I admit quietly.

'So last Sunday – I'd been waiting outside all afternoon. From midday or something, just sitting in my car smoking and drinking. It came to five-thirty and I realized I couldn't stay there all night – I had the party to get to and I didn't want to be late again. I'm *always* late. So I said to myself, "Brian, it's time you faced up to this. Pull yourself together. Just fucking do it." So I got out of the car and went up to the front door. I must've smoked another three fags up there before I found the guts to ring the bell. And then when there was no answer and I tried knocking on the door, it just opened as soon as I touched it. I couldn't understand it – no one had come and gone while I'd been waiting there. It was only later – days later – that I remembered I'd left for maybe ten minutes so I could use the toilet in a garage on the main road, and get another bottle of gin. Whoever it was who forgot to close the door must've gone in or come out while I was gone. So I didn't see anything.

'I pushed the door open and went inside. I'd been there before, used to live there almost, so I knew my way around. I called out but there was no answer. I looked upstairs but there was no sign of anyone around. But I knew he was in there – I'd seen him at the window, and I'd called him and left a message on his answerphone. I thought he'd just been ignoring me as usual. So I went through into the hall at the back of the house – I thought maybe he was in the garden or something.'

He puts his hand through his hair and raises his chin to me.

'John'd tied this rope to the top of the banister and then tied the other end round his neck. He was hanging, this chair tipped over beneath him, he must've kicked it over or something. He was just swinging there. Jesus. His face was purple and the rope'd cut into his neck. It was fucking horrible.'

His hair falls before his face.

'Why'd he do it?' I ask.

'Specifically? Don't know. But he was always really sensitive and he could get really self-destructive when he was depressed. He used to cut himself with razors like that guy from the Manics did, Richey Edwards, remember? The whole thing with the papers'd terrified him. He hated himself for being gay. It took me years to accept it but, I don't know, I don't think *he* ever really did. A picture of him with his tongue down some boy's throat in all the Sunday papers? That on its own'd be enough for him to top himself. And if I know John, the pressure of taking over from me was probably getting to him, too. The new album just ready to come out, no one knowing how the fans and the critics were going to react . . . I'm sure that had something to do with it.'

'Maybe he felt guilty? About what happened to you?'

Brian shakes his head and smiles ruefully. 'Yeah, maybe,' he says.

'Go on.'

'I could see it hadn't happened long ago – he was still warm to the touch. I think I must've fainted, because the next thing I know I'm on the floor feeling really light-headed, with a cut and blood on my head. And then I panicked – big-time. I'd never even seen a dead body before. I suddenly had this blinding flash – if anyone found me like this, with John's body, him dead up there – still warm – I knew what they'd think. I mean, everyone knew we'd been having squabbles. It wouldn't take a genius to figure out that I must've killed him because I was pissed off about the band binning me, losing the court case, my new record getting slated, everyone loving his vocals on their album, everything. Then made it look like it was suicide – very clever, Brian, very clever. And then if the fact we were a couple ever came out, people'd think it was some jealous crime of passion. Me upset about getting dumped for Giovanni or something. John was hardly in a position to explain what'd really happened, was he? So I panicked, I completely lost it. I got out of the house as quickly as I could, got into my car and just took off. I drove onto the M25 and just drove, for miles, pointing the car in the same direction and driving around London until I was almost out of gas. I was just thinking: working out how bad it would look for me if people knew I'd been there.

'Eventually I chilled out. I called Carmen and Lisa, arranged for them to come to the party with us, made sure they'd back me up, say I was with them earlier. They were both totally out of it when I picked them up. They'd been smoking weed all afternoon – couldn't remember a thing. It worked; when the police asked them yesterday, they did me proud. They couldn't be sure about the times, couldn't remember what time they were with me, but they were vague enough to give the police some serious doubts that it could've been me. I feel bad about dragging them in but what else could I do?'

'What about the suitcases in my spare room? I thought you were going to make a run for it.'

'That's just our things. I packed them last night when you were asleep. I was going to take Lisa's over to the hotel this morning, and I was probably going to move in with her after I'd seen you next. But then the police arrested me – threw my timing off a bit.'

The big question:

'Someone sent me a tape from John French's answering machine,' I say slowly. 'You were laying into him on it – threatening him.'

He smiles another sad smile. 'Me,' he confesses. 'I sent it to you.'

'*You* sent it?'

'After the funeral. I felt so *guilty*. You know, seeing the others there, seeing how upset everyone was, then losing my temper again and hitting Marty. And I thought – this's all my fault. All of it. If John and me hadn't argued. If I could've been bothered to *try* during our last tour, and kept clean, maybe it wouldn't have flopped like it did. If I hadn't OD'd and fucked up the recording of the last album, maybe things would've been better. And the worst bit – if I'd told John how much I loved him, maybe he would've found the strength to get through the bad publicity he thought was gonna come our way.'

'But the tape? I don't understand . . .'

'It was when I realized what a mess I was in – stuck in that hallway with John dead, swinging on that fucking rope – I remembered I'd been ringing him up constantly for the last couple of weeks. I wanted us to get back together and I was mad at him for not sticking up for me when they threw me out of the band. And I was usually out of my head when I called him; my messages were all pretty angry. Well, you've heard them now, so you know.' I nod. 'I thought unless I got the tape and got rid of it, people'd come to the wrong conclusion. So I went over to his machine and took it.

'And then after the funeral, when I was feeling like such a selfish bastard, I just had to get rid of it – I had to. I'd been carrying it around in my pocket all week and it suddenly felt like it was red hot. I know that's crazy. So I got out of my head before I could think about it too much, and took it to your office. I thought you'd know better'n me what to do with it. I was feeling so low – I think I half-wanted you to send it to the police and just be done with it. Let *them* decide what to do with me. I was feeling so bad – so *awful* – I just wanted to be punished. That was the only way I thought I could make it up to everyone that I'd let down. I don't think I can explain it any better than that.'

'And the money you bailed me out with last night?'

'It's like I said: an account I'd forgotten about. I still get royalties from some adverts I did in the eighties. Quite a bit of cash actually. The bank wrote to me because I hadn't touched the cash for ages. I just used that.'

'I thought—'

'I know what it looks like,' he breaks in with a wry smile of understanding. 'The cash taken from John's? You thought it was his money I used. I killed him and pinched it. I probably would've thought the same thing myself. You haven't heard the news yet, then?'

'What news?'

'Giovanni got arrested this afternoon. They found the money at his flat. He's confessed that John gave it to him, apparently. That stuff with the papers about John being outted? Gio knew how much John wanted to keep it quiet, so he decided he'd take advantage. Little fucker was blackmailing him. He said he'd spill everything unless John paid him to keep his mouth shut. Ten grand was his price.'

I stand there quietly after he's finished, not quite sure what to say.

I should apologize, but the only thought running through my head is I've got to get back to the office and stop the answerphone tape from going to the police.

'I'm just going to go to the toilet,' I say. I feel sick again.

'I'll be here,' he promises.

THE CHANGING OF THE GUARD

By the time I return, Brian has been surrounded by the heavily made-up members of Monster Munch.

'Hey, Scooter,' Bam Bam says. 'It's the law. Better behave.'

'Scooter's only seventeen,' Mooch tells me. 'He's not allowed to drink.'

They laugh. 'How about this?' Scooter taunts, holding up a transparent freezer bag full of white powder. 'Am I allowed to do this?'

'Shouldn't you be in Japan?' I say.

'Cancelled,' Mooch says. 'Nips wouldn't pay us what we're worth.'

'Not enough lollipops in the rider?' Brian suggests.

'Not enough sherbet, man,' Scooter corrects, tapping the bag.

'We were just saying how we all loved the Black Dahlias,' Bam Bam says, his tone suggesting the contrary. 'They were, like, a big-time major influence on us.'

'And Brian was, you know, one of the best vocalists of 1984,' Mooch adds.

'Although he did kinda lose it after that,' Scooter chips in.

'And, course, he sucks now,' Bam Bam suggests. 'Shame he got chucked out of the Dahlias, wasn't it?'

Mooch nods, 'But it's hardly like Paul McCartney leaving the Beatles.'

'Or not even like Geri leaving the Spices.'

They laugh raucously. I'm waiting for Brian to explode, that now all-too-familiar incandescence surely about to flare. It doesn't happen. He's leaning back against the bar with an expression of mild, paternal amusement. 'Shouldn't you boys be getting off to bed?' he says. 'It's a school day tomorrow.'

They exchange puzzled, disconcerted looks; perhaps they were hoping for more from Brian Fey, the infamous hothead.

'Before you go, boys,' says Brian, 'a bit of advice from someone who knows: you're flavour of the month now but it won't last. You'll get dumped, just like everybody else does. Eventually you'll find out that fifteen minutes of fame just means another fifty years of emptiness. Just bear it in mind.'

Their faces change from perplexed to bewildered, as

if Brian was addressing them in Swahili. 'Come on,' says Mooch, 'let's go. My loser visa's about to expire.'

'Better people to talk to than a washed-up wannabe and a fucking lawyer.'

'Ex-lawyer,' I correct, indignantly.

As I watch them leave – slapping high-fives and touching fists like they were some expatriate white boys from the 'hood – I compare them with Brian, leaning on the bar with a faraway expression. I come to the conclusion that it's better to be a has-been than a never-was, or a never-will-be. Monster Munch will eventually share a page with the other processed bands that have filled the charts recently; Brian was the real deal.

Brian goes to the bar for more beer. I'm going to wait for him to return and I'm going to tell him what I've done, and then go and stop that letter from being sent.

RACHEL AND OLIVER

When Brian doesn't return I skirt the periphery of the dancefloor to look for him. I haven't seen Cohen although he probably wouldn't come to something like this. I don't blame him. Drunken secretaries are staggering around to the ephemeral pop being played by Bruno Brookes, one of the firm's clients, some of them linking hands to form floor-clearing wedges. I steer well clear.

Richard Tanner is dancing with his secretary, looking like he's having the time of his life. I back into an alcove as I spot Wilson and Fulton at a table, deep in conversation. I don't think they notice me. As I'm cowering in the shadows, Rachel wanders past. She's sipping at a multicoloured cocktail.

'Hi,' I say.

Her thoughtful air melts into an awkward smile. 'Hi, Daniel,' she says, 'how're you?'

'Not so bad.'

'What're you doing hidden in there?'

'Oh, nothing much,' I say. 'Just taking a rest.'

'I heard about you losing your job.'

'It's nothing. I needed a change. This's probably an opportunity.'

'That's good. Good you can see it like that.'

'It's just a job,' I say.

'Probably the way to deal with it.'

An awkward pause.

'You look nice,' I say. She's wearing a simple black dress that brings out her figure. And she's got great legs. She looks better than nice.

'You too,' she fibs (since I know I look like death).

We stare uneasily at each other as Dawkins arrives. He sidles up alongside Rachel and slips his arm around her waist. I keep expecting her to squirm away but she doesn't.

'What're you doing here, Tate?' he says to me. He turns to Rachel and says, 'Is he bothering you?'

'No,' she says, 'we were just talking.'

'Do you think you could pop over to the bar and get me a drink, sweetheart?' he asks. 'I'd like a quiet word alone with Tate.'

She nods and pecks him on the cheek. I gape. 'Nice seeing you,' she says to me. 'And good luck.'

'I don't want to make a scene,' the Dork says when she's out of range, 'but if you're not out of here in five minutes I'm calling security. It might've escaped your attention, but you got *fired* today. You don't work for us any more.'

'Us?' I say. 'I never worked for you.'

'If you'd waited another week before showing everyone how negligent you've been that would've been different. By the way, did you see me with Brian? I thought I'd bring him along tonight.'

'You're full of shit,' I laugh. 'Brian told me you just bumped into him outside.'

He smiles at me tensely. 'Is that what he said?'

'And he thinks you're an arsehole,' I add smugly. 'Just so you know.'

'Look – just do us all a favour and fuck off.'

I GET WHAT'S COMING TO ME

'What're you doing with Rachel?' I ask.

'I don't think that's any of your business.'

Surge of dizziness. Lack of breath. Sudden blindness. Shooting pain.

'You know something, Tate,' the Dork says, 'I never thought you'd make such a mess of things. This might surprise you, but there was a time when I thought you were a pretty good lawyer. Better than good, actually. You used to be really on the ball—'

Gasping. Half-stagger. One step towards him. One step back.

'—really impressive. And now look at you. You've been sacked, you look awful and – Jesus – your breath *stinks* . . . I mean, you've completely gone to seed. You're an absolute *wreck*. Have a little pride, man. Pick yourself up—'

Dull headache. It inflates. Shards of pain. Long shudder. Trembling. Legs unsteady. Oh God. Not now.

'—and do something with your life. Although, I have to say, we've all had more than enough of you, Tate. To be perfectly honest, everyone I've spoken to's glad to see the back of you, glad you got the push—'

Bubble of vomit. Taste stained on back of mouth. Another bubble. Another. Another.

'—because watching you mope around the office all day's tedious, watching you fuck everything up and giving the firm a bad name. Failure sticks, Tate, it sticks. You know what Phillip Schofield was telling me earlier? He's got no confidence in you. And that affects all of us. Selfish, that's what you are – *selfish* – and—'

Balance haywire. Sudden fury. With who? Dawkins?

No. Struggle to hear him. Nothing making sense. Sweat slides into eyes. Stinging. No strength. Need to sit. Say something.

'What're you talking about?' the Dork says.

Dizziness. Say something.

'That's gibberish.'

Feel incredibly drunk.

'What?' he says.

Starting to sway. Feet planted but whole body rocking forwards and backwards. Dawkins talking. Hectoring. Shut him up. Colours in front of eyes start to blur and merge. Oh shit. Words stop connecting. Sounds with no meaning. Oh shit. Feeling of detachment. Spaced out like really bad trip. Body heating up. Blood pulsing through veins and head.

Oh shit oh shit oh shit.

'You're bloody drunk.'

Dawkins' face wobbles into line of sight. Looks as if underwater. Ripples passing across surface. Distortion. Deformed. Stagger backwards. Half-swoon. Somehow stay upright.

'Are you all right?' he asks.

Force words out. Legs buckle. Drop onto floor. Bang to side of head. Pocket of people forming. Dawkins on his knees. Looks half-startled and half-revolted. Look up. Brian forging through the crowd. Brian kneeling down. Cohen there. Elizabeth there. Rachel back again with drinks. And Hannah? No. Can't be. Impossible. Must be hallucinating. Must be completely out of it.

'What's the matter?' asks Brian.

His voice stretched and comical. Like tape with dead batteries. Look up. Anxious faces. Richard Tanner is there. Secretaries and lawyers. Shouldering each other for better view. Cohen speaking into mobile telephone. Girl that looks like Hannah still there with hand over mouth. Guy that looks like Vincent Haines behind her. Arm around her waist, leg in a cast.

Try to speak. Nothing comes out. Please no. Close eyes because of strobes from disco. Stabbing pain. Darkness gathering at edge of vision. More people. Brian loops arm underneath shoulders. Pulls into half-sitting position. Propped up against his knees. Brushes hair out of eyes. Please.

Brian asks: 'Can you hear me?'

Need to tell him: letter; tape; ticket.

'Say it again, Daniel.'

Reach into pocket. Ticket. Account number. Money. Explain.

'Come on, Daniel, keep talking to me.'

Sudden movement unsettles balance in stomach. Bring up strange-coloured fluids, thin and opaque, all over lap. Dawkins shoots up and jumps back. Bile all over shoes. Brian has some on him. Ignores it.

Ticket. Number. Letter. Money.

PLEASE.

'Let's have some space here,' Brian is saying.

Blackout.

'Keep your eyes open, Daniel.'

Ticket. Number. Letter. Money.

Two men. Blue uniforms. Approaching. Crowd parting. A leather bag. Liquid warm in lap.

Get to office. Stop letter.

PLEASE, PLEASE, PLEASE.

'Keep your eyes open. Don't go to sleep.'

Blackout.

Brian slaps cheek. Cohen talks to men. His voice a buzz making no sense. The men, nodding. One crouches down. Pulls back eyelid. Shines light into eye. Shines light into other eye. Pain. Can't turn head. Drowsy. Want to sleep. Been a long, long day.

Throw up again until nothing left but spit and phlegm and peptic acid. Sharp tang of vomit in back of throat.

'Daniel – it's me – Brian. Can you hear me?'

Something trips in mind. Pictures spool in mad collage: Hannah in New York; secretaries gawping; Ecstasy memories of Ibiza; Brian on stage; crowds of journalists calling a name; Hannah and Haines; the Empire State; Brian, concern on face; snow, deep and cold and white.

Must get to office. Urgent. But so tired. Just five minutes' rest. That's all. No longer. Sleep. Need sleep to feel better. Sleep it off. Close eyes. Snow expands. Fills hazy darkness. Perfectly clean. Virgin snow. Then nothing.

Blackout.

Whiteout.

'Daniel.'

Can't breathe. Static fills ears. Blind. Exit. Check out. Shut down.

'Daniel.'

Everything wipes clean.

'Daniel.'

Snow.

. . .

SCOTT DOLAN'S GUEST LIST

World's Greatest Showbiz Column

MAN CHARGED WITH JOHN FRENCH BLACKMAIL

An Italian man was charged by police yesterday for blackmailing Black Dahlias' singer John French. Cops said Giovanni Caselli forced French to hand over £10,000 or else he would go to the press with stories he had made up saying that French was gay.

Liar

Unemployed Caselli, 32, claimed he and French were in a homosexual relationship. Police said Caselli had been unable to prove his claim and friends immediately condemned him as a liar and a thief.

'To say John was gay is the biggest load of rubbish I've ever heard,' said stunned Dahlia Martin Valentine. 'The sad thing is, even though he wasn't gay, I'm sure this would've upset John and it probably had a lot to do with his suicide.'

Caselli was bailed to appear before London magistrates next month.

An extract from Media Lawyer

Busy Times for White Hunter

US firm Harris Lambert has poached White Hunter's highly rated media lawyer David Cohen, 28, tempting him with what sources have called 'a very significant offer'. Cohen will become the youngest partner in the firm's London office, heading up their new litigation and arbitration department. Charles Hunter, senior partner at Cohen's old firm, said: 'We're very sad to see David go but this is a great chance for him to make a name for himself. He's an excellent lawyer and I'm sure he's destined for big things.'

Hunter took the opportunity to announce that the boutique media firm has made up corporate lawyer Caroline Lewis to replace Miles MacKay, who died last month. Lewis, 31, emerged after a lengthy selection process that Hunter described as 'difficult'. It has been rumoured that the place in the partnership was initially offered to Cohen, who turned it down before leaving the practice. Hunter was not prepared to be drawn on that suggestion.

No Word on Missing Lawyer

Finally, in a busy week for White Hunter, there is still no word on the whereabouts of ex-assistant Daniel Tate, who disappeared last week. Tate, 27, collapsed at the firm's Christmas party but hasn't been seen after checking himself out of hospital. Hunter said: 'Although Daniel's no longer with us, he still has a lot of friends here at the firm and we're all very concerned about him. We'd all be much happier if he made contact with the authorities.'

Tuesday (Later)

WISH YOU WERE HERE

The sand is gritty and warm as it plays through my toes. I'm walking back to the hotel from the tiny shop in the village along the beach, treading on the soft margin between the wet sand smoothed out by the tide and the fine powder further up the beach. I'm carrying a cut of pork and two bags of black beans and rice, the ingredients for *feijoada completa*, a local dish I'm going to cook tonight. Two pieces of correspondence poke out of the pocket of my shorts.

The cove ahead is empty and, turning, I can follow my footprints back until they disappear around the curve of the bay, the tide lapping at the indentations. Not long ago I was leaving tracks in snow. A group of bare-footed kids kick a thin plastic football around the beach and I watch as it swerves, jerking, in the lazy breeze. The sun is hot, even though it's only just past nine in the morning. It's at my back as I follow the curve of the beach, warming my skin and casting a long shadow ten feet before me.

A NEW ROUTINE

Something – the angle of the sun, perhaps, or the rumble of my empty stomach – reminds me of the time. I sit on a rocky outcrop and put the bag of groceries down beside me. From a pouch fixed around my waist I take out a syringe and a tiny glass bottle of clear liquid. I slide the needle through the rubber membrane on the bottle and draw the insulin inside it up into the barrel and, after rolling up my shorts, inject it into my thigh. I'm told that doing this twice a day will eventually deaden the nerves so that I can't feel the needle and I'll have to find somewhere else to inject: the other leg, my belly, an arm, wherever I can find a vein. For now, the point of the needle as it pushes against and then slides through my skin, brings a brief pain – a reminder. Like all the other facts of living with diabetes, apparently this is just something else you get used to.

The hospital diagnosed hyperglycaemia – a diabetic coma – almost at once. Brian recognized the signs, as Lisa is diabetic. He probably saved my life; the paramedics agreed with his diagnosis and shot me up with insulin. I had all the symptoms: thirst, nausea, fruity-smelling breath, impaired judgment, mood swings, irrational behaviour and, ultimately, loss of consciousness. Stress and my drink problem probably triggered the disease.

'Now you've woken it up, it'll be with you for the

rest of your life,' the doctor told me sternly when I woke up.

ANOTHER DAY IN PARADISE

The surroundings here are extraordinary; the mountains back right up against the ocean and in the early mornings, like now, the sun casts them in a vivid ochre that balances the lush green of the forest vegetation and the cerulean blue of the ocean. The water is so clear here you can see all the way down, stingrays and black-tipped baby sharks basking, and just after the sun rises it casts the water with a gorgeous wash, like spun gold. And the golden sunsets – bloody reds and cadmium yellows – are miraculous.

Things look great: money won't be a problem. Since I couldn't stop the letters to the banks or to the police, I followed through with my plan. It worked perfectly. I reach into my pocket and read this morning's telegram from Sao Paulo for the second time. It's from a branch of Banco América do Sul, confirmation that the sum of approximately two million cruzeiro – £600,000 – has been safely remitted by Banco Bradesco in Rio. Next week I'm going to travel to the bank and make a withdrawal from my account. I'm going to empty it, bit by bit, and move the money into a safety deposit box. I've already washed it through blind accounts in Belize, Cayman and Bermuda.

Once it's stashed in the box, there'll be no way of tracing it. As far as the band and the label are concerned, the money will have vanished.

EVENTS IN LONDON

I set off again. I take out the other letter from my pocket, the one that was waiting for me in an anonymous post-office box in town, and examine it as I walk. The envelope is stamped with a London postmark. I slice it open with my penknife and take out the letter. I recognize Cohen's handwriting. I sent him the details of the post-office box once I'd established myself here, and asked him for the news.

He recounts events at White Hunter before he left. The Dork had no choice but to quit when first Cohen, then Caroline Lewis, were offered partnership in preference to him. He'd told everyone that the job was his and he couldn't bear the humiliation of being overlooked twice. Cohen crossed swords with him at court last week. He's been taken on as a junior partner in a tiny firm of media lawyers south of the river. It'll be a steep drop for him, in terms of both prestige and paycheque. It couldn't have happened to a nicer guy.

I flip through the pages. Cohen hopes I'm OK about Hannah. *Skin Trade* is doing well, and it's rumoured that she's about to take the step up into film. And it *was* her and Haines at the party. Renwick invited them both.

She didn't send me a card while I was in hospital; she didn't visit, either. With the distance between us now I've had to force myself to put her out of my mind. It isn't easy and I still miss her. But I keep myself busy. That helps. It's only when I'm idle that I think about regrets. I've got more than a few. She's still the first thing I think about when I wake up in the morning and the last thing I think about at night.

Cohen reports that Vincent Haines's case came to trial last week. He was cross-examined for two days, during which time he gave a virtuoso display, making a joke of his broken leg and denying all knowledge of the contract he stood accused of breaching. But at the end of the second day, just as the court was ready to adjourn, the other side introduced an audio cassette as vital new evidence. On the tape, speaking to an unidentified interlocutor, Haines was heard to admit that he was in breach of the American contract. The court was spellbound. There was uproar. The Judge quickly found against him and ordered damages in the high six figures.

'And it's funny,' Cohen writes, 'but just after this mystery tape turned up, *Extravaganza* started to run a series of exclusives based on confidential information it'd dug up on White Hunter clients. The partnership went nuts. Six sensitive files with this information in them had gone missing from the office . . . Four of the clients have already sued for breach of confidence. You can see where I'm going with this? You wouldn't happen to know anything about them, would you?'

Smiling contentedly to myself, I fold the letter and slide it back into its envelope.

BEGINNINGS AND ENDINGS

£20,000 of the band's money has already been spent. It was added to the £20,000 Scott Dolan paid me for the White Hunter files, the total spent buying a battered hotel here on the Espirito Santo coast. It's ramshackle and needs a lot of work but progress has been good. The area is popular with surfers and travellers and, once the hotel is in decent shape, it ought to be a busy hang-out.

Nelson loves it, of course. He came with me when I flew out. He basks on the sun-cooked wood and chases insects the size of mice. His favourite thing is to lie on the pier and stare down at the brightly coloured fish that swim around the pilings, knowing that they'll always be just out of reach. His vigil reminiscent of life in the metropolis: the glittering few observed and admired but impossible to catch.

As you round the final languid curve of the bay you come upon the hotel. It's built on a rocky outcrop and surrounded by palms and banana trees, hibiscus and pampas grasses. The walls are weather-beaten wooden planks that need replacing and the roof leaks in several places. It'll be daubed with tar next week. A terrace reaches down from the rocky ledge to abut the beach, and the morning's high tide is already licking up against the rimey wood. Spume clings to the knotted surface and a green-painted rowing boat bobs at its mooring, buffeted by the swells.

I hear the cutting of his saw before I see him. This week, we're replacing the floorboards in the area we've allocated for the bar, and the wood for the job was dropped off yesterday. A hundred planks of teak need to be cut to size and varnished. It's going to be a long, hot day of hard work.

Brian is still gaunt but the sun has tanned him and he's already adding muscle to his frame. He almost looks healthy; he certainly looks better. He waves when he sees me walking through the surf and then, smiling, putting down his saw and brushing sawdust from his arms, holds up two mugs of *cafezinho*, the strong, sweet black coffee we've both learnt to enjoy. Call it a late breakfast.

I managed to pass Brian the ticket to Brazil before I blacked out at the Christmas party. He more or less worked out, from the rest of my gibberish, what I'd done. He spoke to Cohen, who went into the office and stopped the answerphone tape reaching the police. From my computer's hard drive, Cohen then retrieved backups of the faked letters I'd sent to Brian's banks – that gave them the details of the bank in Brazil I was going to divert the Dahlias' cash to; knowing this information, they were able to adopt the rest of the plan.

I was in a coma for six days. Brian and Cohen stayed with me Monday night and all of Tuesday. Brian only agreed to leave when the doctors told him they were keeping me asleep to encourage my recovery, and assured him that I was out of the woods. He left Lisa a tidy sum and an open ticket, and flew out on my unreserved ticket on the Wednesday morning.

Following Cohen's instructions, he arranged for the money from his accounts to be moved between Brazilian banks, eventually withdrawing the cash and holding it in several safety deposit boxes. These tactics would make it nearly impossible for the Dahlias to trace it, once they realized what had happened. After a week he bought the hotel, and had already started to renovate it by the time I arrived.

The days are spent working and the evenings passed on the terrace necking beer (Brian) and fresh fruit cocktails (me). It's a perfect spot. Lizards and crabs skittle out from the terrace when the tide rolls back and when the tide's up, the baby sharks pick lazily at the bacon rind we drop down for them. Nelson sleeps on my lap. Brian bought an acoustic guitar from a trader in the town up the coast, and our favourite thing is to watch the sun sink into the darkening blue of the horizon while he plays a few of the old songs. Watching his fingers flash across the strings, the old familiar strength of his voice, refreshed now that the worry and stress have been sloughed away, my foot tapping out a rough beat on the bleached boards of the jetty, the murmuring of the surf – waves splashing up onto my legs and the salt crystallizing on my bare skin in the late evening heat – the whisper of the breeze in the treetops, the dying sun in my face; I don't know how this could be bettered.

We're confident the place will prosper. After all, the joint proprietor is Brian Fey; surely that must count for something?

THE CONSOLATION OF PHILOSOPHY

During my convalescence, I spent several hours browsing in the hospital's meagre library and found a collection of philosophical musings and quotations amongst the pulp thrillers and cheesy romances. Flicking through the pages, something by the scientist and satirical writer Georg Christoph Lichtenberg caught my eye. He wrote:

> *'The journalists have constructed for themselves a little wooden chapel, which they also call the Temple of Fame, in which they put up and take down portraits all day long and make such a hammering you can't hear yourself speak.'*

I returned to it again and again, before surreptitiously

tearing out the page and slipping it into the pocket of my dressing gown. I took it with me when I left; now I keep it folded in my wallet. A few yards away from the steps leading up to the hotel veranda, I pause and unfold the creased and crumpled page again. I think of my own brief, and inglorious, dalliance with notoriety.

Hannah Wilde, Vincent Haines, the boys from Monster Munch, Sean Darbo, the rest of the Black Dahlias – their pictures still hang in the Temple, but I wonder how much longer they've got left. Brian took time to accept that his moment had passed. But now, as I watch him working happily with a brush and a bucket of creosote, it's clear that he has accepted the changes that Fate has wrought. For the first time since I've known him, he actually looks at peace.

THE WISDOM OF COLE PORTER

It reminds me of something Brian said a week or two ago. The change in his circumstances was something that Brian had obviously spent time considering while he was working on the hotel alone, waiting for me to join him. One evening, frittered away drinking and smoking and watching the bleeding sun go down, he surprised me with an unexpected turn of conversation.

'You know Cole Porter?' he began, apropos of nothing, touching the end of the blunt with his Zippo's flame. 'Gay American dude, wrote musicals, stuff like that?'

'Sure,' I said, wondering where this was going.

He puffed out a cloud of blow-tinged smoke. 'When I was trying to write my own songs for the band, I looked at tunes he'd come up with to see if I could pick up any pointers. There's this one song he wrote, can't remember the name of it now, he said something about "how strange the change from major to minor," something like that. Know the one I mean?'

' "Ev'ry Time We Say Goodbye",' I said, thinking of the classic version John Coltrane recorded – one of my all-time favourites.

'Yeah, that one. I'm probably taking it right out of context, but, I don't know, that line just about sums up everything that's happened since I left the band. Getting from where I was then to where I am now. It took some getting used to, but, you know, I don't care any more. I *like* this. Things've turned out pretty OK.'

I smiled, finished my coconut juice, and took the joint. Nelson sat on my lap, purring. Brian picked up his guitar and started to strum the tune Cole Porter had written sixty years earlier. And, as we watched, the sun melted into the tranquil aquamarine sea.

END OF THE ROAD

As you come closer still you can make out the name of the hotel, painted in broad brushstrokes on a piece of gnarled driftwood the ocean left on the beach a couple of weeks ago. We cleaned up the wood, daubed the hotel's name in thick black paint and sealed it up with varnish. We sat out on the terrace for hours before we came up with the right name, a whole week toking on enormous spliffs and tossing out ideas, like the dead roaches we threw into the ocean. When the name finally arrived, we both knew at once that it was the right one. It looks perfect fixed up on the wall.

We settled on The Black Dahlia.

OTHER PAN BOOKS

AVAILABLE FROM PAN MACMILLAN

MARK DAWSON
THE ART OF FALLING APART   0 330 48499 0   £6.99

JOHN BINIAS
LOCO   0 330 48694 2   £6.99
THEORY OF FLESH   0 330 39062 7   £5.99

PHIL ROBINSON
CHARLIE BIG POTATOES   0 330 49051 6   £6.99

All Pan Macmillan titles can be ordered from our website,
www.panmacmillan.com, or from your local bookshop
and are also available by post from:

Bookpost, PO Box 29, Douglas, Isle of Man IM99 1BQ
Credit cards accepted. For details:
Telephone: 01624 677237
Fax: 01624 670923
E-mail: bookshop@enterprise.net
www.bookpost.co.uk

Free postage and packing in the United Kingdom

Prices shown above were correct at the time of going to press.
Pan Macmillan reserve the right to show new retail prices on covers
which may differ from those previously advertised in the text
or elsewhere.